ECHOES

Diamond of the Rockies

◆◆◆◆◆◆◆◆◆◆◆◆◆

www.kristenheitzmann.com

ECHOES

THE SEQUEL TO
Secrets
and *Unforgotten*

KRISTEN
HEITZMANN

BETHANY HOUSE PUBLISHERS
Minneapolis, Minnesota

Published by Bethany House Publishers
11400 Hampshire Avenue South
Bloomington, Minnesota 55438

Bethany House Publishers is a division of
Baker Publishing Group, Grand Rapids, Michigan.

Printed in the United States of America

Library of Congress Cataloging-in-Publication Data

Heitzmann, Kristen.
    Echoes / Kristen Heitzmann.
        p.   cm.
    Sequel to: Unforgotten.
    ISBN-13: 978-0-7642-2830-8 (pbk.)
    ISBN-10: 0-7642-2830-7 (pbk.)
    1. Triangles (Interpersonal relations)—Fiction. I. Title.

PS3558.E468E28   2007
813'.54—dc22

                                                                2007023687

To Trevor, whose fun and caring nature lights my days.
To Steve, whose smile is like the sun coming out.
To Devin, whose companionship I treasure.

CHAPTER ONE

The whimper came, no more than a note of longing—or fear—in a child's throat. Sofie reacted instinctively, each nerve pulled taut. But when she opened her eyes, there was no warm, damp cheek, no tiny brow wrinkled with sleep-swept worries. She sank back as sorrow, marrow deep, found a familiar fit.

Her wrists stung with memory. The damp bed sheet weighed on her chest like water, pressing her down, rising over her chin, despair so complete it became a force. Shaking, she stared up at the darkness, refusing to give in. *Chi ha dato ha dato.* What's done is done. She could not turn back time, or change one detail of what was, or what had been.

She got up and went into the bathroom. The faucet squeaked; the pipe clunked. Water sputtered, then rushed with a rust-scented stream. Memory pressed again as she stepped over the side of the tub, red-stained water lapping. She turned, and the sting of hot spray drove it away.

After drying her hair, she pulled it into a ponytail, dressed in gray cashmere cardigan, charcoal slacks. Black camel coat, blue and turquoise scarf. She slid her black chenille gloves down the banister of the inner staircase and stepped out to the street her family had lived on for three generations. Belmont. Little Italy of the Bronx. Each shop, each curb familiar; each face knowing too much. A blessing and a burden.

Fog issued from her mouth. Brittle frost crunched beneath her feet. The biting January wind stung her nose. But it wasn't far, just around the corner, a couple of blocks. Shivering, she climbed the steps to the church and slipped inside the massive doors to the sanctuary scented with polish and prayers.

The bands around her chest loosened. Her muffled steps carried her midway down the center aisle, where she knelt among the *donne anziane* in their black scarves and thick stockings.

Mariana Dimino clawed her way, pew by pew, to the place where Sofie knelt. She paused, her eyes a portal. *"Finchè c'è vita c'è speranza,"* she murmured.

Where there's life, there's hope. Sofie let the words penetrate, grateful for the gift. Hope was precious, to be neither hoarded nor spent lightly. And so was life.

The thought resonated as she walked back to her family's apartment building, noting each detail of her surroundings, her cocoon. She felt a metamorphic stirring. It was time for change. She'd go straight up to Momma and—Her cell phone vibrated.

She answered, but no one responded. Whoever was placing the calls waited each time for her to answer, stayed on the line as long as she did without ever saying a word. No breathing or threats, but the silence unsettled her more.

The number was blocked, so she could not return the calls. Could it be someone she had counseled? She'd given none of them her personal number, though she was reachable through the hotline. If they'd gone to the trouble to get it some other way, why wouldn't they say what they wanted?

"I'm not sure what you're hoping to accomplish by this. If you need something, say so."

Still nothing.

"If you won't tell me, I can't help you." She disconnected and looked back over her shoulder. A prickle itched along her neck, the feeling of being watched. Her tendons tightened, even though she guessed it was only a shade from the past.

She went into the hall and navigated past bicycles with train-ing wheels, basketballs, skateboards, snow boots, and other kid clutter. So many children in this building, and she their favorite auntie, with no kids of her own to distract her. Nicky cried upstairs, and her sister Monica hollered for Bobby to quiet him, not even noticing the irony.

Sofie smiled. She'd miss this boisterous scene. She loved them all. She just couldn't stay there anymore. Mariana Dimino's words had awakened her. She'd been going through the motions, lost in a semi-sleep of doubt and regret. But she was alive, and there was hope that she could squeeze through the familial cocoon that had shielded her for the last six years and force strength into her wings.

She climbed the stairs to the second floor. Momma was up; she could tell by the scorched aroma leaking into the hall. This would be the first tug, the hardest squeeze. She rapped the door, and her father let her in as he left for work. "See ya, Pop."

He tapped her shoulder in passing. It would be better to let Momma get used to the idea without Pop's concerns piling on. Even before Tony's death, Momma had done everything she could to keep her chicks near. Only Lance had flown the coop, his rest-less wanderings a constant concern for the woman wiping off the kitsch-cluttered counter.

The open window let the smoke out and the cold in. Black soggy crumbs littered the sink, where Momma had scraped the charred surface from the toast. Chunks clung to the drain like flies.

"Don't worry, Momma. Pop's glad for a full stomach."

"You think Lance would say so?" Her mother shook the towel over the sink and hung it on the rack.

Lance would try hard not to say anything, but if any woman could look inside her children, it was Doria Lo Vecchio Michelli. Lance and Nonna Antonia had run the restaurant downstairs and provided feasts for the family for years. Both wonderful cooks had suffered Momma's kitchen handicap with considerable restraint, but she knew.

"Why are you thinking about Lance, Momma?"

"I always think about Lance. I think about all of you. I worry." She wiped her hands on the apron nipping into her shapely waist. Momma had assets, *Grazie a Dio*. Pop knew what he was getting and what he wasn't.

Sofie drew a breath. "I'm leaving."

"You just got here." Momma ran the cloth under the water and squeezed it out.

"I mean I'm going away."

"Madonna mia." Momma pressed a hand to her heart and turned. "Going away? How can you go away?"

Sofie sighed. "I need to."

"What about school? You worked yourself ragged."

"My dissertation's been approved. I can write it anywhere, check in by phone and electronically."

"But . . ." Momma's face darkened. Her hand slid to her throat. "You found them."

Sofie shook her head. "No, Momma. It has nothing to do with Eric." They both knew she lied. In a sense every day, every moment, every decision had to do with him. "I just need a change. I can't keep waiting for something that isn't going to happen."

"It never should have."

She wouldn't argue. All conventional wisdom came down on Momma's side of the scale. But even with all the pain that had followed, she could not wish it hadn't. "I need to move on."

Momma wrung her hands, but on that point they agreed. "Then go to Lance. He'll look out for you. You look out for him."

At thirty, she shouldn't need her little brother to look after her. He was only now finding his way. But it was as good a suggestion as any, and the other side of the country might be just far enough to forget.

———

Miraculous. There was no other word for it. In the still of the morning, Lance had reached out. Bathed by the golden shaft of sunlight in the dormant Sonoma garden, Rese had taken his hand.

After their strife and disappointment, that small connection felt huge, extraordinary. It was more than he'd expected from Rese Barrett, the woman who'd infuriated and intrigued him, the one he'd given up for a cause, who even now doubted his sincerity, his fidelity. He drew her close, tucked his finger under her chin and raised her face, knowing better but unable to stop the magnetic draw of her mouth.

Her lips parted. "I hope you're not burning that frittata."

He jolted back to reality. This was Rese, and if he thought he was off the hook that easy, he could fagedda-bout-it.

"Have I ever burned anything?" Besides his bridges, time and again.

"Now isn't the time to start."

He threaded her fingers with his. "I won't."

She reached up and touched the moisture under his eyes. The breeze had almost absorbed it, but not quite. He wasn't sure where the tears had come from or why, hadn't really known they were there. Before, he'd have made excuses. Now, well . . .

"Lance, last night . . ."

He looked across the garden. "I guess God wanted to do something." Her stoic face was more than half skeptical. "It wasn't me, Rese."

"The baby's palate was cleft."

He nodded. "The lip looked split."

"Looked?"

"Well, then it wasn't." He spread his hand, recalling his shock when he'd lifted it from the baby's face. Maybe bad light or panic had made them jump to conclusions. Or else God had done something amazing, something heartbreakingly beautiful and terrifying.

Whatever the case, it wasn't a place he could stay. Too sublime, as the psalmist said. He needed something real. "Let's take the Harley for a spin."

"Now?"

"Star can feed the troops."

She sighed. "Lance . . ."

"Just a ride." He needed the road, the speed, the distance. He needed her, but didn't say so. "Baxter can chaperone."

At the sound of his name, the spaniel-retriever mix trotted over and stuffed his nose between their joined fingers.

"That would be animal endangerment."

He rubbed the dog's head. "We'll let him decide."

Rese snorted. "As though he has anything like free will where you're concerned. As though anyone does."

Star stepped through the doorway, her head a white-blond blizzard after the drug-crazed hacking she'd given her hair in the Bronx. He didn't know who had held her prisoner and fed her the cocktail that had left tracks on her waifish arms, but he could see the healing that had occurred here at Rese's Sonoma villa. Not as dramatic and instantaneous as Maria's baby, but real and lasting he prayed.

She rested her forearm across her head and asked, "Is breakfast ready?"

"Nearly." He no longer expected to solve the problems of the world, just to make his piece of it better if he could and get through each day without messing up too bad.

Rese stepped back. "Come inside, Lance."

In the warmth of the big stone kitchen, Rese studied the still-nameless newborn. From his shaggy black hair to his swaddled legs, Maria's baby lay in Lance's forearms, giving off a sweet, yeasty aroma. He had his young mother's flat, square face and low forehead, and his small dark eyes looked up at Lance as though he had all the answers in the world.

Maria, ravenous after last night's delivery, devoured her meal as though she might not receive another. Lance didn't tell her they weren't revoking her meal card. He obviously enjoyed the gusto with which she inhaled his food.

Beaming at the baby in Lance's arms, Antonia cooed, "Such a good strong boy."

How could she know that, when the baby did nothing but stare at Lance? Behind them, Star placed a filled plate on a tray, along with a glass of juice and a foamy latte. Mom wasn't coming down?

This was hardly the uncomplicated environment Rese had envisioned when she'd brought her mother home from the mental health facility, but it wasn't good for her to isolate from the real world. She'd better check in. "I'll take it up."

"That's all right." Star lifted the tray. Somehow she had become Mom's primary caregiver; Star, who'd once believed a dead mother better than her own supremely selfish one. Of course, Mom had not really been dead. That was only the lie people had told to the daughter she'd attempted to kill.

With a sigh, Rese took a bite of the savory frittata and gave Lance the appreciative smile he expected. For him, a meal was more than food in the stomach. It was a cultural event of connection, acceptance, and relationship. His cooking made that comprehensible.

She got up and washed her plate at the sink. Maria brought hers over, uncertain what to do next, though the wet circles on her shirt were an indication. Rese told her, "I'll wash it." The words meant nothing to the Hispanic girl, but she used them anyway.

Maria turned back to Lance, her eyes wonder-lit. He smiled, reducing the girl to mush. Rese shook her head as Maria padded back upstairs to the room originally furnished for guests at the inn, and Lance followed with the infant.

Maria didn't seem to realize she was allowed in the rest of the house, even though Lance had told her she was. She was used to being crammed into a single room. At least instead of six men, she only shared this one with her baby.

Rese turned back to the sink and scrubbed the frittata pan in the hot sudsy water.

Moments later, Lance's breath warmed her neck. "Yes."

She tensed. "Yes what?"

"I want kids."

"What?" Had he forgotten his ninety-year-old grandmother sitting at the table? By Antonia's chuckle neither one of them had. But then his whole family aired their private matters for all to hear.

"You asked me in New York how I felt about kids." He turned her around. "Now I'm telling you."

"You hold one baby—"

"I've held tons of babies."

She expelled a hard breath. "Can you see I'm washing dishes?"

"You look good in suds." He circled her waist with his arms, and her heart took off running. His magnetic gaze turned her to putty, worse than Maria. Amusement deepened the corners of his mouth. Why was he so infuriatingly charming?

Lance Michelli made her feel and think and do things she'd had no intention of doing. He'd broken through her insulation and made her care—not just for him, but his family, his friends, even her own friends in a different way, and most of all herself. He'd shared his faith, his strength, his doubts, his weaknesses. She was so seriously in love it hurt. And it was the hurt she couldn't get past.

His phone rang. With a sigh, he answered it. "Sof. How you doin'?" He raised his brows at his grandmother. Antonia, too, seemed surprised.

It must be his sister Sofie, the only person in his family who hadn't shared her life story—though the one thing she had confided haunted.

"Yeah, sure," Lance said. "Let me call you back." He disconnected and turned. "What would you think of Sofie coming out?"

"To visit?"

"Maybe stay awhile."

Stay. In addition to him and his grandmother, Star and Mom

and a teenage mother and her baby. She'd thought she wasn't running an inn! Thought she'd made that clear. But it didn't matter what she thought. Lance always found a way around.

"Isn't she in school?" A doctoral program no less. Sofie's focus had seemed as tight as her own. She couldn't want to leave that.

"Her dissertation's been approved. She can write it here, then go back to defend it."

"Oh." Rese rubbed her temples and did a mental room check: Star in the Rain Forest, Mom the Rose Trellis, Maria and the baby in Jasmine. Her own suite was downstairs off the kitchen. Since Lance and his grandmother were in the carriage house, that left Seascape for Sofie. Or she supposed Sofie could room with Antonia as she had in the Bronx, and Lance could be back in the room where he'd started—that fateful day he'd walked onto her work site with his earring and his swagger and the cross of Christ tattooed on his shoulder blade so he'd never forget to carry his own.

"It's kind of a big deal, her asking." Lance rubbed his palms together. "She hasn't left home since . . . for a long time."

Rese nodded. Another mouth, another bed. Lance was used to chaos. He fed on it. She was used to solitude, and while she didn't exactly feed on it, at least it didn't overwhelm her. Now she felt like a Jenga tower with one more support beam removed.

"I'm sure she'd kick in something toward expenses."

Or not. Lance was generous, as she'd seen with the change bowl back in his Bronx apartment. He and Chaz filled and Rico drained. Lance wasn't employed at the moment, but with all he did at the villa, he earned his and Antonia's keep many times over.

Dad's life insurance paid for Mom's care; Star applied her trust money from the heiress mother she despised. For Antonia's part, there was still a cellar full of Prohibition-vintage wine, valued up to a couple thousand dollars each bottle. Maria had yet to contribute anything except the infant everyone doted on.

Rese didn't mind being the only one with an actual income. She'd worked since she was just a girl tagging along to Dad's renovations. He'd developed her skill, and she'd made it her craft. Her life.

Buying the villa to renovate and run as an inn had been a knee-jerk reaction to his accidental death. An ill-fated attempt to fulfill his dream of a bed-and-breakfast—a dream he would never have actualized either. They weren't people persons. Yet she was being asked to provide shelter to one more wayfarer.

Of course, with Sofie in the last available room, she could honestly say no to any more strangers. Relieved at the thought, she nodded. "Okay."

"Are you sure?"

"I'm sure." Renovating priceless old buildings took her away and provided hours alone in her zone. The physical labor helped her breathe. Dad's tragic death had almost destroyed it, but little by little she'd reclaimed her birthright. If Lance wanted another body to tend at the villa, it was fine by her.

CHAPTER TWO

M att Hammond stood outside the door. He wasn't responding to a domestic violence call, but the hollering, screaming, and breaking glass didn't sound like a tea party. He speed-dialed 9-1-1 on his cell and gave the address, his name, and position. Another crash followed fresh screams. He banged the door and hollered, but it wasn't likely he'd be heard above the din.

He tried the knob and went in, searching through the front rooms, down low where children might crouch. The noise came from farther back, probably the kitchen, and he caught sight of three kids huddled beneath the drop-leaf table. His shoes crunched broken glass and ceramic shards.

The hulking man swung around, brandishing the jagged edge of a broken beer bottle. "Who are you? Stay back."

"Matt Hammond," he said calmly. "I'm here about the kids."

Donald Price pivoted to get a glimpse, then swung back. "What about them?"

"Why don't you put down the bottle so we can talk."

"Why don't you put yourself outside my house?"

"I can't do that." Not with three kids in danger.

"Show me your badge."

"I'm not a cop."

"What are you?" Price swayed.

"I'm with Child Protective Services."

"Some flunky with the county?"

He'd been called worse.

"Well, this is my house, and these are my kids. So get out."

A woman who had to be Vivian Price appeared in the other doorway of the kitchen, glaring at her husband, a wad of tissue pressed to her cheek. The shaking in her hands could be fear, drugs, or DTs.

Matt told her to stay back. He'd rather deal with a drunk than a meth head.

Scrawny and uptight, she bore the startled look of a recent face-lift. "What's going on?"

"Shut up," Price snarled, then back to Matt, "Go stick your nose somewhere else."

"I need to see the kids."

Price raised the bottle, looking more like a thug than a successful real-estate broker. "I said get out. Leave my family alone."

"Put down the weapon, Price."

"Weapon?" He looked at the edge. "I dropped this. We're cleaning up the mess." He glared at his wife. "Isn't that right, Viv?"

Her tight-lipped nod told another story.

Matt frowned. "What happened to your cheek?"

Her eyes smoldered. "Cut it."

"You cut it?"

Her shaking increased.

"That's what she said," Price barked. "Now leave."

"I need to follow through on some concerns for the children." Matt looked around the kitchen. "How long since they've eaten?"

Price scowled. "What are you talking about?"

Matt looked down at the children. "Are you hungry, kids?"

Two were young enough to nod. The third stared warily at his dad.

"Neighbors saw them going through the trash."

A mewl emerged from Vivian's throat.

"That's a lie." Price raised the bottle menacingly.

"He won't give me the money," Vivian whined. "What am I supposed to feed them?"

Price's lip curled. "I left her with money when I went to the convention. Ask her what she did with it."

With a shriek Vivian launched herself at him. Price brought an elbow down on her shoulder as Matt grabbed the bottle-wielding arm at the wrist to keep him from slashing her again. He should not have been the first one on the scene. Where were the cops?

Price flung his wife to the floor, and Matt slammed the man's wrist against the counter. The bottle flew out of his grasp and smashed on the floor tile. Price lost his footing and went down.

Matt crouched between the angry man and his frightened children. "Listen, Price. You and your wife can fight it out, but not in front of the kids. I'm taking them to a safe place."

"See what you've done?" Vivian yanked a towheaded toddler from under the table and shook her over Price on the floor.

"Enough!" Matt snagged the screaming tot and sat her on the table.

One of the boys crawled out and grabbed his leg, crying. The sharp scent of urine joined stale smoke and spilled beer. The oldest—maybe six?—hung back, wheezing. Asthmatic?

"Leave the child alone." Matt braced Vivian away from the table with a stiff arm since she'd replaced her husband as the aggressor. The bruise on the toddler's thigh was all he needed to remove her. It looked as though she'd been gripped hard, maybe used before as a bone between them.

The call had come in to Social Services that the kids were digging through the neighbors' trash and stunk to high heaven. In this upper-middle-class neighborhood, people found that unusual. He'd gone over to investigate and discovered the escalating situation. Now he needed the kids out of there.

"Stand away, Ms. Price." He took the two youngest into his arms.

"It's his fault," she shrieked. "He wouldn't give me enough.

What was I supposed to feed them?"

"You snorted it!" Price dragged himself to his feet. "Snorted your meth and let the kids go hungry. Ask her. She doesn't get hungry with that stuff in her blood."

The first officer arrived and took in the scene. Matt nodded to him, then herded the oldest boy toward the door. "It's all right, kids. We'll give Mom and Dad a chance to work things out." The first contact was usually investigation: questions, observation, and assessment. This time they'd saved him the guesswork.

———

Four days after calling Lance, Sofie parked her car and surveyed the villa that had once been her grandmother's home in the wine country of Sonoma. The arched and alcoved house, surrounded by a wrought-iron fence, had held its secrets until Lance uncovered them—along with their great-great-grandfather's bones. It still seemed incredible to think of Nonna Antonia anywhere except the Belmont neighborhood where she'd spent her entire life, except the part no one had known.

If Nonna could reinvent herself, surely some of that ran in her granddaughter's veins. Sofie dropped her gaze to the faint blue tributaries just visible beneath her skin. New beginnings were not genetically imparted. Whether she succeeded was up to her.

"Sofie." Lance came around the side of the house and closed her into his arms. "How you doin'?"

She should ask him. Though thinner than she liked, he was not as haggard as he'd been. He had faced down his demons and come out stronger. Was she the only Michelli without the capacity for rebirth? Or had she played that card already? She raised her chin beneath the villa's sheltering shadow. "I'm fine. You?"

"Sure."

"Are you eating?"

"You sound like Momma."

"I was instructed to." She laughed at his sigh. "I guess we don't have to do that out here."

He grinned. "I'm almost convinced she can't see this far."

"She can probably hear." Laughing, she looked up at the house. "It's nice."

"Wait till you see what Rese has done inside. She's a master."

"I saw what she did on Pop's ceiling."

"That was nothing. She's got woodwork in here that'll make you weep."

"Not that you're proud or anything." She slid him a smile. "It's going okay?"

"I screw up one more time, I'm dead. Nail down the lid and dig the hole."

He was the only one who didn't avoid death as though the mere word might sweep her away. He couldn't know how much she appreciated that. "So don't screw up."

"Yeah. My strong suit."

"You only mess things up when you want out. Something tells me that's not going to happen."

He smiled. "I'm glad you're here."

"Me too." Momma had been right to tell her to go to Lance. She'd needed to leave, but none of them could go for long without family. She'd learned that the hard way.

He pulled the two bigger suitcases from the trunk, one of them thudding to the ground. "What do you have in here?"

"Reference books." She grabbed her laptop and a smaller tote.

"Nonna wants you to room with her. She says I talk in my sleep."

"And worse." Sofie laughed. "Remember when we'd find you out in the hall on a mission from God?"

"How would I remember? I was asleep."

"Nonna told us if we touched you the angels would carry you away. Momma stood there moaning with Pop yelling, 'Wassamattah wit' him?'"

"He's still wondering that." He let her into the bungalow behind the main house. It smelled of time and secrets, new wood and old stone, hopes and fears.

"Is this the carriage house you rebuilt?"

"Rese trimmed it out."

"Where is she?"

"At work."

"I thought . . . Aren't you running the inn together?"

"She's back in renovation. Scrapped the inn before Nonna and I returned."

"Oh."

He carried her bags into the bedroom, where Nonna was napping in a big burled walnut bed. They crept on cat's paws, but if they woke her, she wouldn't mind the interruption. He set the suitcases before the large wardrobe that stood at the opposite end of the room.

He whispered, "You can share the drawers. Nonna didn't bring much with her." He ran his hand down the wood. "Rese built this." At her stare, he nodded. "Told you she was good." He pointed to the matching queen-size bed that swallowed Nonna. "You can share that or use the cot in the other room. I know neither one's a great choice."

"We'll figure it out. Thanks." She and Nonna had shared the apartment at home and had an easy way between them, understanding the silences inside each other.

Lance carried her laptop to a table in the other room. She followed him out and studied the portrait on one wall.

"Great-Grandpa Vittorio," he told her.

"He looks like you. Something in the eyes."

"Trouble."

She laughed. "Passion."

"He was murdered."

"Nonna told me."

He straightened. "She did?"

"Before the two of you left. She told me all of it."

His jaw fell slack. "She makes me dig it up and swears me to secrecy, then tells you everything?"

"Once you found the truth, she didn't have to be ashamed."

"She never had to be ashamed. None of it was her fault."

"Sometimes it still feels that way."

His gaze softened. "So how'd you break out?"

As they left the carriage house and crossed the garden to the villa, she recounted everyone's arguments against her coming. "Pop didn't want me driving alone across the country." He didn't understand that once you'd looked death in the face it wasn't as frightening as everyone thought, but she didn't tell Lance that.

"And Momma?"

"Surprisingly supportive, when I agreed to come here."

"Cuts both ways. You can report back on me." Lance led her into the big Italian kitchen. "Our great-great-grandfather built this."

"Quillan Shepard." The first non-Italian in the family tree. A rugged, mining camp freighter and poet whose mysterious lineage they'd never know, but Nonna had spoken of her grandfather with weepy reverence. Sofie circled the room, trailing her fingers over the stone walls. "This has to be original."

"This room pretty much is. The rest was in bad shape when Rese got it. She matched the original look as well as she could, except where she improved it. Look here." As they moved through the doorway of the dining room into the front parlor, he indicated wooden corner pieces wrought in leaves and vines.

"Beautiful."

He touched one like a talisman. "Hard to find craftsmanship like this anymore."

Sofie nodded. "It would be a shame not to use her skill." He must have agreed, though his face showed something else. "What is it?"

He shot her a glance. "Her partner."

"Is he interested?" she asked, raising her brows.

"I don't know. I just hate that she gave up what we'd planned."

"Lance." Sofie touched his arm. "*You* gave it up."

He sighed. "Want to see the rest?"

"Sure."

He headed up the stairs. "I'm here in Seascape." His room had a weathered mariner theme in sea blue and beige that didn't quite suit him, but the guitar in the corner made it his.

Rese's mother's room next to that had shades of rose and cream; lovely, though lacking decorative items that could be hazardous to a schizophrenic. In contrast, the Rain Forest room was heaped with colorful clothing, jewelry, paints and paintings, books of Shakespeare and other sonnets, and a plethora of bright enamel frog sculptures.

"Star's room."

"Of course." It fit the little she'd seen of Star in the Bronx.

Lance closed the door, then indicated the farthest door on the landing. "Maria and the baby are in there, probably napping. She's pretty wiped out."

"Thought you weren't running an inn." She nudged him.

"More like a shelter for misfits."

"I hope it's okay that I—"

"Fagedda-bout-it." He gripped her shoulders. "We're glad you're here. Nonna's ecstatic."

A throaty melody trailed down the attic stairs through the open door in the hall. Sofie turned.

"That's Star. She takes Elaine to the attic when she paints inside."

She hadn't met Rese's mother. "How is Elaine?"

"Some days better than others. She can get agitated, but she's mostly content and more or less coherent. Seems to be glad she's here."

They climbed the stairs to the long attic furnished with colorful beanbag chairs. Rese's mother leaned on a purple one by the window, repeating fragments of Star's bawdy tune. Sofie approached the canvas on which Star had incorporated an aspect of Elaine's face into a floral garden scene, the effect created by the shadows of leaves and petals. "That's wonderful."

Star stopped singing and turned with a serious mien. "Flattery lights like dew upon the leaf, too soon evaporated."

"Or, as Nonna says, fine words don't feed cats." Sofie smiled. "But it really is amazing."

"Then I'll bask in your flattery and thank you."

Bask. How long had it been since she'd even thought of basking? Suddenly the possibility was real that, in this place, with these people—two who were family, three who were strangers, and a mother and infant she had yet to meet—where no one looked at her and saw death, she might make her way through the last of its trappings.

She startled as Elaine gripped her arm. "Have you seen him? Where have they gone? They've all gone. Gone, gone."

"No, I'm sorry," Sofie told her, startled by the words. "I don't know where they've gone." She looked into the white-haired woman's face and saw Rese's features housing a troubled mind. "I'm Sofie. It's nice to meet you, Elaine."

Elaine searched her face but didn't answer.

Star detached Elaine's grip. "Come on, Mom. Come watch the street."

Sofie glanced at Lance. He smiled. She smiled back, thankful once again for an old woman's words. Where there was life, there was most certainly hope.

———————

Still keyed up and more than a little aggravated, Matt went into his house. He wasn't in the mood for company, but Ryan obviously had no qualms about admitting himself, raiding the kitchen, and enjoying the plasma flat screen in the den.

He looked up, all blue eyed and eager. "Hey. Long day?"

And getting longer. "A late call that got complicated."

Ryan didn't press for details, didn't want them, and wouldn't get them anyway. "Grab a beer and join me."

Nice offer, Matt thought, as it was his den, his beer and food Ryan was consuming. "Did you leave me any stew?" He'd thrown the steroid-free meat and packaged organic vegetables into the slow cooker before leaving for work that morning.

"There's plenty." Ryan mopped up the gravy in his bowl with a chunk of baguette. "Good thing one of us can cook."

"You could do a lot of things, Ryan, if you tried." Like patching things up with Becca, his ex-fiancée, instead of mooching off him and pretending it would all work out on its own.

Ryan held up his empty lager. "Mind grabbing me another?"

Matt went to the kitchen. He filled a bowl from the half-empty slow cooker, tore off a chunk of bread, and carried Ryan his beer. The ball game was as good a means as any to decompress, and Ryan probably needed that too.

"This is the night"—Ryan twisted the lid off the bottle—"that the Raiders put one in the win column."

Matt shook his head. "That giant sucking noise you hear? That's your team in the drain."

"And the Niners aren't?"

"I don't take it personally if they are."

"How can you say that? It's your team, man."

"Oh yeah? Does Al Davis call you on Monday morning to see how your weekend went? Does he stress out when your sales are down? It's just a business."

"I haven't evolved into the complete mature man you are, Mattski." Ryan pulled on his beer. "When I was a kid, I thought they'd win the Super Bowl every year. Now I'm not sure they'll ever get there again, but I don't stop hoping. Sure you don't want a brew?"

Matt expelled a breath. "Just watched a man get ugly on the stuff, so I'll pass for now."

"Whether or not you have a beer won't affect what happens to some poor kid whose parents think he's a punching bag. You'll still be the schmuck pulling him out and trying to make something out of nothing. Maybe a brewski would help you forget."

"I really don't want to forget." He kept every face like a collection, small reminders of a world gone wrong. Ryan preferred to look the other way, even when his own house was burning down over his head.

When the game ended and Ryan showed no sign of leaving, Matt put on a jacket and hit the streets. The cold Sonoma night chilled his cheeks and neck as he strolled along, imagining a world where kids were safe. The town was quiet, in tune with the vineyard rhythms. The vines were dormant, cut back to gnarly Ts, and tourists nonexistent.

A car came toward him, a Z3 that stopped in the lane beneath the streetlamp. "If it isn't my favorite bleeding heart."

"Hey, Sybil."

"Contemplating the universe?"

"Yeah."

"I can think of more exciting ways to pass the time." Her silky hair looked like a shimmery veil as she tipped it over her shoulder.

Hard to tell if she was teasing. Her reputation suggested not.

"Buy me a drink and unwind?"

He glanced over his shoulder. "I've got Ryan at the house."

"Converting his sob story to a hangover?"

Matt shrugged. "Not his best of times."

"You cut everybody slack, don't you?"

He shook his head. "Not the mean ones."

"No, of course not." She smiled and zoomed past.

He stuffed his hands into his pockets and turned toward home.

CHAPTER THREE

It was after dark when Lance caught the rumble of Rese's truck outside her workshop. Anticipation rose inside until he heard another truck pull in behind and guessed whose it was. He was out the back door and heading for the shed before he thought of a reason not to. Stopping outside the shed door, he caught the scent of cigarette smoke and low male tones. Brad Plocken, her partner.

Rese said, "Just consider it before you argue."

"I am considering it. That's why I'm here."

"Okay, look." A rustle of papers. "We move this wall and have the staircase line up with the entrance here in the foyer. It draws everything together."

"Our whole budget'll be in those stairs."

"Then adjust the bid. It'll be the focal point of the lobby instead of a necessary transport to the upper level."

"You'd like being the focal point, showcasing your wood-work."

Something banged, maybe a palm on wood. "That's not what this is and you know it. You just won't admit I'm right." Rese rarely lost her cool. In fact Lance had thought the knack for getting under her skin was his alone. He opened the door and took in the two of them facing off, a half-burned cigarette dangling from Brad's lips.

Rese turned. "Can I help you, Lance?"

Her frustration was with Brad, but he hated the tone that made him sound like a child or servant who needed quick direction so she could get back to what mattered. "Sofie's here."

It was an excuse to interrupt, and Rese just nodded. "Okay. Great. I'll be in shortly."

He almost folded his arms and said, "I'll wait." But that would have been childish. As Sofie had said, he was the one who'd given up their plan and left Rese to reestablish things with Brad. Now he had to deal with it. "Need anything?"

She shook her head and put a few more inches between herself and the rugged graying guy in jeans and faded T-shirt. "No. Thanks."

He left them alone together, a slow burn in his gut. Only by grace had he come through the fires of vengeance to the peace of forgiveness. Would he stumble on jealousy now because Rese would smell like Brad's smoke and carry their argument in the tendons of her neck?

Since she worked long and drove far, he'd planned later and later dinners. Even so, he'd fed the household an hour ago, and there was no telling, tonight, how long she'd lock horns with Brad before even thinking of food. Maybe he should invite her partner in for a bite, see exactly what their dynamic looked like.

He'd only encountered the man one other time, and it had been his own neck in the noose that day, not Brad's. In fact, Brad had tried to solicit his help in convincing Rese to work with him again. Unwittingly, he'd done just that. His jaw clenched.

As Nonna made her way to the carriage house through the garden, he tried to look as though he hadn't just plotted a hundred ways to poison Brad's plate. She gripped his forearm and said, *"Tutto è permesso in guerra ed in amore."* Ah, they agreed. All was fair in war and love.

Brad came out of the workshop, shutting the door harder than necessary. He came around and paused. "If I didn't love her,

I'd strangle her." He tossed his cigarette and stalked on by.

Okay, then. Lance didn't proffer the invitation he'd considered. He picked up the butt and carried it to the trash in the kitchen. The aroma of the *saltimbocca* prepared in honor of Sofie's arrival lingered. Rese's portion awaited, but his mood had soured. He left the kitchen and joined Sofie in the long front parlor.

The room had been furnished as a gathering place for guests of the inn when Rese's plans had included him. He plopped down on an ottoman and took up his guitar, thrumming the strings lightly, then striking up a stentorian melody.

Sofie glanced up from her text. "Are you okay?"

"He loves her."

Sofie sat back. "What are you going to do about it?"

He shook his head. "I don't know."

"Are you doing everything you can this time to make it work?"

Valid question. She knew his history. But so many things had changed since he'd walked into this villa and talked his way into Rese's life. He'd changed, become more what he really was, more what he was meant to be.

One thing that hadn't changed was Rese's independence. What would a relationship look like with someone who didn't need him, whose resilience matched his, whose resources he couldn't equal? He ran his fingers up the neck of the guitar in a lilting melody and realized he might be the only one clinging to what they'd had.

Long after Brad had left and Sofie went to bed, he heard Rese come in to shower off a day's work and a head of steam. A song started in his head and he played along.

Knots of steel in flesh like bone, can't let go, can't let it show,
What you feel inside, alone, don't let it show, let anyone know,
How you feel . . . all made of stone . . . alone.

It wasn't about Brad. It was about Rese—the inroads they'd made, the ground he'd lost. It was about trust and how much he cared. She had turned to him months ago when she'd learned her mother was alive, when she'd dealt with her dad's lies and accidental death. Since then, like too many others, he'd betrayed her trust and her love. How could he expect her to try again? She could take care of herself. She always had.

Rese fumed. Why did Brad have to be so impossible? He wasn't stupid. His refusal to accept her plan was one part stubborn and two parts pigheaded. Well, she wasn't giving up. If the diagram wasn't enough, she'd create a model to help him visualize it.

Sleep would never come anyway, now that Brad had decided to be difficult. How had she thought she could work effectively with him? From the time he'd come on as Dad's site manager, they'd knocked heads. After fourteen years, he acted as though she were still twelve.

He'd claimed all the pranks the crew had played on her were out of some weird affection. Their mascot, he'd called her—the best challenge the men had. She clenched her fists. He even claimed he'd had a crush on her once, but she didn't buy it.

He acknowledged her skill but couldn't see past his ego to admit her solution to the staircase was not only feasible but perfect. And accusing her of showboating? All she wanted was to build a focal point of beauty that drew together the different elements and performed a structural purpose. She did not deserve that insult, and he knew it.

She huffed. He'd come to work in a temper and projected it on her. She never inflicted her personal problems on him or anyone. She kept them inside, where they belonged. But Brad had snapped at everyone, then rejected her idea.

Well, she was not giving up. She'd make the model, and when he saw how perfect it was he'd agree. Already picturing the model, she crept through the kitchen and reached for the door. Something moved behind her. She spun, heart thumping with memories of things in the dark, invisible things. "Lance." She pressed a hand to her chest. "You startled me."

"Sorry."

"I thought everyone was asleep."

He turned the light on over the stove. "You didn't eat."

"I'm not hungry."

He glanced at the door. "What are you doing?"

"Working."

He crossed to her. "It's eleven thirty."

"I'm not tired."

He brought his hand to the crook of her neck, thumb and fingers rubbing the taut tendons. "How about a few minutes together?"

"I need to do something."

"I could help."

"With what?"

"This knot here. And this one over here." His fingers read her tension and resolved it.

Her head lolled back. "What is it with him only seeing his way?"

"Brad?"

"He won't admit another plan might work as well or, God forbid, better."

"What's his look like?"

"His . . ."

"I imagine he has an alternative. Oak instead of maple?"

She leaned against the door. He'd made that point before. Was one way right and another wrong, or were there simply two opinions? She sighed. "I feel it when something should be a certain way. I've studied this place, mapped it in my mind. I see it. And I can do it. I know it'll work, but Brad won't agree."

"Dump him." Lance turned her to face the door and sank his fingers into the muscles of her back. As he softened the knots, she felt the animosity seeping away, and in its place came something treacherously close to pleasure. She did not want to feel that either.

"Lance."

"I love you."

"I have enough to think about already."

"So don't think."

"That's how you operate. But I actually have responsibilities. If I miss one detail, Brad will—"

"You want me to take him out?"

His godfather voice didn't amuse her. Not after the true-life vendetta he'd handled at the expense of their relationship. "Not funny, Lance."

He kissed the crook of her neck and sent shivers down her spine. "I think you should forget Brad and get some sleep."

"Like that's remotely possible."

"I'll sing to you."

The times he'd sung her to sleep sprang vividly to mind. "I just got you out of my bedroom; I'm not inviting you back."

"Yeah, but I was unconscious."

"Some people will do anything."

"Believe me, I wouldn't have planned that. I might have groveled at your feet, but I'd never faint." He turned her around.

Tension had drained from her body like rain through sand, replaced by a dangerous longing. But she wasn't ready to risk it again. "You did what you had to, Lance. Let me do the same."

"Don't close me out."

"I'm not." But people she loved had hurt her worse than any stranger could. Dad with his lies, Lance his half-truths. Mom had whispered her love, then disabled the furnace. She wasn't blaming them, but she didn't have to huddle in the dark anymore. She'd find her own way, in her own time. She pulled open the door and went out.

Lance let her go. He'd come back to the villa knowing there was no guarantee Rese would even let him in. Fainting at her feet had accomplished that much, but he'd upset her balance. No telling whether they could get close again. He didn't expect it to be easy. Nothing ever was. He would fight with her the rest of his life if she wanted it that way. Except just now the focus of her ire was Brad Plocken—her partner.

He ran a hand through his hair. What was he doing? He'd landed on his feet—barely, but he wasn't used to standing still.

Months ago he'd burned with purpose, and it had almost consumed him. Now he'd be glad to know what he was supposed to do tomorrow, tonight, an hour from now.

Sofie's phone rang. She'd left it on the table and gone to bed in the carriage house. He glanced through the window, but the lights were out in the old stone building, so he'd see who it was before disturbing her. "Hello?"

A long pause, then a small, soft voice, "Where's Sofie?"

"Asleep. Who's this?"

The phone clicked off.

Carly plugged his phone back into its charger and crept into her room. Daddy lied. She never said that, never said anything to upset him if she could help it, but it was true. He lied. He lied so much maybe he didn't even know he lied. Little tiny lies and great big ones, and nobody knew but her. Nobody cared. But she cared. She wished so much he didn't tell people things that weren't true.

Kids wouldn't talk to her. They stared at her like she was a freak, and she didn't even know what they thought they knew. Even her wonderful Ms. Rodemeyer looked at her with suspicion. Daddy hadn't liked Ms. Rodemeyer's opinions, and when she'd sided with her teacher, he made sure it never happened again.

He told lies, and no one doubted him. No one would believe her if she told them. He was the handsomest daddy in the school. Coolest of the cool.

He didn't just lie *about* her; he lied *to* her. He'd told her Sofie killed herself, but it wasn't true. She dreamed about Sofie. Sometimes the dreams were like a movie. Sometimes they were so real she felt her hugs, smelled her hair and the perfume she'd worn. She hadn't been able to find that perfume, but whenever Daddy took her to the department stores she sniffed the tester bottles just in case.

It had been a shock to find Sofie's number in his cell phone. If she was dead, why would he still have her number? She had thought maybe he knew another Sofie. So she'd called the number and heard the voice. Not another; it was her Sofie. It had hurt too much to speak, and she'd hung up. She'd been afraid to try again for a long time. But then she had, just to hear her again.

She thought Sofie would get mad and tell her to stop calling. But she didn't. She had asked who it was and what was wrong. Asked it like she really wanted to know. Daddy wouldn't want her to say anything, so she hadn't. Not until the man answered. He'd surprised her into speaking when she hadn't meant to. Who was he anyway?

She had hoped Sofie was looking for her, not finding someone else to love. Not forgetting. Now when she dreamed, would there be other people making Sofie laugh? Other people getting hugged?

Tears stung her eyes. She wished she hadn't called. She needed to believe, needed to pretend. Out of the place her stomach hurt, a mad feeling started. It wasn't fair. He had no right to Sofie. Whoever he was, she hated him.

CHAPTER FOUR

M att had turned the Price children over to Cassinia, who'd placed them with a foster family overnight. She would assume the case and oversee visitation and efforts to reunite. Since he had witnessed the domestic violence and been the one to remove the kids, Cassinia stood a better chance of gaining the family's trust, deciding if the parents could provide a stable home, and determining what counseling would be required.

As the investigating agent, he worked on the affidavit for the ex parte custody order. He'd give it to the state's attorney, Diana Myer, and be done until he had to testify at the hearing. If asked, he'd recommend compulsory urinalysis in connection with visitation, anger management for Price, and maybe a psych eval for both. Probably Vivian didn't realize how hard she'd squeezed the toddler, with the meth wiring her as tight as a cable. But that didn't lessen the pain of a grip that bruised tender flesh.

If both parents got sober and straight, they might realize what they stood to lose. Chances of that? He wouldn't guess.

He folded his hands behind his neck and leaned back from his desk. The cubicle he inhabited was no larger than a cell, walled with ugly beige file cabinets he'd inherited from the previous occupants. Most of the stories in the files were the same, an endless line of situations with no good answers. But he'd chosen it.

With a law degree from Columbia, he'd landed a position in a Boston firm and amassed a tidy nest egg by the time they offered him a junior partnership. Three days he'd considered it, then quit the firm to do social work. Certification was cake after the grueling law regime. The job itself, not. There were days—like this—when he wondered at what point he'd lost his mind.

The little faces filled his dreams and wouldn't leave him alone. He needed to stop thinking about the Price kids. The case was Cassinia's responsibility now. He had others to administer: parenting and anger management certificates to copy, a reunification and treatment plan to write, and stacks of statements to wade through, some of it pure gossip from the vultures who hovered every time a call came. The key was finding the truth amid the jealousies, defensiveness, and outright lies.

He turned to his keyboard, unprepared for the memory that slammed in. A small, broken body, as fair as the Price kids, fragile. He gripped his head, elbows to the desk, and willed it away.

Cassinia tapped his doorframe. Her cropped gray hair was shorter than his. Five silver rings adorned the cartilage of one ear, a single hoop in the other, and one more in her left eyebrow. "You're in early."

"Been a busy week. Unfortunately."

"Thought you'd like to know the kids settled in okay, once they'd cleaned up and eaten. Exhausted probably."

He nodded. "Good."

"Exam showed a possible greenstick fracture on Annie's wrist, maybe from a hard jerk. The others were hungry and dirty, but no bruises."

"So only the baby gets it?" His stomach clenched. The weakest member.

"We don't know anything yet. There could be another explanation."

But he'd seen who Vivian had grabbed and shook. "Yeah."

"Had your coffee?"

"I'm off caffeine."

"Well, you look like you could use some."

"Thanks." They shared a smile. "Listen, Cass. Don't pass me the details on this one."

"Okay." Her gaze softened. "Stay tough, big fella."

Yeah. At six-four, 210 pounds, people assumed a resilience that matched his physique. *"Hey, big guy,"* his dad used to say when they sparred. *"Show me you can take it."* And he could. He'd taken a perverse pride in absorbing the blows and giving as good as he got. Pretty soon, Webb Hammond hadn't pulled his punches. *"Watch this,"* he'd tell his buddies and barely give him time to brace. They'd all laugh when he gave it back. Some game. But at least it had been mutual.

He closed his eyes. Anniversary grief shouldn't last twenty years. There ought to be a statute of limitations on guilt. He sighed. *Just get through the day. Get through it and move on.*

—————

Late in the morning, Rese dragged herself into the big stone kitchen Lance was scrubbing down with something pungent. Not otherwise fastidious, he did keep his work space spotless and orderly—the opposite of his mother's chaotic, mouse-infested kitchen. She shuddered. Uncovering that nest in the sagging ceiling had been hideous, but there'd been only one witness—Lance's Jamaican friend, Chaz. He would take her meltdown to the grave.

Lance raised an eyebrow as she sank into a wooden chair at the table. "Bad night?"

She shrugged. She'd spent most of it constructing the model staircase, but it was too late to bring it in for Brad now. He had meetings with inspectors she didn't mind letting him face alone.

Maria joined them with the baby in her arms. She looked tense and wrung out—probably hadn't slept that great either.

Lance stood up and pulled out a chair for her. *"Hola."*

Her response was hardly audible.

He asked how the baby was doing and what she was going to call him. Rese recognized the Spanish phrases he had used every day since the baby was born. Why didn't she just give the kid a name?

This time she murmured, *"Digame usted."*

Lance furrowed his brow. *"Es tu hijo."*

Maria shook her head. *"Es su hijo."* Then she exploded. Spouting an agitated string of Spanish, she thrust the baby into his arms and ran out of the house.

Rese winced at the slammed door. "What was that?"

"I hope a misunderstanding." Lance stared at the sleeping infant. Neither his mother's outburst nor the bang of the door had disturbed his sleep.

"What did she say?"

"That she didn't bear the healthy baby I expected. But I healed him, and he belongs to me."

"What?" Her jaw dropped open.

"She probably means something completely different." He brought the infant's shaggy head up against his cheek with a painful expression.

Something miraculous had happened with the infant. He swore it was God alone, but it had been Lance's hand on the baby's face. No wonder Maria was confused.

"You can't just keep a baby."

He opened his eyes. "I'm not stupid, Rese."

"Yesterday you said you wanted kids."

"Our kids. Yours and mine."

She flushed. "Well, look at you." She waved her hand at his comfortable handling of the infant.

"That doesn't mean I think he's mine."

Rese turned to the door. "Where did she go?"

"I hope just far enough to calm down. But I'd better go see. Here. Hold him."

"What?" She had never held a baby. Neighbors didn't call the daughter of the crazy woman to baby-sit their kids. But as Lance eased the soft, warm bundle into her arms, an indescribable feeling seeped in, a liquefying warmth starting in the pit of her stomach and surging up her torso. Her arms seemed to conform to his shape. His milky breath drifted up, drawing her face to his. She kissed his soft forehead, then looked up at Lance.

"I love you." He kissed her mouth, lingering long enough to arrest her breath, then went out the door Maria had slammed.

Fours hours after Maria left, Sofie paced the long parlor with the baby whose cries squeezed her heart like a fist. His body stiffened and his arms trembled with the urgency of his need. Blood infused the caramel-colored skin of his face, forming tributaries of blue through his forehead to the shock of black hair that sprang from his scalp. Where was Maria?

"Let m . . . e." Nonna said from the overstuffed chair. Months past her stroke, what strength she still possessed had returned, and Sofie nestled the baby into her grandmother's lap.

Rese hurried in from the kitchen with a bottle. "I hope this is right. They had a million kinds of formula, bottles, and nipples, and I have no idea what makes one any better than another."

None of that mattered if they were only tiding him over until Lance found Maria.

"Did you ch . . . eck the temperature?"

"Umm . . ."

"Put a drop on the inside of your wrist," Sofie told her.

Rese did. "Just warm."

Nonna took the bottle and coaxed it into the sobbing infant's mouth. If he didn't accept the artificial nipple, things would get worse before they got better. A baby so new, who'd hardly been out of his mother's arms, knew only what comfort he'd found there. Sofie pressed her hand to her sternum, aching, but the baby started to suckle.

Nonna's face crinkled into a smile. Rese expelled her breath. Sofie closed her eyes, relief washing over as rhythmic sucking replaced the strident cries. Was there any urgency, any helplessness like a disconsolate baby?

She watched him drift off in Nonna's arms. What was Maria thinking? Didn't she know how soon her infant would need her?

Maybe not. There'd been so much to learn. The baby exhaled noisily.

Now that he'd quieted, maybe Sofie could work. She settled into the other end of the parlor, where she'd set up her laptop, reference studies, and manuals. But memories kept pressing against her will. She'd accomplished next to nothing by the time Lance came in hours later, empty handed.

He came into the parlor. "Is she back?"

From her place at the window, Rese shook her head.

He sagged. "I can't think where else to look. I've driven every street in town, and it's getting dark."

Sofie said, "I don't understand how she could leave him. Why would she do that?"

"I don't know." He rubbed his jaw and headed into the kitchen.

Rese turned. "She gave him to Lance."

Sofie set down her note card. "What?"

"She said Lance healed him and he should have him."

"Healed him?"

"He was born with a cleft palate. He wasn't breathing. Maria just sat there screaming her head off, so Lance picked him up and covered his face. When he took his hand away the baby started crying and his mouth was . . . fixed."

Sofie stared. "Lance worked a miracle?"

"He says God wanted to do something." Rese crossed her arms. "But it was his hand."

Months ago Lance had extended forgiveness to the man who'd ordered their grandfather and great-grandfather murdered. He had poured himself into Nonna's troubled past until Momma wrung her hands with worry, but in the process, he had found an acute connection to God. Could that connection . . .

Rese said, "When he and Antonia got here, he passed out at my feet. He could hardly eat. Antonia said he'd been used up by God, but the night Maria had her baby—I'd never seen him so intense."

"He's always been passionate."

"It takes more than passion to work miracles. Doesn't it?"

"I don't know." Sofie slid her fingers into her hair. "There's that part in the Bible that says it's no longer we who live but Christ who lives in us. Maybe there's a spark God can ignite in someone who's willing and open enough to accomplish His purpose. Lance has always wanted to do big things for God."

Rese paced. "Well, Maria's confused." She turned at the window. "Or maybe she intended to leave the baby all along."

"Did it seem that way?"

"No. She held him all the time. But the baby's almost a week old, and she hasn't named him. And she looked terrible this morning, as though she'd cried all night."

"Postpartum depression?"

"I have no idea." Rese planted her hands on her hips. "We don't know anything about her except what Michelle told us."

Lance had given Sofie the bare bones of Maria's previous situation, living in a single room with six migrant workers, any one of whom might have fathered the baby. "She wouldn't go back to where she'd been, would she?"

"I don't know. Maybe they took her back. I only know there's a baby here with no mother."

Sofie looked up. She'd barely seen Maria and had no fix on her mental-emotional state. The thought of her being snatched away from her infant sharpened the ache. Had she left him with Lance for his protection? Could what had seemed selfish be, instead, an act of supreme sacrifice?

A pall fell over the house as night drew on and Maria didn't come back. Sofie walked the colicky infant to sleep in the room she'd chosen to share with him, the room they'd given Maria. White organza and silk sprays of jasmine created a look so pure and pristine it hurt. Innocent. Unblemished.

Gently, she laid the baby down in the white wicker bassinet. She ran her finger over the soft curve of his head, then pulled the yellow flannel over him and patted his back. One miniature fist rested against his cheek. His mouth moved in dreamy suckling.

She stepped away and pressed her hands to the small of her

back. When she'd left New York, she had not for one moment guessed she'd be doing this. Lance didn't like it, but Rese had no experience with babies.

Her own had been carefully excised, yet it came back now with aching detail. The nameless baby needed care. All through the day, other arms had held him, other hearts beat against the pink shell of his ear, but she knew what he wanted. She looked down and whispered, "Where's your momma? How could she bear to leave you?"

CHAPTER FIVE

M att took the call with a sigh. An abandoned infant. Hispanic. One week old. At least he hadn't been found dead in a Dumpster.

He pocketed his keys and prepared to face it. As he reached the door, his pager went off. He checked the number. Becca. He'd call her from the car, give her a chance to vent, then think of a few good things to say about Ryan. Neither mean nor destructive, Ryan merely sat on the irresponsible end of the graph. Could be worse. A lot worse.

He buckled his seat belt and keyed in her number. "Hey, Becca."

"Sorry to call you at work."

"I wouldn't have given you my pager if that was a problem."

"Right. Well, I'm looking for a date."

"Aha." He turned the key in the ignition.

"Friday night is the sales awards dinner, and if I show up alone the stockbrokers will be hitting on me all night."

Nothing wrong with her self-esteem. "I see the problem."

"Will you escort me?"

"Uh . . . Bec. Ryan would love . . ."

"Come on, Matt; you look good in a suit."

He headed toward the address where someone had walked away from an infant. "I can't date Ryan's fiancée."

"It's just an awards dinner and I'm not his fiancée."

"Becca, Ryan's my friend."

"And I'm not?"

"Of course you are." He turned through the intersection. "You both are. Don't put me in the middle."

She sighed. "I thought you'd be there for me, Matt. You let Ryan hang out, but I don't get any of your time?"

"That's not it."

"I need someone big and good-looking to run interference. And I haven't seen you in weeks. This is a reasonable request."

Except Ryan would be devastated. Or furious. Or both. But Becca was his friend too. If Ryan had been busy or out of town, he'd have accompanied her without concern. But she'd given back Ryan's ring—thrown it, to be exact. Technically that meant she was available.

She continued before he could come up with a reasonable response. "I won't call you my date if that feels better. I'll say you're my friend. My good friend, I thought."

He leaned his head against the rest and approached the quiet address he'd been called to. Nice place, but appearances could be deceiving. "All right. But I'm telling Ryan so he doesn't hear it from some third party."

"Not that it matters if or how Ryan hears anything, but go ahead."

"Okay. See you Friday." He parked outside the Italianate villa. The report hadn't been clear on how the baby got there. Had someone left an infant on the doorstep? The place had a welcoming sort of peace about it, and if—He stopped the speculation. Get the facts and work with them. Trying to guess motivations and gauge intentions was part of his job—not imagining scenarios before he even saw what he was up against.

Sofie paced the parlor. Rese had insisted they call the police, but she could have told her it was too soon to legally consider

Maria missing. Just because one day people were there and the next they were not didn't mean a crime had been committed. Not even when someone had waited six years for them to come back.

The police had, however, notified the child welfare division about the baby Maria left behind, and someone from Child Protective Services was on the way. Sofie swallowed the lump in her throat formed by the words *child* and *protective*. She wanted nothing more than to close herself into the carriage house out of sight. But Rese had asked her to listen for the door while she got ready for work and Lance searched the neighborhood one last time.

She turned at the bookcase and walked past the window. Would the person who made protecting children a profession identify that particular failure in another? Would it show like a blemish or stain? Her mind flooded with images of ribbons and barrettes, lacy socks and little pink shoes. She remembered the wiggly weight in her lap, small spongy palms pressed to her cheeks.

"Hear me, Sofie."

"I'm listening, sweetie."

She startled when the knock came. Her pulse fluttered. She made herself move toward the door and pull it open. She didn't know what she'd expected in the social worker, but not the tall man in rolled shirt sleeves who stood there. His brown hair and strong jaw registered, but it was the warmth in his deep brown eyes that undid her.

He offered his hand, a firm, encompassing grip. "Matt Hammond. Child Protective Services."

The woman who opened the door affected him on a visceral level that took him by surprise; the elegant curve of her neck, honey gold hair, and eyes like dark copper pennies with a green aura surrounding the pupils. Her features were defined, her figure exquisite, her expression quick and intelligent, yet somehow veiled. Without realizing, he'd enclosed her hand with both of his.

He released her. "I received a call from the police about an infant?"

She nodded. "Come in. Rese will be out in a minute. Would you like to sit?"

"Sure. And you're . . ."

"Sofie. Sofie Michelli."

The name slid in and locked, fitting her so well he doubted he'd ever forget. The long room, broken into conversational groupings, felt more like a cozy inn than a home. He took a cream-colored chair by the window.

"Would you like coffee?"

"No thanks. I'm kicking the habit—this week." He smiled.

"Is there something else you'd like?"

"I'm fine, thanks. Is this a bed-and-breakfast? I didn't see a sign."

"It was going to be, but Rese changed plans."

He supposed Rese would address the issue he'd been called in for, but conversing with Sofie reminded him of the time he'd asked a girl to the prom and discovered he enjoyed the younger sister more. They'd been laughing too hard to notice the grand entrance his date made, and she hadn't forgiven him all evening.

"I haven't been in this neighborhood for a while, but wasn't this building burned?"

Sofie nodded. "Partially. Rese renovated it."

"He did good work."

A smile touched her mouth. "Here she is now."

Aha. He stood and introduced himself to the woman who joined them, short dark hair framing an angular face.

She said, "I was hoping Lance would be back."

Just as he wondered if anyone there was going to tell him what he'd come to learn, the back door opened and a man of medium stature and somewhat gaunt appearance approached. Matt extended his hand.

The man returned a firm grip. "Lance Michelli."

"Michelli. You're Sofie's . . ."

"Sofie's my sister." He looked around. "Where are Nonna and the baby?"

"In my room." Rese crossed her arms.

Lance took off his jacket and finger-combed his windblown hair. "So, what are we doing?"

She shrugged. "Mr. Hammond just got here."

"Matt. Please." He liked things informal. People at ease were more accurately assessed, and he was about solutions, not control.

"This is an initial interview where I gather as much info as I can about the baby." Since the women seemed to defer to Lance, he directed his attention there. "You told the police the mother has been gone twenty-four hours?"

"Almost."

"And before she left, she asked you to watch the baby?"

"That's . . . what she meant."

A clever sidestep. "What did she say?"

"She was speaking Spanish and got pretty emotional, but that was the idea."

"Spanish is her first language?"

"Only language, as far as we can tell."

"Did she indicate how long she'd be gone?"

"No."

He took out a pad to jot notes. "Baby's name?"

"He doesn't have one yet."

Uh-huh. "Mother is Maria . . ."

Lance shrugged. "That's all we know. Someone asked us to provide her a place to have her baby. She's only been here a week."

"Who asked?"

"Michelle Farrar. She's with a local church."

Matt took down her contact information. Michelle might know the mother's name and whether she intended the safe surrender of her infant. "When was the baby born?"

"The twenty-fifth. Around 2:30 a.m."

"What hospital?"

"No hospital. She had him upstairs. In her room."

Matt looked up. "Who attended?"

"No one. Maria had him before we knew it."

"Has a doctor seen him?"

Lance shook his head. "The nurse midwife came when he was born, and she's done a couple checkups."

"But Maria never took him to a pediatrician or emergency clinic?"

"The baby's fine."

Maybe so, but he was trying to determine her mindset, particularly whether she had abandoned the infant. Sonoma County's safe-haven law only allowed surrender of an infant within three days to a hospital emergency room. Maria may have thought she was leaving her baby in good hands, but he wasn't getting the idea they'd been prepared for her to disappear.

Lance studied the man who'd come on the baby's behalf. Why had CPS sent someone already? If one day was too soon for the police to investigate a missing person, wasn't it also too soon to call it abandonment? He appreciated Matt's interest in the infant's welfare, but Maria was the one they needed to find. Her little baby may not have seen a doctor, but he was hale and hardy and had more arms to hold and soothe him than most babies starting out.

Where was Maria, and who could she turn to? He could not forget her face as she told him the baby was his. The verbs she'd used didn't really translate to *watch* or *look after*, but he couldn't believe she'd given up the baby she had hardly let go of for a minute. How could she disappear so fast? He'd been right behind her. Unless someone had grabbed her. Maybe someone had been waiting. Maybe they'd arranged it.

"Look," he said, meeting Matt Hammond's eyes. "We don't mind watching the baby. But I'm worried about Maria."

"Did either she or—" he checked his notes—"Michelle indicate Maria intended to abandon her infant?"

"No. We didn't press her for details, but she never said

anything like that. Until yesterday, it had been hard to get more than a word or two from her."

"And yesterday?"

He ran his hand through his hair. "She got upset, misunderstood things."

"What did she misunderstand?"

"When she first came, she asked what she had to do to stay here. I told her just have a strong, healthy baby. I meant she didn't have to earn our help, that we were willing to care for her, but she might have thought that meant I wanted the child."

Matt raised his brows. "What makes you think that?"

"She said I should name him. That he was mine."

"Is he?"

Rese stiffened. "She didn't mean Lance was the father."

Matt waited to hear it directly.

Lance shook his head. "I never saw her until a week ago. She meant I should have the baby because . . ." He kicked himself. He hadn't meant to bring up the rest of it. "I helped when he was born."

"I thought she was alone."

"After." Lance rubbed his jaw. "He had some problems. Wasn't breathing. She thinks I fixed what was wrong."

"You resuscitated the infant?"

"He was just lying there, so I picked him up. He . . . didn't look good."

"In what way?"

Lance swallowed. "Well, there was blood and . . . you know, birth stuff, and maybe it just looked like his mouth hadn't . . ."

"He had a cleft palate." Star joined them. In her turquoise beaded top and white caravan-style pants, with her pale skin and hair, she looked like a bleached belly dancer. And in that one sentence she'd undone all his careful hedging.

Matt said, "You are . . ."

"I'm Star." She lighted on the arm of Sofie's chair.

Matt honed in. "You saw what happened, Star?"

"Lance healed him."

Great.

Matt cocked his head. "Healed him?"

"He does that," Star said. "Fixes people."

Lance tried to catch her eye and limit the damage, but she stubbornly avoided looking at him.

"Fixes them how?"

"However they need fixing."

Matt probably thought he'd landed in some Jonesian cult that required impressionable girls to donate babies. The charismatic male with his female devotees. Rese stared her down, but the damage was done, and he suspected Star enjoyed that.

Matt directed his attention back to him. "Did Maria think you cured the baby?"

Lance sighed. "She's overwhelmed."

"The midwife examined the infant? She noted his cleft palate?"

Rese planted her hands on her hips. "She wasn't here. She came after."

"After Lance miraculously healed the infant."

Lance expelled a breath. "I didn't—"

"Does Maria think you worked a miracle?"

"I don't know what she thinks."

"She thinks he walks on water," Star said.

Matt Hammond turned and fixed her with a probing look. "And does he?"

Star formed a secret smile. " 'There are more things in heaven and earth, Horatio, than are dreamt of in your philosophy.' "

CHAPTER SIX

Rese silently groaned when her mother took that moment to come downstairs. Her prematurely white hair sprang out of its straight below-the-ear cut as though she'd rubbed it with a balloon. Why hadn't Star stayed upstairs with her?

Surprised into motion, Matt Hammond got to his feet and held out his hand. "Hello, I'm—"

Mom swept past him with her jerky gait as though he were as invisible as Walter had been to everyone else. Clozapine kept Mom's hallucination away, but her other symptoms were unmistakable. She went to the window and murmured, "Gone, gone, gone."

Rese drew herself up. "That's my mother, Elaine. I'm her legal guardian." That should be all he needed to know.

Matt stepped toward the window. "Who's gone, Elaine?"

Rese almost pointed out the obvious, but Lance touched her hand. She ached in silence as Matt Hammond prodded.

"Is someone gone?"

Her mother looked into his face. "They took her away. They always take them away."

He would realize her confusion. And what difference did it make? He was concerned with the baby's welfare, not Maria's.

And certainly not Elaine Barrett's. Mom had barely known the baby was there.

"Did you see something, Elaine? Something in the yard?"

"They aren't nice, you know. You have to be careful. She wasn't careful and now she's gone. Gone, gone. They took her and she's gone. They're all gone. All gone."

Rese clenched her jaw, ashamed and embarrassed, and angry with herself for both. Mom couldn't help her delusions any more than she could help trying to kill her only daughter, but that particular episode still colored their interactions. Maybe that was why she'd said yes to Brad's offer, why she'd surrendered the daughter role to Star, who had no blood tie whatsoever.

She glanced at the friend she'd had since they were little girls. Though two months older, Star had always seemed like a little sister, running to her to make things right, to take away the hurt, to help her go on. And even though she'd sometimes resented Star's self-centered tunnel vision, she had liked being the strong one. Only in these last months had they found a different balance.

With Mom, Star seemed to thrive for the first time on responsibility, to see outside herself to someone else's needs. They talked nonsense together, and Rese would hear them laughing in the attic like the Looney Tunes she and Star had been called by unkind classmates.

As Matt Hammond questioned her mother, Rese drew herself up. "She's probably said all she knows."

He turned. "Anyone else see someone taken from the front yard?"

She opened her mouth to explain, then caught Mom's face at the window. Why steal her moment? Why say aloud that her word was worthless? Or was it?

"Star?" Matt Hammond moved from folly to foolishness.

"'Let every eye negotiate for itself.' Mine saw naught."

"Mom likes to watch out the window while Star paints." The words were out before she realized she had given weight to her mother's statement. "She probably notices more than the rest of us."

Matt Hammond must have been thinking he'd stepped into *One Flew Over the Cuckoo's Nest*. The strange thing was, she didn't care. The bond she felt with Star and her mother and Lance, and even Sofie and Antonia, meant more than anyone's opinion. They were family, and she'd learned in the Bronx, amid the chaos and clamor of Lance's relatives, exactly how much that meant.

She sent Mom a soft smile, and her mother smiled back.

Matt searched the faces. He didn't know what to make of the supposed miracle healing or Lance Michelli. The man might be a fanatic, except he'd deflected attention—not the sociopathic behavior of a cult leader. Until Star spoke up, he'd seemed normal enough—concerned, but normal.

Matt slid his gaze to the guy's primary relationship: Rese Barrett. She'd been uncomfortable with the talk of miracles and healings, though she hadn't denied the occurrence. She was obviously in love with Lance Michelli. An attraction of opposites? She'd demonstrated loyalty and an instinct to protect. What would she be willing to hide?

The mother exhibited neurodegenerative thought and motor characteristics, but he didn't automatically discount what she'd said. If Maria had been "taken away," they were not dealing with abandonment, and while that didn't affect his taking the infant into the legal, and possibly physical, custody of the state, it might impact things later.

Star's was an odd though appealing lunacy. Even Sofie . . . He hadn't noticed her wrists until the window's light caught the faint scars. They piqued a desire to know more, but that was part of the job. The more details he could gather about each of them, the better he could decide whether to remove the infant from the home where he was being cared for and try to find a different place in an overtaxed system.

Had things in this house frightened Maria enough to leave the baby? He wasn't making assumptions, but if she was in the country illegally, she could have been manipulated with threats of exposure or expulsion. She might not know the infant's American citizenship would give her the right to stay. Anchor babies were a goal of illegals for that very reason. She had nothing to gain by leaving him—unless she'd been forcibly separated.

He wasn't seeing that here. If there'd been any illegal adoption or baby transfer plans, the last thing they'd do was notify his department. Not when they had an undocumented infant. And their concern for Maria seemed genuine.

He finished jotting down his notes. "I'll need to see the baby."

Rese led him into a suite off the kitchen. The infant lay curled in the center of the bed, like an inch worm, knees to elbows. His brownish skin was touched with a slight newborn rash, and he had a full head of black hair. Matt lifted the baby from the bed and examined the square face, the unmarred mouth. Mass hallucination?

The old woman watching over him didn't seem the sort. She fixed him with a rapier look and said, "Don't w . . . ake him." The lag in her speech might suggest stroke, but she was used to matriarchal power.

"I'll try not to." Matt sat down on the chair and unbundled the baby. He checked him for bruises, malnutrition, any sign of neglect. He seemed healthy. "How's he been fed?"

"Maria nursed him." It was Lance Michelli who answered. "He's had formula since she left."

Matt noted the dimples on the infant's fist. "But she nursed him for a week?"

They all nodded.

"Has he been fussy, colicky . . . ?"

"No more than any newborn, and less than some." Again Michelli.

Matt cocked a brow. "You have experience?"

"Nieces and nephews. We all live close, or did. They're in the Bronx." He glanced at his sister, who had followed him into the room. "Except Sof, who just got here."

She said, "Our family owns an apartment building and lives in most of it. Lots of children."

Matt nodded then turned back to Lance. "You said Maria hasn't named him, so I'm guessing there's no birth certificate?"

"Not yet. The midwife's been asking."

It wasn't the strangest case he'd handled and was far from the worst. He'd seen no sign of drugs, no weapons. He wasn't there to judge their religion, only the safety of the environment. And if there was any truth to what Elaine Barrett claimed to have seen, Maria may not have chosen to leave the child. That argued for as much stability in the situation as he could provide. She'd look for her child here, if she could—or chose to.

"Well, he seems healthy. I'm going to place him in the legal custody of the state." He glanced around. "That can include physical placement unless you're willing and able to care for the infant while we sort this out?"

"Of course," Sofie replied unequivocally. "We have six adults here. We can certainly care for one newborn baby."

"I'll need to assign someone temporarily as physical guardian." He turned to Lance Michelli. "If Maria asked you . . ."

He nodded. "I will, but I think she'll be back. If she can."

Matt's instincts told him the same. But he'd been wrong before. People were endlessly disappointing.

After leaving the villa, Matt squeezed in between crates of Gatorade and Ensure stacked on the narrow, shady porch and knocked on the door of the small house. If the place hadn't almost been hidden by the surrounding foliage, the neighbors might have had a serious beef with the pack-rat resident. When the door swung open, he saw that the porch was not an anomaly. Packs of toilet paper rose like insulation from floor to ceiling along both sides of the entryway.

The woman patted the packages and smiled warmly. "For the church outreach."

They swapped TP instead of recipes? Handed it out like

tracts? He extended his hand. "Matt Hammond." There was not one attractive feature on the woman, yet he found the whole of her homeliness oddly charming.

"Come on in. None of this bites."

He could get buried alive in it though.

"You wanted to talk about Maria?"

He followed her down the hall. "I need to find out if she's got family here who would take responsibility for the infant."

"If she does they ought to be drawn and quartered." She tossed a glance over her shoulder. "I mean that in the kindest way."

"Of course. And why do you hold this compassionate opinion?"

They broke free into a kitchen that was amazingly immaculate; the floor, sink, stove, and three feet of usable counter space fairly sparkled. "Would you like a cup of tea?"

He wouldn't especially but said, "Herbal if you have it."

She took down a canister. "I think osmanthus. You don't strike me as needing chamomile."

Without caffeine, chamomile would have him snoring. "You were saying about Maria . . ."

"Ever seen slavery?" She spooned a teaspoon of yellow bits into a steeping bag and pulled the string tight. "I've read about it, watched documentaries. It's a whole different thing to see it in action."

"You're saying . . ."

"I would be shocked if she was in her living situation voluntarily."

Matt crossed his arms. "How did you find her?"

"I take supplies to that part of Agua Caliente." She poured water from the already steaming kettle over the tea bag nestled inside a flowered cup and saucer. "People are packed into those apartments like . . . Well, mostly they're families trying to get by. They work in town, cooking, cleaning, construction, or nearby, picking. But when I asked about the men who had Maria, the women crossed themselves and spat."

"And that told you what?"

"I'm not great with the language, but I know what *diablo* means. If they're the devil's tools, it can't be good for her."

"That's what the women told you? They worked for the devil?"

"Did the devil's work. Make of that what you will." Michelle removed the bag and handed him the tea. "Once I knew she was there, I kept an eye out. They never let her leave the building. Only reason I got her out to have the baby is that they were scared stiff to deliver it."

"Why didn't she go to the hospital? They're required to treat her."

Michelle shrugged. "She was terrified, absolutely refused, so a midwife in the church took her on."

"Can I get that number?" He sipped the tea while she flipped through a personal directory and wrote it on a slip of paper.

"Here you go. But the baby was born by the time Mrs. Sommers got called."

"Did Maria intend to dispose of him?"

Michelle brought a hand to her bosom, stunned by his word choice or the idea itself.

"If her situation was as bad as you say, she might not have motherly feelings for him. She might have thought he'd be better off dead, and . . . maybe that's why she refused the hospital."

Michelle couldn't be so naïve as to think it didn't happen. The birth could have caught the girl by surprise, and then people in the house were there before she could harm the infant. Or maybe she had, and that was why he wasn't breathing when Lance picked him up.

"She seemed fine the times I checked. Sleeping almost constantly, but nursing and changing and holding the baby when she was awake."

"So you'd say she bonded."

"I didn't see anything to make me think otherwise."

He sipped the sharply floral, almost peachy, brew. "How well do you know Lance Michelli?"

"Well enough to trust him with a young mother. Rese had

been attending our Bible study before she started working such long hours."

"Ever seen him work a miracle?"

"What?"

"Star claims Lance healed the baby's cleft palate." He waited while Michelle turned that over in her mind.

"If a miracle happened, it was God who worked it. But I will say this. I've had a burden for that man since the day I met him."

"What kind of burden?"

"To uphold him in prayer. Sometimes protection. Sometimes just lift him up." She poured water over a second bag for herself. "The night that baby was born, I awoke with tears streaming from my eyes and a sense of wonder and delight."

This was getting too weird. "Did you know what happened?"

"Not until now."

"No one else said anything? Not even Lance when you checked in?"

She shook her head.

Why would he keep it quiet? He could have all the zealots hailing him prophet—or charlatan. Not to mention the scores of blind and lame who'd come falling at his feet. Tidy little racket if he played it right.

Instead, he'd low-keyed the supposed healing. There'd been no sign of a cleft on the baby's face, except a faint red line. Where it had closed? He frowned. His job required analysis and observation and a good deal of intuition. It didn't call for superstition.

"Have you heard from Maria in the last twenty-four hours?"

"No." She removed the tea bag from her cup.

"Do you have reason to believe the baby could be in danger?" He drank his tea, eager to be done.

"Maria could be. The baby? I don't know."

He handed back the cup and thanked her, then made his way through packaged diapers, toothpaste, dish soap, canned goods, and the walls of toilet paper to the door. He pocketed the midwife's info. He would call from the car and see if she'd answer some questions. Michelle had raised his concern for Maria, but the young mother wasn't his responsibility—only her infant.

Some ten minutes later, the midwife motioned him into the sunroom tacked onto the front of the house, or maybe it was a porch converted to a solarium. "So what would you like to know about Maria's little son?"

They went over what he'd already been told. Mrs. Sommers knew nothing about a cleft lip. The infant had presented healthy when she arrived.

"Did you suggest Maria take the baby to the hospital to make sure?"

Mrs. Sommers shook her head. "The girl was adamant. No hospital. No *médico*."

"And no birth certificate?"

She shrugged. "Maria hasn't named him."

"This baby's an American citizen. He's eligible for assistance. He's also her ticket to remaining in the U.S. Why would she keep his birth secret?"

She crossed her arms. "Maybe she doesn't want to remain."

CHAPTER SEVEN

Rese followed the sloughing sound and smell of wet plaster to the scaffolding Brad had set up inside the three-story San Francisco row house. Even though the day was wet and foggy, sweat formed a circle at the neck of his faded black T-shirt. She lifted the model onto the scaffold planking at his feet.

He stuck the trowel into the pale blue wall plaster and looked up. "What's that?"

"The way it works."

He scratched the back of his neck. "I'm in the middle of something, Rese."

"Just take a look."

"I'll look at it later. Can't let this plaster dry."

She moved the model out of his way. "Well, we have to make the bid this afternoon, and we should have it in our heads which way to go."

"Yep."

She set the model on the workbench in the center of the room. "Have any more of that mixed?"

"You take over here, and I'll blend up the last wall's worth."

They worked in silence, slathering the walls with plaster, then dragging it to a smooth, pale finish. They'd found the original molds in the attic, so they were casting their own raised moldings to run along the ceiling. White curlicues on sky blue. Very period.

They kept at it until they'd finished both remaining walls, then sealed the remaining plaster to patch air pockets that might open up or crack, though they were both skilled enough she doubted they'd find any. What she really wanted was to deal with their bone of contention. They'd be presenting the plan in less than two hours, meeting the owners of a small Nob Hill hotel, with diagrams and photographs and—she hoped—her model for the staircase.

The original staircase had been damaged years ago in a quake. The previous owners had pocketed the insurance money and painted over the cracks. She wanted to replace it altogether with a gentle spiral that met current regulations and added a beautiful focal point. Brad was stuck on saving the original, which she would have agreed to if it hadn't been a clunky eyesore from the day it was constructed.

She finished scrubbing her hands and dried them off, then let Brad have the sink. Since she had him confined in the narrow bathroom, she said, "Did you look at it?"

"Yep." He stripped the sweaty T-shirt and rubbed it over his chest, then tossed it over his shoulder.

"And?"

"It could take the blue ribbon at a state-fair dollhouse show."

"I don't mean the model. I mean the idea."

"Uh-huh." He splashed water on the dusty tiles with the vigorous rinsing of his forearms. They didn't usually bid after a day's work, but the hotel owners couldn't spare any other time to view the plan.

She grabbed a paper towel and swabbed the floor at his feet.

"Get up, Rese. I'll take care of that."

"I don't want the mud to harden on the tile." She finished wiping and stood.

His glare caught her by surprise. "I didn't ask you to clean up my mess." He grabbed the towel. "Give me some room. And quit trying to fix everything."

She raised her chin. "That's my job. Fixing things." She scowled. "What are you so mad about?"

"I'm not mad." He turned and leaned on the doorjamb. "Just because we disagree—"

"I don't think it has anything to do with that. If you were in your right mind, you'd see the beauty of my plan."

He scowled. "Listen, kid . . ."

She huffed. "That might have worked ten years ago. But probably not now."

He pawed his pocket for a cigarette, found the pack empty and threw it. "Joni's getting married."

Rese stood a second before she realized what he was saying. "Your wife?"

His throat worked. "My ex."

"Oh, Brad."

"Don't get girly on me."

She brought her hands to her hips. "If you had any guts, you'd tell her how you feel. Just swallow your pride and do it."

"You don't know anything about that."

He was right. She was the last person to talk about swallowing pride. "You know what you want."

"No I don't. And you don't either." He pushed off. "I'm regretting opening my mouth."

"Brad . . ."

"Let it go, Rese. We have a pitch to make."

"We haven't even figured out our plan."

"Yes we have." He strode to the workbench and scooped up her model. "I wrote up the bid yesterday while you were having a personal crisis."

"It wasn't a personal crisis. And which way did you bid it?"

"With your fancy staircase."

She followed him to the door. "You'd already changed your mind? Before I brought the model?"

"I don't require show-and-tell. I'm as able to envision something as you are. In case you forgot, I taught you to see the big picture."

"What?"

"I'll admit you're better with the details, but you started out unable to see the forest for the trees."

"Look who's talking."

He glowered. "I'm through discussing my personal life."

"Who's she marrying?"

"Some loser worse than the last guy. She'll be crying on my shoulder inside of six months."

"Then save her that mistake."

"I can't stop her mistakes. Never could." He gripped the door-knob. "Can we go now?"

They climbed into his truck, and he got a clean shirt from the back seat and pulled it over his head. She perched the model in her lap, buckled up, and breathed the scent of smoke and tacos. Three wadded Taco Bell bags nestled at her feet. "Clean out the truck before you propose."

"Not happening."

"The truck or proposing?"

He gunned the engine and tore away from the curb.

"Why is she marrying him?"

He patted his empty pocket, then turned. "Did someone open your head and exchange brains? Since when do you care about anyone's love life?"

Since Lance broke down the walls that had kept her safely contained. "Fine. Buy her china."

"She's dangerous with china." He slid her a glance. "On second thought, maybe I'll get a whole set of that heavy stoneware. She could be out of this in a month."

"And in jail for battery with deadly crockery?"

He tossed back his head and laughed, then turned with a puzzled look. "That was funny."

"Don't look so shocked."

"What's gotten into you?"

Good question. "When's the wedding?"

"Two months. On the Golden Gate Bridge. Is that stupid or what?"

"Might be kind of foggy."

"It's where he proposed, so he thought it would be romantic to say their vows in the same spot. Just the two of them and two witnesses." The truck lurched over the top of the steep hill and they started down.

Rese readjusted the model in her lap. "Did she tell you that?"

"Asked me to be her witness."

Her jaw fell open. "Brad. She's begging you to stop her."

He snorted.

"She wants you to object."

"I doubt they'll have that part in the ceremony."

Rese shook her head. "Are you actually going to stand there while she marries someone else?"

He jerked the wheel, joggled over the trolley lines, and pulled up to a corner market. "I need smokes."

When the door slammed behind him, she realized how hard she'd pushed. Lance was wearing off in more ways than one.

Brad lit up the minute he stepped out of the store. He climbed in and opened both windows. "You mind?"

"No, but I thought you were quitting." He'd tried four times that she knew of.

"Don't nag me on that now."

"I'm not."

He blew out the smoke. "Here's the thing. Just because I haven't replaced her, doesn't mean I can live with her."

"Were you married long enough to know?"

The truck climbed up Nob Hill. "She was eighteen when we married. Lasted until she'd just turned twenty."

"You don't think things might have changed in the, what, twenty years since?"

"Nineteen. And they can't have changed much if she's asking her ex-husband to witness her wedding."

"She's asking you to stop it." She was more sure of that than ever.

He pulled into the small lot outside the quaint fourteen-room hotel. "We're here."

She looked down at the miniature staircase she'd built with meticulous care, then over to him. "Thanks."

"For what?"

She half lifted it. "Going with this."

He smiled for real. "Let's go knock their socks off."

She jumped when he came into the room.

"Carly? What are you doing?"

Her brain scurried. "Um, checking out your phone."

"Why?"

Think. Think. "To see if you had games."

He held out his palm for the phone. "Why would I have games on my phone? I don't play games."

"Drew said every cell phone has games."

"Why would you listen to a skinny wart like that?"

She should have said someone less recognizable. But his was the name that jumped to her head because he was, well, a skinny wart with scaly patches of skin and red hair so thin his scalp showed through. Kids didn't like him much, but she did, and so when Daddy asked . . . He was staring now and it felt like pinpricks in her skin. This was the scary side of Daddy. "I just wanted to see."

"Did you find any?" He pressed something and studied the screen.

"No."

"Is there anything else you want to tell me?"

"No." Could he see what she had really been doing? Did the phone show what calls were made? She hadn't thought about that. She shook her head. There might be, but she hadn't looked.

He drew the air through his nose as if inflating his next words. "You've disappointed me, Carly. Don't you realize you've infringed on my privacy?"

She swallowed. "I'm sorry."

The ice in his eyes lowered the temperature of the room. She would pay for the infringement.

"Does your stomach still hurt?"

"A little."

"Then I think you should go lie down."

"Okay." Her stomach did hurt, and she shouldn't have given in to the temptation of Sofie's number. She had wanted to feel better, but now she felt worse, much worse. She snatched a book on show horses from her desk and tumbled onto her bed. Daddy wanted her to regret what she'd done, but the only thing she regretted was not having had time to hear Sofie's voice.

She'd planned to talk this time, might really have talked to the one person who had always comforted her. Sweet, soothing voice. Soft, tender hands. She could hear Sofie's heartbeat if she pressed her ear to the bed and remembered the chest she'd nestled against. *Oh, Sofie.*

Not like the women Daddy brought home now. Not like anyone—even Ms. Rodemeyer. Sofie would have seen through his lies. She would never have turned her back when someone needed her so much. She pressed the tears from her eyes. Why hadn't she asked where Sofie was living and tried to find her?

But then she remembered the man's voice. Sofie wouldn't come back to Daddy if she had someone else. Or to her if she had other children. A long shuddering sigh shook her chest. She was alone now. Truly alone.

Sofie woke with a jolt and reached into the bassinet. In the dark, her fingers found the sleeping infant. The gentle rise and fall of his chest chased her fear back to the shadows. She rolled back in the dark, lay flat on the bed.

He did not cry out for her; his cries were impersonal need. He did not prefer her comfort to Nonna's or Lance's or Rese's, did not whisper her name in his sleep. He had no name. They were nameless to each other. He wasn't the reason she'd come. Why had she come?

In Belmont, she'd haunted her own streets like a ghost trying to hide and trying to be seen. Waiting to be found. Five years she'd pursued the mysteries of the human psyche, hoping to understand the force that had wounded and interrupted her life. In doing so, she'd given it strength, prolonged his hold.

With an ache, she pictured him. Golden hair like a halo, eyes like the sky, piercing blue. His potent smile. His ardent words, lifting her up and plunging her down. No violence except the silent rending of her mind. And even now she felt the hollow that he'd left.

She touched the ache, brought it out like a memento, studied and stroked it. She missed him. And in the missing found loathing, not for Eric, but for herself. For the damage she'd done. Not willingly, not even knowingly. Yet irrevocably.

Her moan became a name. "Carly." She hadn't known to block her heart. Though the ones she loved had cried beware, her heart had stumbled blindly on. Poor motherless babe; poor lonely man. What need of covenant when need itself is covenant? Grieving man; helpless child. How innocently she'd stepped into the steel bite still piercing her heart with relentless tines.

She clenched her hands. Somewhere out there, Carly slept, dreamed . . . feared. What hands would stroke and comfort, what voice whisper hope and courage?

Eric's. His love for his child never wavered. His devotion never flagged. It smothered. It devoured. It cherished. She could not stem the desire to once more soften Eric's love for his child, to bear his all-encompassing, possessing love.

Dawn touched the window, and she rose. Soon the baby would awaken. His needs were elemental, easily met. Too young to comprehend what he'd lost, he accepted what he had. She went and showered off the nightmare sweat, the scent of remembrance.

Matt rang the bell, and Sofie opened the door with the infant curled over her shoulder like a fuzzy caterpillar in his yellow sleeper.

"Hi." He had made an appointment for the baby with a pediatrician, though ordinarily he'd have directed them to do so.

With the oddities in this case, he wanted answers straight from the source. "Is he ready?"

Nodding, she stroked the baby's back, evoking a soft burp. "He's just eaten."

Matt hooked the baby's splayed fingers with his thumb, cocked his head to meet the roving gaze. "I have an infant seat in the car."

"Let me tell Lance. Here." She handed him the baby.

He cradled the shaggy head in one palm, bearing the weight of his rump in the other. "Well, little guy, you don't look like you're suffering."

The baby scrunched up his face and emitted a bleat. Matt raised him to his shoulder and the baby burped again, dribbling a thin line of milky saliva onto his shirt. He patted the fuzzy back, weaving side to side and murmuring, "'Wynken, Blynken, and Nod one night sailed off in a wooden shoe. Sailed on a river of crystal light into a sea of dew.'"

He turned to find Sofie watching. She'd pulled on a red woolen jacket and had the diaper bag on her shoulder. He raised his brows. "Ready?"

She preceded him out. Something in the way she walked arrested him, and he couldn't help asking, "Are you a dancer?"

She turned at the car. "Why do you ask?"

"You look like it." He buckled the baby into the backward-facing carrier in the center of the second seat.

"Momma would be proud. I went from diapers to tutus to jazz slippers and heels. I taught with her at sixteen, danced a few shows off Broadway and one on."

"Impressive."

She shrugged. "It didn't change the world."

Hmm. That same modesty her brother displayed. He held the door while she slipped into the back beside the baby, then got in and started the engine. "Still dancing?"

She shook her head. "I went back to school."

"What field?"

"Psychology. Behavioral disorders. I'm writing my doctoral dissertation."

"Really." He hadn't pegged her for an academic. She was too—Cassinia would flame him for this thought—sensuous. The Mediterranean cast to her skin, high cheekbones and full lips. Most of all her exotic eyes. Who could concentrate on her lectures?

She said, "We've probably had similar studies."

"I started in law. Came into social work through the back door."

"Did you practice law?"

"Awhile. I took the track where you have no life but work, no religion but work, nothing at all but work."

"And then?"

"Then I thought it would be better to make a difference."

She smiled. "You sound like Lance."

He jolted. "I'm no miracle worker."

"How do you know?"

He framed her in the rearview mirror. "Because there are no miracles."

The doctor's office was crowded with runny noses and coughs. He hated to bring a brand-new immune system into that, but the state required a medical evaluation. He'd filed the birth certificate Baby Boy Doe and obtained a social security number to process him into the system and start his care. If Maria came back, her child was now documented, though still nameless. And if she didn't? Then he'd be worked into the system accordingly.

They were called in, and he watched with Sofie as the baby was weighed and measured, ears, eyes, and reflexes checked. When the doctor ran his finger inside the baby's mouth, Matt said, "Anything wrong with the palate?"

"Bones and tissues are where they need to be. Why?"

"There was some concern of a cleft."

He felt again. "Formation's normal. Hint of a microform here on the lip. That's where the tissues come together just enough but leave this line. This one's fairly insubstantial."

"Any possibility it closed after birth?"

He frowned. "No. The development is early on—six to eight weeks gestation, when the tissues of the head and cheeks join. I'll note this microform, but I'm not concerned."

"So in your opinion, there was no cleft palate at birth."

"If there had been, it would be here still. They don't close on their own."

He didn't look at Sofie. His questions were part of the job, but if she was caught up in the miracle thing, she might not take his persistence kindly.

When the exam was finished, they bundled the baby, and Sofie carried him out to the car under overcast skies. The nip in the air made Matt glad he'd worn the T-shirt as well as an undershirt beneath his chambray shirt. After Boston, though, he would never feel cold anywhere else.

As they settled in to drive back, Sofie said, "You think we're making it up?"

"I just wanted a medical opinion."

"To support your doubt."

"It's a little over the top." He glanced back. "I know he's your brother—"

"I understand your skepticism. What you deal with every day tarnishes the possibility of miracles."

He couldn't have put it better himself. Life was not a magic act. And he didn't get how someone of Sofie's intelligence had bought in. Obviously a lot of things he didn't know. "Has he worked others?"

"He brought Nonna back to life."

He jerked his head around. "What?"

"Do you believe in God?"

"Not really."

"And therefore you don't believe in miracles. But Lance has an intense faith."

"So he's a prophet or something?"

The smile reached her eyes. "He'd say he's a screw-up."

She was baiting him. He turned the wheel and accelerated

through the intersection. "So which is he? Saint or sinner?"

"Both."

"You lost me."

"My brother's failings work in him like yeast, imbuing his thoughts and actions with compassion and decency and a deep desire to bring glory to God. Supposing there is a God, if He wanted to heal, He'd find Lance's hands and heart ready."

Matt parked outside the house but couldn't resist one more question. "What did you mean, he raised your grandmother from the dead?"

Sofie unbuckled and for the next ten minutes told him a story he found hard to swallow—a generational feud, hit men, escapes, and secrets uncovered. The asceticism her brother had practiced in preparation for ending the family's "curse" explained his gaunt condition. And he'd been right about the grandmother's stroke. Her resurrection was actually a recovery, unexpected and surprisingly complete, but not supernatural. Sofie had intended to provoke him.

He shook his head. "I can't say I buy it."

"You don't have to."

"It can all be explained in human terms. Most things people attribute to God can."

She merely smiled.

The whole thing was bizarre, but he'd heard nothing that raised a flag against the baby's remaining with them. Michelli might have a messiah complex, but he seemed to direct it in humanitarian ways. And Sofie showed a tender care toward the infant that he didn't always find in foster situations.

"I need at least one primary caregiver to attend a foster-parenting class. It addresses the challenges in caring for someone else's child." Did he imagine the shadow that passed over her face? "Here's the schedule." He handed her the folded paper from the dashboard, noted the scars again, and wished instead of Lance's story he'd gotten hers.

"Is that all?" Her voice had thickened.

No. Tell me what happened. "Yeah. For now."

She climbed out and expertly removed the baby from the car seat. He watched her all the way to the house, her bearing poised and graceful, all hint of damage erased.

CHAPTER EIGHT

Carly came around the corner from the bus stop and saw Drew hunched down on the curb of his driveway. As she got close, she noted the red patches around his eyes. He hadn't been in school, but that wasn't unusual since he got sick a lot. Except if he was sick he wouldn't be outside, would he? In the cold?

She sat down on the curb beside him. "What's wrong?"

He sniffed but didn't answer.

"Drew?"

He slowly turned his head. "Someone poisoned my dog."

She gasped. "No." Drew's wiry little dog was hilariously homely and highly energized, and it could be annoying, but who would ever hurt it? "Is he okay?"

"He's dead."

Her breath made a slow escape. Tears stung her eyes. "Oh, I'm so sorry."

Drew nodded, accepting the condolence but not really consoled.

She knew how he felt. "My kitten got distemper." Or that's what Daddy had said when she came home and found it gone. "The vet couldn't save it." She had no reason to doubt, and no reason to think Drew's dog had anything to do with her using his name to explain herself to Daddy. It was a stupid thought, a wrong thought. Daddy would never hurt something.

But when she went home and told him, he had that pointed look, the one that said, there's a lesson here. "It probably messed around in someone's stuff. Wouldn't mind its own business. That's dangerous, Carly. But animals aren't smart enough to see that."

She swallowed the baseball-sized lump in her throat, knowing he just wanted her to get the point. The other thoughts were crazy.

"Come here," he said. "I've got something for you." He reached into his desk drawer and took out a shiny pink cell phone. "Your very own." He held it out.

"Really?"

He nodded. "I got to thinking you'd be safer with a way to reach me all the time."

A way for him to reach *her* all the time. But maybe she could get Sofie's number from his phone. Then she wouldn't have to worry about getting caught. She could hear Sofie's voice anytime she needed to. She might even talk to her. Why not?

She wrapped her arms around his neck. "Thanks, Daddy." She'd been so wrong. If he wasn't mad about the phone, why would he hurt Drew's dog?

———

As Star poured water over the ice in the last two glasses, Lance set the steaming tray of lasagna on the table. Rese's comfort food. The dish that had broken through her indifference and forced a response when the last thing she'd wanted was to care about him or anything he did.

They'd come a long way since then, but it had been a bumpy road—with ruts, potholes, construction zones. He was repairing bridges he'd blown sky-high, but in the meantime, she'd found a few side roads that seemed to work just fine. The main one being Brad.

Wearing a white T-shirt and khaki construction vest, the man now sat opposite Rese. Her partner. Her dad's confidant. The one she spent the bulk of her day with. Now, the only night she'd come home for dinner, she'd brought Brad home as a buffer.

Lance sat down and bowed his head, blocking dark thoughts as Nonna raised her thready voice in blessing. "O God, every day you give us br . . . ead, wine, and oil, satisfying us with your generosity. Bless our being together at this table and give us gr . . . atitude toward you and toward all of creation."

A beautiful sentiment. After the soul-searching he'd done, the forgiveness he'd accomplished, he should be able to manage civility. What would it take to completely purge himself of wrong thoughts?

Star passed the endive, arugula, and hearts of palm salad, then the crusty, warm-from-the-oven peasant bread. Lance scooped chunks of pasta, oozing sauce and cheese and spicy sliced sausage, onto the passed plates.

Elaine eyed her serving with covetous glee. "Royal jelly."

Star giggled. "No drones here."

Brad dug in with gusto, but it was Rese's response Lance wanted to see. The first times he'd cooked for her, she'd eaten like an automaton. He'd had to teach her to savor—until he'd made Nonna's special recipe lasagna. Then something inside her had awakened, and he ached to see it again, to know she valued his skill just as she valued Brad's and her own.

Fork poised, Rese announced, "We won the bid."

"What bid?" Star drew it out, while the forkful hung there untouched.

"A turn-of-the-century hotel on Nob Hill."

"A whole hotel?" Star looked from her to Brad.

"It's only fourteen guest rooms, but the lobby's a piece of work." He dug his fork in again.

"It's an architectural gem, except for the staircase," Rese added.

"Which we're replacing." Brad tore off a hunk of bread.

"Since a certain scale model had the owners falling over themselves."

Lance stopped waiting for Rese to take her bite. Foolish to think he could work the same magic twice, even though he and Nonna had customers in the Bronx who'd come for dinner every week for years and ordered the same meal each time and raved as though it were the first.

Rese might appreciate the food, but her mind and heart were elsewhere. He had thought nothing could be worse than losing Tony in one shocking instant, but losing Rese day by day, growing apart as she shared her enthusiasm with Brad and came home weary and spent, was taking more from him than he had.

There were moments, as when she'd met him in the garden and taken his hand, when she'd held the baby, then looked into his face, that he'd sensed a connection. But it was probably no more than peacemaking. He needed to surrender his expectations. God had not promised him a life with Rese, not the way he wanted it, with the passion that had crackled between them and the love he felt so keenly returned in kind. God had only promised to be sufficient.

Okay, then. His heart ached. Every swallow fought him. *Lord.* He bit into the bread, chewed slowly as Rese described an architectural element of their new restoration project.

Restoration. He forced the bread down his throat. He could tell Rese he loved her every day for the rest of her life, but she'd seen him walk away. After a mother who'd tried to kill her and a dad who'd lied about it, with her fears of schizophrenia and feelings of rejection, no wonder she'd rather fix buildings 24-7 than attempt to restore a damaged relationship.

He sipped the wine he'd paired with the entrée. What was he supposed to do? Stop trying? Stop wanting? He closed his eyes. *Lord.* The connection was tight and immediate, the holy presence of God.

"Lance. Lance?"

He opened his eyes and found the faces around the table fixed on him. "What?"

Rese frowned. "Are you all right?"

"I'm fine." He got up and carried the bread basket to the kitchen for a refill but set it on the counter and walked out the door instead.

Rese followed. "Lance, tell me what's happening."

"What are you talking about?"

"Are you sick?"

"I don't think so." He turned. "What did I do?"

"You whispered 'Lord,' then closed your eyes and zoned out."

Great. Was the thought enough to carry him away? "I can't explain it, Rese. I get . . . caught up."

"When you're not even trying?"

"Apparently."

"I thought I'd be the one losing it."

He sighed. "Neither of us is losing it. I just . . ."

"What?"

He drew a slow breath. "I don't want to be in your way, Rese. I don't want you working long hours to avoid coming home."

Her brow furrowed. "What are you talking about?"

"If you and Brad have something going—"

"Me and Brad?" Her hands clamped her hips.

"I thought—"

"No you didn't." She came up nose to nose with him. "If you thought, instead of letting yourself get carried away by your emotions, you'd realize Brad is my business partner. I work long hours because . . . that's what I do. Unlike you, he is perfectly able to keep a professional distance, and besides, he's in love with his wife."

"His wife?"

"Ex . . . wife."

His jaw fell slack. "Then you asked him to dinner . . ."

"To celebrate our success. In case you didn't notice, I'm excited about this project."

"I noticed. But I thought the excitement was . . ."

"Brad?" Her hands clenched. "Lance Michelli—"

He grabbed her fists. "Why won't you tell me you love me?"

"I did." Her jaw tightened.

"You know how long ago that was?"

"You know whose fault that is?"

He groaned. "You think I don't?"

"Lance. You know how I feel, but it's . . . I'm . . ."

"Marry me."

"What?"

He drew her calloused hands to his chest, kissed her knuckles. "Marry me, Rese."

"Lance, be serious."

"I'm dead serious." This was the third time he'd asked. If she said no, he'd have his answer. He wouldn't test the Spirit again.

Tears welled in her eyes.

He cupped her face and kissed her. *"Ti amo."*

She sniffed. "I love you too."

"Then marry me."

"You know what could happen. I might be like Mom."

He held her teary gaze. "For better or worse—no matter what."

"And even if I'm not," she said, her voice tightening, "I'll still be taking care of her."

"Say yes." What would he do if she didn't? But he felt the grip of God.

She drew a jagged breath. "Okay."

Joy anointed him from his scalp to his toes, a warm seeping happiness. "Yeah?"

"Yeah."

He brought his mouth to hers, sealing the promise, transmitting his joy, his desire and passion. He tossed back his head and sang, " 'When the moon hits your eye like a big pizza pie that's amore.' "

She rolled her eyes. "Lance."

" 'When the world seems to shine like you've had too much wine, that's amore.' " He'd teased her before with that song, but he wasn't teasing now. She'd said yes! He captured her hands, brought them to his chest. "I only ask one thing."

She raised her chin. "One *more* thing."

"Yeah. One more." He smiled. "That you come home for dinner, that we can gather around the table as we did tonight and share that time every day."

She threw a glance over her shoulder. "They're all sitting there now."

He turned her face back with his fingers. "Let them sit."

"They'll wonder—"

"Let them wonder."

"Lance . . ."

"It's not much to ask." But he needed it, needed that time, that ritual.

"Okay. Fine. Yes, we'll have dinner together."

"Thank you." He kissed her forehead.

"Now, come on. We have a guest."

"Oh yeah? Who?"

"You know who." She tugged him toward the house. "Maybe now you'll stop sulking and converse with him."

"I never sulk."

She snorted.

Just to make sure, he turned her at the door, kissed her hard, and left her breathless. "Let's go converse."

Sofie breathed the love glow Rese and Lance carried into the room like a sweet aroma. Something had happened. Something had changed.

Nonna pointed at Lance. "You l . . . ook like you ate the ca . . . nary."

"Yeah?" He grinned. "Because we're getting married."

So. After all the hard-luck stories he'd fallen for, all the pretty faces who wanted Lance Michelli—the groupies, the models, the missionaries—at last he'd found the one to hold him. Sofie met his eye and shared his joy, and yet the emptiness inside her yawned.

He rested his hand on the back of Rese's neck. "I can't ask her dad's permission, so I'm asking you, Elaine, and Star, and everyone here for your blessing—even you, Brad."

Rese sent Brad a conciliatory grimace. He returned it with a sideways smile.

Nonna raised her glass. "May you be poor in m . . . isfortune, rich in blessings. May you see your ch . . . ildren's ch . . . ildren."

"Grazie, Nonna. We'll work on that."

Rese flushed. She'd learn there was no point in bashfulness. No subject was off limits to this family. Well, no subject as welcome and wholesome as love and babies.

Star stood and circled the table. "'Thy husband is thy lord, thy life, thy keeper, thy head, thy sovereign; one that cares for thee . . . and craves no other tribute at thy hands but love, fair looks, and true obedience.'" As she tipped her puckish face at Rese, Sofie caught the edge in her expression.

Brad and Lance took each other's measure like two dogs circling, hair rising on their backs. Finally Brad nodded. "If this is what you want, Rese, Vernon would be glad."

Elaine's focus darted around the table—searching from face to face for the husband she missed. Under her breath, she murmured, "He's gone, gone," but it was lost amidst the laughter and clapping as Lance bent and kissed his bride to be.

He spread his hands. "Who's ready for cannoli?"

The baby's cries interrupted the celebration, sounding distant and foreign through the monitor Michelle had lent them. "I'll get him." Sofie went up as the others deliberated between shaved bittersweet chocolate and vanilla crème fillings.

Sofie lifted the infant to her shoulder. He'd eaten right before she sat down for her own dinner, so he couldn't be hungry. He was changed and bathed, exuding only sweet baby smells, but the cries were urgent enough to warrant more than a reassuring pat on the back. His needs were instinctive still, and she tried unsuccessfully to intuit the source of his distress.

She'd made a few passes across the room, gently bouncing the crying baby on her shoulder, when Lance came in. He set a fresh, crisp cannoli on a napkin on the dresser, then took the baby from her and tucked the tiny head beneath his chin. Almost immediately the baby quieted.

She shook her head. All his life Lance had drawn needy, downtrodden people—starting with his grade-school friend Rico. He'd been their champion. Even this infant recognized the healing touch as his eyes slowly blinked back to sleep.

Sofie picked up her sweet. "Matt thinks we need a foster parenting class." They shared a humorous glance, thinking of all the babies and children they had helped raise.

"Okay." He rubbed the baby's back, as comfortable in the role as any man she'd seen.

"What are you and Rese going to do if Maria doesn't come back?"

"We haven't discussed it, haven't discussed anything yet. I didn't mean to propose tonight."

"Then why did you?" She nibbled the edge of the golden cannoli shell, hiding the bittersweet ache his news had caused.

"Couldn't help it."

She raised a quizzical brow.

"I planned to ask her, just not like this. I would have done something romantic, something that showed her I meant it, that I wouldn't mess up." He stroked the baby's head.

"You will, though. Everyone makes mistakes."

He shook his head. "She's had to deal with too many."

"And made her own, I'm sure."

"I guess."

She smiled. It was always harder for him to see someone else's failings. "You should be down there with her."

"I don't want all this to fall on you." He laid the infant back in the bassinet. "You're not getting your work done."

"I'm not sure that matters."

He cocked his head. "What do you mean?"

"These last six years, I've been trying to comprehend what happened. To find the key, the big answer. I thought if I understood, it might not hurt so much."

His face softened, his expression unbearably empathetic.

Their brother Tony's death had hit him harder than anyone but Pop. Loss, so sudden, so complete had left them all reeling. But Tony hadn't chosen to leave. And that was the part of her loss that hurt most.

"Now I'm wondering if it hasn't been years wasted."

"It's not wasted. You've worked hard and you're almost there. You write and defend your paper; you get the degree."

"For what? Am I any closer to an answer than the day he left?"

"Maybe not that answer. But others?"

She shrugged. "I don't know."

"You've been hyper-focused. Maybe it's burnout."

She shook her head. "I don't think so."

"Sof, you don't write that dissertation, Pop'll think I wore off on you."

She smiled. "Maybe you have. And it's as though the sun's coming out after a long, long rain."

CHAPTER NINE

M att could not remember feeling so irritable. Maybe it had to do with Ryan, sprawled on the sofa, swigging a beer as he perused the programming on the various sports channels. Four empty beer bottles, dirty dishes, empty bags of organic blue corn chips, and salsa-crusted tumblers indicated he'd been there awhile.

Matt hung his hands on his hips. "No work today?"

"Nah. I'm a loser. Low aspirations."

"Says who?"

"My beloved."

Matt scanned the mess. "And you're proving her wrong?"

"Who, me?" His blue eyes looked pained. "I've got arrested development."

"You do not." Matt sat down. While he tended to take insults as challenges, Ryan collected them like charms, letting them define and discourage him.

"Her best estimate's about eighth grade."

Eighth grade was when Ryan's dad had taken a job overseas, flying back on odd weekends—except the company wasn't the only start-up his dad had overseen. There'd also been the other family. But Ryan had gotten a lot of mileage out of that already. "When did you talk to her?"

"This afternoon."

Matt tried to gauge whether she'd told him about Friday night, guessed by the number of empties that she had. "Well, get things straight before Friday. Then I won't have to sit through the awards."

Ryan hung his head. "Bec's getting one. Best Service New Accounts."

"Yeah? Good for her."

"She's an achiever."

Matt nodded. "Lots of energy. And she cares."

Ryan sank back in the couch and closed his eyes. "She say what she's wearing?"

"No."

"Probably blue. That cobalt wrap dress? Hot. Really hot. You'll like her in that."

"I'm sure. Too bad she's only my friend. Remember, I introduced you guys?"

"She should have gone for the other achiever who cares."

"Yeah, I never thought of that. She's certainly tall enough." Since Ryan wanted a pity party, he rubbed the sore spot. Heels gave Becca an edge on Ryan's five eight.

Ryan scowled.

Matt spooned half the chicken stir-fry he'd picked up at the natural foods market onto one of Ryan's used plates. "Here you go."

Ryan stuck a fork into a chunk of teriyaki-soaked chicken and a crispy snow pea, eating in sullen silence.

Matt poked his chopsticks into what was left in the carton. "You gonna make Friday an issue?"

"Thinking about it."

"Then hand me the remote. I want to catch the news."

"That's depressing."

"And sports aren't?"

"With sports it's mixed." Ryan tossed the remote. "You wearing that suit?"

Since he'd been scheduled for court, he'd worn a coat and tie to work. He'd probably wear something similar Friday. "Why do my clothes suddenly matter?"

"Suits hang better on tall guys."

He hated when Ryan wanted to wallow and wouldn't allow a solution. "You're saying I'm better in a suit than you?"

Ryan forked a wad of noodles. "Becca thinks so."

"Guess I will, then, especially if she wears the hot cobalt wrap. Maybe I'll get a tie to match, just like prom."

Ryan rammed the noodles into his mouth. "You can be a real jerk."

He sighed. "I'm doing Becca a favor, Ryan. I hate awards."

"But you'll have a good time. You'll be there for her big moment."

Matt nodded. "Yeah, I will. And I'll be happy for her."

Ryan shoved his plate aside. "Couldn't you say no?"

"Why would I?"

"Because I can't stand it."

"Then fix it."

"Yeah. Right." He pushed up to his feet. "Thanks for nothing."

"Hold on. You're not leaving."

"Wrong-o." Ryan wove toward the door.

He had hoped the barbs would shake Ryan out of his self-pity enough to consider what he might do to make things better, but he'd pushed too hard. "Come on, Ryan. Hang awhile."

" 'Cuz this is so much fun? Thanks for the chow. You're a true friend."

"Let's talk it out."

"Nothin' to say."

"You're not okay to drive."

Ryan spun. "Who are you to say if I'm okay? Just leave me alone."

"Let's find a game," Matt said as he placed himself between Ryan and the door. "Gotta be something you want to watch."

Ryan swayed. "Don't feel like sitting with you right now."

He knew what Ryan wanted, but he would not renege on Becca. They were both his friends, and he had to find a way to stay neutral. Right. Like neutral had ever been his position. Matt reached over and took the keys before Ryan even thought to tighten his grip. "See what you can find to watch while I change clothes."

Not the way he'd planned to spend the evening, but he'd hold Ryan's hand if that's what it took. He went into the bedroom and removed his coat and tie. He'd unbuttoned his shirt halfway when he heard an engine, rushed to the window, and saw Ryan pulling away. Must've had a magnetic key box. He shook his head. "Stupid."

He couldn't exactly chase him down, so he turned on the news and ate, then washed the dishes and cleaned up. It wasn't far to the house Ryan's mother had left him. He'd only had beer, and a little food with it. He'd probably be okay. Matt collapsed on the couch and dozed. Later in the night, he moved into the bedroom, convinced he'd done what he could.

His rationalizing fell flat when the call came the next morning to bail Ryan out. Matt returned to the office after depositing Ryan, recipient of his first DUI, back at the house. He had just taken his seat when Diana, the state's attorney, called.

"Looks like we might have found the missing mother."

He shifted the phone to his other ear. "Maria?"

"She answered to that name and matches the missing person's description. She was in the back of a pickup with a load of stolen electronics. The officer who pulled them over noticed that she seemed lethargic. When he told her to climb down, she hemorrhaged. The others are in custody, but she was taken to the hospital."

"She's given birth?"

"Very recently," Diana told him. "And no infant. She claims he's *muerto*."

Hmm. "If this is the same Maria, I'm supervising her baby's case, and he's very much alive."

"I'm reluctant to bring a case against her. The DVD players were reported stolen from the Best Buy bay before she took off from the place you told me she was staying, and it's a good bet she wasn't in the back of that truck because she wanted to be. She's young enough to qualify for CPS herself."

"Let me grab Cassinia and see what we can do."

After wrapping it up with Diana, he tapped on Cassinia's cubicle and explained the situation. On the drive to the hospital, he gave her what information he'd already gathered from the mid-wife and the others—omitting mention of a cleft palate that miraculously went away. Cassinia had less use than he for miracles and more animosity toward those who believed.

She also had a fierce dislike for abusers and obviously sus-pected it in Maria's situation, though no one had proof the girl wasn't acting on her own impulses. He'd made an effort to wait on the facts before forming any conclusions. Cassinia's tight mouth betrayed emotions barely held in check when Detective Brazelton met them in the lobby.

His hooked nose and jowls hung even longer as he told them Maria had been taken into surgery. "Apparently she's still carrying a nonviable fetus."

Matt frowned. "Then she's not our baby's mother?"

"We think she is. It appears she was carrying two—birthed one and failed to expel the other."

Matt's jaw fell slack. "No one noticed?"

"No ultrasound. No prenatal care. According to the staff, the second fetus stopped growing near the fourth month and has been dead for some time. The living infant masked the situation, but she's been septic for a while. If Officer Sheldon hadn't pulled them over, she would have died."

Everyone he'd talked to had said she'd slept a lot, but no one would necessarily find that abnormal after giving birth.

Cassinia drew up her five feet two inches and said, "I'm Maria's caseworker. I want paternity DNA on the fetus so we know who to nail."

"We've already requested it."

"I'll want a sample from the other one as well," she told Matt.

He nodded. The men were being held on transportation of stolen property, but if it turned out Maria had been wrongly transported, held, or coerced, stronger charges would be filed.

She turned back to the detective. "What's the doctor's best guess on her age?"

"She's sixteen. Said her uncle was supposed to get her into an American high school."

"He's a resident?"

"Don't know. She shut down, wouldn't even give her last name."

Cassinia's fists clenched. "The uncle's in custody?"

"Hard to tell who's related to whom. For all we know, he may have passed her off to this group. Is there anyone who might convince her to speak with us once she's able to?"

Matt considered that. "She seemed to trust the man who has temporary custody of her baby. I can tell him what you need." And prepare them for what might happen next. Reunification was the goal. But if she'd abandoned the infant, she might have actually convinced herself he was dead.

At the sight of Matt Hammond's Pathfinder outside the villa, Sofie bundled the baby into his thin green blanket. Did he really have to check the child every other day? The baby's thighs were plump, his hair was clean, diaper dry, tummy full. What more did Matt expect? The alphabet song?

She sighed. The emotionally charged, sleepless nights were wearing, but that was no excuse for projecting her own qualms onto Matt. He had expressed no doubt about her ability to care for the infant, so why did she feel such a need to prove herself to him?

Star, in a flimsy layered dress, beat her to the door. Matt stood in khakis and a terra-cotta microfiber shirt rolled up from his wrists as his others had been. He must find sleeve lengths a challenge with his long limbs. Even so, he looked neat and professional.

He didn't smile. "Hi, Star. Is Lance here?"

"Nope. He and Rese had an appointment."

Sofie joined them, picking up on Matt's serious mien. "Is there a problem?"

"We found Maria."

Her heart skipped. "Is she all right?"

"She's in the hospital."

"What happened?" She pressed the baby to her chest. When had he begun to fit so well?

"It's not clear. We were hoping your brother could talk to her."

"No one in the hospital speaks Spanish?"

"It's not a problem of translation. It's trust."

"Oh."

"She's not—"

Her phone interrupted him. She jostled the baby. "Would you . . ."

"Sure."

She handed him the baby and slipped the phone from her pocket. "Hello?"

Silence. She glanced at it. Another blocked number. "Who is this?"

She heard breathing, but it sounded small and shallow. Her heart quickened. "Who's there?"

"Um."

Her heart lodged in her throat. It had sounded . . . "Hello? Are you there?"

The signal ended. She punched dial-back, but it rang into voicemail. No message saying whose phone it was or any means set up for her to leave a message of her own. She looked up to find Matt watching and released her breath. "Wrong number."

"Been getting them lately?"

Her fingers shook as she pocketed the phone. "For a while. They're pretty random."

"Things that seem random usually have a pattern. And a purpose." He cocked his head. "Has someone threatened you?"

"It's mostly silence." Silence that held a need she could almost touch. "No big deal."

"It upsets you."

This one had. The shaky little voice that murmured, "Um." She'd almost imagined . . .

"Do you recognize the number?"

"It's blocked."

"Is there anyone you've refused, rejected, or torqued off?"

"No." Because the only one had walked away and not looked back. "You were saying, about Maria . . ."

"They took her into surgery to remove a dead fetus."

"But she already had the baby."

"There was another. The infection's pretty bad." He rocked the baby in his arms. "We need Lance to help get some answers."

"I'll tell him as soon as I can. But he and Rese made a point of leaving their phones. It's the first time they've gotten away."

He nodded. "Okay."

"Can we see her?"

"As soon as she's cleared for visitors. But not with this one." He patted the infant's back.

"He might comfort her more than any of us."

"Not if she intended to abandon him. She's claiming he's dead."

Sofie searched his face. "So . . ."

"So we need to proceed cautiously until we get the facts." He slid the baby down to the crook of his arm. "Things are never as simple as we'd like."

With the tiny baby cradled in his long arm, he looked like a guardian angel, the kind that would never let a child be lost or taken if there was anything at all he could do.

Looking up from the baby, Matt caught Sofie's expression. Nothing in the rules prohibited socializing with a caregiver, though his years in law had made him cautious. "Would you like to go for coffee or something?"

"I thought you were avoiding caffeine."

Good memory. "That was last week." It had seemed important then.

"I see." She half smiled. "You accomplished your goal?"

"Close enough."

Star rose up from a high-backed wing chair that had hidden her in the parlor. "There's a latte machine in the kitchen. I'll play barista."

Sofie raised her brows. "It would be easier, I guess, than taking the baby out."

"Sure." He didn't care where the coffee came from. What he wanted was time with her. How long had it been since he'd felt so aware of a woman? How long since that awareness had triggered not only a physical response, but a desire to know, to shield, to engage.

She took the baby from his arms, and he followed her to the kitchen, as well appointed as many restaurants. Near the large stainless espresso machine, Star poured beans into a grinder, humming along with its whine. The noise didn't faze the old woman sleeping in the overstuffed chair in the corner near the stove.

Matt pulled out a chair for her. "Will we bother your grandmother?"

Sofie shook her head. "She's used to commotion. Most of her family lives under one roof."

"In a house like this?" What was it with them flocking together?

"An apartment building. But the families freely overlap."

He thanked Star when she delivered their frothy lattes, sipped his and smiled. He typically took his coffee black and practical, and wouldn't have thought he'd care for the hazelnut flavor, but it wasn't bad. The smoothness of the brew spoke to the quality of the beans and the freshness of its preparation.

"How's your dissertation coming?"

"It's not." Sofie peered down at the dozing infant in her arms.

"Has he interfered?"

"Only because I've let him." She rested her hand over the baby's chest. "I'm not sure that's my direction anymore. I've put it on hold."

"That's a big decision."

"It should be, I suppose. I've worked hard enough toward it these last five years." She trailed her finger up and down the baby's arm. "Now it doesn't seem to matter."

He seriously hoped she wasn't quitting because of an infant who would be returned to his mother if at all possible. "What will you do instead?"

"At some point I'd like to sleep." She kissed the baby's head and smiled.

She was so good with him—better than a confused teenage mother who had convinced herself the baby was dead?

Antonia awoke with a snort and stared. "What's all this?"

Sofie turned. "You remember Matt Hammond, Nonna. From Child Protective Services?"

"I kn . . . ow who he is. What does he want?"

Star let loose a throaty laugh. "What they all want, Grandmother, deep inside that wolf skin." She threw her arms wide. "'Love is a familiar. Love is a devil. There is no evil angel but Love.'"

Sofie said, "They found Maria, Nonna. Matt came to tell Lance."

Smooth. Masterfully unruffled.

"What about our baby?" Antonia's stare sharpened.

"Nothing's settled," he told her. "He'll stay here for now, if you're still willing and able."

Antonia made a sound that mocked his foolishness. "What else would we be?"

"Good." He set his mug on the table and stood up. "I'll keep you posted on Maria's condition. Will you have Lance call as soon as he gets in?"

"He's off with his betrothed." Star swept up his mug.

"They're engaged?" He looked from Star to Sofie. Did prophets marry? Beget prophlets?

Star said, "'Love is a smoke made with the fume of sighs.' And around here, mate, it's catchin'."

"Well, give them my congratulations."

Sofie tucked the baby into her grandmother's arms. "You can tell him when you see him." She walked him to the door.

"Was it a surprise?"

"Yes and no."

He hesitated, then turned. "Does it fit his religion? I don't know how extreme faith works, but—"

"It doesn't cause impotence." Sofie leaned on the doorknob, enjoying his discomfiture.

"I didn't . . ." But maybe he had meant it. Holy men hung out alone in the desert, wearing animal skins and eating bugs. Lance's normal masculinity contradicted his supposed spirituality. Didn't blending the two end in hypocrisy?

Matt fished out his keys. "Thanks for the coffee and the chat. It was . . . interesting."

"Star isn't shy."

He huffed a laugh. "I got that. But neither are you."

"Because I answered what you wanted to ask?"

"Yeah, that. And . . ." And what? What did he really know about her? "You seem pretty open, that's all."

"I'm not allowed to keep secrets." Her hint of a smile was too enigmatic.

He wanted to pursue that. But he had to get back. "Have Lance call?"

"I will." She stayed in the doorway while he reached his vehicle, raised a hand in farewell when he looked back. What difference did it make if everyone in her house was odd? He could deal with that. He smiled all the way back to the office.

CHAPTER TEN

L ance dashed into the hospital. He'd stayed into the evening in Napa with Rese after hiring the broker to auction their wine. He'd coveted a day alone with her and couldn't regret that time even when he'd heard about Maria. He did, however, chafe the slow climb of the elevator that hung, then settled, then disgorged him. He hurried down the hall toward postpartum.

An officer leaned on one elbow at the nurses' station but straightened when he approached. The grip Officer Sheldon applied was harder than necessary. They were about the same height, but the cop wanted to be taller. He spiked his hair and carried himself like a bulldog. Might be a nice guy, but it wasn't surprising Maria hadn't answered his questions. He looked like the kind to boot her back over the border to the *federales* with machine guns.

"Is she awake?"

The officer shrugged. "In and out." He started down the hall.

"Why are you guarding her room?"

"I'm not. Just came after my shift to check in."

His opinion of the man softened. "How is she?"

"Incommunicado." They reached the end room with a sign on the door warning personnel this patient had suffered a loss.

"Hammond at kid services thought you could get her to cooperate. I want the guys that had her."

Maria turned, hollow-eyed and panicked, when he went in. "Señor Lance!"

"Hola, Maria. ¿Cómo estás?"

Her lip trembled. *"Bien."*

"No estás bien, chica." She was nowhere near fine.

Tears washed into her eyes. She darted a look behind him at the cop, then whispered so far under her breath he hardly caught it, *"Mi hijo es muerto."* The urgency caught him in the throat.

Lance glanced over his shoulder. "Can we have a minute?"

When the officer left, he explained about Matt Hammond and CPS. It wasn't going to work to pretend the baby had died—although technically one had, forcing a partial hysterectomy. He didn't know how much of that she'd been told, but tears slipped from her eyes and ran down her face as she took in what he told her now, in Spanish, about the living son she'd left in his care.

"If they find out I lied—"

"Look at me." He leaned in close. "I won't let anything happen to you, or to your baby."

Tears spilled from her eyes. "Is he . . ."

"He's fine." He took her hand and felt her fear.

"I didn't want to—I couldn't . . ." She pressed her other hand to her face. "They will take him."

"No one can take him unless you give him up."

"My uncle—" She lurched up and clenched his hand between hers. "You have to keep the baby. You said—" She gasped with pain and hysteria. "You said I only had to have the baby. And I did. Now you have to—"

"Maria, listen." He placed his hand on her head and eased her back. "I never meant that. He's your baby. Yours. Unless you give him up."

She closed her eyes hard against her tears.

"You can let him go, but not because you're afraid. You're not alone in this."

Her throat worked. "Did you . . . name him?"

"He's your son. You name him."

"Diego," she whispered. "His name is Diego Manuel Espinoza."

Her coarse hair and forehead were warm and damp under his hand. "Diego Manuel will be glad to see you."

She shook her head. "I can't."

"The guys who had you are in custody. Is Diego's father one of them?"

She turned away, and he could swear it was shame that washed over her face.

"Maria?"

"No sé."

"You don't know, or you don't want to tell me?"

Tears welled in her eyes. "Please."

He cupped her head with his palm and rested it there as a tear trickled past her temple to her ear. "Okay." He released a slow breath. "Everything's going to be okay." He held her weary gaze and sent one more prayer to God's ear, then went home to tell Diego Manuel his name.

"This calls for a celebration. Bring wine." Nonna's face broke into myriad lines of joy and laughter.

Sofie shared the smile. The baby in her arms was warm and soft, and now he had a name. Their limbo was past, the cushion of wordless comfort, their knowing without knowing. She needed to prepare herself to part with him, to restore him to his mother. It was right, and she wanted it. But there was no denying her heart ached.

Lance returned to the kitchen from the cellar with a bottle of the family vintage. Star took down glasses, filled two with sparkling water for herself and Elaine, who murmured, "Glad, very glad."

When everyone had been served, Nonna inspected the hue and clarity of the aged wine. "A vintage worthy of the event."

Lance raised his glass with a broad smile. "To Diego Manuel

Espinoza, long life, happiness, and grace." He pressed Rese to his side, and they stood together in repose, upholding each other with joy and satisfaction.

Sofie drank to the baby. God willing, he had suffered no trauma from this separation. God willing, Maria would love him as well when he was returned to her—if. Matt still had his doubts.

Her chest tightened at the thought of him. He was only a man doing his job. He would resolve things for Maria and Diego, then move on to another case and other caregivers. They came from different worlds, held opposing views. He didn't know God existed; she needed to trust God every day. He didn't believe in heaven and hell; she had experienced both.

With a sigh, she passed the baby to Nonna and slipped out to the garden. She had prayed for him, for Maria, and those prayers were being answered. She raised her face in gratitude, and still the pang lingered.

The door opened and Star joined her. "So much happiness cloys."

The bitter edge in her voice came from the place Sofie didn't want to go. "Whose happiness do you mean, Star?"

"Rese."

"Because of Lance?"

"Selfish and embittered, I know. But she's always been there, my sister Looney Tune, my strong and capable friend. I don't know who I am without her."

Her chest constricted. She knew how it was to be so identified with someone that her own self crumbled at the loss. "Your friendship won't change."

Star twisted her arms. "It has. She's changed. We've changed."

And change was hard. She'd found hope in an old woman's words and a new start, but it took work every day to maintain it when habits and thoughts clung like spider webs.

Star sighed. " 'These sorrows make me old.' "

"And yet, we carry on."

"With what?"

"With whatever it is that won't let go."

Star stared up into the night sky. "And what, pray, is that?"

———

Matt waited with Cassinia outside Maria's room the next morning. Lance joined them, and though there was no reason for Sofie to be there, Matt couldn't help a momentary disappointment that her brother had come alone. The stuffed bear holding fresh blooms that Lance carried only slightly softened the antiseptic smell as they entered. Maria's cheeks warmed as Lance drew near, but it looked less like a crush than awe.

"*¿Qué tal, Maria?*" He let her smell the flowers, then set the bear on the stand beside her. "*Estás bien?*"

"So-so," she replied in Spanish.

Matt glanced at Cassinia. They could both follow the basic conversation.

"Worse than yesterday?" Lance cocked his head.

"Better." She raised her eyes. "Yesterday, I lied."

Matt raised his brows, understanding the words, yet surprised when they laughed. From the hospital and police he'd been told no one had made much headway with the girl—no one, it seemed, but this miracle man.

Lance half turned. "This is Matt Hammond, the one I told you about. He's making sure Diego is safe and well. And this is Cassinia. She's going to do the same for you. *¿Comprendes?*"

"*Sí.*" She sent a hesitant glance their way, then fixed her attention once more on Lance. "*¿Cómo está mi hijo?*"

"*Bien.*"

"When can I see him?"

Lance looked to see that he and Cassinia had understood, then answered, "Soon."

Her desire was a good sign, but Matt had told Lance not to force the issue. Right now they needed answers. Detective Brazelton slipped into the room. He was being pressured to release Maria's companions to ICE detention for deportation instead of trying to prosecute. They couldn't be placed at the scene of the theft, and there was no proof they'd known the goods they'd been hired to transport were stolen. Charges of rape or kidnapping would change that, but Maria had yet to admit the kind of treatment Michelle Farrar had described. Maybe the miracle man would get her to tell what they needed to know.

Lance said, "Maria, tell me what happened. Why did you leave Diego?"

She shrank into the bed, dropping her focus to her hands.

"Everyone here wants to help you, but we need to know about the men you were with before you came to us."

"No one can help me. Only me."

Matt raised his brows. *Well, well.*

Cassinia moved toward the bed. "You speak English, Maria?"

The girl looked up with a faint defiance and answered with excellent pronunciation. "I want to see my baby. I want Diego."

Lance seemed as surprised as the rest of them—and not a little amused. But then she'd lived with them a week and not given up her secret.

Cassinia's face showed what she thought of Maria's request. She'd made it clear on the drive over that she thought Maria should not be saddled with the result of the crimes against her. She couldn't say that to Maria, but she'd held nothing back with him. She crossed her arms. "I'm in court in half an hour. I can't be here to supervise."

Matt looked from her to Maria to Lance. "I can."

––––––––––

Lance's call had come as no surprise. Sofie had already packed the baby's bag, anticipating the request a full hour before it came. She brushed Diego's face with her finger as she strapped him into the infant seat in the back of her Neon. Lance had said it was only a visit, that Maria might not even be able to hold the baby. But it was the beginning, she knew. Once Maria had her son in her arms again, how could she ever let go?

Sofie followed the directions he'd given and reached the hospital. With Diego bundled up against her, she headed to the room where mother and son would reunite. Her heart ached, not with envy, but with empathy so deep it became physical. She wanted to reconnect what had been severed, wanted to heal the rift.

She expected Lance, but it was Matt who met her in the hall. His cheeks creased as his smile warmed her. His "hi" seemed to mean so much more. Her pulse skittered. "Hi."

He reached over and cupped the baby's head. "You've got a name now, huh? No more Baby Boy Doe." He seemed truly happy for the baby who hadn't realized what he was missing. A big man with a big heart. Even small things pleased him, and it was having an effect on her she hadn't anticipated.

"Maria's sleeping," he told her. "She tried to resist, but the pain meds knocked her out a few minutes ago."

"Oh." She stroked the baby's back, torn between a few more stolen moments and the satisfaction of returning him to Maria. "How is she?"

"Pulling it together. Gutsy kid."

"Do you still want Diego?"

He looked toward the room. "Lance promised he'd be there when she woke up."

Sofie shifted the baby's weight. "So . . ."

"So go ahead and take him in."

She carried the baby to Lance beside Maria's bed and passed him over without disturbing his sleep or his mother's. For close to half of the baby's life, she had cared for him, letting him into the empty place inside her. But as Nonna said, *"Non c'è rosa senza spine."* Every rose had its thorn.

"You okay?" Lance searched her face.

"Yes." This time she had kept a healthy boundary. "Call when you need me to get him." She fixed him with a pointed look. "Do not bring him home on the Harley."

"You think?" He cracked a grin. "Matt can transport him if you need to go."

"That might be best." She kissed the baby's head and drew back. "Need anything? A magazine?"

He shook his head. "I'm working a song."

He had no paper, no pen, no instrument. But she didn't doubt that inside his mind melody, harmony, and lyrics were taking shape. He made music from life.

"Okay." She smiled. "See you at home." She lingered a moment on the baby, then went out to the hall, where Matt waited. "Lance wondered if you might be able bring Diego home."

He looked at his watch. "I have meetings in two hours, something tonight."

"That's all right. I'll come back."

"Or you could stay. There's a coffee stand down the hall, some chairs."

She looked where he pointed. There was nothing pressing she had to do, if her dissertation was irrelevant, and the direction she'd taken the last five years no longer valid.

"Lance will page me when Maria wakes up. I was going to make some calls, but I'd rather talk to you."

Again she felt a current pass between them. Without a child in need, his watchfulness diminished, but there was something solid and certain about him, so different from Eric's ambiguity; Matt's warm, measured gaze nothing like Eric's first arrested glance outside the theater where she'd performed; their double takes coinciding, and the electricity that followed.

"So . . ." Matt spread his hands. "Could you go for some lousy coffee or a cafeteria snack?"

She smiled. "Okay. Coffee."

They walked down the hall and approached the cart that held two stainless carafes and a short stack of Styrofoam cups. In the corner stood two padded chairs on one side of a window, two on the other. The window looked out on a gravel-covered roof with metal caps like mushrooms sprouting.

Matt poured two cups. "Creamer? Sugar?"

"Both." She looked out the window. Matt assessed people for a living. What did he see in her?

"Do you want to sit?" he asked as he handed her a cup.

She took the chair nearest the window.

He angled the other so they weren't side by side against the wall. "You doing okay? I know the brunt of the baby care has landed on you."

"Not really. Only the nights."

"Nights can last forever with a crying baby."

Her heart clenched. "How do you know?"

He hesitated then said, "My brother. Acute anxiety."

She sipped and grimaced, set the cup on the windowsill.

"I could have Starbucks delivered."

She laughed. "That's all right." She folded her hands and saw his gaze drop once more to her wrists.

She turned them over and looked at the scars. "It's not an original story."

He moved his inspection to her face, not pressing for more, yet he deserved to know, if he thought anything could come of this.

"I fell in love with a man and his baby. We were together four years before he left."

"Who was he?"

"His name is Eric." Her throat worked. "His daughter, Carly, was six months old when we met, four and a half when he took her away."

"How old is she now?"

"Ten. Eleven in March." She looked out the window, her soul as bleak as the pale gravel. "I'd like to send her something, but I don't know where she is. He said I'd never see her again, and I haven't."

"What did you do that was so bad?"

She swallowed the lump in her throat. "I came between them."

"You weren't married?"

"No. I accepted a live-in position as Carly's nanny." She moistened her lips. "I was twenty years old and believed there was only good in the world—my world. Eric was . . . golden. Carly like an angel. I checked her shoulders once for wings." She smiled. Eric had laughed and asked if she'd found them. *"They must grow in later,*" she'd told him, and he hadn't doubted it. They both knew Carly was special.

"It progressed past employment?"

She nodded. The first year they had maintained a comfortable but defined vocational limit. She realized later that he'd been not only training but studying her, and when he applied what he'd learned of her likes and hopes, she fell as deeply as anyone could for another.

"What happened to her mother?"

"Eric said only that she'd died. He didn't tell me how." She had learned early not to ask more than he wanted to tell. And yet he'd gleaned every detail of her life. His probing had felt like caring.

"When he took Carly and left, I . . ." Wanted them so badly it hurt in every part of her body. Even her bones had ached. "Waited and hoped they'd come back. After a while it seemed too hard to go on." She stared out the window. "Not going on took hardly any effort. And I had so little energy left."

Matt's voice was low. "It can feel that way."

"My family found me." She could never forgive the pain she'd caused them. But she made up for it every day, just being there. "It's much harder to live."

"But you are."

She turned back to him. "You needed to know before you thought something might come of this."

"I still think it." His brow had creased but his focus never shifted.

She smiled grimly. "You're a glutton for punishment?"

"I know a good thing when I see it."

She laughed softly. "Your story must be as bleak as mine."

"What makes you think I've got one?"

"You quit law for social work and have no story?"

He stared into his cup, drained and crumpled it. "My dad was a bully. If you stood up to him, he beat you up in fun. You had his respect, which meant he didn't pull his punches."

Hard to imagine Matt being bullied, but he'd been small

once, and he'd gotten his size from someone.

"If you didn't—couldn't—stand up to him, he beat you up in anger." He raised his eyes. "Which still meant he didn't pull his punches."

"Which one were you?" she asked softly.

"Dad's pride and joy." He ran his tongue inside his teeth. "My little brother died at nine."

Her breath made a hard escape. "He killed him?"

"We were outside when Dad started hollering from the house for us to get in there. Didn't know what we'd done this time, but it was certain someone would catch it. I looked at my brother, saw he'd wet himself. That right there marked him as the one."

He clenched his hands. "I screamed at him for being stupid. Called him a baby." His face pinched. "He looked at me with eyes that were a hundred years old. Then he started walking . . . away from the house.

"I hollered at him to come back and be a man. But he just kept walking. I heard the train whistle. We used to throw stones on the track, thought one day we'd derail it and see a spectacular crash. The brush came up chest high almost to the tracks."

She reached out and touched his hand.

"Engineer never saw him coming."

She had not expected anything so awful, but now she wondered why not. Only someone who'd been to the brink could have looked inside her as he did. "I'm so sorry, Matt."

"Never did find out what Dad was so cranked up about."

CHAPTER ELEVEN

Maria and her baby opened their eyes at the same moment, as though they'd sent a signal, one to the other—*I'm here*. Maria gave a little cry and stretched out her arms in a gesture Lance couldn't ignore even though Matt had wanted to supervise their reunion.

Maria started to cry. "He's so fat." She fussed and cooed and stroked his cheeks. "Look at this chin. These dimples." She kissed his hand.

Lance touched the speed dial on his phone to page Matt. The man had made the right call in supporting this. He would have no doubt when he saw them together.

"His hair, it stands up." Maria laughed. "And see how he looks around. He wants to know everything."

"You have good English, Maria." Lance cocked his eyebrow.

She acknowledged his gibe with a sheepish glance. "Because I wanted to attend school here."

"What happened?"

"My uncle lied." Her face clouded with hurt and rage.

Lance leaned close. "Is he Diego's father?"

She shook her head, teeth aligned in a pained grimace. "The others. Whoever sold the most."

Lance seethed. Her uncle had promised an American education, and instead prostituted her?

"He said the school wouldn't take me, so I should cook and clean. I wanted to go home, but he said no." The look on her face made him want to cry. "Then they started waking me." Her voice broke. "I fought. But then it didn't matter. I couldn't go home anymore."

He'd see about that. Most likely she'd been told a lot of things that weren't true, things to keep her quiet and hopeless.

"I had so much anger." She looked at the baby. "I wanted him to die. That night, when I saw his face, I was glad. He was as ugly as what they did. I started screaming, but when you came and took him in your hands . . ." She clutched Diego up against her. "*El amor me demandó.*"

Love claimed her. Tears stung his eyes. He still didn't know how any of that had happened, but when God moved, he didn't stand in the way.

Her eyes filled with tears. "You are a saint."

And wouldn't Pop like that? "I'm just a guy, Maria. What God did for your baby, God did. *¿Comprendes?*"

"*Sí.*" But her face still glowed.

He turned at a sound and found Sofie and Matt in the doorway. He wasn't sure how long they'd been there or what they'd heard. His focus had been tight.

Matt came up beside them. "Feeling better, Maria?"

She nodded. Her arms tightened around Diego.

Matt said, "I want to do the best I can for Diego, Maria. And Cassinia wants the same for you. For us to do that, we need to find your family."

Panic caught her once again. Her breaths came sharp and quick. "My mother didn't want me to come. She thought I was ashamed to be who I was. She said my school was good. My home was good. But . . ." A sob caught in her throat. "I wouldn't listen."

Matt said, "You had no reason to suspect your uncle."

She clutched Diego even tighter. "Don't let them take my baby."

Lance rested a hand on her arm. "No one's taking your baby."

Matt didn't contradict, but neither did he agree. "We have to make the decision that's best for Diego. He is a citizen of this country, and I have a responsibility to him."

"But he doesn't have to stay. He can come home . . . with me, no?"

"Is that what you want?"

"Yes." But her chin dropped.

Lance cocked his head. "Maria?"

She murmured, "I want that, but . . . *mi mamá* might not want me."

Diego yawned and stretched, then started to nuzzle, fussing when the fabric of her hospital gown thwarted him.

Maria raised stricken eyes. "I have no milk." More than a statement of fact, it expressed her shame and failure and regret, none of which belonged on her. She'd been incredibly brave and selfless in rotten circumstances.

Sofie took a bottle with powdered formula from the diaper bag. "I'll have this ready in just a minute." She went out, probably to the nurses' station to hydrate and warm it.

The baby's fussing became a strident accordion cry. Since Maria could not strain herself, Lance lifted Diego to his shoulder and paced the small space until Sofie came back. Then he returned the infant and assisted Maria with the bottle. Diego latched on and sucked as though he hadn't been fed all week.

Sofie tucked a burp cloth over Maria's shoulder. "If you used a pump and let him try, you might get your milk back."

"Yes?" Maria's brows raised hopefully.

Matt shook his head. "That's not a good idea. Nothing's decided yet."

"It's my choice?" Maria said. "To keep Diego?"

"Mostly yes, if care and safety conditions are met. But there are a lot of factors to consider."

She sank wearily back. Diego had guzzled half the bottle and now took a more leisurely pace on the nipple.

Lance nodded toward the door. "Can we give them a few minutes alone?" He sensed Maria's need to reestablish herself with the infant she'd borne and nurtured the first six days of his life. She'd been without him as long as she'd had him, and the loss of those precious days obviously hurt more than she wanted to show.

He followed Matt and Sofie into the hall as she pressed the issue. "Why would you hesitate to encourage her to reestablish a bond so healthy for both of them?"

Matt looked down at her. "Under ordinary circumstances, yes. But we've had no chance to assess her stability or learn why she left him. Whatever her reasons—" He held up a hand at Sofie's intended interruption. "Noble as they might be, she still abandoned her infant with no certainty that he would be safe and cared for."

"She had every certainty. She'd been with my brother a week."

Matt raised his brows, and Sofie conceded the point.

"My responsibility is to Diego Espinoza. It may be in his best interest to return him to his mother's custody, but that determination hasn't been made. We can't assume it and proceed as though the complications aren't there."

"You heard her, Matt. She wants to take him home."

"On a good day. And we don't know that she can go home. What if he's the reason she can't? Would she leave him again? Or worse?"

Lance hung his hands on his hips. "If Maria's family won't have her, she can stay with us. She didn't leave that baby because she wanted to. She thought she was protecting him. And after what they'd done? That's a pretty strong statement."

Matt nodded. "We need time to consider everything—including Maria's mistreatment, if and when we get clarity on that. The fact that she went back to them muddies it up."

"She had no choice." Sofie jumped in. "You heard Elaine. They must have been watching for her. They took her away."

Matt studied Sofie. "Except she verbally surrendered the baby before they *took* her. I'm not saying she hasn't changed her mind, or that she didn't believe she had to leave him. I'm saying we don't know. Give me time to figure it out."

She wrapped herself in her arms. "She's lost half his life already."

"I'll do everything I can to expedite this. But Cassinia will determine whether it's in Maria's best interest to shoulder the responsibility, and what's required for her own well-being."

Lance said, "We all want what's best for both of them."

"Right now that means we keep the status quo until we've learned all we need to," Matt said. "As soon as the baby's fed, Sofie, can you take him home?"

She slackened. "All right. But the sooner Maria tries to recover her milk, the better for both of them."

He looked at his watch. "I'm not going to okay that until we know they'll stay together. She's riding an emotional rollercoaster." He took them both in with a glance. "She said herself she wanted him to die."

Lance wished Matt hadn't heard that, especially if he didn't believe something real had happened for her or the baby, something so profound it had changed her heart.

"I need to go." Matt turned to Sofie, softening his tone. "We'll talk?"

Aha. The flush in her face hadn't come from their disagreement.

She nodded, and for a pregnant moment while he walked away, she seemed subdued. But when she went in and gathered up Diego, she told Maria, "Ask the nurse to help you with a pump."

In response to Lance's questioning look, she said, "That's not nursing him. Yet."

———

Matt slid the suit coat over his crisply pressed dress shirt and tried not to think about Ryan's comments. The last thing he needed was Becca on the rebound. Unlikely, since Ryan was better looking, funnier, and an extravagant gift giver, even if he couldn't afford it. But Becca might be making a point. She was big on object lessons. *See, Ryan, if you behaved like Matt . . .*

He frowned. Maybe he should have said no. But Becca was hurting too. And it said something that she didn't want to be hit on. She wasn't as ready to move on as she claimed. She and Ryan had dated for two years, been engaged for most of a third. He couldn't think of them apart. In his mind, they'd melded.

He checked the knot of his tie and went to pick Becca up. From the minute she got in the car, she chattered with a nervous cheeriness that seemed strange, since they'd known each other so long. "What's up, Bec? Someone spike your tea?"

"I haven't been out to something like this without Ryan for years."

"Well, it's just me."

That eased her nerves, but she turned a frank stare on him. "You shouldn't say *just*. You're not *just* anything."

"I meant we've done this before."

"Not like this, though. Not without Ryan symbolically if not physically included."

Except in his mind, Ryan loomed like a specter ogling every move. "So, you okay?"

"I'm more than okay. I'm great. Never better."

"Someone did spike your tea."

She laughed a little skittishly. "Well, I will be. I mean it too."

"Okay, then."

She'd settled by the time they reached MacArthur Place, the elegant and historic hotel chosen for the event. When she removed her coat, he saw that she had indeed worn blue, but it was a fitted navy sheath, sexy-professional.

"You look nice."

"You think so?"

She had the same vivaciousness that usually defined Ryan, blue eyes enhanced with tinted contacts, and pink, glossy lipstick. One hardly noticed that her nose peaked up and canted to one side, that her hips would carry her weight when she hit middle age, or that she talked incessantly now that the nerves had returned. It was going to be a long night.

"Thank you for being here, Matt. I didn't want to be shark bait."

The guys who'd come without wedding bands did look carnivorous, but that was part of the sales profile. And Becca was no shrinking violet. His presence announced her break with Ryan but told everyone she had no intention of pining. She made a good show, though he guessed inside she was shaky.

She received her award modestly, but her wheels had to be turning. If she could do this, why couldn't Ryan? She was climbing the ladder, while he did as little as possible and still looked for more appreciation and perks than he deserved.

"Congratulations." He kissed her cheek when she settled back down beside him. "It's well deserved."

"Thanks." Her eyes shone. "Thanks for being here."

He squeezed her hand, thinking how much Ryan had wanted to be. Maybe it was the kick in the pants Ryan needed, but it churned inside like bad milk. "Bec . . . Ryan really wanted—"

"Don't." She held up a hand. "Let's have one night without talking about him, okay?"

He didn't remind her that she'd been the one throwing Ryan's name around like confetti. He wanted there to be an answer, but Ryan awakened the helplessness he'd felt for his brother, Jacky. How could he make someone strong? How could he suffuse a survival instinct on those destined for extinction?

She slipped her hand into his. "I feel like I'm out with my big brother."

Good. That was right where he wanted it.

"You've always been there for me." Tears sparkled in her eyes. "A good—no, a great friend."

He squirmed, hoping she wasn't trying to change that.

"So, I want you to know I'm not getting back with Ryan."

There was the train whistle, and Ryan walking blindly through the brush. His throat tightened. "It's only been a couple weeks."

"I wouldn't have broken it off if I wasn't sure. So would it be okay if you didn't try to fix this one thing?"

He nodded.

"Okay, good." She picked up her wine and drank.

The awards dragged on to ridiculous, but he clapped and laughed at the lame jokes and smiled at the anecdotes Becca told about each co-worker. The women at their table asked where she'd been hiding him, and he cringed when she said behind Ryan. They all seemed to support her decision to move on. If Ryan hadn't found stability at thirty-two, would he ever?

Asked about his job, Matt said most of it was mundane and tedious. He didn't say it beat billing politicians eighteen hours a day and feeling slimed by the time he dropped sleepless into bed. Or that the faces that swam in his dreams now deserved his attention. Or most of all, that Dad no longer boasted about Matthew, the big-shot attorney.

At the end of the event, he dropped Becca off and went home, hoping against hope that Ryan had the self-respect to leave it alone tonight. But there he sat in the kitchen in the dark with a bottle of Beam and a bellyache.

He raised bleary eyes. "How was it?"

"Boring."

"Did you talk about me?" His expression was so unguarded it hurt.

"We tried not to."

"Is there a chance? Do I have a chance?"

He sat down and sighed. "She said she's through. It's time to move on."

Ryan scrubbed his face with both hands. "Maybe if I got a better job, drove a better car."

"Your job's fine when you do it, and she doesn't care what you drive. Ryan, you're not putting out your best effort."

"What if I am? What if this is the best I'll ever do?"

"Find someone with lower expectations."

"That's all you can say?"

He shook his head. "I could say a lot. But you had three years to get it together. If Becca meant as much as you say she did, why didn't you try harder?" He crowded the table. "You can only get so far on your looks and your laugh. Then you have to get serious."

"Like you?" Ryan scowled. "You're as serious as a train wreck."

It had to be the booze. Only the amount of whiskey Ryan had drunk would make him say something that carelessly cruel. Matt got up and went to his room and closed the door. He hadn't known Jacky would step onto the tracks; how could he? From out of nowhere tears stung.

He hadn't thought about Jacky so much in years. Telling Sofie had cracked him open. What if he'd told Jack to hide and gone in his place? A beating would have been over and done, but this . . . It never ended. He swore.

Ryan knocked on the door. "Matt?"

"Get out, Ryan."

But Ryan came in. "I'm sorry, man. I didn't think about what I was saying."

"I said get out!"

Ryan slid down the wall and landed with a thump at the bottom. "I didn't mean it. I'm messed up. I shouldn't have touched that bottle. And Bec . . . I don't know what to do." He huddled on the floor. "I'm a loser."

"You're not." Matt sat down on the floor across from him, his back to the bed.

"What am I going to do?"

He sighed. "You're going to crash in the guest room, wake up with a headache, then go face the day."

"Face the day? How?"

"The same as the rest of us." Matt dropped his head back, replaying all the times he'd wanted to run away, give up, give in. Dad boasting, *"There's no quit in Matty."* And he'd wanted to quit, just to wipe that proud smirk off. But it wasn't in him. He survived and went on, and on, and on.

CHAPTER TWELVE

He had wanted that to be the end of it, but Ryan kept talking. It took hours before he finally passed out on the guest bed. Matt went outside and started down the sidewalk. Mist chilled his cheeks as he went, hands in his pockets, step after frustrated step. He had put Jacky away in a safe place, but he wasn't staying there. He was breaking through into places he couldn't be, places that hurt.

Matt moved faster through the dark as though Jacky followed still at his heels. *"Where you going, Matt? Can I come?"* Ragged clouds shuffled overhead, dimming and blotting stars and moon. At last he stopped and looked up. It was late—or early. He lit up his watch. 4:32. But a light was on inside the house. Nights with an infant. He looked up at the window, saw a shadow pass by, pause, then form a sharper silhouette as the curtain was pushed aside.

Idiot. How had he ended up outside this house? He must have walked three miles to get there, and now he couldn't move. Minutes later, the door opened. Sofie, in sweater and soft flannel pants, came down the walk and stopped at the waist-high wrought-iron gate. "What are you doing?"

He swallowed. "Walking."

"In a suit?"

He looked down at himself. "Yeah."

"Are you all right?"

He spread his hands. "I don't really know."

She opened the gate and he passed through. They sat down on the steps. He looked down at his Johnston and Murphy Italian-calf-leather loafers. Not exactly cross-trainers. He hadn't even loosened his tie. "This must look . . ."

"Like you wanted to talk?"

He bunched his fingers into his hair. "Maybe. Not consciously." Had he intended to find her again, pour out a little more, release the pressure just enough? Had he sought out a failed suicide who could understand what no one else could, offer a sort of absolution no one else could? "Talking seems to have punched a hole in some wall, and it's all gushing out."

"That's called catharsis."

"I'm usually on the other end of it." He thought of all the people like Ryan who piled their problems on his broad shoulders as if he were a porter whose purpose it was to bear burdens.

"What is it you wanted to say?"

"I don't know. Maybe that I wasn't always mean to Jacky, if it sounded that way before. Just when I was scared—mostly for him. I know that doesn't make sense."

"Emotions aren't all that connected to reason."

Very true. He dealt with people all the time whose emotions had overridden their sense. He didn't want to see that in himself, but he couldn't seem to stop showing Sofie. "People picked on Jacky, and he didn't know how to give it back, so I let him hang around with me and my friends. Even when they griped, I let him stay. If the teasing got ugly, I made them cut it out. But it was never enough. He always looked like there was something more I could do."

"How much older were you?"

"Almost three years. Looked like more. He took after Mom, slight and fair." He shook his head. "I mean it's genetics. When

Dad married a pale little woman, didn't he realize her genes would show somewhere?"

How would it have been if their looks were switched—if he'd been small, but himself in every other way, and Jacky had looked like Dad? "His wrists were like twigs. Even at nine. And he didn't eat well, probably because he was always upset. At night in our room he'd creep up to my bed to hear me breathing. I'd tell him to get back before the monsters chewed his ankles, but I meant before someone heard him. If Dad knew he was afraid of the dark . . ." He frowned. "I wanted him to get tough so I wouldn't have to . . ."

"Protect him?"

"Be so scared." He swallowed. "I knew what I could take, but not Jacky. He was like a puppy, trying so hard to please he'd end up annoying everyone. And I couldn't control it. I'd learned how to take care of me, but I didn't know how to take care of him too." He pressed his hand to his face. "And in the end, I couldn't."

She put a hand on his shoulder. He felt each finger through his suit coat and shirt. Why had he shown her the ugliness inside? Was that any way to start a relationship? He turned his head. Enough light came from the streetlamp to make out her features, but her eyes were shadowed pools. Impossible to see what she thought or felt, but her touch undid him. He slipped his arm around her waist, leaned in and found her mouth.

Her lips were soft and warm. He deepened the kiss he'd wanted since the first time he'd seen her. Then, without warning, sorrow overwhelmed him, sorrow and loss and the fear that he should have done something all those years ago, something different, something more. He didn't realize the tears were streaming until she pressed her palm to his cheek and pulled his head to her shoulder.

He closed her into his arms, crying silently, less ashamed than baffled. As the tears abated, he kissed the curve of her neck, her hair, the lobe of her ear, the line of her jaw. He clamped her face in his hands, kissed her mouth and felt his life shifting. Jacky was gone, but *he* was alive. Matt wanted to live.

He rested his forehead against hers. "I'm way out of line."

She squeezed his hand. "You needed to let it out." Dawn had lightened the darkness enough to reveal her sincerity.

"I had no intention of coming here."

"The result would indicate otherwise."

"What do you mean?"

"You're here."

He gave a short laugh. "Do you mind?"

"Not too much." She quirked one side of her mouth up.

Since this was a time of bald honesty, he said, "I can't stop thinking about you." The whole time with Becca he'd reined in thoughts of Sofie, what she'd shared, how she'd looked and sounded sharing it. How he wanted to change things for her.

"You don't know enough to occupy an hour."

"I think of everything I don't know." Everything he wanted to. He shook his head, needing sleep, needing to shut up. "I'm making a fool of myself."

"When's the last time you let go and went with your instincts?"

"I'm pretty close to my instincts most of the time."

"For others."

He sighed. "I should transfer Diego's case."

"You can't." She drew back.

"I'm no longer impartial."

"You know what he needs."

"I want you to have him."

She jerked. "What?"

His remark was highly unethical, the entire situation a conflict of interest, but he didn't take it back. "You're wonderful with him—soft, nurturing, strong, and wise. You shouldn't have lost Carly. Wherever she is, she's worse for not having you." He didn't want the hole in her life to gape like his.

"Matt." She took his shoulders. "Maria needs her son. He needs her. I am not part of this."

Her words sank in. Reason wrestled with whatever had taken

over his mind; the erupting grief, no sleep, too many other people's problems, and most of all Sofie herself. He dropped his forehead to his palm, elbow to his knee. A snap at the side of the house made him turn. Lance came around, walking a motorcycle.

Matt stared. "Your brother rides a Road King?"

"Mm-hmm."

"Isn't that . . ." He didn't want to set her off with another challenge to Lance's manhood. What made a man anyway? "Where's he going this early?"

"Church."

"It's not Sunday."

She just smiled.

At the end of the driveway, Lance sensed them and turned. "Sof?"

"It's okay. I'm here with Matt."

Matt prepared to explain what he was doing there at dawn, on the steps with Sofie, but Lance didn't ask, only eased the bike onto the street and started it. As the engine sound died away, Matt drew himself up. "I should go."

"I'll drive you." She got to her feet and tugged him up.

"That's okay." He didn't want her to see how far he'd walked.

"Really, Matt. You must be exhausted."

He threaded her fingers with his. "If you take me home, I'll want to go with my instincts." With their fingers entwined, he bent her arm up her back. He felt her heartbeat as he kissed her mouth until he'd memorized the feel and taste of her, enough to hold on to when his good judgment returned and kicked him hard. "I have to go."

Their hands slipped apart as he took one step down and another. She stood on the porch while he moved down the walk and out the gate. Three miles hard walking might not even be enough.

Sofie shook. Matt had come in the night like a wounded bear to the place he'd sensed haven and healing, probably not realizing his defenses were breached until he got there. She knew how it could sneak up, make you think and act crazy, do things you otherwise never would. He had needed a safe place to grieve, and the vulnerability had felt intimate. He'd acted on that. If Lance hadn't seen them, she would have kept it to herself. Now she'd have to offer some explanation, but how much could she say?

None of Matt's story. Nor the feelings he'd stirred in her. Certainly not that his touch, his mouth, had kindled an alarming response. *Lord.* All Lance needed was reassurance. She was fine; she could handle things with Matt and not . . . get in over her head, not lose herself again, not give up all the ground she'd gained. It was not the same. Matt was as far from Eric as two people could be. She pressed up from the porch and went inside.

Elaine sat at the top of the stairs, pulling her nightgown taut over her knees and feet. "I've always liked this time of day. Before the sun."

"Me too." Sofie smiled and started up. It was a poignant gift when Rese's mother's fog cleared. She wished it could last, wished there were a key that would open the doors of reason that had slammed shut and close the ones that let chaos inside.

It must be hard for Rese. How kind that she'd made a home for her—and kind for Star to be her companion. But then, Star had found haven here and purpose. It was no wonder she feared things changing. They were all refugees, even Rese, in the tides of life. Wayfarers joined by tenuous bonds as deceptively strong as tempered glass. Sofie sat down beside Elaine, who stared at the long narrow window above the door revealing the first blush of sunrise.

Elaine watched the pinking sky, then blinked when the fiery eye burned over the edge of the earth. "They always take them away. You know they do. And he's gone. Gone."

Sofie touched her knee, understanding on a visceral level exactly how she felt. "I'm sorry for your loss."

Elaine turned slowly and peered at her face. Her brow furrowed; her mouth drew in like a drawstring purse. "No one ever says that."

"I'm sure they think it."

"Think it." She turned back to the window and frowned. "Spoiled. All spoiled. Watch now. Watch out. He can see. Everything. He sees everything. He wants . . . everything."

Sofie stroked her shoulders. "It's all right, Elaine."

She let go of her nightgown, groped to her feet, and went back into her bedroom. Sofie heard her murmuring, "Think it. Think. It."

Sofie went into her room and checked on the baby, Matt's words squeezing her throat tighter and tighter. *I want you to have him.* Why would he say that when she'd made it clear how she felt? Or had he read behind her words, seen the aching desire for a child who was out there somewhere.

It was his nature to find solutions, to make things right. She should not have told him about Carly, should not have drawn him into her loss. But then how would he have opened up as he'd so badly needed to? She shook her head. There were reasons people didn't share their pain. It struck a harmonic resonance that started other griefs ringing.

Her arms and chest had formed to Diego's size and shape, but that didn't mean he was hers. *No blood relation.* She had not attached. Cared for him yes, but not attached.

Lance came up behind her, peeked in at the sleeping baby, and whispered, "You okay?"

She nodded, shocked that he was home already. How long had she stood there watching the baby breathe?

"Want to tell me what Diego's social worker was doing here at five a.m.?"

"He needed to talk."

"About Diego?"

"It was personal."

Lance turned her around. "And he came to you?"

"I'm a good listener," she said with a shrug.

"Yeah, but how does he know?"

She smiled. "We've talked before."

"Yesterday? At the hospital?"

She nodded. "He's dealing with something that's needed it for a long time."

Lance searched her face. "You talked to him too?"

She glanced away. "He deserved to know."

"He's interested in you."

"I know."

"Are you okay with that?"

"I'm fine, Lance."

He studied her a long moment. "Okay." He looked down at the baby, then back. "I got Maria's mother's phone number."

"What?" She grabbed his arms. "How? When?"

He grinned. "Which would you like me to answer?"

She socked his shoulder. "Tell me."

"After Mass I went by the hospital and convinced her we needed to know where her *mamá* stood on it all. She really wants to go home, but her uncle's all but convinced her she can't. I hope he's lying."

Sofie walked to the nightstand and said, "Use my phone." But when she reached down, it started ringing. She flung it open before the noise could wake the baby. "Hello?" she answered softly, but the other end was quieter still. Weary and in no mood to play games, she said, "I'm hanging up now."

"Wait. Um . . . sorry."

The line disconnected. Shaking her head, she carried the phone to Lance.

"What was that?"

She frowned. "Wrong number." The same number? The same young voice? Lance had enough concerns, and Matt had overblown it the last time. Maybe the girl had mixed up a number in her directory. She'd clear it up the next time—did she hope there'd be one?

She and Lance walked out of the bedroom and down the stairs while he placed the call to Mexico. He shot her a glance. "Pray."

She stood in the parlor beside him while he introduced

himself in Spanish, then gently explained Maria's situation. In Lance's face she saw the pain he must be causing the listener. She could not imagine being Maria's mother, learning what had been done to her child. She prayed with all her heart.

CHAPTER THIRTEEN

Carly slumped on her bed, the phone open in her hands. *Stupid, stupid.* Why hadn't she said something? Why hadn't she just said, "Hi, Sofie?" Was that so hard?

She'd been so excited about the phone—not so she could call Daddy 24-7 or gab to all the friends she didn't have. But so she could call Sofie. And now she was too scared to say hi?

She looked around the room at the things Daddy had given her: a computer loaded with educational software, more stuffed animals than she could cram into her shelves, books, CDs. Did he think giving her stuff made up for spoiling her chances at friends?

Her private school didn't allow harassment, but ignoring was perfectly acceptable. When her birthday came, she wouldn't have a party with girls sleeping over, telling secrets and laughing all night. Daddy would take her somewhere fancy, like it was a date, and she'd open one really nice present. He thought she liked that better.

She sighed. He'd been so nice the last few days. None of his bad moods. No accusing her of things that she didn't even know about. No icy eyes freezing her inside. It would take a while for all that to build up again, so for now he was the kind of dad everyone wanted.

She fell back on the bed. Some kids never saw their dads. Some dads hit their kids. Daddy just wanted so much from her. Could someone get loved too much? Anyway, he was all she had. She'd read that in a story about traveling players. The girl who did cartwheels on the road to Oxford had looked at her dad playing on the stage and thought he was all she had.

She liked that thought. It helped the loneliness not to hurt so much. She imagined herself in that girl's place. Like the girl in the book, she and Daddy moved *a lot*. He sold things really, really well and made lots of money. But then he'd stop getting along with the people he worked for. So once it got to where he couldn't stand them, they'd go somewhere else. Sometimes when he changed jobs it took a while to find another, and they wouldn't have takeout or go to movies, and once they moved in the middle of the night.

They used to go three or four times a year to see Grandma Beth, who lived in Riverdale in a big white house that looked like a president's mansion, but the last time, when she refused to give Dad money, he'd said in his cold, scary voice, *"If your grand-daughter isn't reason enough, then you won't care if she doesn't know you."*

Grandma Beth had cried. But they hadn't seen her since. Carly sighed. If only she'd been reason enough.

———

Matt woke up with the sickening knowledge that it hadn't been a dream. He'd been drained by Ryan's needs and exhausted emotionally and physically, but that didn't excuse his total meltdown. That could be explained only by two words: Sofie Michelli.

His rubbed his face, rough with stubble, and his eyes, gritty with fatigue. He turned his wrist and read the time. Ten thirty. He was tempted to fall back into bed, but his mind had revved up, and the three hours he'd slept were all he'd get.

He washed up and went to the kitchen, chugged cranberry

juice from the bottle, and stuck a couple of eggs on to boil. He sniffed the remaining sole filet and laid it in a skillet to sauté in olive oil. He tossed in some tofu cubes, sprinkled it all with soy sauce, and sat down at the table, where he had a stack of work waiting.

Half an hour later, Ryan dragged himself from the guest room. "What's that smell?"

Matt looked up. "You?"

Ryan sank into a chair. "Don't tell me . . . fish."

Matt nodded.

Ryan shot up and dry heaved into the sink, spit several times, and rinsed it down. Thankfully he'd done most of his throwing up in the guest toilet minutes before. He collapsed into the chair. "That's cruel, man."

"I don't suppose you'd want the boiled eggs either."

Ryan glared.

"Tofu?"

He dropped his head to his arms on the table. "Just shoot me."

"You know you can't take anything harder than beer."

"Then why do you have it in the house?"

"Because I can. I can also stop before I cause myself damage. I've had that bottle since Christmas three years ago."

Ryan looked at the half inch left in the bottom. "Maybe I should kill it."

"Whatever you think." Matt closed the Walenski folder and slid it aside, took up Diego Espinoza's with a sinking feeling.

Lance and Sofie clearly felt the infant should be returned to his mother, so much so that they would take her into their home again to keep them together. Maria could attend that American high school she'd wanted, he thought grimly, when she wasn't busy raising her son—and dealing with the aftermath of her abuse.

She'd need counseling, which Sofie could provide even without a doctorate; her master's and the field work she'd completed qualified her under the state guidelines if she cared to pursue that avenue. He'd seen for himself what a careful and compassionate listener she was. His jaw clenched.

He opened the folder and studied the top sheet. They'd all been taken aback when the DNA results for Diego and the dead fetus showed two different fathers. The best medical guess was that she'd gotten pregnant with Diego after her body had encased the nonviable fetus like a sort of cyst against the wall of her womb, and the hormones of the new pregnancy had prevented the normal course of expelling the miscarriage.

All that served to strengthen Maria's description of multiple abusers. The best those men and the uncle could hope for would be deportation. Cassinia had suggested castration. He suspected justice would be somewhere in between. But that wasn't his case.

His case was probably right now nestled in Sofie's arms, and she had told him unequivocally not to consider her in the equation. He had worried how she'd handle returning the baby, but she was handling it better than he. She'd made up her mind as to what was right and expected him to execute it.

A pain stabbed his chest. Stress, he guessed. How could he have broken down like that? He'd lived with Jacky's death for twenty years. And in all that time, no one had drawn the poison of it out of him as Sofie had. She'd make one dynamite therapist, though he hadn't gone looking for therapy.

What was it about that place? Was it some safe zone where masks fell away? A haven of healing that drew needy souls. He was losing it. Ryan groaned softly across the table, face in his arms. Matt closed the folder and looked again at his watch. It was Saturday, and normally he'd have nothing pressing, but Maria was being discharged from the hospital.

Though Maria was the reason Lance was at the hospital, it was Sofie who lay heavy on his mind. Had she told Matt enough for him to realize how fragile she might be under the polished exterior she'd formed layer by layer like a pearl? She had moved forward, gone back to school, gotten her feet underneath her.

Leaving Belmont had been a big step, but bigger still would be the new relationship everyone hoped she'd find. Was Matt the guy?

He assessed the big man who joined him outside the open door. No flags came up, but he'd been tragically unaware the last time. Matt seemed nice enough, conscientious, thoughtful. Lance greeted him and said, "I have some new information." He handed him the slip of paper on which he'd written the Mexican phone number. "This is—"

Matt's attention swerved the instant Sofie came out of Maria's bathroom, the look they shared a dead giveaway. If Matt wasn't the one to help her let go, he sure wanted to be. Before either spoke, Maria called for Diego, and Sofie carried the freshly changed infant to the bedside.

Maria seemed stronger than the day before, though he still detected an edge of pain and fear. How had they not realized how sick she'd been? But then, they'd only seen her the day she gave birth and after the infection had taken hold. He hadn't known this brave girl was in there.

She fixed him with a piercing look as he reached her bedside. "Did you talk to my mother?"

Well, that was one way to break the news.

Matt raised his brows. "You spoke with her mother?"

Lance handed over the piece of paper. "That's the number." He'd been trying to tell Matt before Sofie swept him away.

"What did she say?" Maria was breathless. *"Digame."*

Warmth flooded him. "She said she loves you."

Tears rushed to Maria's eyes. She spouted Spanish faster than he could catch it, then said in English, clutching her son, "We can go home?"

Lance glanced at Matt. "We'll talk about that when she gets here."

"Wait a minute." Matt frowned. "She's coming here? How?"

Maria huffed. "She has a travel visa. She is a respected professor at the university."

They all turned to look at her.

"I am not trash." Her voice carried a note of injured fury.

"No one thinks that." Lance rested his hand on the crown of her head and looked into her face. "No one thinks that, Maria."

She stared up, tears brimming, and with a jolt he realized *she* did. *No.* The pain of her violation dragged him down into her misery. The depth of God's love for her and for the life she'd brought into the world overcame him. *Feel it, Maria. Believe it.* She had said love claimed her, love for her tiny son. Now he wanted her to feel that same love directed at her, the love of the Father for His child, the boundless love of God.

"Lance." Sofie touched his elbow. "Cassinia's here."

He stepped back to make room for the gray-haired woman who eyed him guardedly. Matt also had fixed him with a wary scrutiny.

Sofie whispered, "Matt's explained to her about Maria's mother."

He had? When?

"Are you okay?"

He swallowed. "Yeah." But contact was proving hazardous.

Cassinia frowned. "I need to speak with Maria alone. Mr. Michelli, please take the infant."

Lance lifted Diego and followed Matt and Sofie into the hall, the energy between them almost palpable. He quirked the corner of his mouth. "You two want to be alone?"

Sofie glared.

"I can take Diego for a stroll down the hall." The teasing had come naturally, but he was also eager to avoid their puzzled expressions. In fact, a stroll wasn't a bad idea. He'd almost reached the nurses' station when Cassinia came out. He returned and found her steel-faced.

"She swears there's been no coercion, so whatever that eye thing was you had going with her, I guess she's making her own decisions." She scratched her pierced eyebrow. "In spite of the repeated rapes that resulted in Diego's conception, she appears to have formed a protective bond. I'm ordering a professional evaluation, but for now it seems in Maria's best interest that she return home with you." Doubt colored her voice, but she couldn't circumvent the obvious wishes of her charge without a pressing motive.

Sofie smiled up at Matt as though he'd single-handedly accomplished it, and maybe he had. Lance scrutinized him once more. If he wanted to know Sofie, he'd better be prepared to prove himself. *Whoa.* He'd sounded like Pop.

Brad put his knee up on the bench and leaned on his thigh. Rese ignored his stare as long as possible, but the snickers from the other guys at last made her look up. "What?"

"Will you be wearing the white dress and veil and all that?"

Naturally, that brought hoots and exclamations.

"You're getting married? Tying the knot?"

"Rese Barrett in a dress?"

"Who's the sucker?"

"All right, lay off." Brad stilled the outburst.

She lowered her chisel. "We haven't planned anything yet." They'd gone in on Saturday morning to finish the final details of the current job so they could move on to the new project. Couldn't he tell she was in the zone?

"Well, here's the thing: I'd like to walk you down the aisle."

She stared. "You what?"

"I've looked out for you for fourteen years. With Vernon gone, I'd say that qualifies me to walk you down and give you away."

She looked at the other guys standing as dumbfounded as she. If he was pulling something and they were all in on it . . .

"Got someone better?"

She shook her head. She had thought for a moment Mom might, but came immediately to her senses.

"Then what do you say?"

"What is it with you and weddings? Are you still witnessing—" as his face darkened, she shifted tactics—"the other?"

"Don't change the subject."

She looked around the room. "Why don't you guys get back to work?"

"Hey, no way." Their grumbles flowed.

"You heard the lady." Brad didn't have to say *lady* with such irony.

She turned back to him as they grudgingly feigned industry. "So?"

"So what?"

"Are you still standing up at your ex-wife's wedding?"

"What's that got to do with *my* question?"

"I'm trying to find out if you've gone completely nuts."

He expelled his breath. "Your beau asked my permission. I think that qualifies—"

"He asked your blessing."

"Same thing."

"No it's not. You don't have charge of me."

"'You don't have charge of me,'" he mimicked. "Now who's the twelve-year-old?"

"Fine." He didn't have to sound fatherly, either, even if gray threads shone throughout his hair.

He spread his hands. "Why is this a fight? I'm doing something nice here."

"That's what scares me."

"You think it's a prank?"

"Are you wearing a wire? Got a hidden camera somewhere?"

"What's with the paranoia, Rese?"

She crossed her arms. "I don't have good reason?"

"Maybe you do. But this isn't a joke."

The truth was their battles had filled half her life, and she wasn't sure how to take his overture.

Brad cocked his head. "I'm just saying, if you're going through with this—"

"Going through with it?"

"Well, who is this guy? He barges into your life, and now you're getting married?" He dug the pack of cigarettes from his pocket.

"You just had one."

He shoved it back in. "It's not something to decide lightly. I mean look how you sold the company. You can't tell me you don't regret it."

She'd been dazed by Dad's death, hardly known what she was doing, only that she couldn't go on without him. And now here she was doing just that.

He cocked his jaw. "I don't want you to make a mistake."

"Are we talking about me?"

He rubbed his palm over his thigh. "Marriage isn't easy."

"I think we know what we're doing."

"Yeah," he scoffed. "Sure you do."

She clutched his wrist. "Brad. Tell her how you feel."

"She knows."

"She can't. She wouldn't have asked you to be there for her if she did."

He stared a long moment at the floor, then looked up. "What do you see in Lance that makes you think a lifetime together can work?"

His love for his family, his need to be integral, his laugh, his passion. The way he slipped in and handled things. The way he cared. His faith. His faithfulness. But she wasn't about to say all that. "Lots of things."

"Marriage isn't all hugs and kisses."

"I don't expect it to be. Lance can be as infuriating as you."

"You're never ticked off."

"I just don't show it."

"Except the other night in the shed. You got pretty riled about the stairs."

She glared. Lance had broken down so many of her walls, she couldn't hide as well as she used to. "Are you the same person you were nineteen years ago?"

"I hope not." He grabbed the pack from his pocket again and shook a cigarette loose.

"Then why do you think Joni is?"

"I've seen her; I know her." He flicked his lighter and inhaled, then held up and scrutinized the smoking cigarette. "See this? I know it's bad for me, but I can't quit." He took a long, hard drag. "That's how it is with Joni. An addiction I can't shake."

"Maybe you're not supposed to."

"You're hounding me all the time to get off the smokes."

"I never hound you."

"Encourage, then. Call it what you want."

She straightened. "You need to open up to Joni."

He slapped his thigh. "Open up? Did those words even come out of your mouth?"

"Ha-ha."

"Does Lance Michelli know everything?"

"What everything?"

"Like that you offered me a different sort of partnership when you came back?"

She frowned. "I only did that to make sure you wouldn't accept."

"Uh-huh."

"I didn't want personal feelings interfering with work."

"Yeah, so you said. But I don't suppose you've mentioned it to your fiancé."

"Why would I?" She flicked a wood shaving off the carving she'd almost completed.

"Because it's the kind of thing that comes back and bites you."

"Only if you open your big mouth."

"You're missing the point. I'm trying to say there are all kinds of things that can go wrong, and you don't see it coming. Then it goes from bad to worse, and before you know it, you can't fix it all. You don't even know where to start."

She looked into his face. "You start at the beginning. Strip it down to what matters, the essential core, whatever's salvageable. You find the heart of it. Then little by little you build it back up, rub and sand and varnish, paint over the blemishes, maybe even carve a flourish or two."

He released a jagged breath. "I wish it was that easy."

She took the cigarette from his hand and stubbed it out. "Tell her."

His brow pinched. "Then I . . ." He cleared his throat. "It would be right out there that all these years . . ." He bunched his fingers into his hair.

"You've loved her?"

"I told you it's a love-hate thing."

"If she believed you hated her, she would not have come to you for help."

"She comes to me for money and . . ." He looked away.

Rese folded her arms. "The fact is she turned to you. Are you really going to let her walk into another marriage when you're the one she wants?"

Jaw cocked, he shook his head. "She's moved on twice now. I'm the one who can't."

"Maybe she's moved on because you're too stubborn to try again."

"You won't let it go, will you."

"Not when I'm right. You should know that." She picked up her chisel but kept her eyes on him. "I'd like you to stand in for Dad. It would mean a lot to me." To her utter dismay, tears stung her eyes.

Brad looked at her long and hard, then nodded. "Me too."

She played and replayed it all the way home. What would Lance think of Brad walking her down the aisle? Should she have asked Lance first? And why did Brad have to bring up that . . . episode? It meant nothing. It . . . She pulled up to the house. Lance's bike was there. Sofie's car wasn't. They must not be back from the hospital.

She went inside, climbed the stairs, and noticed her mother still in bed. She took in Star's empty room across the hall and headed up to the attic. While her mother chose to stay in her room some days, Star usually managed, with her strange mixture of silliness and insight, to get her out of bed. Rese no longer questioned the relationship they'd formed, Star finding in Mom— impossibly—what she had never known from her own mother.

Love and acceptance. It sometimes seemed as though Star was the true daughter and Rese Barrett the graft. But she didn't begrudge them, not with her own feelings so mixed.

She mounted the narrow stairs to the long attic, which smelled of oil paint and age. Lance had cleaned out the mouse-infested clutter as one of his first tasks for her, and she deeply appreciated it, though his ulterior motives had later come to light. "Star?"

Star stood at her easel and didn't turn. Coming up from behind, Rese saw the start of her new painting slashed down the middle. The paring knife in her hand explained what had happened, but definitely not why.

Rese moved around to see Star's face. "Didn't like it?" Usually she'd paint over something that wasn't working and save herself stretching a new canvas.

"I did." Star's eyes sparkled with tears. "Too much. I should know when things feel right"—her voice quavered—"to 'beware the ides of March.'"

"Did something happen, Star?" She hadn't broken down like this for a long time. The fact that she'd hurt the painting and not herself showed improvement, but still.

Star laid the knife on the easel.

"Is this about Lance? About our getting married?" Star had seemed brittle since their announcement, but Rese hadn't pursued it. Now it occurred to her that Star spent a lot of time with Lance during the day, and Lance was . . . Lance. "Are you in love with him?"

Star's laugh was broken glass. "No more than everyone else."

"Then what? Why the 'Et tu, Brute?'"

Star gaped. "Did that come out of your mouth? A quote?"

Rese shrugged. "You're rubbing off."

"And you knew it, too, the ides of March and Brutus."

"I'm not a total loser." Rese planted her hands on her hips. "Now, tell me what's wrong."

Star bit her lip. "You've really heard me? When I say things?"

"I hear everything you say, Star. I thought we worked this out.

You're my friend—more like my sister."

Star wrung her hands. "I'm afraid I'll disappear."

"How can you, when you shine so brightly?"

She sucked in a sob. "Do I? Do I still shine?"

"Why would you doubt it?"

"Will you want me to leave, when you marry Lance and have his children? I think there will be no room for me."

"We might have to rearrange a little if we do have kids, but—"

"Room inside, I mean."

"Star. Loving Lance has made me a better friend, a better person. I don't think love takes up space; I think it enlarges what's already there."

Star stared into her face. "I like that. I feel so much better." She turned to her canvas and cried, "Why didn't I talk to you before I did that?"

"Because you're Star." A commotion sounded downstairs. "Sounds like Lance is home. Let's hope he has Maria."

"What, hoping for a full house? Where's my friend Rese, and what have you done with her?"

CHAPTER FOURTEEN

Matt followed Sofie and company to the villa, where they were met by women bringing flowers, clothing, and baby supplies. He recognized Michelle Farrar and the midwife. The others were probably church women, as well, informed of Maria's homecoming and there to make it an event.

The tone inside the house was ebullient. Everyone acted as though reunification were a foregone conclusion, and that concerned him since things could turn on Maria's psych evaluation. His doubts, and Cassinia's, were valid, but no one there seemed to agree.

He leaned toward Sofie in the overcrowded parlor and whispered, "Is there somewhere we can talk?" Last night's tête-à-tête hung between them, and he felt the need to rationalize.

"Sure." She brought him out the back door, across the garden to the stone carriage house behind the villa. The place looked ancient on the outside, newly refurbished inside, though the stone floor was probably at least a hundred years old. The glass-fronted sitting room with a wood-burning stove that made him want to settle in and relax for a spell had a more masculine feel than the main house.

"The bedroom is Nonna Antonia's." Sofie motioned to the

door at the end. "I'm staying in here with her until Maria and Diego go home."

"That's not certain yet." He glanced around. "Isn't this close quarters for the two of you? What if Maria stays?"

Sofie shrugged. "There's always downstairs."

"Down . . ."

She stooped down and pulled open a hatch that had been invisible in the floor.

"Holy hole in the donut. A bat cave?"

She laughed. "Close. The tunnel leads to a wine cellar."

"Tunnel? You just energized my inner spelunker."

She pointed to the shelves. "Grab that flashlight."

"Can I go first?" He took the heavy-duty torch and turned it on.

She motioned him down with her elegant fingers. He descended the surprisingly well-preserved steps to the tunnel beneath. A boyish excitement welled up that he hadn't felt since he and Jacky had climbed through the mud hole into a room-sized cavern they'd sworn blood oaths to keep secret. Jacky had kept it to his death two months later. Strange that he could now think of that without the numbing pain.

He turned to Sofie behind him. "Sure this is a wine cellar?"

"A rather large one. The property originally had a vineyard. After learning that caves were used to age the wine in Italy, my great-great-grandfather built the cellar to imitate that here. We suspect his son, Vittorio, added the tunnel during Prohibition."

"A little bootlegging?"

She led the way through a metal gate. "Not successful, as you'll see by the inventory. Nonno Vito was killed before he could sell it—if that was his intention. As I told you before, Antonia escaped the gangster assassins through here."

He'd only half believed the story she'd told him in the car. But this place was proof. "Your grandmother Antonia?"

She nodded. "Our great-great-grandfather died in the tunnel. Lance found his skeleton."

"Down here?" A thrill found his spine as the tunnel opened

on a vast cellar that held stacked wooden casks and fully stocked racks. The torch's beam disappeared among their ranks.

"They had a great year in 1931—an exceptional vintage." She waved her hand. "Each of these bottles should sell at auction for two hundred to two thousand dollars."

He scanned the cellar. "Wow."

"So." She turned. "You wanted to talk?"

"Here?"

"You said alone."

He laughed. Alone must be hard to come by. He sobered as he set the torch on the end of a rack, its reflection on the ceiling casting a glow. "I wanted to explain about last night."

"You think you need to?"

Oh yeah. "I haven't talked about Jacky that way in twenty years. A few people know it happened, but not the details, not the things I told you. When you asked for my story"—he hung his hands on his hips—"it came out like a geyser, and it hasn't stopped. But you have to know last night was not typical."

She raised an eyebrow. "In what way?"

He was glad for the shadows. "I don't haunt women's doorsteps. Or cry on their shoulders." Twenty years' worth of guilt and despair must have needed an outlet. He leaned against the rack. "Some friends of mine are breaking up and I'd spent half the night with each. I just had to get out of the house, walk it off. I don't even know how I ended up outside your window."

"Somnambulism?"

He sighed. "I don't want you to think I'm stalking you or am otherwise unbalanced."

"You feel unbalanced?"

So much so he could topple at any moment. "People unburden themselves to me all the time, but I didn't realize how much I needed to. Now that I have—"

"You think you're through?"

He forked his fingers into his hair. "I hope so."

"Because in my experience grief is layered."

In his experience too. But he was doing his utmost to minimize the damage.

"I heard what happened to your brother, but not to you." Her soft voice sent a wrecking ball to his illusions of finality.

"To me? Nothing." He looked past the light into the crouching darkness that filled with her silence. "Nothing happened. Things . . . got better."

"Jacky's death made them better?"

He closed his eyes, unwilling to agree.

"Your father stopped bullying?"

"Not exactly, but with me it was a weird mix. He took pride in the way I stood up to and even surpassed him. Educationally for instance." His throat tasted bitter. "In a way the boasting was worse."

"You felt guilty he was proud?"

He opened his eyes to find she'd closed the space between them. "He should have been proud of both of us."

Jacky should have had the same chance Webb gave his favored son. But that was long ago, and he couldn't change it. This was now, and he wanted the past behind him, behind them both. All awareness of Jacky slipped away. There was only Sofie, and she didn't hold him responsible.

He slid his fingers into her hair, its honey softness sheer delight. He hadn't asked last night, but this time he had to. "May I?"

She slid her arms around his waist, and he felt exonerated as her lips found his.

Playing with fire could get her burned. But it had been so long since someone had held her like that, kissed her like that. So long since someone had looked at her with desire instead of worry. There, alone in the shadows, she wanted to kiss him and he wanted to kiss her. All of the whys and shoulds flew away, and only their wanting remained.

"Sof?" Lance called through the tunnel.

She drew back and steadied her voice. "I'm here. Showing

Matt the bat cave." Penetrating the dark chambers of his soul that for some reason, he'd opened to her. Exploring the dangers of her own.

Lance approached them through the tunnel with a smaller flashlight that flickered unreliably. "We ought to wire this with ceiling bulbs." He held out her phone. "You have a call." With a wry look, he mouthed *Momma*.

She took it. "Hi, Momma."

"You're there all this time and you don't call?" Her voice carried into the cellar. "How are you? How is Nonna? Is Lance eating? He says he's fine, but is he eating yet?"

She smiled. "Yes, Momma. Lance is fine; I'm fine. We're all fine."

"He's getting married."

"Yes, he is."

"I prayed so hard he would find a nice girl and settle in the neighborhood."

"Rese is a nice girl."

"But so far away. How can I plan a wedding all the way across the country?"

"Let Rese and Lance plan it?"

"You sound like Pop. He wants to know how your paper's coming."

Behind her mother's voice she heard Pop call it a report. "Fine, Momma." It wasn't technically a lie, because she had been working the first few days and might still. "Tell Pop don't work too hard."

"Your sisters miss you. The children miss you. When're you coming back?"

She swallowed a sudden ache for them all. But the thought of walking those streets again, seeing all the familiar faces, and looking, always looking for the two that weren't there . . . "I don't know."

"You sound tired. Are you sleeping?"

She was tired, she suddenly realized. "I've been caring for an infant." Matt had come over after Diego's last feeding, and she'd been up ever since.

"What infant?" There it was, the shock of concern. Flags going up for her in a way they wouldn't for her sisters.

"One who needed care. He'll be leaving soon, and his mother is back now." She glanced again at Matt. "You sound good, Momma. How are things?"

"I could use a teacher for the beginning students. You used to like the little ones."

Sofie smiled. She had loved teaching the young dancers, but she'd made a break from the old neighborhood, the old memories and hurts. She had to give this a chance. "Put out an ad."

Momma groaned loudly enough that both Lance and Matt laughed.

"I have to go, Momma. It's nice talking to you."

"Don't take so long to call next time."

"I won't. I love you." She hung up and looked from Matt to Lance. "So."

Lance hung his hands on his hips. "I was just telling Matt we'll be sending most of these bottles to auction."

Matt scrutinized the space. "What will you do with the cellar?"

Lance shrugged. "Hadn't really thought about it."

Neither had she, but all at once an idea rushed in, maybe from talking to Momma about something that hadn't been spoiled. She imagined the space without the racks, big and open. Mirrors on the walls, a polished wood floor . . . Could Sonoma County support a New York–style dance studio?

As they went back through the tunnel and up into the carriage house, Lance explained how he'd convinced Rese to let him reclaim the stony ruin, what he'd done to make it livable, and best of all, how he'd discovered the cellar beneath. Matt's face mirrored Lance's excitement when he described the cache they'd found under one of the racks. Lance mentioned only the bundles of silver-certificate bills stashed inside, not the dossiers and other personal items. Matt wasn't family.

But it eased her heart to hear them talking. Maybe now Matt would see Lance was a man like any other—except when it came to serving God. In the last year especially, he'd had episodes like today's where he got carried away, oblivious to what was happening around him. But that didn't make him a person of concern as Matt had seemed to think. What he thought now, she couldn't say.

Lance left them in the garden, and Matt turned, catching her in the full scope of his gaze. "I'd really like to see you, Sofie. Not about Diego, and not for a shoulder. Would you want to go out with me?"

Ironic timing after their interludes in the cellar and on the porch the night before. She'd seen it coming, considered it herself. But kissing him in response to some inner urge was not the same as a deliberate decision to spend time together. The reality of forming a relationship threatened her as his arms and lips had not. Relationship was where she failed. "I'm not sure I can, Matt."

"Because . . ."

I'm broken.

"You're not attracted to me?"

Could he think that? What she felt for him was not the mind-numbing, toxic attraction she'd had toward Eric. It was a recognition of his qualities, and a reckless disregard for their differences.

He ruffled his hair. "If you've hated every minute—"

"Of course not. It's just that the last time was destructive."

He searched her face. "I can't undo that."

"No one can."

"But I could buy you dinner. No expectations."

What would that even look like? Eric had been nothing but expectations, spoken and assumed. She had anticipated his wants, deciphered his moods and desires and met them with all her heart.

Matt folded his arms, uncertainty and disappointment touching his features. "It's okay to say no."

Then why didn't she? They were almost finished with Maria and Diego. It was unlikely their paths would cross again. She had provided an outlet for his grief; he'd allowed her to feel desirable in spite of everything. They could leave it at that.

She drew a strained breath. "Dinner would be nice." Another step toward letting go, more monumental really than leaving the neighborhood, when Eric wasn't even there anymore. That was a matter of geography. This step could change the landscape of her heart.

He smiled. "Seven?"

"Fine." *No, no, no.* What was she doing? She'd found her equilibrium.

"Okay, then." He brushed her cheek with his lips. "I'll see you tonight."

It was only dinner. Except she'd been raised in the ritual of breaking bread. Coming together at the table meant shared lives, and she was not sure she could share hers the way he wanted. Heart pounding, she watched him walk away, then went into the kitchen.

Nonna opened her eyes. "Nice man."

"Matt?"

"Who else?"

Sofie leaned on the counter. Matt was nice. He'd weathered tragedy and come out kinder, stronger. Nonna had softened toward him as she never had Eric. But she knew her grandmother didn't judge lightly.

She had endured a brief and fiery courtship, the flight for her life, and a precipitate marriage. Nonno Marco had been an unknown entity, and Nonna had entered the relationship in grief and fear, learned temperance, sound judgment, and abiding love. If anyone understood the terrain of the heart it was Antonia DiGratia Shepard Michelli.

Sofie looked at her beloved grandmother. "Are you all right here, Nonna? Do you miss everyone? Do you want to go home?"

Nonna folded her hands in her lap, blue eyes glistening. On her face the expression Sofie had treasured since her earliest years, wise and mischievous. "What makes you think I'm not?"

CHAPTER FIFTEEN

M att hadn't been this anxious since he'd sat at the counsel table and looked his first jury in the eyes. Why hadn't he let Sofie refuse? If that last relationship had been so bad, he understood her reluctance to try again. How could he think he was the one to bring her through it? Had he brought Jacky through?

For a while he'd been Matthew Hammond, attorney-at-law, with prospects for a sickeningly prosperous future, and even that hadn't been enough to clear away the taint of failure. Now he was just a guy trying to make a difference in one county for a few hurting kids. Some days he wasn't even sure he did that.

What if she'd said yes because she didn't want to hurt him, because she thought he couldn't handle a rejection, because—he gripped his steering wheel—he'd cried on her shoulder. Cried. He almost hit the brakes and turned around.

Since coming back to Sonoma, he hadn't asked anyone out in anything more than a casual way. Now he'd found someone who could be really special and annihilated his chances by baring his soul. She'd bared hers, too, but so much more gracefully.

Once again, the urge to turn around almost took over. But something stronger than anxiety kept him going. He wanted to see her. And it was only dinner, a casual meal with no expectations. Then why did his heart kick like a billy goat inside his chest when Sofie came to the door in black slacks and a soft gray suede jacket?

"Hi." He ran his eyes over her. She wouldn't have made the effort to look that good if she didn't want to go out with him.

"Hi."

"Hungry?"

She nodded, but he caught a whiff of something cooking inside as she closed the door. Steep competition, if that one sniff told him anything. Well, The Girl and the Fig at the Hotel Sonoma served delicious fare. Besides, he told himself again, there were no expectations.

"I like your hair that way." Clipped up in the back with careless chic. Less temptation to his fingers than when she had it lying loose.

"Thanks."

He let her into his Pathfinder. "How's Maria settling in?"

"Fine, though she had a tense time when Cassinia came by. She's convinced the woman wants to take away her baby."

If Cassinia had revealed anything close to that, it violated their code of conduct. Parenthood was constitutionally protected, and Diego's citizenship bestowed that protection upon Maria. But Cassinia did not believe Maria should be strapped with the offspring of her rape, and she may have let it show.

"She scheduled Maria's psych evaluation?"

Sofie nodded.

"What's your assessment of her mental and emotional health?"

"I hadn't seen much of her before she left Diego, but what I've seen of her since seems remarkable. I would never have guessed she's been through that kind of trauma."

"Dissociation?"

"I don't think so. She told Cassinia Lance healed her baby and healed her too."

Great. "Did Lance agree?"

Sofie shrugged. "Cassinia got pretty hostile when he tried to explain. It upset him enough that he took off on his bike with his dog."

"Where did he go?"

"Far enough to think."

"You have to admit it's farfetched. If Lance is miraculously healing people, why won't he say so?"

She shook her head. "Because he's not. Not the way everyone's making it sound. He's not trying to."

"You said intentions were measured by results."

"Okay. He did intend to put himself in God's hands. And he wants to help people." She glanced over. "He's not sure how the healing happens, only that sometimes when he touches people he feels an intense outpouring of love."

"And then whoever he touches is healed, cleft palates and all."

"It appears that way."

"And you think that's what happened to Maria. Lance touched her and all the emotional fallout went away."

"I only know that she doesn't seem destroyed. And she's bonded with Diego, strongly enough to put herself at risk in order to protect him. You tell me if that's the normal pattern."

He couldn't say it was. Not even close. But he was not ready to accept her explanation. Maybe Maria was so deeply in denial, she hadn't begun to face the pain. That made more sense than someone healing her by mistake. But what was he trying to do, pick a fight before they even got inside?

He parked in the plaza near the hotel and went around to get her door. Either she was comfortable being cared for or she'd been raised to expect courtesy—or the guy she'd been with got off on control. The spectrum of women who fell prey to abusers included professionals with advanced degrees and even tough policewomen.

Sofie hadn't said Eric had abused her, only that the relationship had been destructive. She could have been referring to the breakup. He could only guess what the relationship had looked liked before that; had in fact spent most of the day guessing.

As they entered, she said, "This looks nice."

"'Country food with a French passion.'"

They started with cheeses, fruit, and homemade fig cake that she ate with appreciation while she told him how exacting Nonna Antonia had been about her cheeses, how she'd inspected every wheel that came into the restaurant. Next she had the herb-roasted eggplant salad with fresh mozzarella and roasted red peppers, while he had a salad with arugula, pecans, goat cheese, pancetta, and figs.

"Like Momma, my sister Monica has no skill with food. They drive a truck through whatever they prepare. Lance keeps thinking they're trainable. He doesn't realize what an advantage he had, learning from the time he was small at Nonna's elbow in the restaurant kitchen." She took a bite. "Momma takes each suggestion he makes as an insult. But it really hurts him to see the food massacred."

"So he's a perfectionist." Why were they back on the subject of Lance?

"Not in the retentive sense. He's free in his approach, very creative, very talented."

"And that's what he does? Cook?"

"He does a lot of things. It would be hard to find something he hasn't done. But his passions are food and music."

Her pan-seared halibut with crawfish and saffron aioli arrived. She breathed its aroma and lifted her fork. "He and his friend Rico sang together since they were in grade school. They played professionally in some hot spots and landed a top-notch agent who had big plans before Lance quit the band."

"Why'd he quit?"

She looked down. "Lots of things, but mostly Tony's death."

"Tony . . ."

"Our older brother. He was a cop. He died at Ground Zero."

Matt stared at her. "You lost a brother?" He rested both hands on the table, taking that in. "You didn't say anything. When I told you about Jacky."

"I didn't want to dilute your grief."

But she'd been through it, the senseless loss. And said nothing. Compassionate restraint, or that same deflection he'd noticed in Lance? The capacity to diminish, to utterly focus on someone else. "You want to talk about it?"

She sighed. "He died in the line of duty. He was honored, is still honored for that. I miss him." She looked up. "But . . . we're here, having dinner."

So keep it light. She would choose when and what she wanted to tell, as she had in the hospital, but he realized now, she would reveal very little of the woundedness.

He tore off a piece of bread. "What was your favorite subject in school?"

She laughed softly. "Yearbook."

He raised his brows.

"I liked capturing the moments, chronicling the experience."

"Were you the photographer?"

"No, that was Bernie Stein. I did layout. What was yours?"

"P.E. No surprise, huh?"

"Actually, I'd have thought something more brainy, like history, since you went into law."

"Yeah, well, just because I got the grades didn't mean I enjoyed it. What I liked was getting out on the wrestling mat, taking charge on the football field, and dodge ball? Watch out."

"What is it about men and dodge ball?"

"An evolutionary instinct to wipe out the weak." He looked down at his plate. "Actually I usually teamed up with some girl or scrawny kid." He hadn't meant to sound like some adolescent altruist, even though it was true. He'd learned how fragile the weak were.

"Wish you'd been on my team."

A smile tugged the corners of his mouth. "Me too."

"This fish is wonderful. How's your duck?"

He'd ordered the duck confit with roasted potatoes, olives, wilted greens, and capers. "It's great. Want a bite?"

She surprised him by accepting. He held the forkful out as she leaned forward. His whole body warmed as she tasted it. This was a woman with whom he could share lazy mornings and rainy afternoons.

"Delicious. Would you like to try my fish?"

"I've had it. Actually it's one of my favorite things on the menu."

"Then have some." She cut off a soft flaky chunk and held it up.

He cupped her hand and took the bite. "Mmm. As good as always." The contact with her skin an enhancement. "You could write your dissertation on the euphoric benefits of quality cuisine."

"Hmm."

"Have you decided to proceed?"

She shrugged. "I had a crazy thought this afternoon of turning the cellar into a studio. Think anyone here wants to learn how to dance?"

"In the bat cave? Who wouldn't?"

She rolled her eyes. "What is it with you and holes in the ground?"

"A predisposition toward any adventure that gets me muddy."

"Well, it wouldn't look like a bat cave when I was through with it."

"No skeletons?"

She shook her head. "Lance gave him a proper burial."

Someone came up behind him, and he looked up.

Sybil gave him her sexy smirk. "Hi there, softy."

He hated that sobriquet, but she used it with impunity.

She ran a hand across his shoulders, then turned to Sofie. "I couldn't help hearing you mention Lance. Would that be Lance Michelli?"

"That's right."

"Sybil Jackson." She held out her hand, and Matt could have sworn Sofie stiffened.

"Oh."

"He's mentioned me?"

"Mainly your great-grandfather."

Sybil rolled her eyes. "Unfortunate, but I can hardly be blamed. And I did make it right."

Sofie nodded, but not convincingly.

Sybil looked at Matt. "You haven't introduced your date."

He started to rise, but Sofie said, "I'm Lance's sister. Sofie."

"Oh." She turned back to him. "Some of us are slumming over to Boyes tomorrow. Feel like a hot-spring spa?"

"I'll think about it." But not too long. If Sybil got any steamier, she'd accelerate global warming. When she walked away, he said, "What happened with her great-grandfather?"

"He ordered the murder of mine."

"No way."

Sofie nodded. "Nonna's father and grandfather died as a result of his actions. I told you Antonia was forced to flee."

He moistened his lips. "I didn't know Sybil, of all people, was somehow involved."

"She wasn't. As she said, it's all in the past. And she did provide Lance some answers."

"You don't seem too crazy about her."

Sofie toyed with a flat bean. "I'm sorry."

"Why?"

She raised her eyes. "She's your friend."

"In a broad sense of the word. I've known her a long time. She's most interested when I'm with someone else."

Sofie skewered the bean and ate it bite by bite, then dabbed her mouth. "I guess I'm leery of predatory people."

"What makes you think she's predatory?"

Sofie raised a single brow succinctly.

"Well, yes. She does present that way, but"—he spread his hands—"her dad's had something like seven wives, each younger than the last, none of whom have tolerated her very well. She's trying to find affirmation where she can."

"Have you dated her?"

He shook his head. "I haven't pursued any relationship since coming back to Sonoma. It's been a few years of reshaping my life, figuring out what's important."

"So what is important?"

He thought for a moment. "Not money. I was on the fast track for that with my Boston firm, billing hours at a fiendish rate. Now I make enough to get by. Of course, I had little opportunity to spend what I earned before, so most of it is out there earning more."

"So time means more than money."

"Depending on how it's spent. I could hardly think before of doing anything outside of work. Dates were plotted on my calendar for Saturday nights, and I was lucky to remember who and where."

Sofie's brow puzzled. "That doesn't seem . . ."

"Like me?"

She nodded.

"It isn't. I was caught in someone else's expectations."

"Oh." By her expression she knew exactly how that was.

He reached across the table for her hand. "What's important to you?"

"Family. Faith. Joy."

"And you have all that?"

"A measure of each."

His thumb traced the topography of her knuckles. "Is there room for more?"

"There's always room for more."

The waitress came over with the dessert tray. Sofie demurred, but he convinced her to split a chocolate ganache cake with brandied cherry sauce and crème fraiche gelato. "If you hate it, I'll make the supreme sacrifice and eat it all."

She laughed. "And if I love it?"

"We'll arm wrestle for the bigger half."

"You might be surprised," she said, narrowing her eyes.

"Oh, I'm sure you're strong for a girl, being a dancer and all. But I'm afraid it wouldn't be a fair contest."

She raised her chin. "I'm from the Bronx."

"Meaning . . ."

"There are means of prevailing that don't require superior strength."

"Such as?"

"Pressure points."

He sat back and looked her up and down. There were emotional pressure points, too, so incapacitating they could take you down. She had almost capitulated, but she was recovering. He had to believe that. "Thanks for the warning." He smiled, certain that if it came to it he'd put her arm down with no difficulty.

The waitress set the decadent cake between them with two forks. He handed one to Sofie and took up the other. "Ready, set, go." But he let her have the first bite.

She closed her eyes. "Now that's worth fighting for."

He smiled. "I can order another."

"No." She sucked the fork clean. "Sometimes less is more."

"That's one of those phrases created to make you feel stupid. How can less be more? It can be better, smarter, even more efficient. But it has to be more something, not just more."

She smiled. "Would you like some more?"

"Can't exactly have less."

"That depends on less what. Less than me, or less than you've had?"

"And that"—he pointed his fork—"depends on what you meant by more."

She delectably slid the bite from her fork, licking the chocolate from the point of her lip. He felt like a rocket blasting off, all afterburners go. Not good. He could get carried away, and Sofie needed careful handling. With everything in him, he stabilized and took another bite, though frankly he'd rather watch her enjoy every morsel.

———

Carly's hands sweated. *So lame!* She swiped them down her jeans, then picked up the phone again. Just do it. She touched in the number. It connected. It rang. Her heart was racing. This was it. This time she would do it. Because she was tired of being alone, tired of being lonely.

"Hello?"

Carly swallowed hard. "Hi."

"Who's this?"

Sofie sounded a little cautious, like maybe she expected another disconnect. Before she lost her nerve, she said, "Carly." She heard a sharp breath and hoped Sofie wouldn't hang up on her.

"Carly?" It was almost a whisper. Shaky too.

"Do you remember me, 'cuz it's okay if you don't, and I didn't mean to bother you, but . . ."

"Of course I remember you." Now her voice was thick like she might cry. "Carly, is that really you? How did you get my number?"

"From my dad's phone." She didn't mention the times she'd called from his because Sofie might be mad that she hadn't said anything.

"Honey, how are you? It's *so* nice to hear your voice."

Not anything like how nice it was to hear hers. She got warm in her chest and stomach and everywhere. "I um, just wanted to . . . say hi." *I miss you; I love you; I want you to come home.*

"I can't tell you how much that means to me." She sounded calmer now, but in a way it was even deeper somehow.

"So, like, I talked to some guy when I called you before? Was that, is he . . ."

"I think it was Lance. You were probably too little to remember my brother."

Brother. O . . . kay. "Yeah. I guess so. But I remember you, and I just, like, wanted to talk."

"Where are you?"

"In my room."

"No, I mean, where do you live?"

"Carly?" The door opened. Dad came right in. "Who is that? Who are you talking to?"

"Nobody." *Oh yeah, good one—like I'm talking to myself on the phone.* "I mean no one important. Just a friend."

"What friend?"

"Just . . . Sofie."

His face darkened. "Sofie who?"

She swallowed hard. He grabbed the phone. "Hello?" His voice cracked. "Sofie, is that you?"

Scowling, he took the phone from his ear, then closed it. Carly shook from the top of her scalp to the ends of her toes. She stood up from the bed, ran into the bathroom, and threw up. When the heaving stopped, she pushed up from her knees and washed her hands and face in cold water, shivering clear through.

If a meteor had crashed through the roof and smashed her, Sofie could not have felt more destroyed. Matt had hold of both her hands, but she felt nothing. Her hands were numb, her body, everything except the core deep inside that burned, icy hot.

"Sofie." Matt chafed her hands. "Stay with me."

Where did he think she would go? But the moment she moved her head, she realized how she must look. The blood had drained from her brain. A rushing like water filled her ears; her vision blackened. She heard a chair scrape. Matt had his arm around her shoulders.

Things came back into focus. The waitress hovered off to Matt's left. People at other tables stared. Matt crouched down beside her. "You okay?"

Eyes closed, she pressed her fingers to her temples. "It was Carly."

"I heard."

"And . . . Eric."

He clenched her hand as though he could stave off the memories if he just held tightly enough. With his other hand, he motioned the waitress away. "Do you want to leave?"

She nodded. Her head had cleared, and she wanted to get away from the stares, discreet though they now appeared. She stood up. "I'll duck into the bathroom."

He directed her and raised a finger for the check as she walked away. Her heart pounded. *Carly.* The ache was almost physical. She pushed through the bathroom door and leaned on the counter. A shudder passed over her. *Eric . . .* She gulped back tears, then stared hard into the mirror. *Get ahold of yourself.* But she couldn't find herself, couldn't—

"Sofie?" Matt rapped softly on the door.

She pressed back from the counter, forcing deep breaths, then turned and went out. Concern etched lines into his face.

She straightened her spine. "I'm all right. It just took me by surprise."

"Okay." But he cradled her elbow and held on all the way to his vehicle.

She climbed in and buckled her belt, but there was no safety strap that could protect against invisible blows, against the mind's uncontrolled spiraling. Eric had sounded hurt. Angry too, maybe, but the crack in his voice . . .

"Do you think it was Carly calling those other times?" Matt's question drew her back.

"It must have been." Her number was in Eric's phone. They hadn't forgotten her, hadn't wiped her out of their lives. Carly had found her, reached out and reconnected their severed hearts.

"Do you think she's in trouble?"

Sofie jolted. "What do you mean?"

"Will he be angry she called?"

Her hands clenched. "Maybe."

"Do we need to have the call traced?"

She turned. "Can we?"

"Only if you think she's in imminent danger."

"Not like that. He isn't like that." There'd be nothing to see, no signs of abuse.

Matt took the corner harder than necessary.

She tried to explain. "Carly might worry that she's disappointed him." How well she remembered that cavern of disappointment. "It's better to work with Eric, to—"

"Play by his rules." Matt's voice sounded flat.

"Carly must know that. She's ten."

"And that's why you've worried about her the last six years?"

She wrapped herself in her arms. "She sounded . . . so much older."

"Ten isn't old enough to protect herself."

Tears pooled in her eyes. "He would never hurt her."

"He saved that for you?"

She swallowed the swelling in her throat. "He did not abuse me. He just . . . needed . . . a lot." That wasn't a good explanation, but she didn't know how else to say it. Eric wasn't a fiend; he was mesmerizingly charismatic, handsome, and . . . fathomless.

Matt pulled into the driveway and stopped. With the engine running, he got out and walked around. He opened her door.

She slipped out. "I'm sorry. I didn't mean to spoil—"

"Don't worry about it." His face said the opposite.

"Thank you for dinner."

"My pleasure." He closed the passenger door and motioned her toward the porch.

"It's all right. You don't have to walk me in."

He nodded. "Okay. Good night." He made no move to kiss her. If he even thought about it, nothing showed.

She managed a smile, then climbed the steps and went inside.

CHAPTER SIXTEEN

Lance approached the back door with Baxter at his heels, both of them windblown and disheveled. He'd ridden as long and hard as he could, but it hadn't worked its magic, and he guessed it showed. Rese let him into the kitchen and slipped her arms around his waist. "Are you okay?"

He hated that she kept asking that. "I am now." He hooked his arms over her shoulders.

"Want to talk about it?"

He kissed her hairline. Not so long ago, she'd avoided all personal conversation, and he'd been the one making her open up. Now she'd switched roles on him, and he realized how difficult it could be to find the words. "For so long, I've been trying to prove I'm not a screw-up. Even though I'm not a cop like Tony and Nonno, or a working stiff like Pop and Bobby and Lou. Even though Pop still thinks I need to get a real job." He rested his forehead against hers. "I wanted people to take me as I am, but now . . ." He closed his eyes.

"Now what?" Rese nudged him.

"Maria called me a saint. Star looks at me like I'm the fixer of all ills. Nonna says God's had a love affair with me since I was born. Even Rico, who knows me better than anyone—"

"Rico?"

"Remember when he smashed up his wrist?"

She nodded.

"He thinks I healed it."

"But the surgery . . ."

"The doctors pinned him together, but then he drummed."

She grimaced.

"I only held it for a second, just to feel for swelling or . . . I'm not even sure why I took hold of him. When I let go, he looked as if I'd grown another head."

"You've helped people, Lance. You can't expect them not to notice."

He rubbed his face. "Cassinia all but accused me of brainwashing Maria. She thinks I'm on some power trip, making disciples of impressionable girls."

"It doesn't matter what she thinks."

He appreciated the sentiment, but what had really troubled him was seeing behind Cassinia's animosity; the abortions that had hardened her. The pain fueling her insults hurt more than the words, and he didn't know what to do about it. With Baxter between his arms and the wind in his face, he'd begged God not to show him things he couldn't fix.

God's answer? *Know my heart.*

Letting God's love flow through him was a gift he could embrace. But feeling that love rejected? That was asking too much.

"You're not responsible for other people's opinions, good or bad."

He sighed. "Keep telling me that, okay?"

"Have you eaten?"

He shook his head. He'd broken his own rule, had not been there for dinner, making or eating. "I'm sorry."

"Nonna kept a plate for you."

He'd noticed lately that she'd started calling her Nonna like everyone else. "I'm not really hungry."

"Lance."

He put his head to hers again. "Please don't push it."

She stared into his eyes. "I need to know you're okay."

"What would convince you?" he asked with a smile.

"Could you strut or throw a fit?"

He laughed. "Fagedda-bout-it."

"Pierce something?"

"It's not rebellious now that everyone's doing it."

"Oh, the truth comes out. I thought you just liked the look of an earring." She touched the diamond stud in his ear.

"Yeah, well . . ." He pulled her close, dropping his gaze to her lips. "Did you agree to marry me?"

"Refuse that highly romantic proposal?"

He closed his hands around her waist. "You want romantic?" The tiny intake of her breath spurred him as he took charge of her mouth, warming to the subject until Sofie passed by with a hand raised as a shield.

"Sof." He turned only his head.

She lowered her hand. "I'd have gone around if I knew you were making out in the kitchen."

Her words were light, but something in her expression kicked him hard. "Are you okay?"

"Of course." Sofie never could lie.

"What happened? Was he a jerk?"

She looked confused. "Matt?"

"Who else?"

She folded her arms. "No. Matt was fine."

"If he messed with you, Sof . . ."

"It's not Matt, all right?" Her arms tightened. "I talked to Carly."

"What?"

Rese stepped back as his attention diverted.

"She called my cell. I think she tried before and reached you."

"That was Carly?"

"Who's Carly?" Rese asked.

Sofie sighed. "Eric's daughter. He's the one I was with before."

Lance's stomach knotted. "What did she want?" He kept his tone even.

"Just to talk, I guess. We only had a minute, and . . . then Eric came on."

"You talked to him?"

"I should have, but I didn't know what to say."

He snagged his hair with his fingers. "You can't get mixed up in that again."

She looked away.

"Think, Sof. Remember how it was."

"She sounded so sweet. Different, but . . ."

"Don't make that mistake again."

Sadness filled her eyes. "Please don't be Pop, Lance. Or any of the rest of them. You're the only one who didn't judge." She pulled open the door and went out.

"I should've," he said as it closed.

Sofie slipped inside the darkened carriage house, slumped onto the couch, and dropped her face to her hands.

"What is it, cara?" Nonna whispered.

Sofie looked over at her, standing in the doorway in her white nightgown like the old women in folktales who transform into beautiful fairies. "I didn't mean to wake you."

"Waking and sleeping are one breath and the next," Nonna said as she sat beside Sofie. "What happened?"

As pointless as it would have been to evade Lance, it was more so with Nonna. Sofie told her about the call, and Eric's voice at the end. How lost he'd sounded, and hurt. How she ached from the few words she'd shared with Carly and all the lost years. Nonna listened without comment.

"I don't know what to do. If I had found out where she was . . ."

"It's better left alone."

But it wasn't. If Carly knew how badly she missed her, how much she wanted to see her, touch her, make her more real than her dreams, would she be the glue that somehow drew them all back together again? Her heart fluttered. No. Eric would suck her in again, engulf her with his need. Four pivotal years she'd belonged to him. Now she had learned to breathe again.

Yet what about Carly? Sofie ached to think of the child bearing his love undiluted. No one could give Eric enough . . . or could she? Was there a way, something she could have done, could . . . do?

"'As a dog returns to its vomit, so a fool repeats his folly.'"

She closed her eyes. Nonna had minced no words the last time, and yet when everything fell apart, she'd been there, a silent presence holding on, refusing to let her go.

"He could have changed, Nonna. I've changed."

"He's an empty gullet."

"I'm thinking of Carly."

"No you're not. You've tasted his poison." Nonna stood.

"Please. He's a person. He deserves some respect."

"Respect is earned." She went back into her room and closed the door.

She was right. As much as Sofie loved her, Carly was not her burden. A horrible ache seized her. Then whose? Memories came back of Carly's little hands, her precious voice, a smile that took all the strength from Sofie's legs. She'd been so darling, the sight of her could trigger tears, and Sofie wondered if Eric had been that way as a child. Had he realized, even then, the power he had to render people helpless?

Rese studied Lance as he turned back from the door Sofie had passed through. He looked as bleak as she'd seen him. "Are you going to explain?"

"Ever wonder how the devil could be beautiful?"

She frowned. "Have I gotten to that part?"

"Lucifer. Angel of Light. The best of all God's angels."

"That's who dated Sofie?"

"Eric Malden. And he didn't date her. He devoured her."

"Okay, you're scaring me." She had wanted to know Sofie's story. Now she wasn't sure.

"How else would you explain a beautiful young woman, full of life and talent, smart as a whip and loved by everyone, taking a razor to her wrists?"

"I can't."

Lance looked away. "I was touring for a lot of the time they were together. Maybe if I'd been there, looked closer, trusted her less. It seemed to me people were doing a lot of judging and not much loving. I knew how that felt and didn't want to pile on. And with my reputation, who was I to throw stones?"

"What happened?"

"He derailed her friendships, cut her off from her family. He took away her will, her identity, her existence outside of him. And then he left. It took a long time to work her back into the relationships she'd had before. She's only now seeking out new ones."

"So Carly . . ."

"Sofie was her mother for four years. That child was hers in every way that mattered." He shook his head. "We knew she hurt, but she hid how badly."

He cast his gaze to the ceiling, jaw cocked, as memory triggered tears. "Monica found her. The bossy sister who runs everyone's life found her in the tub and hollered to wake the dead—literally. Tony was downstairs with Pop. He staunched the blood and kept her breathing." His voice broke. "While Rico and I played a gig in Manhattan."

"You could not have known."

He lowered his chin and composed himself. "But you can see why I get weary of people thinking I'm something I'm not."

He turned when Star came in, pulled a padded envelope from his jacket pocket. "Here, Star. This came in the mail."

Star read the return address and went still. "Thanks." She took it and walked out.

"What was that?"

"From Rico."

Rese clamped her hands on her hips. "Ashes of her painting?"

"Come on. Rico's not vindictive."

"If you say so." She remembered him searching Times Square

for Star with a hard determination that made her glad they hadn't found her.

"Dangerous, but not vindictive."

"Okay. I have to tuck Mom in. Will you check on Star?" Since it was his friend stirring the pot.

"Sure."

They divided in the hall upstairs. Rese's mother had already fallen asleep, so she made sure the medicine cup was empty, turned off the TV and the lamp. If Mom had too many more days when she didn't want to get up, Dr. Jonas needed to know. Rese slipped out just as Star, wearing earbuds, retreated into her room. Lance looked dazed outside her door.

"Everything all right?"

"Rico wrote her a song."

"Is it any good?"

"No, I said, *Rico* wrote it."

"I heard— Oh."

"See, Rico does rhythm. I do lyrics."

This was touching something deeper, their friendship, their history. And explaining about Sofie had left him raw. He brushed her cheek with his thumb, kissed her softly, and went into his room. Moments later she heard his fingers on the strings.

Rese slipped into Star's room and found her on her back, eyes closed, but her hands moved gently to the music. She sat on the bed beside her, and Star opened her eyes. She patted the mattress, and Rese lay down alongside. She'd expected to find her distraught, but her face had a peace she hardly recognized.

"Listen." Star transferred the earbuds and restarted the CD.

It sounded like the music Star and Rico had recorded in the subway tunnel with Rico on Chaz's steel drum and Star's eerie, wordless vocal. Overlaid was Rico's slightly accented voice speaking one word at a time. "Chance. Perchance. Persuade. Dissuade. Disdain. Explain. Refrain. Sustain. Regain. Renew." Hypnotically the words came, threaded together, a rhythmic heartbeat over the airy, echoing tones.

She thought of Rico with his Jack Sparrow looks, long beaded hair, and quick, nervous hands. Talented. Loyal. Hot-tempered. After Star had betrayed him, he said, "There's no place for you here, chiquita." And Star-like, she'd gone off to hurt herself.

Now they seemed to be caught in a tentative dance of reconciliation. The painting she'd sent incorporating the elements of Rico's life and their time together; his words over the music they'd made. Neither saying too much, only a current between them like the steel-drum vibrations, and in Star's face the fragile stirring of hope.

"Resolution, absolution, revelation, consolation . . ."

CHAPTER SEVENTEEN

M att looked up when Cassinia walked into his office with something more than her usual verve. "What'd I do?"

"She's here."

"Who's where?"

"Maria's mother. Your man Lance just called."

"My man?" He sat back in his chair, wondering why he was getting the brunt of her mood.

"The miracle worker."

"Yeah, I heard that too. Don't put much stock in it."

"Maria does. First her baby, then her. Now he's picked her mother up from the airport and they're driving in."

"He didn't pull her out of a hat. She has a travel visa."

"He wants us to meet them at the house. Maybe you can explain how he got control of both cases?"

"They were helping Maria before we got involved. She trusts him."

"She reveres him."

"After what she's been through, that's not all bad. At least she can differentiate." Which was more than Cassinia did some days.

He'd been all over the board on his opinion of Lance Michelli, but the whole thing was muddied by his feelings for Sofie—

something, thankfully, Cassinia knew nothing about. In the days since their date, he'd tried not to think of her, checking in with Lance by phone a couple times for updates on Diego. According to him, mother and son were thriving.

Cassinia scowled. "I still say she and the baby should not have been reunited until we knew everything."

"You got the eval." And because it affected his recommendations for Diego, so had he. Maria was springing back extraordinarily well, grieving the hysterectomy and clinging to the son she'd borne. She expressed anger toward those who had victimized her, along with a deep desire to go home. If she also clung to her belief in Lance Michelli, who could blame her? "They've had care and shelter there that we'd have struggled to provide."

Cassinia frowned. "And brainwashing. How can people believe that rot? Heaven, hell, and miracles. Fables and fairy tales are harmful when fanatics take them as truth."

Except for her tone, those could have been his words. The ambivalence he felt now surprised him. He just wanted the case closed. He'd recommended the judge sign off on Diego's custodial release. Maria would either return to her mother's care or be emancipated and remain in the States with assistance until she got on her feet—*if* she got on her feet at sixteen with an infant and no family other than those "fanatics" at the villa.

He stood. "Shall we?"

"You're driving; I biked in." The air outside was heavy with mist, but neither rain, nor sleet, nor inclement weather could keep Cassinia from fuel-saving cycling. She wasn't averse to piggybacking, though, if he was already gas guzzling to a mutual destination.

They didn't speak on the way. Cassinia's demeanor in this case, as compared to others, suggested she felt threatened somehow. Things that didn't fit the life structure she'd erected annoyed and frustrated her, but this was the worst he'd seen her yet. She tried to disguise it, but the sooner this whole thing was behind them, the better.

Star answered the door in an embroidered skirt and peasant

blouse. On her wrists and ankles dangled several dozen silver bracelets that jingled when she moved. "Lance isn't back yet with Señora Espinoza. Would you like a latte?"

Not when the word alone conjured his moments across the table from Sofie. "No thanks."

Cassinia gave Star a look that would have withered a true mortal. "I'd like to meet with Maria before her mother arrives."

No doubt to make certain the girl realized this could go either way. But why would Señora Espinoza travel into the States only to tell Maria she could not come home?

"I'll tell her." Star jingled up the stairs.

He waited in the parlor with his co-worker, trying not to wonder where Sofie was. He could complete this visit, even conclude the case, without seeing her. Best for both of them. She'd been essential to Diego's care until Maria returned. Then she'd stepped aside with a willingness that surprised him, given her history of attaching to other people's kids. He shook his head.

Within moments Maria came down alone, concern all over her face. "What is the matter?"

Cassinia cocked her head. "Why do you think something's wrong?"

"My mother is not here yet. But you want to see me?" She reached the bottom of the stairs and stood pretty much eye-to-eye with Cassinia.

"I'm not your enemy, Maria. I'm your advocate. I'm thinking of what's best for you and making sure no one is coercing you. Do you understand coerce?"

Maria nodded. "Forcing me." Her voice broke. "But that was before." Anger filled her eyes. "They will be punished. No one here has done so."

"I don't mean the way you were before. Come and sit." Cassinia took one of the chairs in the parlor, Maria another. She might be harsh in her discussions about this case, but she handled Maria with care and respect, even while questioning her fifteen different ways as to who might be pressuring her to keep the baby or to go back to her mother. Maria's response never varied.

"No one is coercing me. I want my baby, and I want to go home."

The door opened and Lance came in with a stately middle-aged Mexican woman.

Maria jumped to her feet. *"¡Mamá!"*

Mrs. Espinoza opened her arms with a cry, and they embraced for a long time, Maria shedding more tears than he'd seen yet. *"Lo siento, Mamá. Lo siento."*

The woman cradled Maria's head, crying as well. *"Hija querida."* After some minutes, they drew apart. "Where is my grandson?"

"He's here." Sofie spoke from the stairs.

Matt turned, his heart galloping at the sight of her. He couldn't believe the anger he'd felt when she had defended the man who had driven her to attempt suicide. Yet with every step she descended, he wanted to close the gap, pull her close. . . . He forced a flat expression. This was about Diego.

Sofie tucked the infant into Señora Espinoza's arms. The baby protested the shuffling with a squawk, then looked into his grandmother's face. Sofie stepped back, and Matt found that he had closed the gap. She smelled of baby powder and wishes and stood near enough to touch, but he didn't.

"Mamá"—Maria hooked her finger into the baby's fist— "meet Diego Manuel."

Tears coursed down Señora Espinoza's cheeks. "A good name. For your *papá*, may he rest in peace. And where is the priest?"

"He should be here any minute." Lance looked out the front window as he answered.

"Good."

Matt shrugged when Cassinia met his gaze. Somehow the power had shifted to the elegant woman now holding the baby. "You are the godmother?" she asked Sofie.

Sofie declined her head. "I'm honored."

"And Lance." Maria beamed. "He is the godfather."

Matt almost snickered after what Sofie had told him. Godfather indeed.

"Mrs. Espinoza, I'm Cassinia Krantz. I'm the social worker in charge of Maria's case." She looked like a tough gray boxer minus the underbite.

"Whatever illegal things my half brother and his scum were involved in, Maria was not part of it."

"I mean I'm responsible for her welfare, for deciding—"

"*I* am responsible for her welfare."

"Here he is." Lance went to the door to let the priest in. More hocus-pocus. Cassinia looked as though she might spit nails.

Sofie backed up and bumped him with her elbow. She glanced over her shoulder. "Sorry."

He'd answer if he could push the air through his vocal cords.

As the portly priest came in, Cassinia slipped out the door. Matt had too many obstacles between himself and escape, primarily Sofie, whose presence worked in him once again like a drug. Star and Elaine came down, and Nonna joined them from the arched entrance to the dining room. In the press, he touched the tips of Sofie's soft golden-brown hair.

The ceremony was simple—a little water, a little oil, no levitation or tongues of flame. Lance didn't do anything but trace a cross on the infant a few times, so Matt guessed no miracles were on the docket today. Even so, for a baby who'd gone more than a week with no name, things seemed pretty settled by the time the priest packed up his gear.

Maria and her mother and the baby went upstairs. Star and Elaine and Nonna took the priest to the kitchen. Rese wasn't present—it was a work day, after all. And that left Matt alone with Sofie and Lance, and Lance didn't seem inclined to make it a twosome.

He hung his hands on his hips. "Señora Espinoza intends to take Maria home tomorrow. With Diego."

Matt reached into the folder under his arm and produced the judge's order.

Lance read it and smiled. "Thanks."

"It was in everyone's best interest." He and Cassinia had been no more than pawns in this whole business. But he'd take it in place of all the cases where no happy ending was possible. "What was all that with the baptism?"

"Señora Espinoza wasn't sure their parish would accept Diego under the circumstances."

That was the sort of narrow religion Matt knew too well.

"It was also her way of proving she does."

Matt probably imagined the smugness in Lance's smile. Weren't prophets above all that?

"We're putting together some lunch. Do you and"—Lance looked around—"Cassinia want to stay?"

"I guess not." It would take days to decompress her as it was. He couldn't tell if Sofie's expression indicated relief or resignation. But what difference did it make? She'd shown him the one thing he couldn't live with in a woman.

Lance held out his hand. "Thanks for overseeing things with Diego."

"Sure." They shook.

Lance looked from him to Sofie, then went down the hall to the kitchen. Alone with her, it was harder to uphold his convictions, especially when she looked as though she understood and didn't blame him for thinking less of her.

She raised her coppery green eyes. "I'm glad you were assigned his case, Matt. You handled it well."

He'd hardly done anything, and they both knew it. "You took good care of him."

"Babies are easy." She laid on the New York. "They don't argue."

He smiled. "Don't ask for the car keys . . ."

"Don't raid your closet . . ."

"Don't stay out late and forget to call . . ."

They laughed. Her teeth were white and smooth, her lips soft and full. She'd been brave and generous in caring for Diego, selfless in giving him up.

His heart pumped. "Sofie, would you want to see me again? Maybe a drive through wine country?"

"In February?"

"Every season has a purpose."

"Hmm." She folded her arms. "That's biblical."

"Ecclesiastes."

She raised her brows.

"Just because I don't subscribe doesn't mean I'm uninformed. My agnosticism is well grounded."

"I see." Her smile engulfed him. "A drive would be nice."

He was so gone. "I'll call you, then." Warmth infused him as he walked into the drizzly chill, where Cassinia looked as though she'd sucked a persimmon.

She pocketed her phone. "Kid en route to emergency. Five months old. Shaken."

His mood crashed. Why did his enlightened disbelief suddenly seem so useless?

———

Rese settled into a chair at the table. Michelle's Bible studies did not twist her mind as Lance's theological discussions tended to. Michelle's purpose and presentation were clear; the Scriptures she chose to "break open" supported her life's goal to feed the hungry and bind up the brokenhearted. In some ways that was as challenging as the esoteric ideas Lance wrestled with.

Rese shook her head, still wondering how she'd gotten there. Her life had been so insular, Mom's illness at first keeping people from making friends with them, then her own walls thickening with each passing year. The thought of Lance spending all that time improving others' living conditions, putting his life on the line in places like Kingston, of Michelle living in a warehouse of donations for the poor she visited daily, left her dazed.

But as out of place as she sometimes felt, it was nothing to having Star there. They'd all been attending Lance's church on Sundays, an ordeal in itself since there was no telling what Mom would say or do, though people seemed to accept her—amazingly. In a conscious effort to cement their friendship, Rese had asked Star to the Bible study at Michelle's church and hidden her surprise when she'd accepted. Michelle and the pastor's wife,

Karen, had befriended her at once.

Michelle took up her Bible. "In John chapter twenty-one, Jesus asks Simon Peter, 'Do you truly love me more than these?' Peter answered, 'Yes, Lord, you know that I love you.'

"Jesus told Peter to feed His lambs."

Michelle cleared her throat before going on. "Then Jesus asked Peter the same thing a second time, saying, 'Do you truly love me?' Peter said yes. Jesus told him to take care of His sheep."

"So you see," she said, looking at each of them. "Jesus wanted to know one thing from Peter and one thing only. Was he willing to look after the flock? To meet the needs of the poor who would always be with them? That's what loving Jesus means."

Star's eyes were bright. "They do not love that do not share their love."

Karen and Michelle responded immediately, and the discussion turned to whether love existed at all if it did not result in action. Rese sat back and listened, thinking of the myriad ways people in her life made small acts of love every day. Lance had brought Elaine into the kitchen with Nonna and him and put in an opera CD as he began the dinner preparation so that she and Star could sneak out to the church. Even something so ordinary was love. If it was also faith, how could some people not want that?

Her life had grown so full. By admitting one man with a mission to change the world one corner at a time, she had found more than she'd ever expected. She had been a starving sheep and hadn't even known it.

CHAPTER EIGHTEEN

Sofie opened the door to Matt, who stood with hands stuffed into his frayed jacket pockets. After several days of fog and drizzle, the sun shone in a clear, cool sky. The air held a hint of spring. Matt's face didn't. His eyes were dull and a little combative as he greeted her.

She frowned. "Are you all right?"

"Yeah. Why?"

"Only that I thought this was your idea." And he looked as though he'd rather be anywhere else. "You can change your mind."

He expelled his breath. "Sofie, I'm here, and I want to do this. Okay?"

"Okay." It was only a drive, in the daylight, with no shadows to confuse them into thinking it mattered in any way that got complicated. She closed the door and followed him to the car.

They drove in silence to the country highway that wound northeast toward Napa before he said, "Maria and the baby are gone?"

"Yes." They'd said their tearful, clutching good-byes days ago. "You miss him?"

"I'm sleeping through the night—no dirty diapers, no burp

cloths." She stared out at the last of the homes and buildings as they passed into the fields and vineyards along the Sonoma highway and thought of Diego's soft head nestled beneath her chin, the curve of his spine, his warm milky scent. "Yes, I miss him." Funny that Matt should be the one she told. "But he's where he belongs, and I'm glad things worked out."

"According to God's will?" The bite in his tone took her by surprise. He hadn't been sarcastic when they'd talked before.

"I think so."

"Nebulous, isn't it? God's will?"

"I doubt it's nebulous to God."

"Well, correct me if I'm wrong, but it seems things worked out better for Maria and her child than for you and yours."

Hurt bloomed in her chest. "What are you doing?"

"Trying to understand the arbitrary benevolence of your Supreme Being."

She'd never seen him caustic. Even the night he got angry he'd been courteous and composed. "What's the matter, Matt?"

His knuckles whitened on the steering wheel. "I just left a five-month-old whose mother's boyfriend shook his brain into cottage cheese."

She pressed her hand to her heart. "Oh, Matt, I'm sorry."

He clenched his jaw. "Before, I would not have looked for an explanation, not tried to make sense of a baseless act. Now I keep wondering why. As though there could be an answer."

She dropped her chin. "If there is, I don't know it."

"Well, you'd better. Because you opened things up that I didn't need opened."

She shot him a glance. "It helped you to talk."

"No it didn't. I had things under control."

"You hadn't dealt with Jacky."

"Well, now I can't stop. I can't sleep without dreaming. I can't dream without trying to find him, stop him, save him."

She knew the pain of those dreams. "Healing takes time."

"I guess you know. And speaking of which, why did God let you run a blade through your wrists in the first place?"

Her breath escaped in a rush, hurt and confusion flooding her.

"I wouldn't have." His stare pierced her. "Does that mean I care more than the God you think is real?"

She swallowed. "God gave me the people who loved me, who brought me back to life."

"Yeah? Why didn't He give Jacky someone?"

She looked into his face, the need there raw and insistent. "Maybe He gave you Jacky."

"What's that supposed to mean?"

Matt had tried to be his brother's protector, should have been—in his mind—and couldn't. But he hadn't left it there. "Because of him, you've helped other children."

He turned back to the road, hollow-eyed, jaw tensed. "That baby's in a coma. What am I supposed to do?"

"It's too big for you. That's why you're asking. It's why you're wondering if—"

"I just want it to stop."

She understood too well. "God isn't only in the glorious moments, but the dark and hopeless ones as well. Maybe most of all."

"So there's—" The phone tucked on the dashboard rang, and with an exasperated sigh, he pressed the speaker button. "Yeah, Bec."

"I'm giving you a chance to get Ryan before I call the police."

He dropped his head back against the rest. "Come on, Becca, you know he's harmless."

"He's parked a cherry picker—which he no doubt stole from his former employer—in front of my apartment. He's perched outside my balcony."

Matt jammed his fingers through his hair. "Okay. I'm coming." He clicked the phone off and his turn signal on. "I have to deal with this."

"All right."

"It won't take long. One bullet in his skull."

The mood he was in, she hoped he didn't have a gun. "Who's Becca?"

"A friend. She and Ryan both."

"The ones that are breaking up."

"Broken up. Becca's done; Ryan just won't believe it."

"Where do you fit in?"

"Right smack in the middle."

As she'd been caught between Eric and his daughter six years ago and now again. Carly hadn't called back, and her own attempts to reach the child had repeatedly gone to message with no voicemail set up.

They pulled up to a two-story apartment building and easily found the cherry picker, where the blond man perched, complete with megaphone. Matt parked and got out. She got out too.

"I'm not leaving," Ryan hollered down without the megaphone.

"You want to go to jail?" Matt hooked his hands on his hips.

"If that's what it takes. I told her I just want to talk."

"She has the right to say no."

Ryan shook his head. "I know whose side you're on."

"I'm not on any side. I'm trying to keep you from serious unpleasantness."

"Then talk to Becca, not me."

"She's calling the cops. You want to add harassment to your DUI?"

"I only want to talk to her."

Sofie stepped up. "If she hears you out, will you leave?"

Ryan hung his head over the side. "Who are you?"

"A friend."

He looked from her to Matt and back. "Yeah. Okay. If she wants me to leave when I'm done, I'll go." He tucked his hands into his armpits. "But she won't."

He looked like a little boy playing chicken. Sofie turned to Matt. "What number?"

He was watching her with a mixture of surprise and annoyance. "Two fourteen."

She went inside and climbed the stairs. Since Matt's friendship was the rope in their tug-of-war, a neutral stranger might be better. She knocked on the door.

"No, I will not—" The door swung open. The vivacious blonde took a moment to regroup. "Oh. I thought you were Matt."

"He's outside with Ryan. I'm Sofie." She extended her hand.

"Becca Daley. And that idiot outside my window has two minutes to remove himself—"

"He does get points for innovation."

Becca put her hands on her hips and looked over her shoulder. "Oh, he's never lacking that."

"How many of us can say someone staked out our balconies in a cherry picker? Like a modern day Romeo."

"Who are you again?"

"A friend of Matt's. Sofie Michelli."

Becca cocked her head. "Did you two go out to dinner?"

"We did once."

Becca gave a knowing nod. "You want to come in?"

"Sure. I'd like to see him up close."

"Do not be fooled. He's too cute for his own good. And spoiled rotten. He's never grown up and he never will."

"Last of the lost boys." Sofie followed her to the glass doors at the balcony. Ryan was fully visible above the banister. They stood side by side observing him. "He is cute. Great hair."

"He's a loon. Look at him panting like a puppy."

Sofie laughed. "I'm curious what he'd say if you gave him one chance."

"Oh, believe me, I've heard it all."

Sofie folded her arms. "Still . . . you'd have the rest of the story."

Becca looked from her to Ryan. "If I listen, will he leave?"

"He said he would."

She slid the door open. "Okay, dufus. Say what you came to say."

Sofie stayed inside as Becca stalked onto the balcony. Ryan's earnest voice carried in, but not his words. She waited a few minutes, but when it seemed they might talk awhile, she let herself out. Maybe something good would come of this drive.

Leaning against the Pathfinder, hands in his jacket pockets, Matt watched her emerge. He seemed more puzzled than put out. "You got her to talk."

"Women tend to be reasonable and willing to attempt a solution."

"In other words I could have talked myself blue and not budged Ryan?"

She smiled. "They're your friends. You'd know better than I."

"I wonder." His forehead creased.

"What?"

"How can you have all this insight, and yet . . ."

"Be foolish enough to cut my wrists?"

"Let that guy mess with your head until it almost killed you, then make excuses for him."

She looked away from the anger in his eyes. "I wasn't excusing; I was explaining."

"No." He pointed his finger. "You defended him. I know what it looks like."

"Matt, Eric is—"

"None of my business? You're right."

"It's old news."

"Is it?" His face was fierce. "Stop me if I'm wrong, but I doubt you faint at the sound of my voice."

"I didn't expect it. Carly—"

"Is not the whole story. I watched you let go of Diego."

"I cared for him one week. You cannot compare that to four years with a child I loved as my own." She'd taken his previous stabs, but how dare he question her commitment to her little girl? She turned and stalked away.

"Sofie."

Walking faster, she felt her pocket for her cell phone. But it was in her purse, in Matt's car. She would deal with that later.

"Sofie, stop."

She clenched her jaw. There were businesses nearby that would have a phone she could use.

Matt caught up. "I'm sorry."

She spun. "Then get me my purse."

"What?"

"In your car."

His head dropped. "Just listen."

"I've heard enough." She stalked past him. Ryan and Becca were still conversing on the balcony as she tugged the door open and grabbed her purse. The phone and her checkbook tumbled to the floor. She bent and stuffed them back in.

"Sofie . . ."

She shouldered the purse. "I don't need this."

"I know."

"No you don't. You don't know anything about me, except one dark place. I'm sorry I gave you the key. I'd appreciate your staying out now." She shut the door and started off the other way. She'd call Lance. Or Rese. Or anyone.

"At least let me take you home."

She kept walking until the sound and scent and sight of him were gone.

Matt watched her go with a sense of loss disproportionate to the time they'd spent together. An ache of wasted possibilities, and he had no one to blame but himself. He should not have called, should not have thought she could somehow lift his dark mood. Why did he think she'd have the answers? And had he really wanted any?

Some days it sickened him to be human. If there was a God, why had He made such a pathetic attempt with His creation? Why couldn't each life start fresh without the garbage passed on from generation to generation? He got into the car and clutched the steering wheel.

He tried not to think, but it came anyway, a conversation he had not been intended to hear.

"Matt? He's just like him. He'll be fine."

"But Jacky . . ."

"Jacky's a little slow."

"Liz, you have to get them out of here."

"Webb just wants them to be strong."

"Strong? He wants them to be mean dirtbags like himself."

Matt swallowed the bile that rose to his throat. *Just like him.*

Lance parked the Harley and helped Sofie remove Rese's helmet. Since Matt *had* offered a ride, he'd let him live. And until he'd heard exactly what had happened, he'd withhold judgment—but he intended to get the story. Baxter greeted them with leaps and yelps as they walked to the carriage house, then trotted away when their response lacked sufficient enthusiasm.

Lance stopped at the door. "Going to tell me what happened?"

"You don't need to worry. I'm fine." She opened the door.

"Sof." She couldn't expect him to leave it at that. Not after the last time.

"I overreacted to something he said."

Sofie didn't overreact. She weighed and measured and excused. If Matt had pushed her far enough to ditch him, it must have hit a nerve. "What did he say?"

"I don't want to go into it, Lance."

Her counselor had insisted she keep the doors of communication wide open. *"You have a family that loves you. No more secrets."* Did she intend to protect Matt as she'd kept Eric's failings to herself? That past silence had almost killed her. She could not expect him to let it go.

She touched his hand. "Come downstairs a minute."

"As in the cellar?"

"Scared?"

"Get-outta-here. I've uncovered all the skeletons."

She opened the hatch. "I want to show you something."

He followed her down through the iron gate in the tunnel to the huge cellar beyond. Most of the racks stood empty since the majority of the valuable vintage had been transported to the auction house, but the dank smell from bottles that had popped their corks mingled with the scent of old stone and lost hopes. This was, after all, the place their great-great-grandfather had fallen and lain undiscovered until last year. What could Sofie want down there?

She shone the light around the room. "Picture the racks gone, mirrors on the walls, a polished wood floor."

He caught her drift at once. "A dance studio?"

She nodded. "I've been out too long to dance professionally, but Momma's right that I enjoyed teaching."

"You should finish your degree, Sof. You'd make a good shrink."

"I need to let that go, Lance. I wanted to understand how he was, how I was. But the more I learn, the more it draws me in. I've been immersed in the darkness of troubled minds. I can't do it anymore. There's no freedom there."

He searched her face. "Okay. I get that. And I like your alternative." He looked around. "But I don't know that Rese has time to take this on."

"You could."

Part of him balked at the thought of turning Nonno Quillan's sepulcher into a studio; part of him thought the man whose poetry he'd read would appreciate life going on. "I'd have to run it by her. She owns the property."

"Until you're married."

He didn't think in those terms, but she was right. "It is commercially zoned, since she planned an inn when she got the permits. I'll see what I can do."

"Thanks." She smiled. "And thanks for not pushing."

"I still want to know."

She released a soft laugh. "You're a Michelli, aren't you?"

"Not quite as bad as Monica, but . . ."

"I don't need Matt's scrutiny."

He could understand that. "Okay." If Matt had pushed too hard too fast, if he'd expected more than she was ready to divulge . . . Except she'd already told him the worst. Hadn't she?

They went upstairs and found Nonna reading in the kitchen. Lance looked at Sofie, who tossed it back to him. "Hey, Nonna, can we run an idea by you?"

She folded the book closed over her finger and looked from one to the other. He laid it out, Sofie's idea and his own thoughts, being more familiar with the cellar's layout.

Nonna listened, then confirmed his guess with a tearful nod. "Nonno would want that."

Lance watched her gaze slip into the past, where she no doubt pictured Nonno Quillan, the grandfather she had lionized. The strengths and talents he valued most in himself had come from Quillan Shepard. Neither Vittorio, nor even Nonno Marco, whom he'd loved, nor Pop nor Tony had left as deep a mark as the poet he knew only through Nonna's musings and one book of poems. The part of him that sang, the part that prayed without reserve—the best parts of him—he attributed to the man who'd found victory through crushing adversity.

CHAPTER NINETEEN

When Rese drove in a few hours later, Lance met her at the truck. "Want to come down to the cellar a minute?"

"No way." She crossed her arms.

"Come on. It's a great make-out spot."

She gave him the look of death. "Except for the time Mom tried to kill me, I've never been so afraid as in that stupid cellar. I'm not going down."

He unwrapped her hands from her sides. "I'll be right beside you."

"What can you possibly want down there? The wine's gone, so is the money, and there's no one left to bury."

"Sofie wants to make it a dance studio."

Rese stood dumbfounded. "She wants to dance in a tomb?"

"It's not a tomb, Rese." He should never have made her believe that, though it had been for a while. "People die in lots of places. That doesn't mean they can't ever be used again. Is a studio possible?"

"Anything's possible."

"So can you take a look, gauge what it would cost, factor materials, and make a decision?"

She shook her head. "Walter's down there."

He was pretty sure she didn't really believe her mother's invisible companion lurked in the cellar, but she said, "I felt him. If Chaz hadn't come—"

"Honey, there is no Walter. I promise you."

She opened her mouth and closed it. "Did you call me honey?"

He drew her toward him. "Rese."

"The last time you called me honey you broke up with me."

"I never broke up with you."

"Hah."

He slipped his arms around her. "I was taking care of business." He caught her mouth and took care of it again. "I didn't want you trapped in something that could hurt you."

"And now you want to take me to the cellar."

"I promise nothing will happen." He threaded her fingers with his. "We'll take a look around, see what it needs . . ."

"It needs to be sealed up."

"There's some great workmanship down there." He inched her toward the door. "You'll appreciate it."

"I'll appreciate your dropping it."

"You don't want to be afraid of this, Rese. You're too tough for that. What if Brad knew?"

"He does. I made him retrieve the money we used to outfit the business."

The silver certificate bills had been stashed there by one of Nonna's forebears, but she and Brad had made use of them. "See, if Brad can do it, you can."

"Not fair."

But they'd made it inside the carriage house and he opened the hatch.

"Lance . . ."

"If Walter's down there, we'll boot him out, once and for all. But he's only in your mom's mind. You know that."

"He was pretty firmly in mine as well."

"You were an impressionable child."

"I was an adult, alone in the dark with—"

He kissed her. "You'll be fine." He took the flashlight in one hand, hers in the other, and started down the stairs.

"Why do I let you do this? Why do I always let you talk me into things I don't want to do?"

"Like hiring me?"

"Right."

"And kissing me?"

"Well . . ."

"Come on, you were steamed that first time." They made it to the bottom of the stairs.

"Because you worked for me and would not respect my authority."

"I've always respected you, Rese."

She snorted.

"It's true." They'd reached the gate.

"Lance . . ."

He pushed it open. Just past that point, he'd found the remains of his great-great-grandfather. So had Rese, though he'd warned her not to go down there.

She balked. "I don't want to do this."

"Come here." He took her into his arms. "We can beat this, and you'll be stronger for it. Or you can turn around and go back." He kissed her forehead. "I'd like your input, but if you can't, that's okay."

"I don't know anything about dancing or studios."

"You know about floors, walls, and ceilings." He could do it without her, but he wanted to share anything he could, because even though she'd accepted his proposal, it still stung that she spent so much time doing what she loved with Brad.

She exhaled. "I suppose you'll be wiring it."

Electrical was the one element she wouldn't touch. He knew enough to get light and sound into the place. "I'm the man."

She looked through the gate. "You're sure we're alone?"

"If we're not we'll just do some house cleaning."

"Do you think Walter was a demon? I mean the Walter I felt?"

He'd encountered a principality or two in his travels—and on the night he and Chaz had prayed for Star. "It's possible." He took her hand. "But we have the victory."

"That's what Chaz says." She looked unconvinced.

"He should know. In Jamaica people still practice obeah. Voodoo." Chaz had not been shielded, but rather trained to recognize and vanquish the enemy in a land of dark arts. In the cellar, Lance didn't expect to meet anything worse than mice, but he didn't say so. Mice were the other thing Rese couldn't stand.

She looked into his face, her brown eyes resigned, her callused palm tight inside his. "Okay. Show me what you want to do."

He smiled. "Now that's a dangerous statement."

"To the cellar."

"Oh, that."

She tugged his hand.

Laughing, he shined the light far enough out to push the darkness away as they moved in among the empty racks. No bogeymen so far. "You okay?"

She nodded.

"Feel anything?"

She shook her head. "It's different with you."

"Alone in the dark anyone can get worked up."

"I don't think I imagined it."

"Then you probably didn't." He shined the light around.

"But what if—"

"You're not crazy."

"For Mom, Walter was so real she could touch him. She danced with him." She shivered.

"He's not real." But he searched the room again, picking up her tension. Her mother's delusions were clinically explained by sound medical diagnosis. But he closed his eyes and slipped into prayer. *Lord, if there's anything here—*

It hit him like a brakeless Mack truck. A sense of oppression and fear. Why was it there? It had no right or reason, unless . . . His anger erupted. He spoke without conscious effort, one hand outstretched against the darkness as Rese clung to the arm that held the flashlight. He prayed hard and deliberately that she would no longer be a target, that whatever had preyed on her fears would be bound and broken. "In Jesus' name, be gone."

Rese gave a little cry.

He opened his eyes. "It's all right." He turned, shining the light up and around. "Now, then. Sofie'll need some framing on the walls to attach mirrors, but I'd hate to lose all this hand-cut stone."

"Lance." Her breath came sharply.

He turned. "It's an action, reaction thing. God seems to have a plan for us. Satan would like to scare you off, but this is our home, our life. Together."

He took her into his arms, wanting to light the place up and dash the darkness that had keyed into her childhood trauma, masquerading as her mother's companion. Light bulbs wouldn't really affect such things, but it seemed right anyway.

She pressed her hands to his back. "You're thin."

"I'm working on that."

"Why does it have to be harder for you?"

"I don't know that it does." He kissed her temple. "You have a suggestion for flooring?"

"I'll always go with maple over oak."

He nodded. "Bright, durable, regular grain. Let's pace it out so we can estimate lumber."

"You're sure everything's gone?"

"At Jesus' name every knee must bow, every tongue confess Him Lord. They'd rather take off than go through that." He could feel her hesitation. "Come on."

She walked with him the length and breadth of the cellar. As he walked, he silently claimed the ground for God. Only the musty scent and the silence remained. Rese ran her hand over the end of a rack. "These are in good shape for their age."

"We can offer them on eBay."

"Lance, I never apologized for spending the money."

"What money?"

"Your great-grandfather's. From the cache."

"I gave it over to you."

"I know but . . . it wasn't technically mine."

"It wasn't technically mine either." It had gotten too complicated with overlapping deeds and letters of intention that might never have been possible to sort out.

"Does Nonna know?"

He shrugged. "She has what she wanted. Peace."

"And you?"

He drank in her features, the trust and love he saw there. "I have what I wanted."

Carly huddled under the covers. She hated her new room—too cramped, too white. Dad said she could pick a wallpaper border and curtains, but the landlord wouldn't let them paint. She'd outgrown pink, but she didn't want plain old white. She didn't want the new school, or the new neighborhood either.

She had left Drew and the other sort-of friends she'd made, and now she'd have to start all over. Why bother? What was the point when anytime someone got close, Dad ruined it? First he would start dropping hints about her spending too much time and thinking too highly of certain people—un-Daddy people.

If she didn't take the hint, it got worse. She guessed but hadn't actually caught him swiping things. They just disappeared after someone had been with her, so it seemed like she'd taken it, but she didn't—ever. Except once when she'd been very little, she'd come home with a bunny sticker that her friend said she took. Maybe that was where he got the idea.

Not that anyone would believe a dad would take the things he took. He didn't want them. He wanted them to think she did. When she denied it, she looked like a thief *and* a liar. So of course no one wanted to be her friend.

The worst part was that she had made them move this time. After she'd talked to Sofie one stupid time, he had left her with the single mother of one of her fellow students and been gone for two days. He hadn't told his boss or covered his appointments and—duh—had no job when he got back. Of course, he would dazzle the next boss, so it wasn't a problem for him.

She did not dazzle anyone. She didn't dare.

Daddy looked in. "Hey. Want to talk about the other night?"

She didn't pretend to wonder which one. "Okay."

He came and sat on the end of her bed. She looked for the icy anger, but what she saw was worse. She'd hurt him. It came off him in waves and smothered her. His face was so miserable, she gulped back tears. "I'm sorry, Daddy."

He took her hand. "I hoped you'd forgotten."

"Forgotten Sofie?"

"You were so little."

"I don't remember a lot." Just the place inside that ached with loss.

"You got her number without telling me."

Now she totally expected to see the ice in his eyes, but they looked far away instead. The way he kept staring at the wall scared her more than his disapproval.

"I'm sorry. I didn't think . . ." *you'd want me to.* "I didn't know if it was *that* Sofie. And—"

"You've been talking to her."

She shook her head. "Just once."

"I saw the calls."

"But I only talked once. The other times I just listened to her voice."

He studied her, then said, "I tried to find her."

"What?" It fell out on a whisper.

He nodded. "After your call, I went back to her place, her neighborhood. But she wasn't there."

No. She had to be. How could he look and not find her?

"She's moved somewhere."

It was a lie. Another lie. Anger burned up her throat. She was going to throw up.

He took her phone out of his pocket. "Would you like this back?"

She couldn't speak. It was too hard to keep it down. And what did it matter, if Sofie was gone? But she nodded.

"Carly, it's all right with me if you want to talk to Sofie."

"It is?" She couldn't hold back her shock, even though something strange appeared in his expression. If he had known she was calling . . .

"But I'd like to know what she says, okay?"

Carly gulped. Tell him everything? Somehow that felt wrong, more wrong than when she'd sneaked her calls. But was it? "Okay."

"Good." He smiled. "What do you want me to order for dinner?"

Sofie turned a slow circle in the middle of the cellar as movers from the shipping company carried the old racks out through the side exit Lance had discovered and excavated. The rumble of dollies on the wooden ramp recalled the rolling barrels of the bustling vineyard that had once spread over the DiGratia property.

Nonna had described the rows of vines, the smell of the earth, the grapes hanging redolent with promise. All that remained was the house, carriage house, and cellar Quillan Shepard had built on the section given him by his father-in-law, Angelo DiGratia.

"Lend me a hand here, Sof?"

She gripped the other end of the rack, but they'd only moved it a couple feet when Lance set down his end. "Whoa."

"What?" Then she saw the hole in the floor that had caught his attention. "Is that where Vittorio's money was?"

"Nope. Haven't seen this one." The narrow rectangular gap in the stones had been completely hidden by the rack that had stood atop it. "And I don't think that money was Vito's. He worked in a bank. He wouldn't put cash in a hole."

"Nonno Quillan's?"

"He built the cellar. He hated bankers. Makes sense to me."

She retrieved one of the lights from the near corner and shined it into the hole. Its narrow shape left the bottom in darkness, but Lance reached in.

"Anything?"

With a keen expression, he pulled out a number of notebooks. She moved closer to see. Five gray notebooks tied with string. "Lance," she breathed.

He carefully untied one. The notebook fell open to a hand-written page arranged in stanzas. His hand shook as he flipped to the front, turned page after page, and closed his eyes. "It's his poetry."

"Who?"

"Quillan Shepard. Great-great-grandfather Quillan. He had at least one book of it published, but this . . . these must be his originals."

She picked up another and untied the string. "This one looks like a journal. It's prose. Are you sure they're his?"

"Who else?"

She shook her head. "Why does this feel better than a pot of gold?"

"Because it's our past. Our heritage." Lance looked up, his eyes rife with emotion. "He's here, Sofie. In his words."

"Can we read them?"

"If not us, who?"

She nodded. "I'll carry these up while you finish here."

"Tonight," he said. "With Nonna."

She carried the books up and set them on the table. Her great-great-grandfather's life. Maybe in there were the answers she wished she had, something that could make the hurt of not reaching Carly again make sense. Because Matt's words had sunk in. It did seem that God chose when to act and when to hold back His hand. And where did that leave her?

"'If travail has a purpose, let me find it now. If honor needs a taker, O Lord, me endow. If wisdom is a garment, let me wear it well; if goodness needs a champion, help me dark dispel.'"

Lance looked up from the tablet he read from. Seated across from him in the parlor, Nonna fixed him with a keen counte-nance. She had come alive when she'd seen Quillan Shepard's notebooks, and she leaned forward now.

"That became his m . . . otto, and he kept it to the letter. I have . . . n . . . ever known such a strong-m . . . inded man as my grandfather." She sat back, looking bemused. "You remind me of him."

Lance raised his brows. "That's a fine compliment, Nonna. I hope to live up to it."

"You'd better."

Sofie said, "Here's his version of the train robbery." She read aloud how Quillan Shepard had confronted the outlaws and recognized one from his past. His description had brought about the man's capture—the man who had left him holding the bag in a bank robbery he'd known nothing about until it was too late. "What adventures he had." Sofie's eyes shone.

Star drew a long breath. "'Take heed before you give your heart, for given once, 'tis ere more lost. And though it beats within your breast, each steadfast beat now bears a cost.'" She looked up. "I've found a new bard worth quoting." And her eyes shone.

Lance looked at the three of them, then at Rese, who also seemed caught up. Quillan Shepard had been larger than life while he lived, and now four generations later he was still lighting up the room. That was a legacy.

CHAPTER TWENTY

Rese went down the stairs with a surprising lack of spine-crawling. The part of the wine cellar accessed by the mechanical door in the kitchen pantry had been preserved exactly as it had the time she'd beat her fists against the door, desperate for escape. But Lance had wired and installed two light fixtures that made her previous panic seem overblown.

She went through the door to the next section. In a few weeks, he had framed in a huge studio. She inspected the carpentry—not perfect, but not bad. She might have taken more care with the cuts and joints, but construction didn't require the exacting skill she gave her finish carpentry. This was Lance's and Sofie's project, and the best thing he'd accomplished was tossing the monster that had dogged her in the dark of the cellar, and in fact most of her life, even before Mom disabled the furnace. The Presence that had saved her that night, Jesus, was protecting her still. His name enough to ban Walter—or whatever it really was—into the abyss.

She shouldn't confuse Mom's delusions, her own childish confusion, and whatever it was Lance had taken authority over. They were not necessarily one and the same, any more than Star's fairies could be confused with fairy tales. She was learning to differentiate—to discern, Lance called it. But it would never have occurred to her to command the thing in prayer and have it obey. She wondered even now. Would she have to fast and be completely commanded by God before her prayer had the power Lance's carried? He said no, but she wasn't sure.

He'd shown her place after place in the Bible where spirits were driven away, and even the disciples had seemed a little giddy and unprepared for the effect they'd had. One story had scared her, the one where an evil spirit left and seven came back in its place. But they didn't seem to be multiplying in the cellar—thank God.

In the far end of the studio, she found Lance on his knees laying the floor, except he wasn't working. His eyes were closed, his hands suspended at his waist. He didn't hear her approach, and she wavered between interrupting or going away. But then he opened his eyes.

She smiled uncertainly. "Hey."

"Hey." His voice rasped.

"You okay?"

He cleared his throat. "Sure."

"That doesn't sound very sure."

He sat back on his heels and brushed sawdust from his jeans, then sighed. "I'm worried about Sofie."

"The thing with Matt?"

"No. I saw something."

She looked around with a shiver. "Down here?"

"Yes." He shook his head. "No. I was down here, but it wasn't."

Fear rippled through her. "What did you see?"

"Sofie. Falling."

She searched his face. "You mean you imagined it?"

"I was working there on the floor. I thought about Sofie and started to pray. Then I saw her falling."

"From where?"

"I don't know. It wasn't like a movie. Just an image. A flash."

"Maybe you dozed off."

He slanted her a crooked glance.

"What, then? A premonition?"

"It wasn't some psychic thing. More like a message."

"From God."

"Why pray and not expect an answer?" He ran his hand through his hair. "Rese, I'm worried about my sister. I lifted her up to God, and He responded."

It shouldn't be so hard to get her mind around it. But she was far more comfortable reading about and praying to God than hearing—or in this case—seeing an answer.

Lance swallowed. "The day Mrs. Espinoza came? And Cassinia got so bent about the baptism?"

"I wasn't there."

He went on as though she hadn't spoken. "The next time she came back I saw why she'd been so upset. I knew, when I had no way of knowing." His eyes held an intensity, startling even for Lance.

"You knew something about Cassinia?"

He nodded. "God showed me."

"What did you do?"

"Nothing. I couldn't do anything."

"That's why you took off on the Harley."

He paced. "God showed me how it feels when someone so hurt closes off any hope of healing."

"You realize how that sounds, right?"

"I'm not trying to do this. I am a guy laying a floor, cooking meals, playing songs."

She bit her lip. "Have you said no?"

He turned back to her. "You remember Ground Zero? I told God then that whatever He wanted to do with my life, it was His." He swallowed. "How can I say no now?"

She sighed. "You can't. It's not in you."

He forked both hands into his hair. "You don't know how badly I want to run." The ache caught her hard. Would he leave again? Had she fooled herself? He gripped her arms. "You'd have to come. You and Baxter on the Harley. What do you say?"

She looked into his face. "Where do you think you could go? Do you really think even a Road King can outrun God?"

He tipped his head back, eyes closed, then pulled her close with a smoldering gaze. "Sometimes I can't believe this thing I have with you."

Sometimes she couldn't, either, but she kissed him softly. "Believe it."

————

The driving rhythm and throbbing tones of one of his harder songs reverberated from the CD player throughout the studio as Lance attached the mirrors to the framing on the stone walls. He'd been so in tune with Rico that the music had emerged from them as one tight harmony. Chaz hadn't joined the band yet, and though he'd added versatility and depth when he came, the early songs with Rico had possessed a gripping energy.

Lance tightened the fastener and checked the glass panel's stability, then moved on to the next. He didn't often listen to the CDs they'd cut, but Rico had been heavy on his mind since the package came for Star a few weeks before. He glanced over his shoulder to where she stood on the ladder, transforming Sofie's ceiling into sky.

"So, Star." He spoke over the resounding fade of the final chord. "You going to play me Rico's song?"

She swept the brush across the ceiling over her head. "Why?"

"I'd like to hear it. He's never done lyrics before." Curiosity over what Rico had produced was driving him crazy, but if it was too personal, he'd understand Star keeping it to herself.

"They aren't lyrics like yours." She drew the CD out of her shirt like a class ring hanging from a string around her neck, then tipped the disc, catching the rainbow hues on its surface and sending them around the room. She looked at him. "It's us. Rico and me, singing."

"Yeah?"

"When we played the coffeehouses? And in the tunnels?" She threw back her head. "'I did never know so full a voice issue from so empty a heart: but the saying is true "The empty vessel makes the greatest sound." ' "

"You're not empty, Star."

"I was." She took the CD off the string and inserted it into the player.

Lance held his breath as the first tones of their music emerged. Then came Rico's voice with a single word and then another. He recognized immediately the overlay he'd given it the first time Rico had let him listen. Rico had taken that idea and inserted words of his own, words that spoke to Star, to their loss. She bit her lip as the words filled the room like a benediction.

He looked into her tearful turquoise eyes, then hugged her softly as she sank into his chest.

She murmured, " 'True, I talk of dreams, which are the children of an idle brain, begot of nothing but vain fantasy.' "

"You never know." He cupped her head, recognizing her childlike hopefulness. Whether or not his best friend and Rese's got back together, using a language only they spoke, they'd begun to reverse the damage. He squeezed her and let go. "Thanks for letting me hear."

———————

Matt tossed another handful of small tight mushrooms into the bag and twisted a tie around the end. Those, along with the steaks, covered his portion of the meal. Now he just needed a wine. He moved toward the rows and rows of choices in the Sonoma Market—local, semi-local, regional, imported.

Everyone would bring a bottle of something, and some of them took it much too seriously. Jen, for instance, was a wine snob of the most random sort. She liked only what she liked, but wines fell in and out of her favor faster than her mood swings.

With the basket draped on one arm, he neared the wine section and stopped. These last weeks he had managed to muffle the disappointment and regret, but seeing her there caused a raging return of both. "Sofie."

She looked up from the two champagnes she was comparing.

He could tell her not to waste her money on the one, but seeing her full-on constricted his throat.

"Hello, Matt. How are you?"

"I'm . . . good. And you. You look good." Wonderful, sensuous, desirable. And so achingly strong and fragile. "Are you?"

"Yes. Thanks."

He nodded to the champagnes. "Celebrating?"

"The completion of my studio. We converted the cellar."

"The bat cave?"

"Hardly a cave anymore. You wouldn't like it."

Yes he would. He'd like any space that contained her. *Oh man.* "Getting dinner?"

He looked into his basket. "Yeah. Having some friends over. I should"—he cocked his head over his shoulder—"be there when they arrive."

"Always a good plan." She smiled.

He might breathe again in a few years.

"It's nice seeing you, Matt." She returned her attention to the bottles she'd removed from the refrigerated case.

"Don't get the Santa Lucia."

"No?"

"Too young a vineyard. Nothing interesting yet in the grapes."

"Thanks."

"Sure." *Turn and walk away. One foot, then the other.* "It's a . . . kind of an . . . open gathering tonight. You'd be welcome."

Her smile took too long and didn't reach her eyes. "We're having a gathering as well."

"Right. Your studio. Congratulations."

"It's only the construction completed. I haven't opened for classes or anything."

"I'm glad things are working out for you."

"Thanks. And for you."

He thought over his day: a runaway who believed the streets treated him better than the kids in his private school, the five-month-old who'd been transferred to a permanent coma facility, the ongoing mess with the Price children, whom the police had removed again. Cassinia was on leave for a family emergency, and since he'd handled the rough part last time, it had fallen to him again. After all that, he should have expected to run into Sofie, but he hadn't, and so hadn't steeled himself.

"Yeah. So . . . maybe another time."

She settled the alternate choice into the crook of her arm. "Thanks again for the advice."

He stepped aside to let her pass, then moved into the wine shelves himself. If his mind would clear he could make the decision quickly. As it was, he stood there dumbfounded by the task.

Sybil rounded the far end of his short aisle. "Are you choosing white or red?"

He watched her slinky approach. There was something to be said for uncomplicated. He should get sloppy drunk and fulfill her every wish. "White."

She smiled. "Dry?"

He reached into the shelf and grabbed a vintage he could count on to be generally accepted.

"Hmm." She tilted her head. "I'll bring something more robust."

"Good. I'll see you soon."

Maybe Sofie had gone already. Maybe she'd still be in line. He didn't know which to hope for. No, that was a lie. The second definitely, just to see her a little longer. She'd been unequivocal, though polite, in her refusal, so there was no risk in looking. But she'd either come only for champagne or was somewhere else in the store. Did he have time for a search? Maybe some slivers under his fingernails while he was at it? He paid for his groceries and left.

Sofie drove home with a stone in her heart. She hadn't realized how much hope she had packed into the possibility of a new relationship. Someone like Matt, whose warm brown eyes welled with appreciation without that other aspect lurking behind, wanting more than she could give, wanting . . . more.

She carried the champagne to the carriage house and down the rebuilt stairs to where everyone waited. What she had envisioned, they had created. It was no longer a smuggler's cave but a dancer's dream. Lance opened the champagne and poured flutes for them all.

Sofie raised hers. "For the talent, heart, and effort that went into this, my thanks." She met Rese and Lance's eyes, Nonna's and Star's and Elaine's. "For your love and not saying I'm totally foolish, my deepest gratitude."

"Salute." Lance raised his glass.

"Salute!" Their voices rang.

She wrapped an arm around Nonna's shoulders and whispered, "Grazie."

"For what?"

"Everything."

"Oh, that." The old woman laughed. "It's nothing."

The weight that had descended in her encounter with Matt peeled away. She couldn't change what he thought of her, but knew condemnation for what it was. She looked around the room. In fact, it illuminated her true friends.

CHAPTER TWENTY-ONE

How could seeing her for three minutes so totally dominate everything? He kept thinking of things he could have said, questions he didn't ask. He kept seeing the look in her eyes when he'd invited her over. Right. She'd love to come be insulted again. He turned as Becca handed him a piece of cake.

"Here you go, gloomy-face."

"Thanks, Bec." He took the cake. "Where's Ryan?"

"He told me to find out what's wrong with you."

"That's funny, Ryan worrying about me."

"It's the new improved Ryan."

"Right." Since Sofie had gotten the sparring partners to talk, it seemed Becca hadn't been as through as she'd claimed. He had taken her at her word and tried to get Ryan to save what dignity he had. Instead Ryan had made a complete fool of himself and earned another chance. Go figure.

Not as good at fixing lives and relationships as he was busting up families that didn't work. "Say, Bec. What was it Sofie said to you that day Ryan hijacked the cherry picker?"

She tipped her head to the side, thinking. "Only that Ryan was original, and I'd have a great story to tell. I figured at least life wouldn't be boring."

Matt smiled. Sofie had seen the outrageous behavior as clever. Maybe she valued that kind of thing, or else she guessed Becca might. He would have sympathized with her righteous anger and demanded Ryan leave. Sofie had seen the alternate route.

"So what's eating you, Matt?"

Ryan joined them but didn't enter the conversation.

"Nothing. I ran into someone."

"In your car?"

"No, Becca. Not literally." Though it felt like it. "Just saw someone who . . ." he'd ruined his chances with. "It's no big deal."

"It was Sofie Michelli." Her eyes drilled into him.

He crossed his arms. "Why would you think that?"

"Am I right?"

"Who's Sofie Michelli?" Ryan looked from one to the other.

"I said hi to her in the store—that's all."

"You should have invited her."

"Who is she?" Ryan butted like a fly against their interchange.

"I did." Matt shrugged. "She had something else going."

Becca cocked her head. "Oh yeah?"

"She's opening a dance studio."

"Really? Cool." Becca hooked her arm through Ryan's. "We'll take something. Salsa, maybe."

Right. Malibu Barbie and Ken dancing salsa.

"You should too, Matt. Help her get going. It's not easy starting a business."

"I know how to dance. Learned in charm school." It had been all but required to move in the circles he had navigated for a while.

"Bet you didn't learn it all."

"No, just enough." He turned. "Hey, Domino, have enough steak?"

His square-built buddy had never met a cut of beef he didn't love. Running into him was like hitting a brick wall in their pickup football games, but if you could topple him, he fell flat on his back, and you didn't want to be under him when he landed.

Sybil slid past Domino and curled her fingers into the crook of Matt's arm. "Hi."

"Want some cake?" He held out the plate he hadn't touched.

"Can I eat it too?"

Becca tugged Ryan away. Smart. He gently extricated his arm. "Excuse me. I need to let in some air."

Every three months or so they got together, and even when he hosted, Becca usurped the entertainment portion of the evening. As he opened windows, she began arranging teams for the Cranium game she was crazy about that mostly drove him crazy. She'd understand.

He slipped out the door. After striding less than a block, he hooked back around and got into his car. He didn't want to end up there on foot in the middle of the night. Again.

He parked along the curb in front of the villa, then stood outside the gate before glimpsing her in the glass-fronted carriage house. The night smelled faintly of mist and the wet leaves sloshing under his feet as he walked the length of the iron fence to the driveway and turned in. By the look on her face when she answered his knock, it could be a short conversation.

"The time in the store wasn't enough to totally ruin your day, so I thought I'd—"

"Finish the job?" She stepped out and pulled the door to the frame without letting go of the knob behind her.

"There I was in the middle of my party, eleven people in my house, and I just walked out."

"How long before they notice?" she asked, raising her brows.

He laughed. "Right away, I'm sure. Becca was dividing the crew into teams for Cranium. Have you played?"

She shook her head.

"Sort of a charades–Trivial Pursuit amalgamation."

"You don't like to play games?"

"Only when there's something to hit, catch, or tackle."

"Which of those did you plan to do here?"

He dropped his chin. "I deserved that." He cocked his gaze back up. "Any chance we could start over?"

"That doesn't really happen in my experience. Forgive and forget isn't as realistic as forgive and remember."

"Probably healthier," he agreed. "Keeps you from making the same mistakes."

"To a degree. Which parts were you hoping to erase?"

"Anything that's upset you, everything that's hurt you, and the rest of whatever's made you mad."

"Wow. Doesn't leave much."

Her wit had a bite. "I could fill in the gaps."

"Why?"

"Because . . ." He pressed his palm to the jamb, leaned and studied her. "I'd like to show you I'm not always a jerk."

"I don't think you are."

"Really?"

"Really. I think you're warm and caring and good at what you do. I'm sure your friends are disappointed you've ditched them."

"They'll proceed without me. Ryan and Becca have reconciled, by the way, thanks to your pep talk."

A smile flickered on her lips. "There still seemed a lot of effort on both their parts—hers to prove she didn't care, his to prove he did. So much energy must count for something."

"I should have noticed the lack of apathy."

Another flicker of a smile. "You take things at face value. If Becca says she's through, she's through."

"What I really want to know is . . . are we?" He swallowed the knot in his throat.

"That depends." She raised her chin and searched his face. "What is it in me that you can't tolerate?"

His breath made a hard escape, and with it the candid answer. "You made me think of something." Of the times people had hinted, warned, begged. "How she always made excuses."

"I'm sorry?"

"People told her things were going south with us boys, but she always made excuses for him. 'He's not like that' was her favorite."

"Your mother?"

He nodded. "She wanted to be like the other church ladies, with a solid husband, a happy family, everything right and proper in God's view. She submitted and supported him in everything."

Sofie listened with her luminous eyes fixed on him.

"She was proud of him." His voice ran over the gravel in his throat. "Right up to the day Jacky walked in front of a train. Even afterward she made excuses. I live with the guilt of what I said that day, but I was just a kid. She was his mother."

He clenched his hands, his big hands. *"Matt's just like him. He'll be fine."* Pain streaked down his neck, his spine, lodged in his lower lumbar region. "She still calls it a tragic accident."

Sofie clicked the door all the way shut. "Come into the main house for some tea. The others are over there already. I was just turning off the lights."

In other words she didn't want to be alone with him. But she brushed his hand with her fingers in passing.

He opened reflexively, wanting to capture her hand, to trap and imprison it. Instead he followed her to the main house. Music washed out when she opened the kitchen door; a male and female voice, and a guitar played exceptionally well. It came from the front room, and there was laughter intermixed. He wouldn't mind joining them if it meant he got to stay, though Sofie made no move to leave the kitchen.

She poured him a cup of tea. "Milk?"

He shook his head.

She got herself a cup, too, brought them over and sat down at the table. He sat down diagonally from her. The room smelled of herbs and laughter, and another song began in the parlor, a very complicated picking on the guitar that made his high-school strumming seem babyish. "Who's that playing?"

"Lance. But you don't like to talk about him."

"He's really good, isn't he?"

"I told you that. If he hadn't quit the band they'd be on their way up. I'm not sure Rico will ever forgive him for that."

"What did he do instead?"

"He joined the Peace Corps."

Matt laughed. "A man of contrasts."

"Like you."

"No. I'm pretty much what you see." Then why did Cassinia call him a tough guy and Sybil call him a softy? Why did he work so hard to mask the man he'd worked so hard to be? He stared into his tea.

Sofie sipped, then set her cup down. "You think I'm like your mother."

"No." She'd jolted him out of his introspection. "You're nothing like her. She's . . . bland."

Sofie tipped her head. "Then why—"

"I'm afraid you'd let me be like him."

"What?" It came out on a breath. "You can't be serious."

"I am." He sat back and crossed his arms. "You look at pictures of us, I could be a carbon copy. In the courtroom, I could make a witness cower. I like being in control, going into bad situations and taking charge."

"You do it to help those who can't help themselves."

"Dad thinks he does the same." He clenched his jaw. "He doesn't tolerate weakness and stupidity. Neither do I."

"You don't tolerate cruelty either." Her liquid gaze washed over him.

He took her hands. "I'm sorry I hurt you."

"I've already forgiven you."

"Before I apologized?"

She nodded. "I don't harbor grudges. It only makes the wound grow deep."

He tightened his hold. "I'd still prefer you forgot all the bonehead things I've said and let me start over. I want to get to know you, spend time with you—watch movies, play games, take walks, whatever you like to do."

"That's all?"

"I'd like badly to kiss you."

One corner of her mouth drew up. "Not to be confused with kissing me badly."

He laughed. "I hope not. I'm pretty rusty though."

"Didn't feel rusty to me."

"I can do better. With practice." Drawn by her incredible mystique, he leaned in, then drew back as Rese Barrett came into the room.

She stopped short. "Oh. I didn't know anyone was here."

Sofie shrugged. "Seems to be where people linger. What is it about this kitchen?"

"Memories." Rese folded her arms.

Sofie breathed deeply. "Is it the same in all the places you renovate?"

"Some more than others."

Matt looked up. "Ever find one haunted?"

She frowned. "Only Sofie's studio."

"The bat cave?"

"Bat cave?"

"Matt's name for it." Sofie laughed. "Doesn't fit anymore. It's fun and elegant and light now." She turned to him. "Lance even excavated an outdoor entrance."

"No more trapdoor? I'm seriously disappointed."

"It's still there," Rese said. "And the old stairs at both ends, the iron gate in the tunnel, and the mechanical door in the pantry. Too much history to lose all that, but I suspect the entrance we opened was original to the working vineyard, sealed up later."

"That's what Lance thought too," Sofie said. "It had been buried on the outside, probably since Prohibition."

"Uh . . ." He honed in on the thing that had really struck his interest. "What mechanical door in the pantry?"

Rese took a plate of cheese and apples from the refrigerator. "You show him. I don't like that door." She headed out of the room.

Sofie got up and opened the door of a pantry the size of a small bedroom. Jarred peppers and tomatoes lined the shelves, along with wheels of cheese in hard rinds. He ducked around the restaurant-quality cookware hanging from the ceiling. At the back wall, she stooped and reached beneath the lowest shelf. He heard a click and then a whine as the wall swung open.

"Holy secret door in the wall." How many places could boast invisible doors and hidden cellars? "What's not to like about this?"

"Rese got trapped behind it. Alone. In the dark."

"She doesn't strike me as skittish."

"Everyone has trigger points."

He looked through. "Can we go down?"

"Will it ruin it for you?"

"I don't know."

"Only the two ends still look like a cellar."

"I think I can take it."

Sofie flipped a switch. A bare bulb lit their way without spoiling the ambience. He descended the wooden stairs to an area that still contained racks of old bottles. The musty scent triggered his penchant for underground places.

Ahead, a wall had been framed and finished with a door. Sofie opened it, flipped another switch, and let him into a magical space of mirrors, polished floors, and a ceiling painted midnight blue with stars and comets and meteors that blended at the midpoint into clouds and daylight.

"I'll put the sound system here." She motioned to the right of the door, where the wall was unmirrored, and a CD player was plugged into the wall.

Reflected in all the mirrors, it seemed as though she surrounded him, and he'd baldly lied when he'd told himself she didn't matter. He was more than enamored. He was smitten. He wanted her more than he could recall desiring anything in his life.

Catching his expression, she folded herself into her arms. "Do you want to sleep with me?"

His breath escaped. "Yes."

"Is that all you want?"

"No. But it's high on my list." No sense denying what he'd already shown her.

"It isn't going to happen."

"Okay."

"Don't you want to know why?"

"Why doesn't matter." He'd rather not hear that she wasn't attracted to him or interested in furthering a relationship. He didn't want her to say she no longer trusted him or . . .

"If Eric and I hadn't made the relationship intimate, I might not have gotten so caught up, so vulnerable." She sighed. "I won't make the same mistake again."

"I'm not Eric."

"Maybe not." She turned back. "But I can't trust you to decide what's right for me. I won't."

He nodded slowly. "Well, then . . . may I have this dance?"

She arched her eyebrow. "You're asking a former Broadway talent to dance in her own studio?"

He bent and pressed play on the portable CD player, without knowing or checking what she had in there. "It won't be what you're used to."

A smile touched her lips. "Makes me wonder what's under your Clark Kent façade."

"You think I pretend to be nice?"

"I think you pretend to be mild." She rested her hand on his shoulder with such poise it threatened every ounce of his self-control. But she'd made herself clear. Look but don't touch. Touch but don't incite.

He recognized the voice and guitar that started on the CD, a ballad Lance and another voice sang with that same gripping pathos he'd heard earlier in the house. Sofie waited for him to lead, and he did, the responsibility weighing as it never had before.

CHAPTER TWENTY-TWO

B rad held the carved corner molding up against the juncture of ceiling and wall as Rese drilled the screw almost invisibly into a hollow in the pattern she'd repaired and refinished. From down below came the whine of saws and *pfftt-pfftt* of nail guns. She tried to block the sounds and focus on the task before Brad noticed anything wrong. She had control of it. But it wouldn't hurt to distract him. "Have you talked to your wife?"

"Ex." Brad shifted his hold. "And yeah. I talked to her."

"Really?" She hadn't expected that. She lined up the second screw. "And?"

"She called me a liar and pushed me out the door."

Her jaw dropped. Well, that just showed how pathetic she was about relationships. As if she hadn't realized it first thing that morning—with her mother. "Brad, I'm sorry."

He rubbed a fleck of something off the wood and slanted her a glance. "Then she came over to the house and demanded to know if I was serious."

"And you said yes?"

"I said I wouldn't joke about something so terrifying."

The sound of a saw set her teeth on edge and dizziness threatened, but she blocked it forcibly. "How romantic."

"Yeah, sort of ticked her off." He lifted the next section and held it in place. "When she got through pounding my chest and telling me I was the last person she'd ever marry—and we all know the fallacy in that—we made up and . . ." He shrugged.

"And what?"

"I'm not giving you the details."

"I don't want the details. I want to know if she said yes."

"She said maybe."

"Yeah?"

"Maybe Friday. If she can stand me that long."

She gripped the drill, trying to block the sounds from below. "Brad, that's . . ." Downstairs someone hollered. Her head spun.

"Rese?" Brad gripped her arm. "What's wrong with you?" He held on as she dropped to one knee.

"I need to get down." Stupid to think she could climb down eighteen feet of scaffolding, but the need persisted.

Brad crouched beside her. "Are you sick? Pregnant?"

"No, I'm not pregnant." She gulped back tears. She had never willingly cried in Brad's presence, though that one time silent tears had spilled when she'd been all but catatonic.

"What, then?"

She swallowed. "It's Dad's birthday."

"Oh man." He dropped down to sit beside her. "I didn't think. I'd have told you not to come in."

"Not come in? The whole reason I'm doing this is because of him."

"I thought it was me."

She pressed her hands to her face, fighting the tears with everything in her.

"That was a joke. Sorry. I don't know how to handle you like . . . this."

She could not stop the thoughts. Dad's big, capable hands. His strong back and sharp eye. The high standards that had formed her and Brad both. She had learned more from him than in all her courses at school. He hadn't been affectionate, but he'd been proud. And he'd carried her to safety on the worst night of her life.

This morning her mother had looked at her as though she should have died, her eyes deep, deranged wells. She had clawed her arms and demanded, *"Where is he? What have you done with him?"* Was it even Dad she'd meant?

Over a year had passed since he'd died. Some days it didn't impact her at all. Some, like today . . .

"Don't go into that weird no-talking place, okay?" Brad jostled her.

"He should be here. He should not be gone."

"How long have you had the dizzy spells?"

"Since I came out of that weird no-talking place." Three weeks of shock, and then the long road back to proficiency in her chosen field.

"You didn't say anything? How many times have you been up on this stuff alone?"

"I can handle it. It's not usually this hard." But Dad would have turned fifty-two, and she wished he were there, working beside them.

"Flashbacks?"

"Not as many."

"Rese, doggone it. You should have told me."

"Lance knows. He's talked me through it."

"Well, that's great, except he's not here; he won't be here when you fall."

"I won't fall." Her head spun with the coppery scent of blood, so much blood. She shook as Brad took out her phone. "What are you doing?"

"I'm getting Lance."

"He's an hour away." Too far. Just as help had been too far the day she'd tried to keep her father's life from seeping away.

Brad called anyway. She pressed a hand to her forehead. She had never told Brad about that day, but they talked now. She told him everything that had happened. And then he told her things, and she told him others. For her father's birthday, they gave each other memories, some painful, some funny, mostly respectful, but not even his foibles were left unturned. They disagreed and argued and remembered. And then Lance was there.

He burst into the Nob Hill hotel and saw Rese side by side with Brad on the scaffolding near the vaulted ceiling. "Rese?"

She looked down. "I'm all right."

Brad shifted his position. "She's dizzy."

Lance frowned. Since she'd gone back to work with Brad, he had assumed she was over the flashbacks and dizzy spells. He'd been wrong. He climbed the scaffold, thinking what might have happened if Brad hadn't been up there with her.

"You didn't have to come," she said as he pulled himself onto the platform. "If Brad had just let me go down . . ."

"You got her?" Brad said, rising to his feet.

Lance nodded.

Brad pulled the cigarette pack from his pocket. "I'll have a smoke; then one of the guys can help me up here. Rese, you go home."

She shook her head.

"I mean it. I don't want to be filing insurance on another accident."

Rese pulled herself up by the scaffolding. "I will not quit."

Brad expelled an exasperated breath. "Go on. Get out of here."

She raised her chin. "He mattered to you too. If you can keep working, so can I."

"It's not a competition, Rese. Will you tell her?"

Lance looked into her face. He wanted to take her home, but if she needed to work through it, he'd give her that. "Rese?"

She turned to Brad. "What do you think Dad would say?"

"To you?"

"To any of us."

Brad hung his hands on his hips. "He'd say earn your pay or I'll let my daughter run your crew."

That surprised a laugh from her. "I deserved that position,

even if you did get along better with the guys. I got more out of them."

"That's about what Vernon said."

She drew herself up. "I am not wasting his birthday crying."

"Well, I've got a job to do. I can't be watching that you don't fall."

Lance studied the operation. "You go ahead, Brad. Rese and I'll tackle this."

They both looked at him. He'd never intruded on their work before, and he half expected to be refused. Though he and Rese had worked together on the carriage house, since partnering with Brad she'd kept her professional life separate.

But she planted her hands on her hips. "We'll finish the cornice."

Brad stood a long moment, then shrugged. "Okay."

———

Driving home with Lance's motorcycle in the back of her pickup, Rese felt surprisingly whole. She and Brad had aired things that had been simmering in silence. Dad had not been perfect, far from it, but he had mattered to them.

So much of her work happened alone, and she loved the zone where her craft comprised her entire focus. Yet working with Lance had been wonderful—his smiles, his self-deprecating jokes. It brought back the first weeks they'd spent together restoring the carriage house and finishing the villa, planning the inn, its entertainment and marvelous meals.

She'd kept him out of this part of her life, afraid, maybe, that he'd pervade it so completely she'd have nothing of her own. But now she wondered why that had mattered so much. She glanced at Lance beside her. "Tired?"

"Yeah, actually. That was a lot of lifting."

It would not have fazed him before, but he was still regaining his strength and muscle. Physical labor might help that. "Lance, would you want to . . . do this again?"

"Work with you?" The look on his face sent a pang to her heart.

"Well, Star's home with Mom, and Sofie and Nonna can put together some pretty good meals."

"Pretty good?" He laughed. "Nonna's the master I learned from."

"I didn't want to hurt your feelings." Though he hadn't been anywhere near as sensitive about his cooking or anything except Brad since he'd come back. He'd been incredibly content with what little praise and attention he got. Where was the earringed pirate who had swung into her work site and taken over her mind?

"If we win one more bid, we'll need extra hands, and you know what you're doing."

His voice grew hoarse. "Would you like that?"

It surprised her how much. "I wouldn't turn you loose on anything that mattered."

He grinned. "There's the woman I know and love."

Good thing she wasn't standing. He'd just turned her to pudding.

"Okay." He nodded. "Put me to work."

"Don't you want to know what it pays?"

"Fagedda-bout-it. It's the benefits that count."

She frowned. "We will maintain a professional relationship."

His eyes creased. "Oh yeah, that."

"Like you got it the first time."

He tipped his head back recalling. "Weren't you the one who wanted a repeat of that particular violation?"

"I did not."

"Came to my door loaded for bear and hoping for an encore."

"If you can't behave, it won't work."

"Don't worry. I won't blow your cover."

"What cover?"

"Everyone knows you're tough as nails. I won't tell them you melt like a Popsicle in the sun."

"You are so not getting this job."

His smile raked her. "Get-outta-here. You need me."

"Like a banged thumb."

He laughed. "Okay. I promise to behave."

"Define *behave*."

He thought for a minute. "Hands off unless we're alone."

"Hands off period."

"Aw, Rese."

"Lance." The man was impossible. What had she been thinking to even open the door?

"Okay. Your rules. Home is under control, at least for now. Star's doing better."

"Much."

"Did you hear Rico's song?"

She nodded.

"You did?"

"The first night. After we talked."

He scowled. "How come I had to wait for weeks?"

"You don't know the secret Star handshake."

He leveled her a long stare. "Probably better."

She smiled. "Yep."

"So what do you think about Matt?"

"Matt." Where had that come from? "Want to narrow the subject?"

"No. Give me all your impressions."

She tipped her head. "He's handsome."

"Okay, skip that part."

"Reliable. Conscientious. Strong. Big hands." Her throat choked suddenly. "He reminds me of Dad."

Lance rubbed her shoulder. "You okay?"

She nodded. "I don't know where that came from."

"I never saw your dad, but I can imagine the similarities."

She smoothed the emotion back down. "Why do you want to know about Matt?"

"He's starting to matter to Sofie."

CHAPTER TWENTY-THREE

Sofie looked over the simple flyer she'd created announcing the new studio and classes. She had decided to start small, to distribute flyers around town, put an ad in the paper. Beginning and intermediate ballet training three hours each afternoon and Saturdays. She imagined the girls coming in their pink leotards and tutus, their slippers and tights, hair pulled up and twisted into tiny knots atop their heads.

And suddenly Carly was there, all sweetness and twirls, dancing into Eric's arms.

"Look, Daddy, I'm a swan."

"Yes. Yes you are. I see that."

"Sofie's a swan too. Are you a swan?"

"No, Carly, I'm the lake you and Sofie swim in."

Carly collapsed in giggles. "You can't be a lake, Daddy." But he'd looked over, and Sofie knew he was exactly that. He upheld and contained them. She moved freely within his boundaries, gliding on his love, trying not to make ripples.

Until the lake went dry and she'd been left flapping in the mud, and then even that was too hard, too futile. But as she'd told Matt, God had given her people who cared. People who needed to believe she was looking forward, taking back her life.

Who wanted to believe she could never hurt herself again. Even her change of plan had motivated Lance, so that he and Rese and Star had completed her studio in record time. Anything to keep Sofie productive.

She hadn't told anyone back home yet, or the doctoral committee at Fordham, that she'd quit working toward the goal that had seemed so essential a short time ago. Burying herself in her studies had been as mind-numbing as any drug. With that gone, she had time to think, to remember. To wish. To regret.

She clenched her fists. *Carly!* One phone call was not enough! She'd told herself if she was meant to play a part in Carly's life then the Lord would not have allowed everything that happened. But every night since Carly's call, she'd lain awake praying her cell would ring, that Carly would say, "Hi, umm, are you busy?"

And she'd say, "No, Carly, I'm never too busy for you." How could she be? What single thing could be more important than the child who had thrown herself into her arms, kissing her face, her eyes, her nose. *"I love you, Sofie. I'm all filled up with love."*

An ache like a hole in her stomach nearly doubled her. Who was she to think she could teach anything? The physical and mental discipline of dance was supposed to reflect a sound and ordered mind, an artistic, joyful spirit. An instructor should be someone students could respect and depend on. Her gaze slid from the flyer to her wrist, the skin raised in angry reminders of failure too deep and encompassing.

With a cry, she tore the paper down the middle. No one should entrust their children to her when she'd lost her own. Though no court would acknowledge it, Carly was her daughter. She had been grafted into her heart and then torn away. How had she thought that could heal?

She'd failed. Even if she'd been forgiven, the Lord would not entrust fragile lives to her. He had returned Diego to his damaged teenage mother, who had risked herself to save her child. She would not have offended someone who had the power to disappear.

A knock came at the door. Star and Elaine were in the attic,

Lance and Rese at work. Nonna probably didn't hear and shouldn't have to respond. With a sigh, she left Rese's office and opened the door.

"Hi." Matt held out a single rose, the fragrance of its pink-tinged ivory petals preceding him.

She took the bloom. "It's lovely."

"You're lovely."

She frowned. "This isn't a good time, Matt." Their dance had ended with a promise to talk, but she could not put on the face he wanted to see.

"What's wrong?"

She had not energy or desire to explain. She inhaled the rose's bouquet and said, "This needs water." She took the rose to the kitchen and prolonged its freshness in a vase. But it would die, severed as it was from the plant that had sustained it.

Matt had dressed casually in jeans and a three-button, placard-front sweater that fit well the breadth of his shoulders and length of his torso. His hair looked freshly cut. The concern in his eyes pained her.

"So." He spread his hands. "Want to take a walk?"

A walk. Innocuous. Undemanding. The counselors had told her she must have a plan, even if it was only to get up and get dressed. She had surpassed their expectations. But today it might be all she could do to put one foot in front of the other.

They stepped into the windy briskness of spring emerging from winter. Matt took her hand, his large palm and long fingers engulfing hers as they headed down the sidewalk along the quiet street. For a moment she felt utterly cared for, like a little girl certain nothing bad could happen as long as the big, strong hand held on. Then she recalled it was Matt, and the strength and surety of his grip called out other feelings.

He lacked Eric's debilitating magnetism, yet he drew her nonetheless. Could she care for him, surrender any part of herself? How would she know where to stop? Where Matt ended, and she began? She looked down at their hands, intertwined but not melded. Her fingers enclosed but not invisible.

As they passed by the blue frame house next door, Matt cocked his head. "How long has that been empty?"

"I think the owner died several months ago. An old woman—Evvy something. She helped Lance find some pieces to Nonna's puzzle. He did some gardening for her."

"I don't see a For Sale sign."

Sofie shrugged. "I don't know who has it now."

"Think it's got a bat cave?"

She smiled. "You like old houses."

"I like things with staying power."

Staying power.

A gust of wind carried the scent of pastureland when they reached the end of their street. It was almost at the edge of town, with a few fallow fields on which a horse and two goats grazed. A bird sang. She couldn't tell what kind.

He said, "Want to talk about it?"

"I'm not sure I've made the right decision."

"About teaching dance instead of completing your degree?"

She had meant something bigger that included leaving New York, giving up, starting over.

He slid her a glance. "When I changed careers, I must have wondered a thousand times if I'd made a mistake."

"How do you know it was right?"

He shrugged. "I feel more comfortable in my skin."

A smile tugged her lips.

"If I'd accepted a junior partnership, that would have set my course. I could have made a lot of money and wielded no little power."

"But . . ."

"Disguising the misconduct of shady politicians was too close to what I'd grown up with. I guess I got tired of lying."

"So you made the right decision."

"I did."

She drew a shaky breath. "How long did it take to know?"

"Longer than you've given it." He squeezed her hand. "Just take the first step."

"I designed a flyer."

"Did you post them?"

"Not yet."

"Put them out. See where it goes."

"I might not get enough students to fill a class."

"Well, then I'll reconsider."

She raised her brows. "Amid the pink leotards and ribboned slippers, you might prove a sizable distraction."

"Isn't that useful with all that lifting and tossing?"

She laughed. "There's not much tossing, but a good deal of catching."

"Plenty of tossing on the TV show. But they're past the form and discipline, I guess, on to the turning loose." His smile sent a quiver down inside.

"Dance forms that appear haphazard are still rigorously defined."

"I see." He stopped and turned. "Now, why don't you tell me what's really wrong."

Pain broke through her mask, too close to the surface already for her flimsy restraint. "Why hasn't Carly called back?"

"You know why."

"He won't let her?"

"Maybe he took her phone."

"Why can't she use a friend's?"

He brought her hand to his chest. "If he had a hold on your mind, Sofie, what kind of power could he wield on hers?"

She knew what kind. She'd seen it when Carly had only been a preschooler. They'd spend the whole day in effortless relationship, but the moment Eric came home, Carly would fixate on him, painfully focused as if there could be no triangle, only a linear sort of love between Eric and any other point.

"I lost her, Matt." The self-reproach in her voice tore at him.

"I know." Some days he awakened with the feeling that Jacky had leapt the tracks like young Superman outrunning the train, that he'd been hiding out while big brother Matt fixed things at home and would walk back in, forever nine, with his lopsided grin and clear blue eyes. "But she's alive. She's with her dad." And either Eric was a threat or he wasn't. It couldn't go both ways. "Carly didn't say she needed help."

"What if she tried, and I missed it?"

"She's eleven, Sofie. Not four." But he could tell her mind still churned. He sighed. "Maybe I can do some checking."

"Find her?"

"I could see if she's in the system. If there have been any reports of abuse or charges against Eric, whether she's had foster care."

She shook her head. "No way."

"In six years, things could have escalated. Maybe he caught her before she could tell you."

"She wasn't upset."

"Was he?"

She looked away. "Why can't I let go?"

He had a guess. "You tell me."

She didn't answer.

"Sofie." He nudged her chin back. "You've been on hold ever since he walked away. Don't you think it's time to get on with your life?"

Her brow furrowed. "That's what I came here to do."

"Then don't look back." He pulled her close as the wind gusted around them. "Open your studio. Teach people to dance. Stop looking for answers that don't exist." He caught her face between his hands. "Fall in love with me."

"What?"

"Why not? I'm more than half in love with you." He leaned in, but she put her fingers to his lips and eased back.

"I need to start dinner." She slid her hair behind her ear.

"Isn't that Lance's job?"

"He's working with Rese now."

He arched his brows. "That should test their compatibility."

"You don't think people in love can work together?"

He raised a branch for her to pass under. "It stresses the relationship."

"I suppose." She shrugged. "Rese is exacting."

"Lance better know his stuff."

"He hasn't done the kind of fine finish work she does, but he built homes with Habitat for Humanity and did other construction with Food for the Poor and the Peace Corps in El Salvador, Guatemala, and Jamaica."

"He gets around."

She half smiled. "He's been told that too."

He caught her drift. "No way."

"He started notching kisses on his wall in elementary school."

"Doesn't that disqualify him from messiahship?"

She glared at the joke. "Nothing disqualifies a repentant heart."

"So as long as he regrets it—"

The wind tossed her hair across her face. "Repentance requires reform. He gave up what he loved because the temptations were too many."

"Well, now he's got Rese."

"He's not sleeping with her."

"Come on. They're getting married."

She looked into his face. "He wants his marriage to honor God. Wants his life to."

"Well, I don't think sex is the great evil. Not between people who love each other. Or who might."

"It forges unions that go too deep without grace to sanctify them."

"What does that even mean?" They reached the villa and he held the door for her.

"My explanation will be useless to you."

"If it's true, it should make sense outside of religion."

"You're saying there aren't social, psychological reasons for restraint? No physiological benefit to committed, monogamous intercourse?"

He followed her through the entry to the kitchen. "There are, obviously. But, Sofie—"

She opened the oversized refrigerator and studied the contents. "Separating the physical and emotional from the spiritual—"

"Everyone is physical. Not everyone is spiritual."

She took out a paper-wrapped package. "Everyone is spiritual. Ignoring or denying it doesn't change reality."

They'd reached an impasse. If everyone had some invisible part that went on when the physical and emotional ended, then there had to be a reason for it, an eternity with or without a Supreme Being, or an endless recycling until achieving perfect annihilation, or any of the other myths created to explain the unexplainable. But in his experience, religion frequently did more harm than good—especially for people like his mother.

Matt rubbed his face. How had he ended up in this bastion of virtue, where people suppressed natural desires and broke natural laws?

Sofie pulled out a skillet. "Veal scaloppine?"

He lowered his hand. "Sorry, I don't eat veal."

She looked surprised, and the irony struck him that he'd at last turned the tables.

"Why not?"

"I can't support an animal being crated up for months and fed iron-deficient formula to make it weak and tender."

She leaned against the counter and scrutinized him.

He returned it defensively. "What?"

"I know how to pick the palest pink-flesh, white-fat, milk-fed veal. I know what makes it that way, but I hadn't thought—I like that it matters to you."

"A lot of things matter to me. Religion isn't the only basis for a moral compass." He folded his arms. "I'll eat the vegetables or whatever you make to go with it."

She wrapped the veal back in its paper and took a different package out. "The chicken is free-range."

He nodded. "Good. Thanks."

"Scaloppine?"

"Whatever you do will be great. I'm not picky—in the usual sense. Can I help?"

She took out a marble board and stainless-steel mallet. "Want to pound it thin?"

"Sure."

Her fingers brushed his hand as she transferred the utensil. "Sofie." He took the mallet, then he took her hand. Whatever their differences, there was no denying his interest. "I'm glad you came here to start over."

She looked into his face. "I am too."

He resisted the urge to kiss her and wondered if there was some spiritual deposit made by his sacrifice. That probably required an account.

CHAPTER TWENTY-FOUR

L ance sniffed the air as he followed Rese inside. Chicken, probably scaloppine. Sofie or Nonna had been busy he noted as he reached the kitchen and received the full effect of the aromas. Even Star sat cutting garnishes out of thinly sliced vegetables. It felt strange surrendering his kitchen, but working with Rese was where he needed—and wanted—to be. At least for now. He didn't mind being grunt labor if it included him in that part of her life.

And the girls could handle meals just fine. He kissed Nonna's cheek, then noticed Matt in the dining room with Sofie. They shared a soft laugh, gazes meeting as they plunked down the silverware. Matt saw him and straightened. Then Sofie looked up.

He searched her expression, but she seemed all right, maybe more, so he gave Matt a nod and said, "We got a letter from Maria." He held up the envelope.

Nonna turned. "What does she s . . . ay?"

"I'll read it when Rese comes out." He glanced toward the suite where she had gone to wash up.

"Then, here." Nonna handed him the wine and corkscrew. "While you wait." Never mind that he'd worked a nine-hour day. No one stood idle in Nonna's kitchen.

Rese came out just as he slid the cork free. "Where's Mom?"

Star shrugged a shoulder. "She stayed in bed."

"Doesn't she feel well?"

"She didn't want to talk about it."

"We'll get her down for the meal." Lance drew her to his side as Sofie and Matt came into the room. "Let's hear what Maria says." He tore it open and handed three photos to Rese to pass as he read.

"Dear Lance and everyone,

"I want to say how thankful I am for your help, and for getting me home. As you can see, Diego is eating always. He is so big. One day I hope I can show him pictures of his godparents and all of you. Mamá says that is a hint.

"I am better now, stronger all the time. I think of the good things you did for me. Those are what I remember when I wake afraid and angry—that Lance (I know he says God) made my baby well and Sofie made him happy and that you were all so kind.

"One day Diego will do great things, and I will tell him it was because of the good people God put in his life. I will go back to school soon—my own school that Mamá said was good enough. There are so many people to watch Diego while I am gone. They all want to hold the miracle baby.

"God bless you, and I send my love. Maria"

The pictures came around to him, and he studied the fat cheeks of his godson, Maria's teenage smile, and the last photo that could hardly contain everyone in it. She was back where she belonged, with loved ones to help her deal with all that had happened. He looked across at Rese. "Guess we made the right call, taking her in."

She nodded. "Good thing we weren't running an inn."

"And that Sofie arrived to keep Diego." He looked across at his sister, who turned to her suitor.

"And that Matt gave us physical custody."

Matt smiled, and for the first time Lance considered him part of them, part of the fabric God wove.

"All things according to God's w . . . ill," Nonna said.

"Amen," he breathed, then waved the photos. "We need refrigerator magnets next time you're out, Star."

She formed an elfish smile, and he could only imagine what she'd come back with. The crazier the better, as far as he was concerned. "Smells good. Let's eat."

Something had changed, though it took most of the meal to put his finger on it. Then Matt realized he must have passed some test, crossed a portal into the heart of this family. Lance had exchanged wariness for an irresistible geniality, and even Antonia looked on with kindness.

Their acceptance touched him, and he was reluctant to do or say anything that would once again mark him the outsider when every person at the table—even Elaine, whom they'd coaxed down to join them—seemed a part of the whole. In this house, no one got marginalized. It was more than a meal they shared; it was a sort of communion.

He stayed deep into the evening, not wanting it to end, not wanting to leave them. They talked philosophy and Shakespeare, history and politics. Even religion, but not the kind he'd heard before. When Star asked something, Lance quoted the prophet Isaiah, talking about a world where lions lay down with lambs, then claimed that time was now. He called it the kingdom of God overlapping the world of sin, the city of God in the midst of fallen creation. A reality inside a reality.

Matt hoped the man wasn't crazy. But if they were all mad, why was sanity prized? The laughter was real. And the love. They were all disarmingly real in a way he'd never experienced. Maybe everything outside these walls was the illusion.

At last Elaine rose and informed them it was time for bed. She issued a number of warnings they all took in stride; then Rese went up with her to prepare for the night. Antonia had long since slumped down and was snoring softly in her chair.

Lance rubbed his hands. "Guess I'm on cleanup."

Star stood to help him.

Sofie's affectionate look slid from her grandmother to him. "Matt, will you help me get Nonna to her room?"

He stood, grateful for such an intimate opportunity. He hadn't been part of a family for a long—Well, never. Not a family like this that loved unreservedly, accepting the foibles and flaws of each member—especially the weakest.

Sofie gently nudged her grandmother awake, and as he gave the old woman the strength of his arm, his eyes teared. He fought to keep Sofie from noticing, but by the time they'd conveyed her grandmother to bed and went back out to the cold night, she'd caught on.

"Are you all right?"

He pressed through the tightness in his throat. "If there's a heaven, I think it looks like tonight."

She smiled up at him with such pleasure, he caught her face between his hands.

"Sofie, I need to kiss you."

She shrugged one shoulder. "Then kiss me."

She trembled as he took her mouth with his. Not a desperate kiss, no grief outpouring. It was a connection borne of the night's camaraderie and deep desire. He kissed her slowly, a man to woman kiss, expressing what he felt, what he wanted, who they were, who they might be together.

He stopped when she drew back.

"I can't."

"It's just a kiss."

"I know you want more."

He caressed her face. "Sofie, I want anything that includes you. Whatever that looks like; whatever you make it."

She stared into his face unbelieving, but he meant it. He'd court her like a squire if she wanted that.

He squeezed her hand. "I'll call you tomorrow."

Lance woke with a jolt, senses heightened. *Lord?* The urgency remained. He slipped out of bed and went into the hall. Grief struck him, but it could be any of his companions and each would require a different mode of action. He listened until he heard the soft sobs from Sofie's room, then went to her door.

He didn't knock, just slipped in and knelt beside her bed. He cupped the back of her head and whispered, "Sof."

She didn't withdraw or hide her tears. When at last she turned, he asked, "What is it?"

"I'm afraid if I let go, she'll be lost."

"Carly?"

"I dreamed I was holding her over an abyss. Her hands were slipping out of mine. Behind me voices demanded, 'Why can't you let go?' as if they couldn't see she'd be lost if I did." She drew a jagged breath. "It was so real. The feeling that I had to hold on, no matter what anyone said, what anyone thought."

"Dreams can be deceptive. Have you prayed?"

She shrugged. "I say the words, but . . ."

"Then let me." He took Sofie's hand and rested his other palm on her head. The Father's love came immediately, but it seemed to drain away. *Lord.*

It was a leak Sofie refused to close. Her connection to Carly? Guilt over her attempted suicide? A lingering desire for Eric? He didn't know what caused the rent in her spirit, but she had to be willing before it could heal, and he sensed that now was not the time. What comfort she could accept, she'd received. He opened his eyes and saw that she'd fallen back to sleep.

Matt stood with Sofie at the top of the deep-green forest overlooking the sparkling Pacific. After spending the evening before with her family, he had picked her up for a day in the bay area. A brisk wind rising from the ocean below tossed her hair and battled for his breath. In the face of such majesty he didn't know what to say anyway.

He had not been joking about heaven last night. If eternity was anything like the evening he'd spent with Sofie's family, he could almost accept it. Seeing Lance unguarded had explained the way people like Maria viewed him. His charismatic presence emphasized the things he'd talked about, the kingdom of God on earth, a new creation.

Matt shook his head. He got it, but it wasn't that easy to change the mindset he'd methodically developed since leaving home. Many of his friendships and nearly all his work relationships would be impacted. There would be fallout he couldn't even foresee.

But he put it out of his mind as Sofie bent beside him and peered over the cliff. "Does the height scare you, Matt?"

"I'm used to it. Ever since seventh grade."

She nudged his ribs. "I mean the height of the cliff."

"Oh, that." He looked down. "I wouldn't walk a tightrope over those rocks, but heights don't bother me."

She leaned on the concrete pillar that held the metal cables surrounding the overlook. "What does? Snakes, spiders?"

He grinned.

"Come on. What makes Matt Hammond tremble?"

"Tremble?" He turned her around, bracing her against the barrier at the top of the cliff. "You make me tremble."

She pushed his chest. "I mean scared tremble."

"So do I."

"What, I scare you?"

"Half to death."

"Why?"

"You're like a siren luring me from my course."

She folded her arms. "What course?"

"My certainty. My reality. Even my mundanity."

"You're hardly mundane."

"I get up. I work. I eat. I sleep."

"You change lives."

"Yeah, maybe." He studied the shape of her eyes, the arch of her brows. For beauty like that, a man would do anything. "I thought I had it all figured out. Then came you. I'm telling you, Sofie, the first time I saw you I could hardly breathe."

She smiled. "Is that why you wouldn't let go of my hand?"

"I think time stopped for a while. I can't be blamed for that."
She laughed. "And that's scary?"

"Scary is not wanting it to start again. Today only has twenty-four hours, but I want every one of them to go on and on."

"Very poetic."

"And I'm not. See? You've brought something out that's never been there."

"Not true. I saw you with Diego. I heard the rhymes you murmured. Wynken, Blynken, and Nod."

"But that's not me. It's Eugene Field." He half smiled. "My favorite poet."

"Why?"

He shrugged. "The guy loved kids, understood the magic. And losing his son almost killed him." He stared out over the sea behind her, words coming to his mind.

> "Last night, as my dear babe lay dead,
> In agony I knelt and said:
> 'O God! what have I done,
> Or in what wise offended Thee,
> That Thou should'st take away from me
> My little son?'"

His chest squeezed. Had Dad ever searched himself for blame? Had he questioned a God who gave someone such unfit power over smaller lives? His voice graveled.

> "Upon the thousand useless lives,
> Upon the guilt that vaunting thrives,
> Thy wrath were better spent!
> Why should'st Thou take my little son
> Why should'st Thou vent Thy wrath upon
> This innocent?"

Sofie searched his face. "You're saying God's unfair?"

"I'll leave that for another day."

"Then what?"

"Field asked what he'd done to make God take his child."

Sofie went still. "What had he done?"

"I don't know. What mattered was he asked."

Sofie could not get Matt's words out of her head. It surprised her that he'd committed to memory the agony of a man wrestling with God when he didn't believe God was there. But the poem had shown Matt a model he admired, one that contrasted with the example his own father had set, the example he was afraid he'd follow.

He needed someone to take the blame for what had happened, but both adults seemed to shun the guilt until he was the only one holding it. She knew that burden too well. Maybe that was why they'd connected on a deeper level than she'd expected.

She rested her head on his shoulder as they drove back to Sonoma. His broad shoulders would bear the weight of her past if she let them. But could she?

Lance's prayer last night had lulled her back to sleep, but it had not provided the release she'd hoped for. The dream had been so real, and Matt's was one of the voices she'd resisted. Was it fair to raise his hopes? Yet the thought of letting him go brought another unexpected pang.

She lifted her head when he parked outside the villa. They'd spent the entire day together, and like Matt, she didn't want it to end. "Are you tired?"

"No."

"Do you want to come in?"

"And what?"

She flushed. "I don't know. Talk?"

His eyes went over her. "You know what I'd really like? And it's not what you're thinking."

"What?"

"I'd like to watch you dance."

"Alone?"

He nodded. "Without me in the way."

He was asking more than he realized. Dancing had been the hardest thing she'd given up for Eric. She had told herself when

Carly wasn't so little, so needy, there would be time. But time hadn't been the issue. She couldn't divide her passion, and he'd seemed worth the sacrifice. Only when they were gone, when she'd tried to get back to the level she'd been, had she recognized how much she'd lost in those four years—not merely strength and agility, but the will and the hunger to get it back.

Matt wouldn't know. He had nothing to compare with what she did now, no trained eye to gauge before and after. She took her keys from her purse as he came around to let her out. The new key opened the new lock on the old doors Lance had unearthed and Rese had sanded down and refinished. The doors opened into the center of the studio. She went to the CD rack at one end and thumbed through until she found the one she wanted.

He raised his brows. "Shrek?"

She set the system to play the tenth track and moved to the center of the floor. She could think of nothing that better portrayed her life than the troubled strains of what had been, and what was now. As the music filled the room, she started to move, bending and arching, reaching and pleading. She knew what she had lost, but danced now in appreciation for what she'd kept, giving him, and God, the best she had—her own broken hallelujah.

When she stopped, Matt's eyes had pooled. He reached out a hand, and she went to him. He closed her into his arms. "You are . . . so beautiful . . . it hurts."

CHAPTER TWENTY-FIVE

Rese had never seen Brad in a suit, and since he'd worn jeans to his wedding, she guessed she never would. With flowers in her gray-streaked black hair, Joni paced the ladies' room down the hall from the court in a broomstick skirt and camisole top.

"It's a mistake. We're making a mistake. We'll kill each other."

"It's not a mistake." Rese pushed open the door for Joni to exit.

Out in the hall, Brad seemed strangely calm. He'd always had confidence in the decisions he made. No matter how hard he'd dug in his heels before, once he'd made up his mind, everything was good. But when Joni saw him standing there, she turned back around, pale as a ghost in spite of her over-tanned skin.

Rese blocked her retreat. "The judge is waiting."

"I can't."

"You were willing to marry someone else on a bridge."

"Because Brad . . ."

"Exactly." Rese crossed her arms, hardly believing she was playing this role with someone other than Star. Joni was older, more experienced, and probably wondered where Brad's business partner got off talking to her that way. But Brad had asked her to witness the vows, and she couldn't do that if his fiancée wouldn't speak them.

Joni drew a shaky breath and faced Brad. "So. We doing this?"

Brad took her hand. "You change your mind now, I'll kill you."

Joni shot her a glare. "I told you. Didn't I tell you?"

Rese followed them into the courtroom and up the aisle as Lance came up beside her. He leaned close and whispered, "Think they'll go through with it?"

"Of course."

"Sure?"

"They want to be married."

His hand closed around hers. "Well, so do I."

Her heart jumped. "We'll talk about that later."

"We'll seriously talk about it."

She directed her focus to the judge, who took his place before them. His wide bald head, framed by two bulbous ears, reflected the ceiling lights. Several chins connected his face to his tight black robe. Only his voice was thin as he addressed Brad and Joni.

Lance whispered, "Don't you want to be Mrs. Michelli?"

"Yes, Lance, I do." But she knew what he expected. He had friends all over the world, and he'd assured her his mother would die if every living relative wasn't invited. Then there was the issue of Rico standing up for him, with Star being her maid of honor. None of it was as simple as Lance tried to make it.

Brad and Joni faced each other. After so many turbulent years, they were recommitting their lives in spite of everything that had gone wrong. Brad put the ring on Joni's finger and spoke his vows with a hoarse confidence that made Rese proud. Joni's voice was hardly audible as she slid the other ring onto Brad's thick, callused finger.

Rese hoped with everything in her that Joni meant it as wholeheartedly as Brad. Then they kissed, and a sweetness came over her. They'd put back together what they'd torn apart. It was the phase of restoration she loved best, replacing tenderly repaired or remade parts to their former positions, bringing completion and wholeness to the project.

Lance's breath warmed her ear. "You need time to get a dress made and all that?"

"Actually . . ." Her throat squeezed. "I thought I'd wear my mother's."

He turned and searched her face. "You have it?"

She nodded. "Dad saved a few important things."

"Then what are we waiting for?"

She shrugged. "There's the judge."

"And put Momma in the grave? She's already a wreck over Sofie."

She hadn't been serious. As glad as she was for Brad and Joni, a courthouse and judge were not the way she and Lance would make their covenant. Of that, she was sure.

"One month." His dark eyes glittered dangerously.

She huffed. "Okay, Lance. One month." And then she laughed. So what if he invited the whole world? She was marrying Lance Michelli, and nothing would ever be simple again.

Brad and Joni had a flight to catch so the hugs were brief, but even so, when they drove away, Lance said, "How many packs a day do you think she smokes?"

"Why?"

"I'm just wondering."

From anyone else she'd accept that. "Is she sick, Lance?"

He shrugged. "It was just a feeling."

"Is there something you can do?"

"There's always something we can do."

"I mean to make it right."

"That isn't up to me." He took her hand. "Besides, we don't know anything for sure."

"Does God show you things that aren't true?"

"No. But not everything I think is God."

Witnessing Brad and Joni's wedding had affected him more than he'd expected. He honestly didn't know if he could have taken it if Rese hadn't agreed to set a date. She didn't know what it took every day to be close to her and not act on each and every impulse.

They had re-created in the Sonoma villa what the Michellis had in Belmont. A family of individuals, working and sharing lives. But he wanted to be one with her, to share his bed, his body, his being. Hugging Joni, he'd realized once again how fragile life was, and how their days were numbered. He didn't want to squander even one.

Michelle had come by the house to pick up the car seat they no longer needed for Diego. Maybe to make it official, or simply because he couldn't hold it in, he told her, "One month from tonight, I'm making this woman my wife."

"Well, hallelujah." She squeezed them both. "And if that's the case, I have news for you. Maybe I should wait until it's a done deal, but this might prove useful beforehand."

"Let me guess." He quirked a smile up one side. "Toilet-paper flowers."

She took his teasing with good grace. "You'd be surprised how grateful people are for that particular item."

"Not surprised at all, some of the places I've been."

"Lance, let her talk." Rese nudged him.

"As you know, your neighbor Evvy was a pillar in our small church and a dear friend to all."

Lance nodded. That birdlike woman had possessed an intense zeal for God and a meddlesome nature that equaled any he'd suffered. He'd adored her.

"Well." Michelle beamed. "Evvy left you her house as a wedding gift."

He and Rese turned simultaneously to the big blue house next door. It had been vacant since Evvy died, and he'd wondered why no one had put it up for sale or taken possession.

"But"—a pucker pinched Rese's brow—"what made her think we would get married?"

"Oh, she had a way of knowing things." Michelle smiled.

"Yeah," Lance agreed. "She told me I was in love when I still thought Rese the orneriest female I'd ever met." When Evvy went on to glory, things had been anything but rosy between Rese and him.

"You were the ornery one. You're still ornery."

"The truth is, she put it under the care of the church with the one stipulation—if you two got married it would revert to its original ownership. She said the property had belonged to your family, Lance, and shouldn't have been divided. She intended that you put it to good use."

Of that, he was sure. Evvy was never faint of heart—he'd taken her on his Harley, and she'd loved every minute. Nor had she hesitated to decide what was best for everyone. Or to scold them into it.

Michelle clasped her hands. "Now that you've set a date, I thought knowing might help you plan."

An idea struck him. "If we took down the hedge between the properties, Rese, we could have the reception here—and house some out-of-town guests."

"It's empty," Michelle told them. "Evvy donated all her belongings to the sharing fund, so you'll have to furnish it."

He shrugged. "Blankets on the floor of her attic and ours'll do for the kids."

"All six thousand of them." Rese planted her hands on her hips. "But the Bailey House on Nob Hill pulled out all the iron beds. If they haven't sold them already, I can probably work a deal for the lot and run it through the company. If we don't keep them all here after the wedding, they'll work for any number of projects."

He could tell her mind was turning. She couldn't wait to get inside and see what could be done with the old place. As soon as Michelle left, he raised his brows. "Want to have a look?"

"What do you think?"

"I think your fingers are tingling."

She tugged him next door. "Are you finding this as hard to believe as I am?"

"Nah." He picked up the hide-a-key rock along the walk and unlocked the door. "Evvy loved me."

Rese huffed. "Who doesn't?"

He followed her inside. "Rese."

"What?"

"We should think about this in long terms. What we might be meant to do here."

"Before I start tearing out walls?"

He smiled. "Something like that."

Turning a slow circle, she drew a deep breath. "One thing I've learned with you, Lance, is that renovation isn't an end; it's a means."

Carly climbed onto the cold, smooth counter in the dark. She had a flashlight stuffed into the pocket of her pajamas, but enough city light filtered through the window to manage without it. Holding her breath, she reached into the super-tall cabinet. Dad had looked so strange earlier, when she'd walked in on him, that she'd expected to find the box gone, but her fingers touched something. She stood up and took the black and gray box from the back of the top shelf.

She was so dead if he caught her up there, but his snores carried down the hall. She didn't think he'd fake snoring. He hated hearing that he did it at all. If one of the women who came over mentioned it, he never saw her again.

She climbed off the counter and tiptoed back to her room, pausing to listen before slipping inside. Gripping the knob, she eased the door shut with the faintest click. She only closed it at night, but even then it was always open in the morning, since Daddy checked in on her. Maybe more than once.

Please don't let him look now! Her heart thumped. But nothing happened.

She slipped the lid off the box and shined the flashlight. The box was filled with photos. She lifted the top one and studied the woman. She didn't remember her . . . but could it be . . . ?

Swallowing the lump in her throat, she set the photo on her bed and picked up the next. Same woman; same street. She was talking to someone there, tucking the hair back behind her ear. The picture was fuzzy, like Carly's brain. Why couldn't she remember?

She looked at the next and the next, dug into the box and checked the ones farther down. Her hands shook. They were all the same person. It had to be Sofie. She reached into the bottom and pulled out the very last picture. An ache filled her throat. The woman looked much younger, holding a baby with such a look of love it brought the tears before Carly could stop them.

She swiped them away so she could see. Was she the baby? Was that how Sofie had looked when she'd held her? The flashlight flickered. She looked toward the door, listened hard. Dad had stopped snoring. She couldn't put the box back if he might be awake. Trembling, she slid the picture back into the bottom and picked up the others on the bed.

But the two from the middle—she couldn't remember where they'd been. She should have held their places. Panic rose in her chest. Her stomach hurt. She looked on the backs, but there were no names or dates that she could see by the fading flashlight.

She put them on top and closed the box. In the morning she'd find where they went . . . somehow. And get the box back . . . somehow. She slipped it under her bed and crawled into the covers. Her foot bumped something. The flashlight.

She sat up and dragged it under the blanket just as the floor creaked in the hallway. Had she closed the door when she went to bed? He'd know if she hadn't. He'd know she'd been up. She pressed her face into her pillow, closed her eyes.

The door clicked and swung open. Dim light from the hallway leaked in. She sensed the shadow that came and stood over her. *Please let him think I'm asleep! Wait. Better to move. He'd think he disturbed her.* She made a sleepy noise and shifted her face on the pillow, not opening her eyes or she'd have to talk.

He stepped back. *Go away, go away, go away.* It should be comforting to know he watched her sleep. Her daddy cared enough to watch her sleep. But right now, she wanted him to go back to bed. He didn't close the door, but the light in the hall went out. Still she didn't move. She made her breath sound sleepy, even though it wanted to rush.

Tick. Tick. The clock on her bed stand. Were those long spaces seconds?

Don't move. Wait. Her stomach hurt. Whatever was in there wanted out. Another creak. Shuffling in Dad's room. Water running. Her breath slowed without her working so hard. After so many ticks she ached from listening, a soft snoring started up again.

She swallowed. Tomorrow she'd take care of everything. He'd never know. But what was he doing with a box full of Sofie?

CHAPTER TWENTY-SIX

The flashing of his message machine caught his eye when Matt walked in. The quiet house tempted him to leave it until morning and simply savor the time he'd had with Sofie. Now that Ryan no longer needed him, no one had trashed the kitchen or cluttered the house. No one waited for answers he didn't have.

He went into the bathroom, then into his bedroom to stretch out and replay each incredible hour of the day. But instead of lying down, he headed back to the kitchen and pressed the message button. *"Matt, it's Sybil. Join us for a drink. Murphy's."*

"Too bad I missed it," he muttered. He hadn't had this much attention from Sybil since . . . ever. She liked the bad-boy types. Like Lance. Earrings. Attitude. What would she think if she knew Lance worked miracles?

The second message started. *"Yeah . . . uh, Matt, this is Dirk Brant. Need you to come down to the hospital and take custody of Annie Price."*

His stomach lurched as the officer continued briefly. The call had come over an hour ago, but he was the only available caseworker. Cassinia had extended her leave as her mother's decline accelerated. No point leaving just to turn around again for the funeral. They had fences to mend if they could.

He got his keys and headed for the door. This shouldn't be any different from other cases, but the parallels stunk. Donald Price, a church member, well known in the community; the youngest, weakest child taking the brunt of the abuse. At least Vivian didn't match the pattern—a lush and meth head. Anyway, it didn't matter. He had a little girl waiting.

The hospital reflected the quiet of the hour. He made his way to the curtained cubicle where a nurse's aide held the sleeping toddler. He'd have to hear about her injuries before he could take her out of there, and the ER doc met him almost immediately.

He said, "She has a medial fracture of the left humerus." It had been cast and strapped to her body by an impossibly small sling apparatus. "Probable concussion." The man rolled her slightly in the young aide's arms. "Contusions here and here." He straightened. "They say she fell down the stairs. That these grip marks came from panic when they tried to catch her."

"They?"

He shrugged. "They're backing each other up. I'm not sure how the story hashed out in the end. Check the police report."

"Could she have fallen?"

"It happens."

"And that could explain the injuries? All of them?"

The doctor looked back at the child. "No history? It's possible."

"But this is a third strike," Matt reminded him. "What do you think happened?"

"I think she got tangled up in a scuffle and dropped down the stairs. I think they waited awhile before coming. Ms. Price didn't look good herself. Said she slipped getting to Annie."

Vivian Price wasn't his problem. From what he'd seen, she did her share of bruising the toddler, might even have shielded herself with her daughter. Matt looked for a long moment at the fair-haired waif. He had to take physical custody, place her in a foster home. Damage was being done to the other children, he knew only too well, but with no visible evidence of abuse and no further incidences of neglect, they had no grounds to act on their behalf. Only Annie. He reached and with utmost care lifted her from the aide's arms.

"She just fell asleep." The aide seemed reluctant to surrender her, though anyone who worked as hard as she did without much compensation had to have a caring heart.

Annie stayed asleep as he tucked her head over his shoulder.

The doctor finished writing. "This second concussion is near enough the first that the previous bump may not be healed. You'll need to wake her every hour. Check her pupils and responsiveness. If she doesn't wake completely, throws up or seems dizzy and disoriented, bring her in."

Disoriented? She was two years old. How could she be anything but? She might remember him from the first time he'd removed her from the house, though more likely having some huge guy shaking her awake in the middle of the night would scare her to death. "Okay. Car seat?"

"We have one checked out for you at the front."

"Thanks."

Before exiting the parking lot, he knew he wasn't taking Annie to his empty house. Sofie could say no, and might, but he drove to the villa anyway. The house was dark, but light poured from the small window in the shed. Someone was up.

He debated locking Annie in the car while he asked, then kicked himself for thinking it. No matter how safe it seemed, no place was safe enough. Cradling her against his chest, he reached the shed and knocked.

Rese opened the door. The smell of fresh wood surrounded her, and curls of it stuck to her jeans. She hadn't put down the chisel. She looked from him to the child.

He swallowed. "I need to ask a favor."

"Who is she?"

"Annie Price." Lance and Sofie had participated in the foster training and their approval had come through, even though Diego had left before it did. There were others he could have contacted, but . . .

Rese tossed the chisel to the workbench and brushed the wood shavings off her hands. "Bring her inside."

They went in through the kitchen and down the hall to the front room. Rese glanced over her shoulder. "Wait here. I'll see if Lance is still awake."

He doubted it. He'd been surprised she was. He stood at the bottom of the stairs while she knocked at the first door on the landing. A different door opened, and he heard Sofie.

"What is it, Rese?"

Rese turned. "Matt's here."

"What?"

"He has a little girl—"

Sofie rushed into view. He hadn't thought how this would key into her past, only that she'd be a soothing presence to Annie. But Sofie stopped, stunned, at the top of the stairs. He wished with everything in him he'd thought his decision through.

She gathered herself and came down, Rese on her heels. "What happened?"

"She got banged up in a family squabble."

Pain washed Sofie's features. "She's so little."

"It's the little ones that get it." His arms tightened reflexively.

Sofie looked into his face. "What's her name?"

"Annie."

"Is her arm broken?"

He nodded. "She may have fallen down stairs. Mom's a meth addict; Dad gets angry."

Sofie leaned in and breathed the child's scent. Tears sparkled in her eyes.

"I'm sorry," he said. "I didn't think."

She slipped Annie from his arms. The child's eyes fluttered. A soft whimper. Sofie soothed her. "What's there to think about?"

He loved this woman. "She'll need temporary placement as this gets sorted out."

"Of course."

"I'd have kept her at my place tonight, but she's got a concussion and needs to be checked every hour." He touched Annie's little hand. "I thought some big guy waking her all night might be more than she could handle."

Sofie's mouth pulled sideways. "You're not the stuff of nightmares."

"Should be just this night on the concussion."

Lance came down behind Sofie, sleep rumpled in a T-shirt and flannel pants. "You okay with this, Sof?"

She nodded.

"Sure?"

"Yes." She shot him a sharp look.

Only half as sharp as the look Lance shot him. The protectiveness was back, that tension between his family and someone who might pose a threat. He hadn't considered Annie a threat, but given Sofie's past, maybe he should have. At any rate, he fit the bill.

"If you need anything, Sof, come to me." Lance touched Annie's dangling hand with one that had closed a cleft palate.

Matt couldn't help wondering how much it took for a miracle. Had something happened already?

They all climbed the stairs to Sofie's room, and she laid Annie down on her bed. The toddler opened her eyes, fear and confusion rising in their blue depths.

"Hi there, Annie. I'm Sofie."

The tot's eyes darted to Matt and the others, then back.

"I'm going to take care of you tonight, honey."

With one arm, Annie tried to push up from the bed.

Sofie helped her. "See, that's Matt and Rese and Lance." She stroked the curve of her little back. "And you can sleep right here with me. I won't let anything happen." *Please, God.*

Annie whimpered. Sofie eased her down, caressing her head and neck until she fell back to sleep. She looked up and caught Lance's extreme concern. Understandable. Turning back the clock, with her fair hair and blue eyes, Annie could be Carly.

She formed a smile. "It's okay."

He knew it wasn't.

Matt couldn't have realized the resemblance, but he had to be catching the drift. When Rese and Lance went out, Matt approached the bed. "I needed to bring her somewhere."

"I'm glad you did." But the ache in her chest felt like knives. "If it's too much . . ."

"It's not." She looked back at the child, tears burning. "It's just so wrong."

"I shouldn't have brought her here. Let me—"

"Stop. Just because it hurts doesn't mean I want you to change it." She willed him to get it. "I want to do this. Do you understand? I *want* to."

He nodded. "All I thought was how good you'd be for her."

Because he didn't know. He thought it was Eric who'd messed up her life when it had been her choice to question, to argue. Her choice to risk losing her little girl.

"You should go. She'll be fine."

He hesitated, but she pressed him out. "Good night."

He drew himself up. "Good night."

When he'd closed the door behind him, she slipped into bed beside Annie. The soft, shallow breaths whispered in her ear as she lowered her head to the pillow near Annie's. What was wrong with the world? She rested her hand on the child's arm and cried herself to sleep.

Rese settled back behind her workbench. Lance had followed her to the shed and paced it now with the caged energy she'd seen before. He would want to talk it out. He always did. They could hardly have turned Annie away, but it had him seriously worked up.

She rested her hands on the bench. "Okay, what."

He turned back the other way, shaking his head. "She's a dead ringer."

"What?"

"Annie. She looks just like Carly at that age."

"Oh." No wonder he'd looked at Matt as though he'd like to take him down. "Do you think Matt knew that?"

He caught his hands in his hair. "I don't know what Matt knows or how he thinks or what he wants."

She gave up believing she could work and went over to him. "Maybe it's good. Maybe she needs to do this." When he didn't immediately agree, she rested her hand on his arm. "I mean, I didn't want you crashing into my life and plans, but I've come to terms with it."

He cupped her elbows with a crooked grin. "Get-outta-here. I'm the best thing that ever happened to you."

"Best painful, annoying—"

"Fagedda-bout-it." He slid his hands around her waist and kissed her.

She kissed him back. "Nonna says everything according to God's will."

He settled his hands in the crook of her neck. "When did you get so wise?"

"I always have been. You just wouldn't admit it."

He laughed. "Okay, okay. So what do we do about this little girl?"

Good question, but she'd given up trying to anticipate the turns each day could take. "People seem to think we have something to offer."

"Do we?"

She shrugged. "It worked out well for Maria and Diego. Maybe you can . . . help Annie too."

He pulled her into a hug. "Maybe we all can."

CHAPTER TWENTY-SEVEN

Carly raised her head from the toilet and wiped her mouth. "I can't go, Daddy."

He rubbed the back of his neck and gave her a look of concern and frustration. "I can't leave you here alone, and I don't know anyone yet to trust you with."

She pushed up from the floor, holding her stomach. "I'll stay in bed and sleep. I could sleep three days. You can call me every hour." She looked into his doubtful face with the sorriest one she could make. "Please, Daddy. I'll die if I throw up at school."

He softened. "I'm worried about you. These stomachaches— I should take you to the doctor."

"You have to work. Maybe tomorrow. Grandma even said I have a weak stomach."

His eyes narrowed. "Grandma doesn't know anything."

Bad move. "I just want to stay in bed."

"You wouldn't lie to me, would you, Carly?"

She let all her hurt and frustration show. "Daddy."

He pulled her into a hug. "Of course you wouldn't." He stroked her hair. "You'd never lie to me. You know how wrong that would be."

Her stomach squeezed tighter. She wasn't lying. Not really. He had to believe her. He had to.

He sighed. "I'll figure something out. Let's tuck you in. What can I leave you to eat?"

"Nothing. Maybe some crackers."

"Animal crackers?"

She was too old for them, but Daddy kept buying them because she couldn't quite say so. "Okay." She climbed into bed and pulled up the covers. "I love you, Daddy." And she did. That was what hurt so much. Her stomach squirmed. Maybe she really was sick. Maybe she was totally messed up.

She wanted to cry every time she realized she didn't remember how Sofie looked. She wanted to remember. She had to. She could not put the box back without seeing every picture, without putting Sofie's face where the blurry feeling of her remained.

Her dad kissed her head. "I'll come back on my lunch break. Maybe you'll feel better by then."

"Okay. Thanks." She closed her eyes, opened them a whole minute later to find him still looking at her. "Can I have a drink of water?"

"Sure." He went to the kitchen, filled a glass, and brought it with the animal crackers. "You'll be okay?"

She nodded. "I just want to sleep." She was so tired—tired of being on guard, tired of being lonely, tired of it all. "Bye, Daddy."

He left, then five minutes later came back in. She hadn't moved. She knew better. He went out again. She waited. Five, ten minutes. Even then she didn't move. She wasn't sure she could make herself take the box out.

He could walk in any minute, say he'd changed his mind about leaving her alone. He'd never left her alone before. Never. Not without someone he'd picked especially, someone he knew would never cross him, someone completely gaga over him so the whole time all she heard was how nice her dad was, how hand-some, how cool. And he was, but sometimes couldn't he leave her with a family?

He probably didn't want her to see what it was like. He picked single moms or single women who would throw themselves at his feet if he told them to. Sometimes they were pretty and nice; sometimes they were overstressed and nasty to their own kids, but never to her, because they wanted him to come back. That felt worse than if they'd been mean to her. She hated how the kids glared, knew what they were thinking. It wasn't fair.

No one ever yelled at her; no one ever hit her. What kind of kid was she to think she had problems? Yeah, my dad loves me too much. They'd feel real sorry to hear that. She pressed her face to the pillow. It wasn't like he molested her. So why, why did it feel so wrong?

Carly slipped out of bed. She had actually dozed and come awake with a jolt, thinking she'd slept through the day and not looked into the box. It had only been forty minutes since Dad had finally gone.

She listened hard as she pulled the box out from under the bed. She'd hear the car, wouldn't she? Clutching the box to her chest, she climbed back under the covers. They didn't offer any safety, but it still felt like it. Didn't monsters go away under the covers?

Swallowing hard, she lifted the lid of the box and set it to hold the pictures. She slid her hands in and lifted the whole stack, flipping them so the oldest were upside down on top; then one by one she turned over the pictures and studied them, warmth spreading inside her. There were others of Sofie with her. In each she got a little older, and Sofie stayed just as beautiful, just as wondrous as she'd imagined.

Photo after photo she studied, until she came to one of Sofie alone. Then another and another. These were taken from farther away. She frowned, turning them over in a hurry to find what she suddenly guessed she wouldn't. Her heart ached. She wasn't with Sofie in any more of the pictures.

It must be when Sofie went away, but then why did Daddy still have pictures? They went on and on, almost all of them on the same street or in front of a church with two towers. Sofie didn't face the camera, or else she was so fuzzy it was hard to tell.

Then came some that looked like the pictures Dad took now with his new digital camera, and they were automatically dated. There were a few of Sofie in a crowded room and the date was last year. Last year? She shook her head. It must not be Sofie. It couldn't be. But the next was more recent still, only a couple months ago.

And then she remembered he'd gone to find her after their phone call. Daddy had known where she was. All this time, he'd gone there and taken pictures. Her throat swelled with tears. Was he seeing Sofie without her?

She chewed her lip. No. Sofie never looked like she knew her picture was being taken. A lot of times it was almost the back of her head. It didn't make sense. She flipped quickly through the rest of the stack, stuck the two that had gotten out of place back into the middle anywhere, and closed the lid.

Waves of anger shook her as she slipped out of bed and went to the kitchen. She climbed onto the counter and shoved the box back onto the shelf. But her hand touched something else. Another box. More pictures?

Before she could grab it, a sound nearly sent her stomach through her throat. A key opening the front door. *Daddy.* She closed the cabinet and slid one leg down, then scrambled to the floor and looked frantically for some reason to be there. She groped for a glass and hurried over to the sink, praying he wouldn't look inside her with that cold stare.

She had barely made it to the sink when a thin, nervous woman she'd never seen before stopped outside the kitchen.

"Carly?"

She turned. "Who are you?"

"Paula." The woman flashed an anxious smile. "I work with your dad."

Oh right. For the whole week he'd been at the job.

"He asked me to stay with you."

And she'd done it. No doubt he'd given her instructions to report back, but that was how much he cared. She held up the glass. "I needed a drink."

Paula took a canvas bag off her shoulder. "Water might irritate your stomach. I brought 7-Up. And saltines."

Wow. A fairy godmother.

Paula poured her a small glass of soda. "Carbonation soothes an upset stomach. But don't drink it too fast. Just little sips."

"Okay. Thanks." She started back to her room, but paused in the doorway. "Umm . . . just wondering, but how could you leave work?"

"I've been there long enough." She waved a hand. "I can take a sick day."

She'd use a sick day to care for a kid she didn't know? Daddy must have poured it on. "It's nice of you to come, but I'd've been all right." Better. Much better by herself.

"Oh, honey, after all you two have been through? It was the least I could do."

No telling what he'd said. The dead mother for sure. He always started with that. And by the hollow she felt inside, it might be true. He would not have mentioned Sofie; he never did. Because the one good thing that had ever happened to both of them didn't create sympathy.

Carly felt sorry for Paula. Her dad would give her enough to keep her hoping, so he could call on her again and again. But Sofie had been the only one he'd really gotten close to—if the photos told her anything. "I'm going back to bed."

"Okay. Tell me if you need anything."

She lay down, thankful for the reprieve from school, where everyone expected something from her, and from Dad, who expected even more. That woman, Paula, had no idea. But now there was no way could she get into the other box. She'd have to wait for night.

––––––––––

As Star let him into the villa, Matt breathed the savory aroma of coffee and some delectable breakfast that drew him to the kitchen. He found Sofie there with Annie on her lap, sitting across from Lance at the table. The rest of the house seemed quiet, but Elaine and Antonia must have been there somewhere. Did Elaine ever go out?

Her level of disability was severe. With her volatility, she would not function in even the most routine employment situations. Sofie had explained that the tasks they gave her there were an opportunity to participate without any real expectations.

Lance looked up with a friendlier expression than he'd worn last night. "Hungry?"

Matt had hoped he'd ask. "If it's not too much trouble."

When Lance got up, Matt turned his attention to Sofie. She looked tired, but not too ragged. He dropped his gaze to Annie. With two fingers stuffed into her mouth, the toddler watched him with the wariness he'd expected, but when he stooped next to her, she didn't draw away.

"Hey, punkin." He touched the hand her sling held toward him. "Does your arm hurt, or your head?"

Annie just stared.

Sofie stroked her hair. "I called the doctor's office. They said she could have Tylenol."

Lance delivered an individual crock with some kind of baked egg dish that smelled as though it would settle in and hold him from the inside out. Matt thanked him. "This is excellent." As delicious a meal as he'd tasted.

"Thanks." Lance crossed his arms. "So what's the plan?"

Matt looked from him to Sofie and back. "If you're open to keeping Annie while we investigate, I'll go to the office and make the petition."

Lance cocked his head. "I stayed home this morning to sort things out. But I'm working with Rese now." A subtle change came over his features. "Annie's care will fall to Sofie, and I'm not sure that's a good thing." Honest and direct.

"I have other options if—"

"I'll keep her." Sofie tightened her hold. "As long as she needs me."

The fact that Annie wasn't crying for her mother was telling. He guessed she didn't get a lot of positive attention from Vivian, who was either working at the spa or tweaking on meth. Sofie's was probably the softest touch she'd had in a long time.

He wanted to make sure Sofie was okay, but he didn't want to do it in front of Lance—who wasn't. Understandably. If he had considered the parallels before he'd brought Annie over, he might have chosen differently. Or maybe not.

Sofie knew how to say no, had no qualms saying so to him. She could have refused him, but it didn't surprise him she hadn't. Who could resist Annie Price? She had a chunk of his own heart that as a rule he tried not to surrender. He couldn't think of a better place for the little one to weather this storm than here with Sofie, but she still could have said no.

"So." He dabbed his mouth. "I'll swing by later with supplies." The hospital had sent him home with a few diapers, but she'd need more. Maybe a stuffed animal or something to cheer her up. At two she'd no longer be on baby food, but perhaps some toddler-friendly snacks.

"Okay." Sofie smiled. "Come for lunch." Seemingly on the same wavelength, she added, "Macaroni and cheese."

"Sounds good." He stood up and stroked Annie's cheek with one finger. "Be a good girl."

She said nothing, only burrowed a little closer.

He straightened. "Later, then. Thanks."

Surprisingly, Lance pulled on a leather jacket and walked him out. Not surprisingly, he didn't prevaricate. "My sister's a beautiful woman inside and out. I understand your feelings for her, but . . ." He took his Harley keys from his pocket. "You hurt her, I'll rip your heart out."

Matt did a double take before Lance grinned, then walked off toward the bike. A joke. It had been a mob-style joke delivered in a Bronx accent, but he'd only half convinced himself of that when the Road King roared to life and Lance raised a hand in passing. Yeah. A joke.

Annie hadn't said anything all morning, not one word, only whimpers when she wanted something and little grunts when she didn't. Nothing like Carly, whose vocabulary at two had caught people's notice wherever they went, who had vocalized while dropping off to sleep such things as, "Sofie, what does precocious mean?"

Annie had just turned two, a stage that seemed especially tender. Sofie taped the diaper on, noting the tapering of her soft thighs into her hips, her round belly with the little nub of navel—and the bruises behind one leg and the small of her back. Without thinking, Sofie bent and kissed them, drawing the pain and injustice into herself.

Annie's arms came around her and she lifted the child, pressing her to her breast until their heartbeats met. "You are loved. You are beautiful. You are a child of God." Those were the words Nonna had spoken to every one of them, every time she'd held them close.

Annie reached and Sofie picked up the flannel that had comforted Diego not so long ago, tucking it between them in a soft mound that molded to their shapes. Annie plugged her fingers into her mouth, and Sofie breathed the scent of her shampooed hair. She had bathed her in the sink, careful not to wet the cast.

She carried her over to Nonna, waiting in the overstuffed chair in the corner by the stove, but Annie would not release the hold on her neck. Sofie had never known a tyke to refuse Nonna's grandmotherly care. Maybe it was too much for the child to absorb another pair of arms, another lap.

"You sit." Nonna pushed herself up. "I'll cook."

An outsider might be appalled by a ninety-one-year-old woman giving up her seat, but Sofie obeyed, knowing Nonna chose to fill her remaining days in the same way she'd filled her others. While Annie became a limp weight on her chest, she watched Nonna boil macaroni, salt, and pepper and set it aside. She made a white sauce into which she dumped freshly shredded cheddar and farmer cheese, stirring until it pulled like shiny golden velvet from the spoon, then layered it all into a buttered baking dish and sprinkled the top with Parmesan, thyme, and rosemary.

Slowly, she slid it into the oven, then straightened and reached for her cane. "I'll rest now," she said and headed for the back door.

Sofie mouthed a thank-you as Annie pressed closer in her sleep, one hand clinging to the collar of her shirt. She rested her chin on the child's head and closed her eyes. Last night had been difficult, but Annie showed no dizziness or disorientation today. In her wordless way, she had communicated her needs.

Sofie kissed her soft, fair hair, then let the drowsiness overtake her. The next thing she knew, someone was touching her shoulder, and she opened her eyes to Matt.

"Hi." He smiled. "I didn't want to startle you."

"Hi," she whispered over Annie's head.

"Brought some things." He set a couple bags on the table. "Diapers. Snacks. What smells so good?"

She glanced toward the oven. "Mac and cheese. Nonna's."

He feigned a long Irish sigh. "Think she'd marry me?"

Sofie laughed—which woke Annie, who looked at Matt and started crying. Some men would back off, leave the crying tot to her, but he crouched down to render his height nonthreatening. "Hey, punkin. Got you some animal crackers. You like them?"

Sofie's stomach squeezed. They'd been Carly's favorite. She used to empty the box for her and lay the animals out in a line like a parade. She would name each creature and make its sound—inventing something for the rhino and giraffe. Then Carly would pop the cookie into her mouth with a smile of complete joy.

He pulled a box from the bag and made a production of opening it in front of her, unfolding the paper lining and pulling it apart. "What's in here?"

Annie leaned. Matt reached in and held up a monkey. Sofie heard its noise in her head but refrained from making it aloud. This was Matt's show. Annie took the cracker and sucked its head, staring at him.

He stood back up. "How's she been?"

"Sleepy. Probably stress and Tylenol. But I think the concussion's better. She doesn't seem confused or disoriented—only . . . quiet."

"Star said you got some rest."

She must have come and gone without disturbing them. "Ever sit with a sleeping child in your lap?"

He smiled, then sobered. "Here's the thing. The dad's pulling strings, says he's tired of being harassed by our department."

"Good connections?"

"Good enough."

"What about the hospital?"

"He's not denying Annie took a tumble, but he claims there's no way it was anything more than an accident. The ER doc says her injuries are consistent with a fall down stairs and someone grabbing to catch her."

"Her mother's drug record?"

He shook his head. "Irrelevant. No one drew blood last night."

Sofie swallowed. "So you're taking her?"

"I'm waiting to hear."

"If the parents told them all that last night, why did the police call you?"

"Because of previous incidents. I had to be informed."

Sofie frowned. "They've done this before?"

Matt nodded. "We've removed her and her siblings twice."

She pressed her fingertips to her forehead. "And I'm supposed to let her go back to that?"

"If that's how the judge rules."

An acid burn climbed her throat. "Then you shouldn't have brought her."

"We have to strike a balance, Sofie. Sometimes people need help. Sometimes they get it." His doubt hung as thickly as hers. "Parental rights are constitutionally protected."

"Where are the other children?"

"Home. There haven't been signs of abuse on any but Annie.

Possible neglect; hunger, fear, but hey, they're all one happy family." His voice grew so thick, she searched his eyes.

"Will she be okay?"

"Ask your brother the prophet, if he's not too busy tearing out
my heart."

Sofie raised her brows. "Something I should know?"

"Nah. Just a little man-to-man talk."

"Matt—"

"Doesn't matter. I don't intend to hurt you."

But people did hurt each other, even precious ones like Annie.
Like Carly. People who had the power to hurt the most had the
most responsibility not to. And yet they did. "Would you mind
taking her for a minute?"

"Sure." He eased Annie into his arms, and this time she didn't
protest. Animal crackers were amazing things.

"I'll be right back." She used the bathroom, washed and patted her face with a cool washcloth, letting the sorrow slip away,
then rejoined Matt in the kitchen. The timer went off and she
removed the macaroni from the oven. As it set, she sliced some
tomatoes and sprinkled them with fresh minced basil from the
garden that Lance protected well enough it stayed green and
savory all year.

While Matt walked around the room with Annie perched in
his arms, Star came down humming, and Elaine followed, reciting
single words. "Explain. Refrain. Sustain."

Sofie glanced at Matt. Annie had a grip on the finger with
which he tapped her tummy, then her nose, then her kneecap.
Her smile melted them all.

Walking Annie, Matt's thoughts went a direction he hadn't
intended. He was thirty-two years old. His job was getting to
him, his past churning up in a way it never had before. He had
kept previous relationships superficial, but there was nothing
lightweight in his growing feelings for Sofie. And holding Annie
triggered paternal instincts that alarmed him.

He hadn't consciously decided not to reproduce, but he'd kept the possibility so far at bay the yearning caught him now by surprise. He had committed himself to the welfare of children in a big and general sense. But to create one of his own, to pass on a part of himself, to take on the task he watched people botch with sickening regularity, that was terrifying. So why did holding Annie make him wonder what a child of his and Sofie's might be like? Imagining Sofie's features or his own on a little one he came home to every night was shaky ground.

Antonia came in, leaning on her cane. She gave him a glance, then took her place at the table. These people, this place, had impacted him. The faith that underlay everything they did looked more like the real thing than anything he'd seen, and knowing them, even such a short time, had awakened things he'd maybe never felt. The way they cared for each other made him want to do better, be better.

Tax collectors and prostitutes had probably felt that way, hanging around Jesus and His disciples. They've got something. It looks good. We want the same. Did he?

Sofie set down the steaming pan of gooey mac and cheese. He hadn't known it could be made from scratch. While he rarely ate out of a box, his normal routine was to throw stuff in the slow cooker before he went to work, add a salad or fruit, and call it dinner.

He boosted Annie up on a couple of phone books. She dug into her cooled macaroni with a spoon and her fingers. He used a fork, but his first bite brought an irrepressible groan. Antonia smiled. Nothing new to her, he assumed, but she still seemed to appreciate his reaction.

Without Lance the meal had a different tenor, but he didn't feel awkward as the only man. They were only people sharing a meal, sharing a moment he could tuck away like a precious keepsake. Afterward, he helped everyone clear, wash, and put away, while Nonna held Annie in the big stuffed chair.

"Put the green with the green," Elaine told him as he scooped macaroni into a container to take with him. "Very important."

"Psychological tests," Sofie murmured as she passed by. "IQ

or deductive reasoning, I'd guess. That particular battery seems to have stuck."

He smiled at Elaine. "Okay. Thanks."

"They're always watching."

He nodded. "I'll be careful."

When they'd finished cleaning up, Sofie walked him out. "Thank you for coming by."

"It's better than anything else I'd be doing. But is this keeping you from things?"

"Nothing that matters." She took his hands. "Right now Annie needs to be loved—intensely."

"I knew that's what she'd get here."

"I didn't mean it before, when I said you shouldn't have brought her. I just don't want to think of her being hurt or frightened. I had such a magical childhood, I wish . . . I know it's not reality to expect that for everyone."

"Not yet." Maybe in the new creation Lance had described, a world set right, ruled justly. But for now, "We can only do what we can do."

Sofie raised up on her toes and kissed him. "Go save the world, Superman."

CHAPTER TWENTY-EIGHT

Carly waited long past the point she was sure Dad had fallen asleep. Did she dare press her luck two nights in a row? She'd gone back to bed after Paula came, exhausted from the strain of trying to figure things out. But just as she had been about to fall asleep, a thought had stabbed her like a knife. If the first box was full of Sofie, could the other hold her mother?

Her stomach still ached with the thought. She had to know. He hadn't moved the boxes the first time, but he could anytime. Then she'd have to find them again, or worse, never see inside the second one. She pushed herself up in bed. She had to. She could say she was hungry. She'd hardly eaten all day because of the weirdness and pretending she was sick. He'd believe she'd gotten hungry.

She eased her bedroom door open and listened. Daddy's snores were soft and uneven. Was he faking? She gulped her fear and moved into the hall. He had let Paula stay for dinner, but it was too soon to keep her overnight. He'd have her help him out a lot more before he let her think it was serious.

She slid against the wall until she was across from his door. He never closed it. His snores ended in a soft snort. She froze. Did he feel her there? She couldn't see his eyes in the dark. Her heart pounded. He could be looking right at her. *Move.* She came off the wall and walked softly but normally to the kitchen.

She couldn't look sneaky. He'd see it right off. He'd know. *He'll know anyway!* She had to risk it, had to see inside that box. She didn't miss her mother like she missed Sofie. Duh. She'd never known her. But she'd like to know what she looked like. There was not one picture anywhere of her.

She pressed her palms to the counter, sprang up and banged her knee. She sucked back the cry, squeezing her face tight as pain spread, then lessened. She let herself down. She hadn't yelled, but he might have heard her bump. She went and stood next to the refrigerator. If she heard him, she'd open its door.

Silence, and more snores she could barely hear. She edged back to the counter, carefully pulled herself up. Her knee hurt, especially when she knelt on it. She swung open the cabinet door and almost lost her balance. Then she stood up and reached into the top shelf.

She had convinced herself they wouldn't be there, that he'd have read her mind over dinner and known what she planned. But they were. She felt the one she'd put back, then reached over for the other. Her hand froze at a sound that came from down the hall.

She dropped into a crouch, but not off the counter. The snores came louder, almost as loud as the pounding of her heart. She straightened, grabbed the box, and lowered it to the counter. She slid off and landed on her tiptoes. Clutching the box, she crept back to her room.

A second sick day would not happen, and she didn't have the nerve to look at them now. Carefully, she buried the box in the bottom of her backpack. Maybe during recess . . .

She climbed into bed and actually slept, dreaming of different women she kept asking, "Are you my mother?" Daddy was relieved the next morning when she got ready for school with no hint of stomach trouble. She had important plans.

It seemed forever before she finally got the chance. They weren't allowed to go out to the parts of the playground near the street, but she'd located a gully by a couple trees just past the basketball court where she could crouch down and look at the pictures. She glanced over her shoulder, then trotted down and slid the pack from her shoulder.

No one was falling over themselves to play with her. She'd come into the school after all the friendships were made, and it wasn't like she tried. So no one came running over to ask what was in the box. No one noticed at all.

Even so, she stayed on guard. Like she could ever let down and relax. Like she ever stopped worrying. Her stomach hurt. She ignored it, set the box on the ground and opened the lid. The top picture was of her, just outside this school, talking to the principal. Must have been that first day after Dad dropped her off.

She put the picture on the lid and picked up the next. Her again. Was that what filled the box? Nothing wrong with Daddy taking pictures of her, except they weren't the kind of pictures he'd put in an album. She hadn't known they were being taken, didn't even seem to be the point of the picture. It was the people she talked to and smiled at that he was more interested in photographing.

People she'd liked, people who had mattered. And these were labeled with dates and names. But not like *Carly, age six, with her friend Sandi.* They said *Gutter Boy, Future Trash, Brown-Nose.* On the ones with teachers snapped on various playgrounds were names like *Know-It-All, Conniving Hag,* and worse names that made her blush, names Daddy wouldn't think she knew.

She studied a picture of the school counselor, Ms. Baker, walking out of the school. Ms. Baker had suggested counseling for stress she had picked up on in third grade. It was only Ms. Baker in that picture, and she looked shocked and upset. On the back, Carly read one of the nastier names, and the next picture showed a car with the tires slashed.

She gulped. The pictures went on and on. Mixed in were shots of icy stairs, ambulances . . . dead pets. She lunged up and heaved, her stomach a hard knot as it expelled everything she'd eaten. She threw the pictures back into the box and shoved it deep inside her pack.

She almost stood up, then realized he could be out there with his camera, taking pictures of her betraying him. Her whole body shook. What was she going to do? Her stomach heaved every time her mind replayed the picture of Drew's dog. She hadn't wanted to believe it. She had taken Daddy's present and pretended she didn't know what happened to her friend's dog. Her face flushed with shame.

"Carly?"

She looked up into the playground teacher's eyes. "I think I'm still sick."

The teacher, whose name she didn't know and didn't want to, looked at the evidence. "Come with me. I'll take you to the nurse."

She staggered, and it wasn't pretending. The woman put an arm around her shoulders. "Honey, when you're feeling bad, you should tell someone."

Carly nodded. The nurse would know she'd missed school yesterday. They'd believe her. As bad as she felt, it might be true. But they'd call Dad. He'd come. How could she look at him?

They reached the nurse's office. She studied the older woman's face and said, "My dad's in meetings today. He said I had to call my caregiver if anything came up."

"Is she on the approved list?"

"Uh-huh." Yeah, right. I'm not allowed to see her, but Daddy gets to all the time.

"Okay. You have that number?"

"In my phone. Can I use it?" At the nod, she took it out of her pack. They didn't allow kids to use cell phones during the day, but it wasn't against the rules to have it. And this was a health situation. Her throat had dried out like an old hollow stick and tasted like barf. Tears stung her eyes, but she didn't let them fall. She picked the entry from her list and pressed Talk. *Please answer.*

"Hello?"

"Um, Sofie?"

A student came in with a cut hand and the nurse moved over to tend to him.

"Carly, I'm so glad you called. I've tried—"

"I'm sick at school and . . . can you come get me?"

The pause was too long. Maybe she didn't want to. Maybe she didn't care. Had Dad ruined her for Sofie too?

"Honey, I don't know where you are, but I'm in California."

The weight of disappointment crushed her. "California?"

"Carly, are you in trouble? Is that why you didn't call your dad?"

She gulped. "Yes."

"Is he the trouble?"

"Yes."

"You need to tell someone at the school—"

"They won't believe me. He tells them I lie. They *always* believe him."

"Is there someone you can trust? Anyone you can go to?"

He'd made sure there was no one, scared them or hurt them, or made them believe she was bad. Who could she—Grandma Beth. She might not love her enough to give Daddy money, but she wasn't asking for money. "I could try my grandma."

Sofie's relief was obvious. "Okay. See if she can come get you. Call me either way." Grandma Beth wasn't in her phone. She had to dial information and ask for the city, then give them her name. She wrote the number on a scrap of paper, then looked at the nurse, busy with blood and Band-Aids.

Carly touched the number pads. Her grandma might say, "Sorry, you're not reason enough," but when her voice came on with a brusque "Hello?" Carly said, "Grandma, can you help me?"

Sofie closed the phone, overwhelmed with sorrow. Six years she had stayed in the neighborhood waiting for something she thought would never happen. Now it had, and she was too far away to help. She grabbed her phone as it rang again, but it wasn't Carly, it was Matt.

"Sofie, I'm sorry. I have bad news."

Bad news? She shook herself. "What news?"

"The judge has released Annie to her family. My supervisor's going to moderate, and they'll all find a solution together." His voice was tight, speaking the words but not buying them. "We'll be over in about ten minutes."

"Okay." She went out to the garden, where Star had amazingly gotten Annie laughing and playing. Elaine watched from the bench with a faraway look that might have been memories of her own little girl, though Rese was not blonde and fair.

"I hate to interrupt, but they're coming for Annie."

"Blast them for fools." Star held the one-legged pose as though she'd been frozen, then came stiffly to rest like a doll. Annie laughed. Such a magical sound.

"Come on, sweetheart. Let's get you changed and ready."

By the time they arrived, Sofie had Annie waiting with the stuffed bunny Matt had brought. She kissed the child's head and whispered through a throat that felt parched, "You are loved. You are beautiful. You are a child of God."

Annie raised her face and gave her a sweet kiss right on the mouth. Tears stung. She handed the toddler to Gail, a portly fortyish woman who'd been around this block before. Still, Sofie said, "If there's anything else I can do . . ."

Gail nodded. "Let's make this as smooth a transition as we can."

Sofie tucked the child into the car seat in Matt's Pathfinder, but he surprised them both by handing Gail the keys. "You go ahead. Swing back when you've delivered her."

"You're not on board?"

"It's your call."

"It's Judge Harrel's call. Personal feelings can't interfere with our decisions."

Matt nodded. "See you when you get back."

Her mouth formed a tight line. Annie's cries came from the car. When had she started to cry? Sofie pressed her hands to her head, loss overwhelming her as they drove away.

Matt caught and pulled her close. "Lance was right. I shouldn't have done this."

The two situations melded in her mind and she moaned, "Carly."

He stroked her hair. "That's not Carly, Sofie. It's Annie Price."

She shook her head. "Carly called. She's in trouble."

He moved his head back and studied her.

"I was waiting to hear back when you called."

"But you haven't?"

She shook her head. She should have. What if that call for help was the last she ever heard from her little girl? "She wanted me to pick her up at school, and she couldn't call Eric."

"That's hardly an emergency."

"She couldn't call Eric because something's wrong." It had been there in Carly's voice. Something raw. "I need to go."

"Sofie."

"I should never have left New York." She pulled away and went inside. "I'd have been there when she needed me."

"You didn't even know she was still in the state." He followed her inside without an invitation. "At least talk to Lance. See what he says."

She climbed the stairs. It didn't matter what Lance or anyone said. Carly's call was not a simple request for a ride home from school. Something had happened that was bigger than she could face alone. Sofie pulled one of her suitcases from the closet, hardly noticing which clothes she folded in.

"You have no legal recourse."

"I know where her grandmother lives." If Carly had gotten through, if Beth had picked her up, maybe, just maybe, she'd see her little girl again.

Expelling a breath, he raised and dropped his hands. "Okay. If you're set on this, I'll take you to the airport."

"That would be nice. Thanks." She flicked him a grateful glance.

"We'll stop by my place first. I'm going with you."

"What?" She scooped her cosmetics into a bag and straightened. "Why?"

"Maybe I can work with CPS out there."

"But you have all this business with Annie."

"She's Gail's responsibility now. Frankly some distance will be good."

Sofie looked for an argument, but if he could help her with Carly, she'd be so grateful. And more than that, she realized. "You can leave your car with Gail. We'll take my Neon."

He opened his phone and got the number for the airline, asked for a direct flight to LaGuardia. Two tickets. Family emergency.

"She should be here any minute," Carly told the nurse, pretending it was her make-believe caregiver on the way.

"You have to wait here until you're signed out." The nurse explained school policy, but what good were policies that gave all the power to adults who could do things like . . .

She gripped her belly. "My stomach hurts. I need to go to the bathroom."

"Okay. Let me give you the pass." She handed her the red cardboard cross that was the health pass, easily recognized through classroom doors so kids didn't get hassled on their way to throw up. Carly scooped up her backpack, hurried out, and headed for the bathroom, then passed it and went out the side door. She couldn't let grandma sign her out. Even if she was on the people-approved-to-pick-up-kids list—and she wouldn't be—even if they didn't double check, and they might not, if Grandma signed the sheet, Daddy would know. Carly hurried around to the front and ducked into a brick alcove to wait for her grandma.

After a few minutes, a car pulled up, the same silver car Grandma had driven before with the fuzzy steering wheel cover. Carly hung her pack over her shoulder and hurried over. Her grandma took a long look, then popped the locks and Carly climbed in.

Tears clogged her throat. "Thank you, Grandma."

"Do you need to go to a doctor?"

She shook her head. Had she really thought she was sick? But then, it was Sofie who had understood. "Can I please go to your house? I have to show you something." Before she lost her courage.

Grandma Beth reached over and squeezed her hand. "Okay, honey. I'm glad you called."

They drove in silence, but Carly couldn't help stealing glances. It had been at least three years since she'd seen her grandma, though she didn't look that different. Same blond hair, cut round on her head, same glasses, or maybe not. She didn't look mad. She might be sad. What would she think when she saw the pictures? What if she told Daddy?

Carly could not even think how awful that would be. Maybe this was a mistake. But what was she going to do? It took so long to get through the traffic to Grandma's house that her stomach was in a knot. One fingernail had started bleeding, and she hadn't even realized she was biting them. The box felt like lead in her lap. Why had she thought she could let anyone see?

She couldn't. It was too awful. And if Daddy knew she'd shown someone . . . Grandma didn't care about her. Why should she trust her with something this big? Oh, why wasn't Sofie here?

When they pulled into the garage, Carly started to leave her backpack in the car, but her grandma said, "Don't forget your bag."

Okay, so she'd bring it in. She slung the strap over her shoulder. The house was bigger and nicer than anything she and Dad had ever lived in. Soft carpets, and the yellow and cream furniture looked new. Everything was in place, but not the way Daddy kept his things with everything practically labeled. Grandma's house looked happy and comfortable.

They went into the kitchen, and Grandma took out a package of fig bars and poured her a glass of milk. She stepped back. "So let me look at you."

Carly shrugged. "It's just me."

"Eleven now?"

"Mm-hmm."

"I sent a card. It had twenty dollars inside. I don't suppose you got it."

Carly shook her head. Dad had taken her to a fancy place and worn a suit. She'd ordered spaghetti. He'd tried to get her to have something she couldn't even pronounce. Then he'd said it's your birthday, have whatever you want, and he'd looked like he wanted to give her the world. The spaghetti was . . . spaghetti.

Her grandma cupped her face and raised it. "You have your father's eyes."

She gulped, not sure that was a compliment. Everyone gushed over Daddy's eyes, but they didn't see them when they got scary. "Is that good?"

Grandma Beth smiled. "You've always been good."

Not a direct answer, but it made her feel better. She bit into a fig bar, suddenly hungry. The milk was cold and fresh. Maybe everything tasted better in her grandma's blue and yellow kitchen.

Grandma's mouth gathered into fine lines. "How is he?"

The cookie stuck in her throat. She choked down the rest of the milk, miserable again. "Um . . . fine."

Grandma sat back. "I haven't lived all these years to fall for that."

Heat crawled into her face. Carly wished she hadn't eaten the cookies.

"Honey, you didn't call me from school because everything was fine. And as glad as I am that you did, I'd like to know what we're up against."

Carly saw the warmth in her grandma's face, and the concern. "I found something. A box full of pictures . . . of Sofie. A lot of them were taken when she didn't know it." After seeing what was in the other box, she was pretty sure of that. "I think he's been watching her."

Grandma's brows raised. "They split up six years ago. Longer than they were together."

"I know. But I know he's seen her because I saw the pictures.

And he told me he went to see her and she wasn't there. He was really upset."

"And that's why you called me?"

Her stomach turned. "No. I . . ." She wrapped her arms around herself. "I found another box."

They sat a long moment in silence, both knowing, she guessed, that once she brought it out, everything would be different. She had the crazy thought that if she had kept it to herself, put it back in the cabinet with no one knowing, it wouldn't be true. He'd just be the dad who loved her too much. Not . . .

"What was in the other box?"

"I'll show you." With leaden fingers, she reached in and pulled it from her pack, set it on the table.

Grandma was more confused than anything else at first. "Who are these people?"

"My friends and teachers. Some of my friends' parents."

She got to the picture of the car, then more people, then the icy stairs Mrs. Warren had fallen down when the rest of the sidewalks were dry. The ambulance. The pets. Grandma pressed a hand to her forehead. "Did you know this was happening?"

"Nobody knows. They think I'm the bad one, that I lie and steal things. But I don't." Grandma had to believe that. "Except I did lie about being sick, and I did take the box. But I meant to put it back until . . ." She'd seen the awful things it held.

"When you were here that last time, I had two little dogs."

She suddenly remembered them. Little tan and gray things that yapped and stood on their hind legs for a biscuit.

Grandma's eyes teared. Her hand slid down to her mouth. "I didn't want to believe . . ."

Carly gripped her stomach. "No."

The phone rang. They stared at it. Dad must have realized she wasn't at school. Maybe the nurse had called to say she'd disappeared. The whole place could be in a panic. Lockdown. Maybe even police.

Grandma Beth picked up the phone. "Yes?"

Carly held her breath.

"Yes, she did. I told her you were not getting more money from me." A pause, then a throaty, "No. She's not." She hung up, turned with a hand at her throat. "Now we're both in trouble."

CHAPTER TWENTY-NINE

Lance stood up from the final knob he'd installed in the ladies' powder room door and pressed his hands to his lower back. All the crew had gone home, including Brad. Try as he might, he could not see the reason he and Rese had not.

"Lance—"

He shook his head. "We're done."

"Are you the boss now?" she asked, sitting back on her heels.

He reached down and raised her to her feet. "Yep."

She brought her hands to her hips. "Says who?"

"Says I. In case you haven't noticed, there's no one left to impress. You have proved you can work longer, harder, and better than any man standing. Me included."

She raised her chin. "I'm not proving anything."

"Get-outta-here. I know."

"No you don't."

He hung his hands on his own hips. "Okay, then what are we still doing here?"

"We're . . . I . . . there's something I want to tell you."

"And it couldn't happen in the truck on the drive home because . . ."

"I didn't think of that."

"Well. Now that—"

"Besides, I just want to say it."

It took a lot to rattle her, but she looked anything but comfortable. And if she'd wanted to say it, why hadn't she? "Okay."

She looked away. "After you broke up with me—"

"I didn't—"

"Don't say it, Lance. You told me we couldn't be together, and I couldn't run the inn without you, so I decided to go to work with Brad, and I needed to know that—He'd made a comment about . . . a crush, and I had to know whether . . ."

"You're killing me, Rese. Say it before my mind runs off with the wrong idea."

"I kissed him."

His heart thumped. "You kissed Brad or the other way around?"

"It got . . . mutual. Then he realized he didn't want to, and I hadn't wanted to anyway, so—"

"You didn't want to but you did?"

"I had to know he only wanted a business partnership, since mixing business and personal with you had been a big mistake." She looked into his face. "Brad thought you should know."

"He did?"

"He said it was the kind of thing that could come out someday and cause problems."

Lance tipped his head. "If not for that, were you ever going to tell me?"

"I'd forgotten about it."

He raised his brows, doubting by half she'd done anything of the kind.

"I mean it, Lance. I'd learned what I needed to, and his kiss did not burrow into my heart and soul and thoughts and take over everything like yours do. That's all there was to it."

"Not much of a kisser, huh?"

She glared. "It just didn't mean anything."

He slid his fingers into the soft, short hair at her nape. "Thanks for telling me."

"So, you're okay?"

"I'll be reestablishing my territory."

She flushed. "I'm sure you will."

But before he could, his phone rang. He gave serious thought to throwing it out the window, but it was the home number, so he answered. "What's up?"

Star said, "Where are you guys?"

"Just finishing. Why?"

"Annie's gone back to her miserable parents."

"How's Sofie taking it?"

Star's pause didn't sound good. "She's gone."

His heart hit his ribs like a hammer. "What?"

"Carly called her, and she went to New York."

"When?"

"Earlier. She went with Matt."

"With Matt? Are you sure?"

"I gave his supervisor the message."

"Thanks, Star. We're on our way." He hung up, tension knotting his spine as he told Rese what had happened. "I have to—"

"No." She crossed her arms.

"Rese." She hadn't even heard him yet.

"Matt's there."

"Yeah, but Matt—"

"I'm sorry, Lance. But if you go back to solve another family crisis, then stay there."

His gut clenched. "Rese, don't do this."

"*You* don't do it. Because I can't. Not again." Her hands clenched. "I know you think I'm being unreasonable."

He shook his head. "I don't think that." The last time he'd put his family first it had almost destroyed their future. The fact that she'd been willing to try again meant more than he could express, but still. He saw her need in her eyes. She wouldn't express it that way, but she'd been wounded. Badly.

Lord. Fear for Sofie formed a dull throb, but he'd have to trust someone else to step up for her, someone who didn't even know God was there. *You know what you're asking? Of course you do.* He dropped his forehead to Rese's. "Okay."

Her breath made a sharp escape. "Okay?"

"I'm not going to do something you ask me not to." Her disbelief revealed the damage still there. Her chest rose and fell with emotion, and he drew her into his arms. She'd been tense already over the thing with Brad. Now was not the time to press her—if there ever was a time.

"Come on." He exerted the effort it took not to try to change her mind. "Let's go home."

The cab stopped outside the two-story house in the upscale neighborhood north of the Bronx. A light illuminated the porch, but the rest of the house was dark like its neighbors. Sofie sagged. "She's asleep."

He considered their options, but it was Sofie's call. "You want to wake her?"

She pressed her fingers to her eyes. "I don't know for sure that Carly's grandma has her."

They'd come an awfully long way on that assumption, east through three time zones and not a few air miles, but maybe morning would be a better time to find out what was happening. Sofie gave the driver a different address.

They left the suburb and headed south past the botanical gardens through some less-than-prime real estate to an urban neighborhood. When the cab stopped once more, Matt climbed out in front of a four-story building, brick with white decorative elements. The sunken first floor appeared to hold a restaurant, but a sign in the window said Closed Indefinitely.

Sofie joined him on the sidewalk as the cabbie set their two bags down. She paid the fare, and Matt picked up their bags, checking both ways over his shoulders. This was her place? A street he wouldn't like to walk in the dark? Not what he'd pictured.

Sofie touched his arm. "If Momma wakes up, don't mention Carly."

"What's the cover story?"

"I'll figure that out if we have to."

The building was quiet as she unlocked the door and entered the long hallway.

He followed curiously. "Neat old place. Got a cellar?"

She smiled. "Yes. But it only holds an ancient furnace and a sump pump."

They climbed two flights of dim stairs and stopped in the hall, where two doors stood opposite one another near the front of the building. "I'll see if you can stay with Chaz and Rico tonight." She tapped one of the doors. "My apartment's across the hall, but if I let you have Nonna's room, Momma will have a heart attack."

"Not a good first impression." He had certainly not planned to meet her family at this point. But he hadn't intended any of this. With Cassinia still out, his supervisor was not enthusiastic over his emergency departure. But he'd been rethinking his career and every other element of his life. Were the decisions he'd made still valid? This break might be as much for him as Sofie. But then he watched her biting her lip and admitted it was all about Sofie.

The door opened and a tall black man with a generous smile welcomed them. "Hello, Sofie." He wore a tuxedo, and in response to Matt's curiosity said, "I only just got home from work."

Matt nodded. An upscale restaurant, he'd guess.

"Chaz, this is Matt Hammond."

"Hello."

Matt shook a hand equal to his in size.

Sofie said, "I was wondering if he could stay the night with you and Rico."

"Rico has moved into Lance's room, but there is a bed available in mine." He turned his warm gaze on him. "You are welcome to it." Then to Sofie, "Momma will be glad to see you."

She went inside. "How are you, Chaz?"

"Well. Always well. And you?"

She gave him a half-hearted smile, not hiding from this gentle giant whose accent Matt put somewhere in the Caribbean.

The apartment had a long front room with a small kitchenette, two bedrooms, and a bath at the back. Musical equipment took up much of the main room. Someone could do some serious jamming with all that.

"Rico's out running sound for a show. He'll be late." Chaz turned. "Would you like something to drink? Some tea?"

"That would be nice," Sofie said.

Chaz put a kettle on the hot plate. "So." He motioned them to the table by the front window, filled with speckled city night. "To what do we owe this visit? Or are you back now?"

She looked into his face. "I'm here for Carly."

So the cover story didn't apply to Chaz. Matt watched the interplay as she told him about the phone call from Carly and her certainty that something was wrong.

Chaz listened with a focused sympathy, then said, "Maybe she had an argument with her father."

Matt sat back. He'd suggested the same, but Sofie shook her head now as she had then. "She wouldn't argue with Eric. That's not . . ." Tears welled in her eyes. "Something's wrong. I heard it in her voice."

She seemed to have an uncanny link to the child. Or else she wished she had. The situation with Annie could have heightened the effect of Carly's call in a way that not even the child intended. But that's what they needed to find out. He had come to support Sofie, but it went deeper than that. She might believe Eric harmless, but something in his gut said otherwise.

———

Sofie opened her eyes in the apartment she'd shared with Nonna since she had begun the road back from the brink of death. Carly was part of before, and the doctors would strongly caution her. But she would not ignore the child's cry. A tenuous connection had been reestablished, and not by her. She had no choice but to respond.

She rose and showered and went across the hall. Matt was

awake, Chaz informed her from the table where he sat with his Bible open.

"In the shower," he added.

She sat down by him to wait, playing yesterday's call over and over in her head. Carly had said her dad was the trouble, but what did that mean? Eric would never raise a hand to her. She was the outward projection of himself, and he protected himself at all cost. So why did Carly's call leave such an awful foreboding?

"Would you like to pray?"

She raised her eyes to Chaz, realizing she'd chewed her lip raw. "Yes."

Chaz reached over and took her hands. "Heavenly Father, all things are in your control. Let us be instruments of your will."

She swallowed. "Please protect Carly wherever she is, and . . . please let me see her. Don't punish us further for my mistakes."

Chaz tightened his hold. "In your mercy grant us all we ask. Amen."

She opened her eyes. Matt stood behind Chaz in khakis and a black cotton sweater with a cautious but respectful expression. Chaz offered them tea, but she stood up. "We'll get coffee out."

Matt preferred it. She hoped he had slept better than she, but his eyes suggested not. Espresso sounded good.

As they headed for the door, Rico came in. Having run sound for a show, he'd probably also torn down and loaded the equipment—and partied. He seemed relatively sober and highly energized.

"¿Quetal? Sofie." He looked both surprised and pleased.

"Hi, Rico. This is Matt." Matt towered over the wiry Puerto Rican with black hair that hung past his shoulders and rings in both ears. She could almost hear the wheels turning in his head. This was the prophet's best friend?

But Matt had laid off the sarcasm. He'd seemed more open and less antagonistic to their faith lately, maybe due to his growing feelings. Still, what kind of man would drop everything to help her find Carly?

Eric had controlled every part of their lives—his, hers,

Carly's—but every part eventually came back to him. Matt had the capacity to put her first, and she wasn't sure what to do with that.

She looked up. "Are you ready?"

He nodded. "Sure."

Sofie touched Chaz's shoulder. "If Momma asks, will you let her know I've borrowed her car? I'll explain everything later."

Chaz raised his brows. "She will want to see you."

"She will." It was a minor miracle that they'd gotten this far without Momma's knowledge. But explanations would be painful. One mention of Carly would send Momma spinning, and there was no point until she saw whether something could come of the situation.

If she had overreacted—but her heart said no. God would not torture her with possibilities. Not this possibility. Maybe it was for exactly this that He'd allowed her to hang on.

They stopped and bought coffee and hazelnut biscotti. Mary Cavalla beamed as she passed the cups over the counter. "Nice to see you, Sofie." She sent Matt a curious stare.

"Thank you." Sofie didn't satisfy her curiosity. If it got back to Momma that others had been introduced before her, she'd be heartbroken. Besides, she didn't know what to say. Matt wanted a relationship. He'd made that clear. Until Carly's call, she'd felt herself opening to him in healthy and wonderful ways. Now she didn't know what would happen.

They headed north to Beth Malden's house. No telling what Carly's grandma had been led to believe about her, but it didn't matter, because Carly was there. *Please, God.*

"Worried?" Matt's voice sounded calm, but he was feeling out the situation.

She nodded. "Carly said no one at the school would believe her. That Eric tells them she lies. Why would he do that?"

"To keep her from saying anything." His mouth drew down. "Or maybe she does lie. This whole thing could be a manipula- tion—"

No way. Her little girl was light and sunshine. "She's not like that."

"You said the same about Eric."

"I said he wasn't violent."

"Not even when he's angry?"

"He's never lifted a hand against her. I've never heard him raise his voice." But his ice-cold anger had sent dread coursing through. He could punish her with a glance. Or make her never want to hurt him again.

"Why are we here if he's no threat?"

A valid question. She came to a stop in the light traffic heading away from the city. "Because Carly needs me."

Matt shook his head. "You can't have it both ways."

She sighed. "I need to do this for her. Whether or not Eric is in the wrong, Carly asked for my help. That's all."

"Okay. But I'm not just along for the ride. If I see trouble, I won't step back."

"I wouldn't expect you to."

They passed the Bronx Zoo and the botanical gardens. "We visited Grandma Beth so often after going to the zoo that Carly thought the animals were hers." She smiled at the memory. "Beth was so tickled she didn't correct the misunderstanding. She'd say, 'How did you like my giraffes today?'"

"Would you say she was domineering? Overbearing?"

Sofie shook her head. If he was looking there for an answer to Eric's issues, he was wrong. She turned into the neighborhood. "She didn't like us being together unmarried, but neither did Momma. Sometimes I thought—"

She rounded the corner and gasped. Where the house had been silent the night before, police cars, a fire truck, and an ambulance now blocked the driveway and clogged the street. She veered the Fiat to the curb and flung the door open, running. *No.* Tears stung her eyes.

She rushed up to an officer. "What is it? What happened?"

"Resident was attacked, house burgled."

"What about the child?"

"Don't think there were any kids."

There had to be. Unless Eric had taken Carly before emergency teams arrived. Everything seemed to slow around her. Her own words and motions. "Please, I have to go inside and look."

"You think there's someone else in there?"

"I think there might have been."

"This is a crime scene. The woman was hurt pretty badly."

She didn't have to scour her mind for places Carly might be. She knew. "Please let me look. If Carly's in there . . ."

He called to someone to escort her as Matt came up with her purse and keys. She sent him a silent thanks, then followed a female officer into the house. She went into the cheerful living room, now tumbled and strewn with broken knickknacks. Her feet crunched shards of china as she passed through to the kitchen. Drawers were yanked out, cabinets emptied. None of that mattered. It hardly registered.

Playing hide-and-seek, there was one place Carly had chosen more than any other. Sofie pulled open the closet door, pushed past the mops and brooms and vacuum to the enormous ironing board hanging upright near the back of the space. She tipped it sideways and looked down as time came to a halt.

"I knew you'd come." Carly raised her face from her knees.

Sofie drank in the sight and scent and feel of her little girl. Carly. *Oh, Lord!* Carly. She was no longer an adorable four-year-old, but no flicker of doubt entered her mind. They knew and were known. Pain seared her chest. "Come out, honey. Tell us what happened."

CHAPTER THIRTY

M att had shown his credentials, and even though he was way out of his territory, they allowed him into the kitchen, where Sofie sat with a girl who won his heart the moment he saw her. Golden and spindly like a new foal, she had what he could already tell would be a great beauty. But there was something achingly sad in the eyes she raised to him.

Someone had wrapped her in an afghan, and Sofie had one arm around her shoulders. Carly looked small for eleven. Hair like spun gold. She'd be the last kid he'd pick out to have problems, but he knew it didn't work that way. Dysfunction had no boundaries. Hidden sins no restrictions.

Carly looked from him to Sofie. "That's not your brother."

"My friend, Matt."

Disappointment washed over her face. Had she read more into *friend* than Sofie intended? Did she want Sofie completely to herself? Ah. Maybe she'd hoped for a reconciliation with her dad. Not happening. *Sorry, kiddo.*

The female officer who had shown Sofie in came and sat at the table. Her blended ethnicity formed an attractive, tough exterior, but she gave the girl a soft look. "My name's Peggy Mantero."

"Hi," Carly said.

"So, Carly. Whatchu doin' here?" the woman asked. "Come to see your grandma?"

Carly nodded, but Matt saw immediately that wasn't the whole story. A flush pinkened a swatch across the child's cheeks.

"You do that often?"

She shook her head. "Not for a couple years."

Smart kid. Tell the truth when you can. Neighbors would say they hadn't seen a granddaughter around much.

"Why now?"

Carly swallowed. "Can I talk to Sofie first?"

The cop sat back. "Did you see what happened?"

Carly shook her head. "I heard it."

"I need you to tell me what you heard."

"I will, but . . . I have to talk to Sofie first." The hand on the table trembled.

Technically the officer shouldn't question a child without a parent present. He'd point that out if he had to, but he guessed Officer Mantero knew kids had a thin trigger. Shut them down and it took an awful lot to open them up again.

"Okay." She stood up. "I'll give you a few minutes and come back."

Carly looked as though she wanted him to go too, but Sofie said, "Matt works for Child Protective Services. He takes care of kids in trouble, all kinds of trouble. That's why he came."

Not really, but he let it go.

"I'm not in trouble. I mean I didn't do anything wrong. Or . . . I guess I did. I shouldn't have come here. Now Grandma—"

"This isn't your fault." Sofie looked firmly into the girl's eyes.

"She said we were both in trouble. But I didn't know she'd get hurt." The regret in her voice sent a pang to his chest.

Sofie's voice stayed smooth and calm. "Why were you both in trouble?"

"I ran away, and she told Daddy I wasn't here."

Sofie rubbed her shoulders. "I'm sure you had good reasons."

Did she believe that, and still consider Eric harmless? Maybe. Good kids ran away from good homes. Even in stable families things got blown out of proportion. His gut told him that was not the case this time, but there was still a difference between abusers and controllers. Carly might have been fed up, though not endangered. Then why hadn't she come out when Grandma got hurt? And why had Grandma lied?

Sofie leaned in. "Can you tell me why you ran away?"

Carly brought a black and gray box up from her lap. "I found two of these. The other box was all pictures of you, Sofie. But I don't think you knew they were being taken."

Matt asked softly, "You mean like someone watching her might have taken from a car or something?"

She nodded. "At first they were pictures of us, you and me. But then I wasn't in them anymore. It was only you, and you never smiled for the camera. The last ones had digital dates. They weren't taken very long ago."

He did not want to hear this. "How long?"

Carly shrugged. "I don't remember exactly. A couple months, three, maybe."

"Three months ago someone took Sofie's picture? Without her knowing?"

Carly shrugged again.

Sofie shot him a warning glance. "That's okay, Carly. You don't have to worry about me."

"Daddy said you . . . killed yourself."

Sofie sat back unguarded, something raw in her expression as she unconsciously drew her arms deeper into her sleeves. Had the man actually told his daughter Sofie was dead by her own hand?

"I didn't believe him. But why would he say that?"

Sofie composed herself. "You said that was a different box. What's in this one?"

Carly lifted her chin slowly, her dread obvious. "Other people he watched." Tears sprang to her eyes. "People he hurt."

Matt eased the box from her and lifted the lid. The first photos looked like surveillance on his daughter. Could be an obsessive control disorder, needing to know where she was, with whom, and that she was safe. Then he got to the shots of vandalism and emergency teams, dead animals.

That took it way beyond the pale. Sofie must see that. The names on the back of some of the photos seemed to correlate with the deeds preserved in the following photos. For someone who never raised his voice, Eric certainly expended his rage. Accidents like the icy stairs had obviously caused injury. And they hadn't heard yet what had happened here.

"One of the dogs was my friend Drew's. I think two of the others might have been Grandma's." She put her face in her hands and started to cry as he shoved the pictures back into the box.

Sofie nestled Carly's head against her shoulder. "You were brave to call, Carly. It was the right thing."

"I love my dad." Carly's plaintive voice hurt.

"I know you do." Sofie stroked Carly's golden hair, and he heard the unspoken *so do I.*

What did this guy have that generated that kind of devotion in people he'd victimized? Did men like that exude a scent, some pheromone that interacted with a female's brain chemistry and drew her to the most dangerous of the species? Matt frowned. What made him think he could break that connection when neither of them seemed to want it broken?

He walked away from the table as Officer Peggy Mantero came back. Carly reluctantly left Sofie's embrace when the officer sat down and took a digital voice recorder from her pocket. She turned it on and tapped it, then replayed back the tap.

"This is going to record what you tell me, okay? About what happened here?"

Carly nodded bleakly.

"So go ahead."

"We had just finished the supper dishes when the doorbell rang. Grandma asked if I wanted to talk to my dad, and I said I couldn't. Not yet. So she told me to stay out of sight and went to answer the door."

Matt noted the fairly direct line of sight between the front door and the kitchen. "You knew it was your dad?"

"We were just guessing."

"How come he didn't see you here?"

"I got into the closet."

"You thought it was your dad so you hid in the closet?"

Carly flushed and nodded.

"Then what?"

"Daddy asked Grandma if I was there, and she said, 'Go see for yourself.' He went upstairs and I guess she did too."

"You stayed in the closet?"

Carly looked down at the floor. "I should have gotten out."

Sofie laid a hand on her arm. "No one's saying that. Officer Mantero just wants to make sure she knows what happened."

"That's right, Carly. You might have seen something if you'd gotten out. But if you were in there the whole time you probably just heard things."

Carly gulped back fresh tears. "I heard them talking."

"Talking how? Yelling? Fighting?"

"No . . . Daddy never yells."

Matt met the glance Sofie flashed him before returning her attention to Carly.

"Did your grandma yell? Like, 'Get out of here' or something?"

Carly shook her head. "They talked real quiet. I couldn't hear the words."

"More quietly than we're talking? Maybe low and threatening?"

Carly looked at Sofie, then back. "Sometimes Daddy's scary without—I don't know how to explain it. He doesn't act mad, but I know something bad's going to happen."

"Does he hurt you?"

She shook her head.

Peggy's expression turned skeptical. "He never hurts you, but you hid in a closet?"

Matt shared the skepticism. Surprisingly Carly sent him a pleading glance. As though he could explain something like that. He said, "There are different kinds of hurt. Some are silent."

Carly nodded, tears pooling in her eyes.

"How does he hurt you?"

"He makes people hate me."

"Why would he do that?"

"So he doesn't have to share."

They all sat, silently processing that. Mantero said, "He didn't want to share you with your grandmother? Isn't she his mom?"

"Yeah, but we couldn't see her anymore because she wouldn't give him money."

"Did he need money?" She looked around the ransacked house.

"Sometimes he has a lot and sometimes we have to move."

"Right now?"

"He has a new job. But he gets tired of people and finds reasons to leave so it looks like their fault."

Sofie turned away. That must have struck a chord. He hoped it sank in that whatever had happened wasn't her fault either.

"So he talked to your grandma. Then what?"

Carly drew a jagged breath. "She must have tripped."

"She fell down the stairs?"

He thought of Annie taking a fall with resilient bones and the injury she'd suffered nonetheless. He didn't know how old the grandma was, but even a middle-aged person would not fare well on the long staircase.

Tears slipped down Carly's cheeks. "I heard her yelling and falling."

"What was she yelling?"

"Just . . . yelling." She pressed her hands to her face. "Then she was kind of crying."

"Did your dad call for help?"

"I don't know. He went all over the house opening doors and drawers."

"Looking for money?"

"I thought he was looking for me."

"Did he call for help after he finished searching?"

"I don't know. No one came."

"So then what happened?"

"It got quiet. I waited."

"For what?"

Carly's answer was almost inaudible. "Him to go."

Matt shared a look with Sofie. They'd come by late, and though the house had looked peaceful, an old woman had been lying in pain while a child exhausted by fear huddled in the closet. Why hadn't Carly called for help? Too afraid her father was still inside the house?

Eric had caused his mother bodily harm. Maybe he believed the injured woman would not implicate him. Maybe she wouldn't. Either way, his daughter had not risked discovery even to help her grandmother.

As though she'd read his thoughts, Carly looked up at Officer Mantero. "Is Grandma going to be okay?"

"I don't know. As soon as I know something, I'll tell you. But you've got to give me something too, Carly. Because I don't see how a man who can push his mother down the stairs doesn't hurt his daughter sometimes too. And I don't mean spoiling your friendships."

Carly's head shook adamantly. "He's never hit me or . . . anything."

Officer Mantero refused to accept that. "So maybe he's too close. Maybe he does other things."

Again the furious denial. "He loves me. But not like that."

Silence from the cop.

Carly's fingers whitened on the box about which Peggy Mantero had surprisingly not inquired. "If he's mad he punishes me by . . . hurting other people."

The officer raised her brows as Carly pushed the box over. "I found this. That's why I couldn't talk to him. I was upset. But not because he hurt me. Because he hurt them."

Sofie gasped as a glimmer of understanding caught her by surprise. For six years she had thought Eric was punishing her. Had he in fact been punishing his little girl for daring to love someone else? Had he taken away the one person Carly might have loved better than him?

She looked down to hide the sudden tears and missed Officer Mantero's reaction to the photos. The contents of that box were only now sinking in. Could Eric truly have—But he had. And recorded it. Why? Certainly not for Carly to have seen. She knew beyond a doubt he had never intended that. So if they were for Eric alone, did the pictures act as a conviction . . . or a reward?

She silently groaned. How could she reconcile that with someone who had made her feel so cherished, so essential? Or was that also obsession? If he'd been watching her all this time, no wonder she'd felt that creeping in the back of her neck. But why hadn't he come to her?

Did he prefer to see her suffer as he'd made these others suffer? He had told Carly she'd committed suicide, yet he'd known she was struggling back to some hope of normalcy. Had he hoped she would find it? Or did her struggle gratify him? It was too bizarre to contemplate. Their relationship had delved unhealthy depths, but she'd never suspected . . .

Matt's voice broke through her thoughts. "I work for CPS in Sonoma. Sofie's a qualified foster-care provider."

"In Sonoma, maybe. I'm not sending this child to California. She's a witness."

Sofie looked up. "I live in the Bronx. I was in Sonoma on a professional sabbatical, but my official address is not far from here." She gave the street address of her Belmont apartment. Though she hadn't planned to return permanently, Matt would have to understand her first duty was to Carly.

He said, "I'll have Sonoma CPS fax you Sofie's paper work. I can personally vouch for her."

He must have understood or he wouldn't be paving this road for her. He made an impressive advocate, but Officer Mantero still waffled.

"Carly will need protection—"

"That a local foster family may not be able to provide."

"And you can?"

Matt drew himself into the vigilant stance Sofie had noted before. "It's what I do."

And so well. God must have put Matt Hammond in her path for this moment. Her heart rushed with gratitude. She hoped he knew how much it meant.

The officer looked from Matt to her to Carly. Maybe it was the child's silent plea that settled her. "We'll go by the station and get that fax. If everything clears, I'll release her to you until we know how it's going with her grandma."

Sofie gave the policewoman her cell number, and Matt, one of his cards. Sofie stood and gathered Carly to her. "Should I take her to the hospital to see Grandma Beth?"

"Better wait for now. We'll let you know."

Outside, Sofie handed Matt her keys and said, "Do you mind driving?"

"You'll have to direct me."

"Of course." She got into the back seat with Carly, kept an arm around her shoulders. Could this beautiful girl truly be the precious child she'd lost? If only she hadn't come back to her in such heartbreaking circumstances. But then, maybe these were the only circumstances that would have allowed it.

The police had kept the photos, and she hoped never to see them again. If Eric's disorder had gotten so extreme, he had to be stopped. But that didn't mean she wanted him to suffer. And she was certain Carly didn't either. She pressed a kiss to Carly's head. "Are you okay?"

Carly shook her head, misery written on her face. "I wish I'd never seen anything. I wish I didn't know."

"He needs help, Carly. If you hadn't told us, others might have gotten hurt."

She gulped big sorrowful tears. "I didn't want to get him in trouble."

"He got himself in trouble."

Why had he done such cruel and senseless things? Where was the man they'd known, and loved? Had that capacity for cruelty always been there? Or had something in her, in their relationship, held it at bay?

When their souls were rent apart, she had turned the pain on herself. Had he vented it on others? Or was it all part of a compulsive disorder? Could he be reacting to threats he felt he had to control?

She remembered his arms closing around her as he whispered, "What are you doing out here?"

"Just looking at the night."

"Don't you think that makes you a target?"

She had turned, humor touching her lips. "A target for what?"

He'd laughed. "Come inside, where nothing can happen."

She had teased him with all the things that could happen to someone inside until she sensed he no longer found it amusing. Then she'd gone in, where he felt a greater measure of control, and thought how wonderful it was to have someone so concerned, so watchful.

As Matt parked behind the building, she bolstered herself to go in. What would she tell Momma? Pop? Any of them? No matter what they thought or said, she had to take care of Carly.

They went in through the back and up the stairs. No one accosted them. Sounds of young children came down from above, but neither of her sisters appeared. Pop would be at work, of course, and if Momma had walked to the studio as usual, she might not have heard anything—yet.

It felt like a reprieve. When it came, the outcry would be extreme. How could she get involved again with what had almost killed her? How could she do that to herself? To them?

She unlocked the apartment door and let Carly and Matt inside. Blue shadows underscored Carly's red-rimmed eyes. Sofie rested a hand on her shoulder. "Are you hungry?"

Carly shook her head. "Just tired. I didn't sleep much."

Of course not, crammed into the closet with the awfulness of what had happened. "Do you want to lie down?" At the weary nod, she took the child into Nonna's room, pulled back the blanket and crocheted coverlet. Tucking her in, Sofie ached with tenderness. "Can I bring you anything?"

"No thanks. But . . . you're not leaving, right?"

Sofie caressed her face. "No, sweetie. I'll be right outside." Facing Matt. She started to close the door, but Carly called, "Please don't."

She left a gap. "Okay, honey. Rest now."

Matt stood at the window that overlooked Nonna's once-bustling restaurant. This time of the morning only Arthur Avenue's Little Italy markets had shoppers. The street below was quiet except for the occasional car. She joined him.

He slid an arm around her. "She's a sweet girl. This must be eating her up."

Of all the things he could be feeling, concern for Carly had come first. She raised tear-swept eyes. "She's strong."

"Even so, it's not easy, what she did. I've seen battered kids defend their abusers. She turned evidence on the only person she has."

"I don't think she foresaw all of this."

"No doubt. But once she realized people had been hurt, she didn't keep it to herself."

"I think she would rather he'd hurt her."

"You're probably right." He turned her in his arm. "Sofie, how can you hang on to someone like that?"

"He's not— He wasn't like that."

"You must have seen something or you wouldn't have felt the need to shield Carly. Why did you come between them?"

"I can't think about that, Matt." Recalling that day was like stepping into quicksand.

"But you'll admit things weren't right."

"They weren't easy."

"It's never easy. But you said yourself it was destructive."

"Self-destructive. I hurt myself, Matt. No one else did that to me."

"It's healthy to take responsibility for your actions. It's not healthy to ignore all the instigating factors."

She pressed a hand to her face.

Matt turned back to the window. "He spied on you."

He hadn't let go anymore than she.

"He enjoyed your suffering."

"He shared it."

"As he shared the pain of his other victims? The ones whose pets he killed, whose accidents he caused?"

"That's not the man I knew." A tear trickled down her cheek as the memory came.

"I have never been happy before, Sofie. You've taught me happiness."

"Don't be silly," she'd laughed.

"I'm not."

"What about Carly, then? Weren't you happy to have her?"

"I was afraid. Loving her hurts."

She hadn't pressed him to clarify, because she'd understood. It was possible to love too much. But now she realized Matt was waiting for an explanation. "When he said there was no one else in the world for him, he meant it. He never looked at anyone else. In a neighborhood where guys check out every woman they pass, his eye never wandered. He made me feel . . . peerless."

"Because you were. How many friendships did you maintain?"

"I meant—"

"I know, Sofie. But what you're saying is he isolated you."

Matt didn't understand that for the first time in her life she hadn't been one of many, the third sister sandwiched between two brothers, lost in the crowd of cousins, aunts, nieces, nephews. "He cherished me."

"As he cherishes his daughter. He has photos to prove it."

She understood Matt's position. He couldn't understand hers.

"I believe you loved him, Sofie. What I don't get is how you can excuse what he's done. Now that you know."

"I'm not excusing it." How could he think that? "I'm horrified."

"But . . ."

"When you love someone it doesn't stop because of things

they do. There's more to him than this, and—"

"And that's what you want."

"No." She gripped his hands. "I could never be with him again. But it doesn't change the fact that I did once love him, just as Carly does, even though she can't bear it anymore."

He released his breath, unwilling to force the point. "He'll come looking."

She shook her head. "He has no reason to believe I'm here."

"He knows Carly called you. He didn't find her at Grandma's, even when he pushed her down the stairs."

"You don't know that. It could have been an accident. He might have turned suddenly, or maybe she blocked his way as he tried to get by."

Again he didn't press the point. "He can't go back to work, can't go home. He'll go to places he knows, people who will help and defend him. He'll have a version of what happened. He'll believe it. And it'll be his mother's word against his—if she pulls through, and if she accuses him."

"Carly—"

"Do you think Carly will sit across a courtroom and say anything that could hurt him? Her testimony makes it an accident. The only witness heard no sign of struggle, no raised voices. She hadn't even had time to think when she answered as much as she did, and she defended him. Once she realizes the trouble he's in . . ."

"What about the photos?"

"Maybe he hired someone to protect his daughter. Maybe that person photographed anything suspicious that happened with the people she knew."

"But the names."

"The names suggest maliciousness, but it's only circumstantial. There's no proof he committed the crimes, only that he documented them."

Matt had practiced law. He would know. And it all had such a terrible ring of truth. Sofie pressed her fingers to her temples.

He raised her chin. "I know you want to protect Carly, but

you've put yourself in the center of the storm. Who's going to protect you?"

She swallowed back the tears that filled her throat. "I can't leave her alone in this."

"I know."

"Can you—will you—stay?"

He searched her face. "I have to know that if it comes to it, you won't take his part against me."

"In what way?"

"In any way. Eric is not innocent in this. He is not a victim. He's a victimizer. If he finds you, he'll manipulate you. If you plan to give in, I'm going home today."

She shook her head, blinking back the tears. "I won't." She had worked too hard to come back from that place.

"I might not have his Svengali lure, but I want a chance with you."

She couldn't think of that now.

"I'll fight for you. But I can't fight what's inside you."

No one could.

"So tell me now, Sofie. Tell me if you're here to get him back."

Her heart hammered. Did Eric want that? Her chin trembled. It would never be the same. She could not erase what she knew. "No, Matt. That's not what I'm here for."

Some of the tension left his shoulders. He drew her in and kissed her. Her heart rushed. Warmth flooded her. She reached her arms around his neck, and he raised her off her feet. She soaked in the size and strength of him.

"Um . . . Sofie?"

They startled and turned. Her feet found the floor. "What is it, Carly?"

"My stomach hurts."

"Let me make you some peppermint tea." She went to the cabinet and drew out the box she'd kept there for Nonna. Carly came and sat at the small table in the kitchenette with her glance flicking between them. For just one moment, she wondered if the child's stomachache had anything to do with Matt's kiss.

CHAPTER THIRTY-ONE

Rese pulled the helmet onto her head. Sofie's leaving had agitated Lance to such a degree she hesitated to climb astride his Harley. She knew too well how he worked out his anxiety. But it was the least she could do when he'd stayed—and not blamed her for it. At least she didn't think he blamed her.

She wrapped her arms around his leather-clad waist as they eased out of the driveway and took off for the wilderness of upper central California's wine country. Her own constricting leathers provided protection against road hazards, a timely reminder as Lance opened the throttle. She forced her body to meld with his, matched his motion and let her tension melt away.

Lance knew his limits. He knew his vehicle. He knew God.

When he'd taken them as far as he needed to, he slowed, swerved the bike to the side of the road, and stopped. Her thigh muscles complained of clenching, but she'd survived his therapy fairly well. He took her hand and pulled her through a loose wire fence. She recognized the stretch of pasture along the Petaluma Highway where he'd attempted their first date, a picnic she'd been too aggravated to enjoy.

He led the way to the single windblown tree, took off his

jacket and laid it on the ground just as he had that first time. "Remember this place?"

"How could I forget?" They'd fought, and he'd driven like a maniac back to the villa. Too shaken up to fire him on the spot, she had intended to the next morning. Somehow he'd talked her out of it. Or she'd talked herself.

She sat down on the jacket. "What are we doing?"

He knelt behind her, rubbing her neck and shoulders. She'd obviously not relaxed as thoroughly as she'd let herself believe.

"This is where I was going to propose to you—pack a picnic and everything."

"To prove how wrong I was?"

"Nah. Just to bring it full circle."

She melted into the massage. "I'm glad I didn't fire you."

He kissed the crook of her neck. "I was pretty cocky."

"You still are."

"Yeah, well." A breeze carried the scent of grasses, and she guessed what was coming before he said, "Rese . . ."

"I know."

He leaned around to see her face. "You know what?"

"How worried you are about Sofie." He had hardly eaten, and it took great effort to get his attention, even while he worked.

He sat down, stretched his legs to either side of her, and encircled her shoulders in his arms. "I am worried."

She leaned back against him. "Are you going?"

"Not unless you say so."

"Lance . . ."

"I'm not asking you to. I just wondered if you'd prayed about it."

She half turned in his arms. "Yes. Maybe my prayers aren't as . . . effective as yours, but I have, Lance. And I don't think you should go."

"Because . . ."

"It's how I feel. Michelle says when you're peaceful with an answer, it's probably right. I don't have peace about you going."

He raised his knee to support her position. "I don't either."

"You don't?"

He shook his head. "First it was that you didn't want me to.. So I prayed the Lord would change your mind."

"I'm not sure that's fair."

His smile pulled sideways. "God must agree. I have the impression this isn't my fight."

She turned farther in his arms. "I didn't believe you'd listen to me."

"It would be hard if I was hearing something different. But don't ever be afraid to speak your mind."

She raised her brows. "Has that been an issue for me?"

He laughed. "Get-outta-here. You're the mind-speaking master."

"And just for the record, that title fits more than one of us."

———

As Carly sipped her tea, the door burst open. Matt spun, adrenaline surging, but it was a woman with auburn hair whose Mediterranean allure matched Sofie's. It had to be her mother. He instinctively stood up straight.

"Momma." Sofie met her with a hug.

He could see from where he stood the return embrace was not superficial. This woman had a fierce affection.

She gripped Sofie's face. "What is it? What's happened?"

Sofie covered her mother's hands with hers. "Momma, you remember Carly." She turned carefully for her mother to see the girl at the table. Carly looked miserable.

"Little Carly?"

"And this is Matt Hammond. Matt, my mother, Doria Michelli."

The woman was shorter than she'd looked coming in, her posture giving an illusion of height. He took a step and held out his hand. "I'm honored to meet you." Honored? Who said that kind of thing?

Her grip was firm. "Are you friend or lover?"

"Matt's here to help, Momma."

Her attention hadn't wavered, so he shrugged. "A friend who'd like to be more."

"An honest man. Heaven be praised." Her next look skewered him. "Don't touch my daughter."

"That's pretty much what she said too."

She pressed a finger to his chest. "You do it right, you'll be thankful. God will bless you."

He barely held back the "Yes, ma'am" before he came off a complete fool.

Doria turned to the child. "Little Carly. Let me look at you."

Carly didn't bear scrutiny well. He could almost believe she didn't realize her attributes. Or she intentionally downplayed them. Maybe she realized it was dangerous to attract attention. That kind of automatic response took time to develop, suggesting a previous or ongoing suspicion that it wasn't a good idea.

Doria hugged the girl, then told Sofie, "I want to talk to you."

When Sofie stepped into the hall with her mother, Matt looked at Carly. "Are your ears burning?"

Carly reached up and touched the pink shell of one ear.

He leaned close and whispered. "It means they're talking about us."

"Oh," she whispered conspiratorially. "Is that bad?"

"Let's listen." He strained, eyes squinted. "Hmm. 'Carly's a sweetheart, but that big guy . . .'"

She giggled, but too soon her expression changed again. "I'm the troublemaker."

He sat down at the table across from her. "You didn't start this."

She squeezed her hands into fists. "I miss my dad. I don't want him to be hurt."

"I know."

"I didn't want anyone to be hurt. And it's all because of me." She dropped her face to her hands. "Those poor dogs."

"Did those people threaten or upset you?"

She sat a long time, groping with her answer, then gave a sad shake of the head. "No. They were nice. They were my friends." She sank lower into her chair. "He doesn't want me to have friends."

She'd said that before, but her dad's actions took it to another level. It was one thing to perceive a threat—real or imagined—and protect his daughter from potential danger, another altogether to target people who'd been kind or concerned about Carly.

She pressed a hand to her stomach.

"Your tea might help."

She took a sip. "So you want to marry Sofie, right?"

Her directness caught him off guard. "We're nowhere close to that."

"You're only sleeping with her?" Not as innocent as she looked.

"That's not really your business, but you heard what I told Mrs. Michelli."

"You didn't say you weren't. Only that Sofie said the same thing."

He studied the child. "You're a careful listener."

She shrugged. The fact that she'd learned to be suggested the need to. Maybe she knew more about her dad's behavior than she'd like them to think.

"Your dad's had girlfriends?"

She sniffed. "Not exactly." She didn't elaborate. Maybe she was differentiating between sexual partners and someone who mattered. If he was spending all his affection on his daughter, he'd only have loose change for someone else. So what had Sofie cost him?

And what might Carly cost her now? He realized he didn't want Sofie to come with baggage. Sweet as the kid seemed to be, she was the child of the man who'd almost ended Sofie's life. And what manipulations had she learned and absorbed? Or inherited?

He sat back and looked toward the door through which the women's voices carried wordlessly.

She followed his look. "What's going to happen?" Vulnerability brought a catch to her voice.

"What do you want to happen?"

"I wanted Sofie back, but in an 'I know I can't have it' way."

"Like a dream?"

She shrugged.

"Do you even remember her?"

"Duh. I remember everything about her."

"Good memory. It's been a long time. Most kids, those memories fade."

She shot a look right into his eyes, gauging his temper? "If I didn't remember her, why would I call?"

"Why did you call? Your dad ask you to?"

Her jaw dropped. "Right. I got in so much trouble when he found out."

"What kind of trouble? What did he do?"

She clamped her mouth shut as blood rushed into her face. A second later she ran to the bathroom and threw up. Could be stress; could be she actually was sick the day she called. She was a little young for an eating disorder, but with her high stress level, it wouldn't be too surprising. Instead of coming back to the table, she went into the room Sofie had given her and lay down. She didn't close the door.

Sofie came back into the kitchen. "We're having dinner with Momma and Pop. Lance would tell you to be warned."

"Warned?"

"Momma has a heavy hand with seasonings."

"That's what you were discussing? Dinner?"

She came and sat with him. "She wants to see for herself that you're not planning to eat me alive and"—she lowered her voice—"that Carly hasn't lured me here to get back together with Eric." She looked toward the bedroom. "She's feeling bad again?"

"She could be bulimic. She purged and went to bed."

Sofie's brow creased. "Did something upset her?"

"You mean did I? She didn't want to tell me what happened when she 'got in trouble' the first time she called."

"Oh." Sofie looked down at her hands. "I shouldn't have dragged you into this."

"I don't recall any dragging." He reached over and took her hand. "I'm here because I want to be."

"And I appreciate it." Her long-lashed gaze swept up to his. "But Carly's confused, and Momma's frantic. Pop will be worse. And I haven't even started on my sisters and aunts and friends and neighbors. I wish we could take Carly and disappear."

"That's called kidnapping."

She smiled grimly. "Is that all?" She laid her other hand over his. "Momma thinks you're handsome."

"What do you think?"

"The first thing I noticed was your eyes, the warmth and compassion. Then your hands, the way they cradled Diego, the way they swallow mine."

Not exactly the instant visceral attraction he'd felt for her.

"You seeped into my awareness—the line of your jaw, the breadth of your shoulders, the creases that form beside your mouth when you smile."

He'd smiled more since meeting her than he could remember.

"You're handsome and you're good."

If she followed that with "and I love you like a friend" . . .

"God gave you a great capacity to care."

Care and love were two different things. She had to know he was way past caring.

"You defend the most vulnerable every day."

But not because God expected it. He'd been dedicated as an infant, submerged as an adolescent. His first adult step had been to reject his father's faith, the avenue of control Webb used to bully weaker souls. Matt might be like his dad in every other way, but he would not be a hypocrite. "I don't do it to satisfy some judge in the sky. I do it for the sake of each kid."

She felt him withdraw. She had tried to tell him what it was that drew her to him, but maybe she saw good things in people that weren't there—and missed the dire ones that were. "I better check on Carly."

He didn't object.

Carly lay curled like a kitten in the bed. She opened her eyes. "Daddy?"

"No, honey. It's Sofie."

"I dreamed I was little. Like in the pictures? And you and Daddy and I were all together."

"I've dreamed that too."

Carly scooted closer to her. "I don't feel good."

"How long has it been since you've kept something down?"

Carly shrugged. "I guess I have the flu."

She didn't push it—just took Carly's hand and held it between hers. "Would you like a book to read? I have some of my favorites from when I was a girl, or the twins might have something newer."

"Who are the twins?"

"My nieces Lisa and Lara. They're a little younger than you. They live upstairs." When she'd had Carly before, there had been almost no contact with her family, and of course Carly would have been too little to remember if there had been.

"I'd like one of your favorites, Sofie."

She went into the other room, where the bookshelf held the stories she'd discerningly accumulated. The top shelf held the treasures of childhood: *Heidi, Black Beauty, The True Confessions of Charlotte Doyle*, books that had opened new worlds. She took down *Island of the Blue Dolphins*, gravitating at once to the story she'd read over and over about one girl's courage after being left alone on an island with wild dogs and nature to contend against.

Carly might identify with Karana's isolation and her strength. She brought the book in and found Carly sitting up. "Would you like some more tea?"

"No, thank you." She accepted the book and studied the cover.

"Have you read it?" Sofie asked.

"No."

"It's a Newbery award winner." Sofie rested her hand on Carly's knee under the blanket. Carly looked up at her with such longing, it closed in and swallowed her until nothing else existed.

It was her dream come true, Sofie caring for her, touching her, smiling. Her wonderful voice, her beautiful face. Daddy should never have made her go away, but she would fix that now. Sofie knew they needed her. When Daddy came, she'd see.

"I know I'm too old, Sofie, but . . . would you read it to me?"

Sofie's surprise was swallowed by an affectionate smile. "I'm not sure anyone's ever too old to be read to. Nonna loves it, and she's over ninety."

Carly settled into the pillows and drew up her knees. She was sad for the people who'd gotten hurt, so sad. But she pressed it out of her mind—Daddy, her grandma, the pictures. None of that was real. Only Sofie. Only now.

The woman she'd imagined for so long opened the book. Carly took in every word Sofie spoke and tucked it deep inside. She might only have minutes or hours or days. It wouldn't last. It would be spoiled like everything else, because Daddy loved her too much. Unless, unless she could convince Sofie to come back to them.

It was the only way. She couldn't take it alone anymore. Daddy needed Sofie too. Why else would he have taken all those pictures? They might be the only two people in the world Daddy loved, but together they could make him happy.

She should not have called Grandma. Thoughts of what happened made her stomach a hard ball. She should have waited for Sofie. But now she was here, and when Daddy came—

Matt stuck his head in the doorway. "I'm going to take a walk around."

Sofie nodded, acknowledging him with only a small smile. Carly could hardly bear the joy that jumped up inside. She wasn't too late. Sofie didn't love Matt. He might love her, but it wasn't too late to stop her loving him.

CHAPTER THIRTY-TWO

M att walked out to the street. He wanted to know the basic layout of their location—entrances, visibility, hazards. The building had an alley down one side, but it was connected to the next unit on the other. Four stories, and Sofie had mentioned a cellar. Fire escapes down the front, and as he reached the corner, he saw the same down the back.

Safe egress in emergencies, but not that hard to access from outside. He could do it if he had to. He didn't know how athletic Eric was, but in any case, the entire building could not be contained. He'd focus on Sofie's part of it.

The interior doors lined up, so he could watch from Chaz's side. He could even sleep in the hall if it seemed prudent. Chaz and Rico might help. They obviously cared about Sofie. Wouldn't Lance's closest friends protect his sister?

Matt headed upstairs through the door he'd propped open, letting it lock behind him, and knocked loudly enough to be heard over the drumming that came from the room where he'd slept last night. Rico pulled it open. "Don't have to knock. It's open."

Matt looked across the hall. "Sofie's too?" He recalled Doria walking in unannounced.

"Everyone, I think. If it's locked you can get the key from Pop."

"Pop?"

"Roman. Sofie's pop. Second floor."

"He has a key to all the rooms?"

"He owns the building, man." Rico twirled his drumsticks.

"Anyone else have any keys?"

Rico looked toward the stairs. "Bobby and Monica, Lucy and Lou up there. Dom and Vinnie in back. Chaz and me. Why?"

Matt shrugged. "How much do you know about what's happened with Sofie?"

"You mean before?"

"Before and now. She has Carly."

Rico's eyebrows shot up. "Carly? She was a baby last I saw her. Hair like a doll, eyes like an angel."

That description could still be applied. But was it accurate? "What about Eric?"

"Smooth talker. Movie-star looks." Rico cocked his head. "Sofie fell hard, but things didn't work out so good. You coming in?"

"Sure." Matt stepped into the room. "Where's Chaz?"

"Delivering flowers."

"Thought he worked in a restaurant."

"He works three jobs to send money to his father's church in Kingston."

Matt groaned. Would every person in the building bang the religion drum? He hadn't expected it from Rico. "The police are looking for Eric."

"What for?"

"Assault."

"On who?" Rico flopped onto the couch.

"His mother. She was hiding Carly."

Rico's eyes hooded. "If he knows Sofie's here, he'll come."

"You mean if he knows Carly's here?"

"Yeah, sure. But he's been here before, looking for Sofie."

"When?"

Rico crossed his ankles on the table. "Different times, hanging around in his car."

"Did he have a camera?"

Rico shrugged.

"Would anyone else have seen him?"

"Everyone would have seen him."

"Think he talked to anyone?"

"A few weeks ago, he was asking. But she was gone."

"Did they tell him where?"

"No way." Rico shook his head. "Everybody knows what happened before."

"They'd keep her secret? The whole neighborhood?"

"This part, yeah. Anyone who knows her."

Matt thought about that. "If we passed the word, would people keep an eye open?"

"Both eyes. But they're mostly old people like Dom and Vinnie."

"Even better. He won't suspect anything."

"You want them to call if they see him?"

Matt took out the half dozen cards in his wallet. "Give them my number. Sooner or later he'll guess Sofie's got Carly. I don't think there are too many others the girl could turn to." He'd isolated her in the same way he'd cut Sofie off from people who might have guessed things were wrong. "I don't know how long he'll evade police."

"Not that hard, man. Not around here." Rico looked like he knew.

No matter. He needed his help. What manpower could the force realistically commit to Carly? Best-case scenario, they'd snag Eric before he caught up to Sofie, but he couldn't count on that.

He'd had kids swiped right out from under supervising eyes or beaten up with neighbors right next door. Matt clenched his jaw. He'd never been through police or military training, but thanks to his father, he could fight.

"So you'll pass the word on the street?" It would go better from someone they knew and trusted. Rico didn't look the sort people trusted, but he guessed in a clannish place like this, he'd been accepted or he would have been gone.

Rico fanned the business cards like a poker hand. "I'll pass your number."

"They should also call the police, but I don't know what kind of response time . . . What?"

"They won't call the cops." Rico hunched forward. "We take care of our own."

Matt hooked a thumb over his shoulder. "I better get back." Though he doubted he'd been missed. Reading to Carly, Sofie had looked happier than he'd ever seen her. He tried to imagine the impact of losing a child, then six years later having her back.

Then he tried to imagine what could happen next. Sofie had no claim to Carly. With no priors, unless the grandma died, Eric would probably weasel out of jail time. Distraught and frantic to find his child, he'd overreacted. They both had. A jury could buy that.

If his mother recovered, and any of the rest actually stuck to Eric, she'd be next in line for Carly. If she was unable or unwilling, he supposed Sofie could be named guardian. Eric wouldn't let go without a fight, though maybe he'd used Carly as bait to bring Sofie back. He had to have learned she'd slipped his vigilance. The whole thing could be a setup.

Matt crossed the hall and went into Sofie's apartment, locking the door behind him. Her voice trailed from the bedroom, but it didn't sound as though she was reading anymore. They were conversing. How did one catch up on six lost years of a child's life?

Matt sat on the couch and used his PDA to contact the office, bring up his mail, check on a few loose ends. He had a note that Cassinia's mother had died and sent condolences, then ordered flowers to be delivered. He hoped she'd made peace with her mother before it was over, wondered if he'd ever do the same.

He contacted Officer Mantero for an update.

"Mrs. Malden's in fair condition. Two fractured vertebrae, a crushed disk. Bruises and contusions. She won't be getting up anytime soon."

"Any word on Eric?"

"A neighbor thinks she saw him coming out of his place with a suitcase, but doesn't know him well enough to say for sure."

"Sounds like he's on the move."

"We've got surveillance on your girlfriend's neighborhood. If she hangs tight with Carly a couple days, we'll get him."

He liked her optimism—especially the girlfriend part. "We've alerted the neighbors. They know Sofie and they know him."

"Good. How's the kid?"

"Not great. Better with Sofie, though."

"What's the deal there?"

"She lived with Eric for four years. Raised Carly from infancy until they had a disagreement and he took his daughter and left."

"Must be rough."

He didn't tell her it had almost been deadly. He thanked her for the update and hung up. Then he settled in to wait and wondered what, really, he was doing there.

A while later Carly went into the bathroom. He heard the shower start up with the groan of old pipes. Sofie joined him.

He slipped his arm around her. "You doing okay?"

"Yes. It's strange but . . . wonderful too. Having Carly."

Strange and wonderful having Sofie. Only he didn't. Not really. Not as long as her heart and mind were tied to Eric and his child.

Tucked into the crook of his shoulder, she raised her face. "I apologize."

"For what?"

"Saying things you didn't want to hear."

He frowned. "You have a right to your beliefs."

"Just don't impose them on you?" She half smiled.

"Don't imagine something that isn't there." The situation with Annie had reaffirmed his doubt about a supreme being. Lance claimed that the kingdom was now. If it was, it just wasn't enough.

Sofie sighed. "If there's no arbiter of good and evil, what separates moral from immoral choices?"

"Things either hinder or benefit society or individuals. It has nothing to do with some eternal condition after death."

That close to her face, he wanted to kiss her, kiss away all thoughts of religion, all piety, all inhibition. If he claimed her body, would her heart and mind follow? It had with Eric. He cupped her chin and kissed her mouth. "It's about you and me and what happens now."

The water turned off in the bathroom.

"And Carly."

He dropped his forehead to hers. "She's not yours, Sofie. You know that, right? They're not going to give you Eric's little girl."

"I can't let her down again."

"Sofie . . ."

She drew back. "I took the coward's way out last time, but God's given me another chance. Can't you see?"

"A chance at what?"

"Being in her life."

He shook his head. "There's no good way that can happen. Only if her grandma dies or you hook back up with him."

When she said nothing, he pushed up from the couch. "I thought you didn't want that."

"I don't." She dropped her face to her hands. "But you should have heard her, Matt. I'm all she has."

He could just imagine. "She's certainly her father's daughter."

Indignation ignited Sofie's eyes. "She did not intend any of this. How could she?"

"Whether she planned it or not, she's working you." He paced.

"Stop it."

"She said she wants you back. You and her dad and her, together again."

"Don't."

He threw out his hands. "She's playing on everything in you that's kind and giving and wounded. And you're letting her, just like you let him. They're two of a kind."

"Get out." The soft tone gave her words impact.

He'd gone too far. But he'd spoken the truth. He walked out the door, down the stairs and out to the street. He walked past stores and restaurants that seemed to be a page out of a time long past, skinned rabbits and sheep's heads staring out from display windows, an enclave of unreality. Sofie lived in an imaginary world. And liked it there.

He went back inside along with a handful of kids, climbed the stairs to the guys' apartment. He gathered his toiletries, put his clothes into the suitcase, and carried it out to the hall. Sofie's door was closed. He didn't knock. If he found Rico he'd tell him to direct the neighbors' calls wherever he wanted. Just keep him out of the loop.

From her window, Sofie saw him on the sidewalk, his suitcase beside him. He put his phone to his ear and placed a call. In the time it took the cab to arrive, he never looked up—not even when he climbed in and directed the cabbie. Her throat tightened. She hadn't meant to send him away, but she could not hear the things he'd been saying.

Somehow, some way, she would be there for Carly. From the moment she'd seen her in the closet—*"I knew you'd come"*—nothing else had mattered. She had to believe there was a way. God would not have brought her there, Carly would not have found her, unless they were supposed to be together.

Matt could not understand. He had not walked Carly through long hours in the night, had not thrilled over her first laugh, first words, first steps, had not melted in the glow of her. He hadn't seen the wariness creep into her being, the incomprehensible knowledge that more was needed from her than she could give. He hadn't worked day and night to meet a fathomless need so that the child could be spared a burden too great for so tender a heart. Matt couldn't know what it was to be utterly desired.

But she knew. And Carly knew. And when she went into the bedroom and found the girl, wet and clean, talking on her phone, it didn't surprise her at all that it was Eric she'd called.

Lance groaned through the mask as he moved the orbital sander over the wood floor of the hotel hallway. His spirit writhed with the swelling oppression. *Lord.* If it wasn't his responsibility, why was it weighing on him so painfully? Had something changed? Had he heard wrong?

He reached the wall and shut off the sander, dragged his phone from his pocket and keyed Sofie's number. *Come on, come on. Tell me you're okay.* When he got her message again, he called Matt.

"Matt Hammond."

Hope choked him. If Matt was fine, Sofie was fine.

"Leave a message after the tone."

His arm fell to his side. A million reasons they might not be answering. Don't read more into that than there could be. But the weight was crushing him. He sank to his knees. Fingers locked behind his head, he dropped his chin to his chest. *Tell me. Show me. What do I have to do?*

"Lance?" Rese's voice penetrated.

He pushed up to his feet, shakier than he'd been in a while.

She came to him, touched him. "What's wrong?"

He found his voice. "I don't know."

She searched his face. "Is it Sofie?"

"That's my guess. I'm worried."

She had said she would tell him if she thought he should go, but she didn't say that now. "Lance, even if you were there, what could you do?"

He swallowed. "I don't think I'm supposed to be there."

Her shoulders relaxed. "What, then?"

"Come here." He took her hands and leaned his shoulder to the wall. "Pray with me."

"Here?" She looked down the half-sanded hallway where he'd been working alone. "Right now?"

"Unless you want me on a plane doing someone else's job."

"What are you talking about?"

He wasn't sure he could put it into words. "This isn't my fight. Yet. Or maybe it is in a different way. I've always been the one out there laying it on the line while someone like Chaz covers me in prayer."

"This time you're covering someone else?"

"Yes." His heart swelled that she'd gotten it. "It's not easy standing back. I'd rather be there guarding Sofie, making sure nothing hurts her, no one hurts her."

"You like that position of control."

No denying that. "And God knows I'll take it if no one else does." He brought her fingers to his lips. "So help me?"

Her uneasiness showed. God had invaded her professional space, the space she guarded above all others. But this was right. It was necessary.

"What are we praying for?"

"Matt." He said it with no forethought. It was just there. He closed his eyes, pictured the man Sofie had allowed into her life. Did Matt know the magnitude of her struggle? Without faith, what would he fight with?

Lance squeezed Rese's hands. He'd expected to pray protection for Sofie, and that was part of it, but his burden now was for Matt. He didn't know what had happened, or what might, only that a battle raged. He spoke without planning one word, letting his spirit lead.

When he looked up, Rese's eyes were still closed, and that glimpse of her in prayer excited him like nothing else. He expelled his breath. "I love you."

Her eyes opened. "Amen?"

A full smile grabbed his heart. "Yeah." He didn't always sweat the formalities. "Thank you, Rese. You don't know what that means to me."

"I think I do." She leaned in and kissed his mouth. Affection in the workplace—another breakthrough. "Think you can finish this floor now?"

"You are one terrific motivator."

She rolled her eyes. "Don't get used to it."

"Sir?"

Matt jolted.

"Did you want to book this return flight?"

He looked at the woman who had brought up his options on the computer at the ticket desk. He swallowed. One touch of her finger and he'd be headed home—back through security and onto a jet, back to his work, his life.

The people behind him grew restless. He had told Sofie he wouldn't let her hurt herself, and now he was leaving her in circumstances that could do nothing else. What if there was something still that he could do? Not for his own benefit, but simply for hers.

Had it helped to tell Jacky to stand up to things like a man? If Sofie couldn't help herself, would he let her walk into a train too? He looked at the woman, looked at the clock, then picked up his suitcase and stepped out of line.

Sofie's face filled his mind. Her expression when she told him to leave had been angry, but behind the anger there'd been resignation, the kind that saw no way out. *"If there's no arbiter of good and evil, what separates moral from immoral choices?"*

Had his contention that things either hindered or benefited society or individuals with no eternal consequence removed the final obstacle to choices that could prove dangerous and self-destructive? If she believed she had to help Carly at any cost— His stomach clenched. He'd been blinded by jealousy. If she wouldn't forget Eric, then forget her. He'd even resented the little girl.

Matt raised his hand for a taxi. Where were his grand ideals now? He'd been just like his dad, trying to make Sofie tough enough. She should be able to say no, able to let go. When it was her very softness, her compassion, her desire to give that had caught him so deeply.

The cab ride took days. Traffic formed a solid wall. The driver spoke no English, knew no alternate routes. Matt clenched and unclenched his hands, wishing for the first time in years there was somewhere he could turn, someone who could help. Matt couldn't remember his dad ever praying except in front of others as a person of importance.

He rubbed his temple. In the back of the sweaty cab, he groped for words to reach a being out there somewhere who might be listening after all. "God help me," he murmured, then realized they were the words he needed. Everything in him repulsed the urge to say it again, so he modified it to, "Help Sofie. Help me help Sofie." That he could live with.

CHAPTER THIRTY-THREE

The cab brought him to the building as the setting sun reddened the bricks and turned the windows brassy. A chilly wind bent and unbent the spindly branches on the trees along the curb. Young men and women clumped at intervals along the sidewalk. A few checked him out as he exited the cab, gripping his suitcase, and realized he couldn't get into the building.

A bell beside the outer door rang somewhere, he hoped. After a long wait, a dark-haired woman appeared with a cranky toddler on her hip. Her face was an older, sharper version of Sofie's, and her voice had the harsh New York bark. "Yeah?"

"I'm here with Sofie."

"Oh." She swung the door open. "You're Matt?" She craned her neck up. "Say hi to Nicky. Nicky, this big man is Sofie's friend Matt."

Matt hooked fingers with the tot. "Hey, Nicky."

Nicky turned away, disinterested.

"I'm Sofie's sister Monica."

He just wanted to get upstairs and make sure Sofie was all right.

Monica led the way. "Did you come to meet the family?"

"That's . . . part of it."

"You staying awhile?"

"Not sure yet."

"How come Sofie hasn't come up to say hi?"

"She's, um, working on something."

"She's always working on something. If she were an animal, she'd be a beaver."

"I'm a beaver," Nicky said and tried to gnaw his mother's neck.

"Cut that out." On the second-floor landing, she said over her shoulder, "Hope you're hungry. Momma's cooking."

He'd forgotten all about that. He might have been on a plane eating granola while Doria served a special meal without the guest of honor. "Yeah, thanks."

Monica continued past his floor. He debated between Rico's and Sofie's doors, tried Rico's first to ask if anyone had seen Eric. The apartment was empty. He went across to Sofie's door and knocked.

Carly pulled it open and did a fair job of hiding her disappointment.

Sofie came up behind her. "Matt."

"Can we talk?"

Sofie patted the child and scooted her back inside, then stepped into the hall. Knowing Carly's ear would be to the door, he caught Sofie's elbow and walked her into Rico's apartment.

Her anger seemed spent, but she withdrew her elbow with practiced ease. "I thought you left."

"I'm not leaving."

Emotions crabbed across her face. Surprise, relief, dismay.

"You're not the best judge of things right now, Sofie. I told you I wouldn't let you hurt yourself."

"And I told you this isn't about me."

"But you're part of it."

She sighed. "You said there's no good way this can turn out. I accept that."

"Sofie."

"Carly's been lost to me for six years, Matt. Six of the hardest

338

years of my life. It breaks my heart to think how it's been for her."

If he let himself, he'd find the place she was in. Psychological abuse could hurt more than bruises. That was why Jacky had despaired. Not the whippings that left welts, but the ones that didn't show. "We'll help her together. It's what I do for a living, remember?" She didn't resist when he pulled her into his arms. "Trust me."

"Matt . . ."

He caught her face and tipped it up. "In the cab coming back, I prayed. I don't know, maybe you're right. Maybe there's a whole bigger thing than us."

Tears pooled in her eyes. But he had the distinct feeling she was thinking too little, too late. Had something happened?

"What's wrong?"

"Nothing."

He felt her deceiving him. Why? Pressing her head to his chest, he wanted to cry himself. She'd let go of Diego and Annie, one for the right reason, the other because she had no choice. But she had a choice now, and she would not let go of Carly. And any way he looked at it he saw trouble.

He might not only be protecting her from Eric, but from herself as well. Okay, then. God help him, he'd do it. And if that was the best prayer he could manage, maybe God would still hear.

He stroked her hair. "I need you to trust me, Sofie. And I want to trust you."

She didn't answer—unwilling to lie, he guessed. But he'd taken all the ground he could and had to stop pushing. He raised her chin, looked into her eyes. "It smelled like dinner downstairs. Think we can get Carly to eat?"

Sofie formed a faint smile. "If anyone can, it's Momma. It's just easier to say yes."

He wondered if she realized the parallel. Didn't matter. He was there to help her say no. She reached for the door, but he caught her arm. "I'm sorry. For before."

She nodded. "Me too." The sadness in her voice suggested that she meant for more than before.

Sofie's mother was nothing like Grandma. She talked a lot. She hugged a lot too. She made spaghetti. A lot of it. And big meatballs. And soggy green beans, though she said, "You don't have to eat those. Have more spaghetti. And ice cream for dessert. Save room for that."

Eat more and save room? Carly smiled, and for the first time in too long, her stomach didn't hurt.

"You're spindly like Sofie used to be. I always told her, 'Eat,' but she'd say 'Momma, I'm full enough for three Sofies.'"

Carly loved hearing about Sofie as a kid. Like she was her real mother and Doria her real grandma. But that thought made her stomach hurt again because it made her think of Grandma Beth falling. *Just don't. Just pretend all this is real.* Because it was all she was going to get and because the tears were too close.

Sofie hadn't yelled about her calling Daddy. She had looked at her with sad, sad eyes like she knew and understood how it had to be. The feeling that gripped now in her chest was the deepest love she'd ever felt. And Sofie loving back didn't hurt.

She stared at her plate because the tears had come anyway, and she tried to blink them away before anyone could see. She was so tired of hiding. Just for once she wanted everything to be okay. But she couldn't pretend it was okay. Nothing was okay. Nothing ever was.

Her stomachache got worse. Daddy would be so mad. Someone would get hurt. Sofie? She couldn't bear to think it. Maybe Sofie could stop him from hurting anyone. Maybe she really could. Wouldn't having Sofie back make him forget the rest? Wasn't that enough? It had to be. It had to.

"Ice cream, Carly?"

She looked up and shook her head. "My stomach hurts."

For a while, Carly had seemed happy, even silly with Momma. But the weight of it all must have settled back. Her stomachaches were troubling, and Matt could be right. She and Momma had watched for eating disorders in their dance students, and this would have raised flags. She doubted Carly's issue was body image. More likely the child just wanted to disappear.

She remembered the feeling too well. *Don't need me so much. Don't see in me what's missing in yourself. I can't ever be enough.* Lord God, how had Carly stood it? By bingeing and purging?

She would need to talk to her. Bulimia had detrimental effects on the body that didn't show—electrolyte imbalance and stress on critical organs. Carly hadn't binged at dinner though. She'd eaten as normally as anyone could under Momma's prodding.

Matt too. He'd pleased Momma. The pang returned to Sofie's chest. This could have been different, his meeting Pop and Momma, his seeing what she'd come from, the haunts of her youth, the people she loved.

She hadn't realized she wanted that, hadn't admitted how much he mattered. The time they'd spent together with Diego, with Annie, with each other had formed a bond. But she couldn't let it get in the way.

He wanted to trust her, but he shouldn't. She didn't trust herself. Because she knew, had known for six years, that if this time came she'd take it. She would die for Carly. She almost had. Maybe she was meant to.

She smiled at Pop, his surreptitious glances betraying fears that underlay his relief that she'd gotten involved with another man. She realized guiltily that Matt made a great decoy. Strong, intelligent, good-looking. Who would suspect she'd want anything else? When their gazes crossed, he seemed determined to fill the role her family assumed. Suitor and protector. She should not have let him get so close.

She told them about her decision not to complete her degree. No one hollered. No one criticized. What did they care if she became a doctor? She had a good man now and no longer pined for the destructive one.

But there was still the problem of Carly. And so Eric hovered over the gathering like a malignant spirit. She could feel his hunger. And something inside her responded. It had always been so; it always would. Strange how there was almost a peace in that.

_____

While he had thought the plan was to keep Carly safe until the police apprehended Eric, Matt had considered Rico and Chaz's apartment adequate. If he'd guessed right that Sofie had been compromised, even across the hall was too far. So when she had tucked Carly in and come back out, he said, "I'll sleep here on the couch." It was short enough he'd be bent up by morning, but he'd hear and see anything that happened in the apartment. "I cleared it with your dad while you and your mother did the dishes."

She raised her brows. "You didn't clear it with me."

"I am now."

"It could give Carly the wrong impression."

"The wrong impression would be us together in your bed."

Her throat flushed, a sign that she still felt something, even if it was discomfort. Her performance at dinner had been amazing. But then, she'd had years of fooling even herself. He had no idea what could be done about that, but right now he was keeping her alive. That was all.

If Eric thought she had come between him and his daughter, the rage that fueled the vicious acts in the photos might be nothing to what he showed now. If he was trying to get her back, the emotional fallout could be as bad.

Sofie looked at the couch. "You'll be very uncomfortable."

He quirked his mouth. "Got a better offer?"

She didn't rise to the bait. She had sunk even further into the place he couldn't reach. And the way he felt now, he doubted they'd strike sparks anyway.

She sighed. "You take the bed; I'll have the couch."

"Thanks, but I'd rather be out here, near the door and windows."

"You're not serious." She crossed her arms. "You think he'll come in through the windows?"

"I think he could."

"There are windows in the bedrooms too. But that's not happening."

"How do you know?"

"I know him, Matt."

Then she looked away, and he thought it must be how it felt to love an addict. To see her going down that path of destruction and be helpless to stop it. "What do you want me to do?"

She pressed her knuckles to her lips. "I can sleep with Carly. You take my room."

He considered that. The bedrooms were separated by the bath. He wouldn't see the hall door from in there, but he'd be closer to his charges. "Okay."

She lowered her hand. "I know this isn't how you wanted things to be."

"Is it what you wanted?"

At least she looked torn. "You knew I would do what Diego needed. And Annie. When Eric took Carly six years ago it was as though she'd been kidnapped. One day she was there and then she was . . . not. I'd gone to church. When I got back they were gone. I never said good-bye, never asked for pictures. Except for what I had in my wallet, he took everything that was her."

"Why didn't you hate him?"

Her brow creased. "I did. Part of me did. But . . . I . . ." She swiped a tear from her eye. "Knew how he felt. That he couldn't let anything come between them."

"You mean anyone?"

"You don't know what it's like to lose a child, Matt. I can't imagine his anguish."

"Can't you? Didn't you lose her too?"

She blinked back her tears.

"Or is it worse for him because she's also the object of his obsession?"

Her hands closed into fists, but he pressed on. "Have you forgotten the pictures? His mother in the hospital?"

She paced. "Of course not."

"Then what's changed?"

She looked over her shoulder. "What are you talking about?"

"This morning you were as horrified by all of it as I am."

She expelled her breath. "You said yourself, it won't stick. And if he thinks he'll lose Carly—You should have gone home."

"I'm not leaving."

"Matt—"

He pulled her into his arms and kissed her. "I'm not leaving. Even if you tell me to."

She rested her fingertips on his jaw, touched the corner of his mouth, and looked into his eyes. "Thank you."

"You don't need to."

"Sofie?" Carly's call was soft, but it may as well have been a bell clanging.

He nodded toward the bedroom. "Go ahead."

She stepped back. "I'll get a few things from my room."

"Okay. Good night." Tonight he'd be sleeping with the door open—and not just to catch someone sneaking in.

CHAPTER THIRTY-FOUR

As Sofie showered, memories arose like the steam, a vapor she breathed and absorbed through her pores. Feeding the ducks in the rain in Central Park, Carly darting among them like a yellow-booted duckling herself, Eric stomping through puddles with her as though he'd never known the splash and abandon of wet shoes and laughter.

Eating Gray's Papaya hot dogs on the Throgs Neck Bridge in the fog. Perched on his shoulders, Carly proclaiming, "I see dolphins in the sky." And Eric trying to catch them as the fog rolled by.

The lightness of his step on the stairs coming home. Taking Carly on his knee and unraveling his day like a storybook, then hearing—entranced—their exploits while he was gone. Sofie lifted her face to the water. She had perfected the recanting of their day so that nothing alarmed, only amused, so he did not feel slighted. *"We went to the park and thought how high you could toss Carly into the sky."* And he would glow as though he'd been there, thrilling them. Thrilling her.

Eyes closed, she remembered the first time he'd brushed the hair back from her cheek. The scent of his breath; the tremor in his hand. It was, she now admitted, not only the loss of Carly that had driven her to despair. Four years of Eric's unyielding adoration had left a terrifying void. She didn't know how to be without him, or who to be—or who she'd been before.

It was as though she'd been wiped clean and refilled. Eric's Sofie never raised her voice, soothed rising tensions with a word. Eric's Sofie never complained, never disagreed. She'd learned how to deflect his anger so that it dissipated like a vapor that only she breathed, leaving the air pure for him and for his child. And when his sunshine smile warmed her and the ice melted away, she'd been validated as never before. Sometimes her heart had felt too big for her chest, as though she could not contain the love there but had to store it up in every part of her. And he'd radiated the same.

"I have never laughed before. I have never lived before. You are my life, Sofie. My life's breath."

It was as much the loss of him as of his daughter that had drained her desire to live. No wonder Carly couldn't be without him. No surprise she'd reached back, in spite of what she'd learned. Could she blame the child for believing Eric's love outweighed everything else?

Did it matter that its edge could slice? That its ice chilled to the marrow? The resuscitating benevolence had wiped clean every error. Except the last. She had not allowed it when he had turned his icy stare on Carly, freezing her soul with the depth of his disappointment. Sofie had stepped between them, revealed her loyalty to his child. And nothing was ever the same again.

Sofie brushed her wet hair into a ponytail, dressed and slipped out of the bathroom. She hadn't heard Matt get up, but he stood by the window with bristly jaw and tousled hair. Sweatshirt, flannel pants, long limbs, and bare feet. Even his toes were long and knuckled. She absorbed the sight of him, the strength and comfort.

He turned from the window and murmured, "Morning." His voice had an endearing sleepy coarseness.

She smiled painfully. "I didn't know you were up."

"Just."

She joined him at the window, slid her hand into his and looked into his eyes, eyes that had told her so much the first time she'd seen him. He was a wonderful man, not at all the person he feared he might be. She wanted him to know that. She raised her chin, but he dragged his palm down his cheek.

"I'm rough."

She didn't care. She drew his face down and kissed him. Seconds stretched as his arms enclosed her and their mouths communicated everything they couldn't say. *Be strong. Forgive me.* Her spirit quaked. She drew back and touched her chin made tender by his whiskers.

"Sorry."

She looked once more into his eyes. *Don't be.* "I'm going to church. Will you stay with Carly?"

"Let's have some coffee."

She shook her head. "I have to go."

"It's not even Sunday. I don't think missing one day—"

She reached up and touched his lips. "I want to." It was not what she'd intended, but things had gone beyond her control. And who knew what God intended? Who could presume to know? What she hadn't forgotten was that she owed Him a life. She had tried to throw it away and He'd restored her. She had lain in pain, begging *Why?* But now she knew. It was hers, still, to plead for Carly.

Matt said nothing as she walked out. There was nothing he could say. She went downstairs and out the door as she'd done so many times. Most mornings she'd tagged along with Lance and Nonna, no one else sacrificing the last of their sleep to go to church before school or work. But they three had needed God's touch on their day.

She wished she could glean the anticipation, the hope she'd found in the morning ritual. But she felt alone. Was Matt right that everything came down to doing right for society or an individual? If there was no arbiter but herself, her heart and mind were resigned. She hadn't known this moment would arrive, not until Carly made the call. Then helplessness had surrounded her like the water in the bath.

She walked the blocks to the church, thinking of the love she'd found within its walls, the comfort of an all-powerful, all-seeing protector, an all-loving, need-satisfying being. Was it that intensity that prepared her for Eric's? Had she placed on his shoulders God's mantle?

If, as Matt claimed, there were only human reason and relationships, all she could do was trust the love she had for her child. Maybe that was the true light of the world, the only truth.

Others joined her on the sidewalks and passed through the doors. She went inside. The scents of candles and polished wood, the whispers of prayers surrounded her as she knelt and made the sign of the cross. She slid into the next to last pew.

Her lips did not move in prayer; her eyes went neither up toward heaven nor forward to Christ on the cross. They stayed on her hands, on the scars across her wrists, small ropes of bondage. *Lord.* She had no sense of holiness, only loss.

Moments later he slipped in like a shadow beside her. "Hello, Sofie." His voice strained as though it hurt to say her name.

She turned to the face so handsome, so compelling she couldn't look away. Even haggard, he had a raw appeal that caught her by the throat. She remembered how it was to belong to him. To be ravaged by his hunger. But it wasn't hunger she saw now.

His gaze sank like a spear into her heart. "Where's my daughter?"

She drew a jagged breath. "She's safe."

"With him?"

She startled. "What?"

"The man you're *with*. Does he have her?"

She focused on the altar as blood rushed in her head.

"Did you think I wouldn't know?"

She trembled. "I thought you wouldn't care."

"Sofie." He closed her hand into his. "I have missed you every single day."

She impaled him with a glare. "Then why did you only watch and take pictures?"

His head jerked up. "You know?"

"A whole box of them, Carly said."

He exhaled. "So that's it. She saw the pictures. I should have known she'd look for you."

She couldn't tell him she'd seen the other pictures. If he thought she knew . . . what? He'd be embarrassed? Angry? Enough to hurt something?

He swallowed. "I let her call you. I could have stopped her, but I didn't. Once she'd figured it out. I didn't keep her from you because I know how it is to lie awake, aching for your voice."

"You knew where to find me, Eric. We could have talked."

He shook his head with a look of such profound betrayal it staggered her. What could he possibly hold against her?

His whisper rasped. "You left me."

"What?" She could hardly breathe.

"Tried to go where I could never find you. You tried to take your life from me."

Her chest quaked. "You left *me*, Eric."

"I wanted you to see how it would be without us."

Tears welled in her eyes. She had seen.

"But you, you would have made it so we could never come back." His voice broke.

Guilt hit her like a tidal wave. "I never meant to hurt you."

"You meant to destroy me."

She quaked as the awful possibility echoed in her mind. Had she? She pictured the razor in her hand. Had it been Eric she had cut from her, draining his love until it could no longer hurt? Maybe it wasn't giving up, but striking back.

Had the cut of that blade been the first act of independence she'd accomplished in the four years she'd known him? She looked into his face and saw the damage. Her action had broken him in a way he hadn't been before. Had she tipped him over an edge, a point of inhibition past which he'd do anything to protect Carly and by extension himself?

"I won't ever hurt like that again." The chill in his voice turned her heart to ice.

"Eric—"

"I want Carly." Stone-cold, like a voice from the grave.

"The police are looking for you."

"I know."

"What about your mother? Eric, please tell me you didn't push her."

"I didn't." Remorse moved over his features. Maybe it was real, maybe not. "She should not have kept Carly from me."

She read the implication. "You'd hurt me too?"

"Don't make me."

She took his hands. "Let me keep Carly while you deal with this. Get the help you need. You know you can plead out. You were always persuasive."

Out of nowhere, his smile lit up like a single star in a curtain of clouds. How she had loved that smile. He brought her hands to his mouth and kissed her fingers. "Come with us."

Six years she'd waited, six years begged God to restore what she'd lost. And Eric had been waiting too. She dropped her forehead to their joined hands, tears spilling over their fingers. "I can't."

For all their sakes, she could not allow him to follow this course. She felt his hands tremble. When she looked up, all emotion had left his face except the hard, cold anger.

———

Matt gripped his phone as an unidentified call came. "This is Mary Cavallo. I'm in the coffee shop across the street. That man you wanted to know about is leaving the church with Sofie."

His chest constricted. He hadn't wanted to think it. Even as she'd walked out, he'd hoped. But he didn't have time to regret. "Which way are they going?"

"The way she walks home."

Eric was coming for Carly. Well, he wouldn't get her. That little girl deserved a chance at an untortured life. He called the police, then hurried to the bedroom, where Carly sat up, sleepy-eyed.

She pushed the hair back from her forehead and eyed him. "Where's Sofie?"

"She went to church." He walked to the window, checked the lock, and studied the fire escape going down to the courtyard.

"She was supposed to take me."

She hadn't said anything like that, but the implication bruised him. Had Sofie planned for the three of them to simply walk away?

Carly threw off the covers and climbed out in a nightshirt that would have been short on Sofie but dangled just above Carly's skinny ankles. Before he could tell her to get dressed, she snatched up her clothes and darted to the bathroom. Good. Soon he wouldn't count on her cooperation.

When she came out, he took her across the hall to Rico and Chaz's apartment. The door was unlocked when they went in, but he locked it behind them. "Sit down."

She frowned. "What are you doing? Aren't we going to the church?"

"Did Sofie know your dad would be there?"

She looked triumphant. "We were supposed to meet him. Both of us."

He knew better than to take anything she said at face value. Maybe the kid had hoped for that, but Sofie knew better. Had she gone to confront Eric? Or to reconcile.

Chaz came out of his room. "Is something wrong?"

"Eric has Sofie."

Carly shook her head. "It's not like that."

"Is Rico up?"

"I'll wake him." Chaz moved to the other bedroom.

Matt squatted down before Carly. "Listen to me, kiddo. You know what happened to your grandma."

She started to shake her head again.

"And your friends and their pets."

She put her hands on her ears.

"I know you can't stand the way things were, and you think Sofie can change that. But she can't. She tried once and almost died trying."

Tears sprang to Carly's eyes.

"Your dad needs help, but he can't get it as long as you and Sofie enable him."

"You don't understand."

"I understand more than you think."

"No. You're just a big, stupid person, and you've ruined everything. Why did you have to be here?" She lunged.

Her shove hardly budged him, but her fear and rage and desperation came through. He grabbed her as Chaz and Rico came out, planted his palm over her mouth when she started to scream. Though it went against everything in him to manhandle her, if she bolted, he'd lose any control of the situation he might have. Her life, and Sofie's, could depend on it. "Check the windows. Can you see them?"

Chaz moved from one to the next. "No, mon."

Matt's phone rang, but he didn't want to lose his hold on Carly. He shot Rico a glance. "In my pocket."

Rico took the call. "That was Lynette Funio. Sofie and Eric are just around the corner."

"Split up, front and back. Try to see if he has a weapon." A warped part of him hoped he did, that Sofie wasn't willingly participating.

"I see them," Rico called from the bedroom. "They're walking close. I can't tell about a weapon. Maybe, maybe not." He paused, then, "Sofie unlocked the door."

Matt clenched his jaw. She was bringing Eric up. Maybe she had no choice, or believed she had none. It didn't matter. Even if she wanted this, he had to stop them from leaving. Eric was dangerous. Where were the cops?

Since they would probably check Sofie's apartment first, he turned Carly over to Chaz and went to stand by the door.

Behind him Chaz said, "Why do you struggle? We're trying to help you."

It wouldn't work to reason with her. Not now. He only hoped he could get through to one of the others.

Rico joined him at the door. The man was small but street tough, and Sofie had suggested he'd seen his share of fights. If they had to muscle her away from Eric . . . A commotion sounded outside the door. Lots of feet on the stairs in the hall. Kids' voices.

"They're going to school," Rico said beside him.

"Down from upstairs?"

Rico nodded.

Could they use that? No, it would risk the kids. The noise died down. He listened for other footsteps. Eric's. And Sofie's. Had they reached this floor? Gone into her apartment? He waited.

His phone rang. Sofie's tune. Rico handed it over. Matt set it to speaker. "Sofie?"

"Eric and I are on the roof." Her voice sounded shaky. "If you don't bring Carly up, he'll throw me off."

His stomach clenched. He hadn't even thought of that. But now he imagined the critical injuries of a four-story fall. Injuries or death.

"He wants Chaz and Rico, too, where he can see them."

Matt looked to see if the others had heard. They obviously had. He tried to process that into a plan, but his reasoning was blocked by thoughts of Sofie falling. Everything came back to that. "We're coming up."

He needed to think, but Chaz had removed his hand from Carly's mouth, and her crying overlaid the pounding in his ears. He took her arm. "You need to stay with me." Something in his tone must have told her not to struggle, or else she realized she was getting what she'd wanted. He asked Rico, "How do we get to the roof?"

Rico led the way up the stairs to the top floor, through a door to a narrow flight up. The next door opened onto the chilly morning. Matt hoped for sirens but heard only kids on the street below. Eric held Sofie near one edge. No sign of a weapon. Once he released her, how did he think he'd get past them all? Something wasn't right.

Carly tugged, but Matt didn't let go. He moved her to the center of the roof, Chaz and Rico flanking them. "What's the plan here, Eric?"

"Give me my daughter."

"It's not safe over there. It's my job to keep kids out of hazardous situations." As he spoke he scrutinized the man Sofie would have died for.

Eric looked to be sizing him up, as well, then shifted his attention to the child. "Come here, Carly."

Matt held her tight. "Let Sofie go."

Eric snapped his focus back. "Sofie doesn't want to go. She wants her little girl."

A chill spread through him as he looked into Sofie's face.

"Let her go, Matt," she said.

"You know I can't do that. Let's all go down—"

Eric stepped onto the raised edge of the roof, his knuckles whitening on Sofie's arm. "If I go, Sofie goes."

"Daddy!" Carly shrieked.

The wind tossed Eric's hair. Murder-suicide was not beyond him. Matt caught the thought like a blow to the chest. Eric didn't plan to get out of there. Sirens sounded—not near but coming closer. Matt clenched his jaw. If he could hold him off until the cops arrived . . . Carly yanked free and ran.

"No!" He charged after her.

Eric teetered. Sofie screamed. Carly lunged for her dad as he lost control. Wheeling, Eric grabbed onto her. Sofie clutched them both as he fell. No time to think, only act. Matt dove on top of Sofie and caught hold of Carly's arm as she dangled over the edge. The child's screams pierced his ears and covered the sound of Eric landing.

He groped his other hand down to Carly's shoulder joint and heaved her up as Chaz and Rico caught and pulled her over. The sirens drowned Carly's screams while Chaz dragged her away from the edge. Matt rolled off of Sofie and pulled her down from the four-inch rise. She gasped with pain, and he guessed he'd broken or bruised her ribs, collarbone maybe. But if he hadn't landed on her, they'd have all three gone over.

CHAPTER THIRTY-FIVE

On his knees in the hall, Lance prayed. The fierce knowledge that lives hung in the balance had gripped him, and he'd kept on without stopping until it let him go. Now, spent and stiff, he opened his eyes. Afternoon had yielded to evening, and no sounds of other workers reached him. He turned.

Rese sat against the wall, her expression more querulous than concerned. "Are you back?"

Pain shot up his thighs from knees that felt numb. His hamstrings pulled as though he'd run for miles. "Yeah." He pressed a fist to the small of his back.

"Can you move?"

He sat back on his heels, drawing his toes forward, a burn running the length of his Achilles tendons. "I didn't finish the floor."

She shrugged. "You were doing something else."

He eased back against the opposite wall and drew his legs out from under him. "I could have finished this hall."

"You will."

She was taking this better than he'd expected. He tried hard to avoid any hint of preferential treatment, so maybe no one had noticed his lapse.

"Randy came up to take the sander, since you weren't using it."

Lance noted it standing where he'd left it when he had dropped to his knees.

"He shook your shoulder to tell you."

Randy was a Saxon behemoth. How had he missed that mitt on his shoulder?

"A few years ago, someone broke a Seagram's bottle over his skull in a bar fight. He has chronic headaches and recurring double vision. This was a bad day." She raised her head. "Until he touched you."

Lance took that in. He'd been so deep in prayer the contact hadn't registered.

"He came downstairs with a weird look on his face. Said his head was full of butterflies. Then it cleared and he was pain free."

She wasn't expecting an explanation, so he didn't try. All he knew was that God had impressed him to pray. Sofie and Matt had been primary in his thoughts to begin with, then the awareness of God had overwhelmed everything else.

"The guys wanted to go up and see. Randy guarded the stairs."

He dropped his gaze to his hands. Rese had taken a chance, letting him into her professional life. Now this. "So I'm a freak?"

"No more than I've always been. But . . . watch out if they want a new mascot."

"Fagedda-bout-it."

"Actually that's one role I wouldn't mind passing on."

He doubted he'd ever replace her legend. He'd seen enough to know the crew revered her work but still considered her a challenge to work for. Teasing her, even if half their efforts were wasted, restored the balance. No telling what they'd think of him.

She tipped her head back against the wall. "Ready to go home and see what's for dinner?"

"Okay." He managed a grin. As much as he would enjoy whatever Nonna and Star had cooked up, he longed to take raw ingredients and create something himself, longed for the aromas and textures of his art. And if it kept him in the shelter of Quillan Shepard's kitchen, where the Lord's sneak attacks went unremarked, so much the better.

He'd never shirked life, but he'd never been out of control either. Maybe this intensity in prayer would fade. He got the idea he could stop it if he wanted, but did he? What if his prayer today had been a channel of grace and power in a situation too far out of his hands to even know? Sofie still had not taken his calls. It wasn't like her, but she had Matt, and maybe he'd underestimated their connection.

And if it wasn't Sofie it could be someone else. How could he tell God thanks, but no thanks? He pushed up from the wall, met Rese in the middle, and took her hands. "Tomorrow, one sanded floor. I promise."

Sofie held Carly in her lap as a monitor counted each beat of Eric's heart. His crushed and battered organs were shutting down one by one, and after six years of waiting, these moments would be all she had. No words, no explanations, no apologies.

Now she knew the terrible wound she had caused the ones she loved by spurning her own life. The wound she had caused him. A betrayal worse than his. No wonder he hadn't forgiven her. How could she ever forgive herself?

She'd gone on, but the life she'd returned to had been the grand gestures of a specter trying to be seen among the living. Bold words, trying to be heard. Echoes of love and life she could no more contain than her veins had held the blood. Lance's prayer had passed through her. Nothing was real but the child in her arms. Eric's child.

A rattle started in his throat. Carly turned her head. "He sounds different."

She stroked her back. "He can't fight much longer."

"Why don't they do something?"

"They can't fix all that's wrong." Nothing had, or ever would. As they'd waited on the roof, he had called death their final unity, and she'd seen the depth of his illness, how it had hollowed him into a shell of the man he'd been or could have been. She had told him in the church that she couldn't go with them, but Eric had known she would not have let Carly go alone. They were bound together, survivors of a consuming love. And now co-bearers of this grief.

As Carly's soul-deep sobs covered the last of his breaths, Sofie couldn't stop the prayer that came to her lips—hope more tenacious than her weary mind could disregard. *Lord have mercy. Christ have mercy. Lord have mercy.*

Carly cried. Sofie rocked her, ignoring the pain in her ribs, seeking it. Together they mourned Eric's passing, sharing the grief—and the guilt. What if she'd said yes, if they'd gone in together for Carly? What if she'd told Matt to let it go, to stop fighting for her? Such painful words, *what if.*

A nurse came in and turned off the machines, then went back out. Somewhere police waited to be informed; other authorities to be notified. She would speak with Eric's mother when that was possible. Plan a memorial. Carly would need that. Then sorrow overtook her and nothing mattered but the loss—and the terrible freedom in its wake.

––––––––––

How could anything hurt so much? In the room at Sofie's, Carly squeezed herself. She was dying. She had to be, wanted to be. She had made Daddy fall. Because Matt wouldn't let go, she'd fought and run, and then . . . It kept going through her mind like a slow-motion movie. His arms wheeling, his body twisting, her daddy grabbing hold. For help. He'd wanted her to help, to catch him, to save him.

But she'd gone over too, and if Sofie hadn't held her, she'd be dead. She wished she was. She deserved to be. He had never hurt her. He only wanted her safe, and he'd tried to make her happy, tried his best to always make her happy. He couldn't help it if she wanted friends, and now she knew she'd been so stupid. What good were friends?

It was Daddy who had mattered. Now he was gone. She bent over with sobs. What if Sofie left her too? But then she was there, soothing, holding, crying with her.

"I know it hurts, honey. I know."

She knew because it hurt her too. She was the only person in the world who had loved Daddy too. And he'd loved her. It would have worked. They could have been together, if Matt had just let go!

Sofie rocked her in her arms and didn't make her stop crying the way Grandma had. She knew it would never stop. She had made Daddy fall, made Daddy fall, made Daddy fall. But it wasn't her fault. *Oh, please, please, please, don't let it be my fault.*

She pulled away, ran to the bathroom and threw up. There was hardly anything inside. The reflex had come so often since Daddy took his last awful breath, that there was nothing left to throw up, but she wanted to. She wanted to get it all out. All of it. All the bad feeling. All the pain. All the guilt. All the regret.

Why, why had she called Grandma? Daddy wouldn't have been in trouble if she hadn't. It was Grandma's fault she fell down. She shouldn't have gotten in his way. Stupid woman. And stupid Matt. Stupid, stupid Matt.

Sofie rubbed her back. "Come on, Carly. There's nothing left in your stomach."

She washed out her mouth. Sofie was wrong. The hurt was left. As hard as she tried she couldn't get it out. It was there just as strong. *Daddy.* "I want my Daddy."

"I know."

Why didn't she say she wanted him too? She looked at Sofie, saw the hurt in every shadow. She might not say it, but she wanted him. Because how could they live without him?

Carly gulped. "What will I do without him?" Who would she even be? No one. "I'm nothing." Worse than nothing.

"No, Carly. You're everything. And I love you."

"Don't leave me."

"Never."

But how could Sofie say that when they both knew it was her fault Daddy fell, and all he ever did was love her too much?

Matt rubbed his face. He had hardly slept for two nights; vigilant the first, regretful the next, wondering what he could have done differently. A longer reach. A better grip. He hadn't known Eric, hadn't liked what he'd known. But Sofie and Carly, who had suffered the man's warped affection, mourned him now, and he'd have avoided that if he could.

Maybe God had helped him help Sofie, and thrown Carly in too. He hadn't prayed to help Eric. Maybe if he'd asked better, known how to ask or been willing to, things would have turned out better. He nodded to Rico, doing crunches on the incline bench by the wall, then sank into a chair beside Chaz, whose Bible lay open on the table. "Any answers in there?"

"All of them."

Naturally. He should have asked Chaz to pray. Maybe Chaz had. Maybe two out of three was the best anyone got, and for that much he was truly grateful. He didn't want to think how Sofie would be if Carly had been lost. That was the real answered prayer, but he hadn't prayed it. "Seems a little muddy."

Chaz sat back. "The enemy loves confusion, twisting a little bit of truth with a little bit of lie. The key is to search with the heart. Thoughts are too easily bent."

"Hearts can be pretty bent too."

Chaz spread his long fingers. "If you seek with true desire, mon, you will find what you need."

"I'm worried about Sofie."

Chaz fixed him with a penetrating gaze. "It is for Carly that we must fight."

Carly? She wouldn't let him within ten yards of her and by extension, Sofie. He'd been the one restraining her. He'd forced the issue on the roof. Or had she?

No. Eric was responsible for his own death. He'd been willing to take their lives, as well, to inflict pain on them for resisting his control. Matt clenched his fists. "He's still controlling them. But they can't see it. Or won't. And that makes me the bad guy."

"That stinks to high heaven, 'mano," Rico called from the bench.

Chaz said, "I promise, if you look, you will find your answers."

"I'm not even sure I know the questions." He straightened. "But I do know my being here is complicating things."

"The little girl wants somewhere to focus her anger."

"I'm a pretty big target."

"It is herself she blames. She would rather it were you."

He understood that too well. "It'll be better if I'm out of sight for a while."

"Better for whom?"

He shrugged. "All of us."

Rico sat up and toweled his neck but offered nothing beyond his succinct summation. It did stink, the stench of wasted life as foul as anything there was.

Matt wasn't sure where to start untangling his thoughts and emotions. If God had a role to play, he wanted to approach it reasonably, and reason fled in Sofie's presence. He'd fall to his knees and confess anything if it would break the hold Eric wielded from the grave.

He went into the bedroom for his suitcase, then told Chaz, "I stripped the bed. If you want me to wash the sheets . . ."

Chaz smiled. "We will wash the sheets, mon. It's Rico's turn."

Rico grunted from the floor, where he was doing one-handed pushups at an impressive rate.

"I'll just talk to Sofie, then. Let her know I'm taking off."

"I pray your flight will be uneventful."

"Yeah." He took that to mean the airline flight. Because he was not running away, only . . . what? Across the hall, he tapped the door.

Sofie opened it, her hair brushed and shining, her blouse crisp; an attempt at normalcy for Carly's sake, no doubt. The veneer failed at her eyes, hooded with weariness and weeping.

What exactly was she mourning? A death? The chance to reunite? He wanted to ask but didn't. "How's Carly?"

"Overwhelmed with regret."

That had to go for both of them. "And you?"

She lifted a shoulder. "I'm thankful I can help her through this."

He searched her face. She had broken before, but now she had something to hold on to, and it seemed to be giving her strength. Throat tight, he nodded.

"It's what I came for, Matt. What I was made for."

If she believed that, there was less getting through than he'd thought. "Have you spoken with her grandma?"

"Very briefly. She's in a lot of pain." Her voice caught. "There's no way she can keep Carly right now."

"Then you're staying until she can?"

Sofie nodded. Otherwise she'd go into the system, and he was the first to admit how overextended and shaky some of the options were. Even a quality foster home would not provide the love Sofie lavished on her.

No question this was best for the child, at least in the short run. But Sofie? Back in the environment that had bred despair, with loss once again slicing her like a razor? What happened when it came time to let Carly go?

He released his breath. "I have to go back to work. I'm catching a flight this morning."

She showed as much relief as disappointment. If Carly blamed him completely, Sofie wasn't far behind. They'd both been thrown into a tailspin of guilt and regret, grasping for a scapegoat to ease their pain. He'd take all the blame if it freed them to live their lives. But it wasn't working that way.

He pressed back from the jamb. "Anything I can do before I go?"

Something flickered in her eyes that would have encouraged him days ago. Now he realized it was false hope. "No. Thank you, Matt."

He cradled her cheek, sank his fingers into her hair, aching for her to tell him to stay. But of course she didn't. He leaned in and kissed her mouth with pain deep inside. "I'm sorry. I wish things were different."

"I know." Tears sparkled in her eyes.

"Bye, Sofie."

She drew a jagged breath. "Good-bye, Matt."

Whether from Chaz's prayers or not, the flight back was uneventful, the following days at work, not. Cassinia had returned, and they had their hands full, compiling documentation to answer a suit Donald Price had filed for harassing his family.

It should have been dismissed outright, but Price had gotten to someone who'd pushed it far enough that it wasn't going away before they'd been seriously inconvenienced. And the department would think twice before interfering in that household again. Matt shook his head. Did bullies always win?

CHAPTER THIRTY-SIX

Rese stared. She had furnished the four bedrooms in the house next door with two full-size iron beds in each to accommodate guests coming in for the ceremony. The other old-fashioned beds she'd acquired, some full and some single, had been lined up in the villa attic, dormitory style, and now—frighteningly—Mom had taken residence in one by the window.

Star giggled uncontrollably, having tugged her up to see. "It must remind her of the nuthouse."

Rese looked at her mother all tucked into the narrow bed. "It'll be a nuthouse when all the kids get up here."

Star twirled. "She'll think they're elves and pixies, come to play."

"And what will they think?"

Star leaned close and whispered, "Fairy godmother."

Rese crossed her arms. "You'll tell them that?"

"If they don't figure it out for themselves," she said, her eyes bright.

"Right. Well, I guess she can stay. She seems to like it better up here."

"And you can offer the Rose Trellis to Roman and Doria."

Rese laughed. "Good idea. Right next to Lance."

She looked once more at her mother, comfortably ensconced in the bed of her choice, then started down, with Star on her heels. The lower levels of the villa had always been planned to accommodate guests and wouldn't take much effort when the time came. The parlor held conversational groupings, the dining room having small tables they usually combined, but that would be angled separately along the walls for the reception.

Things were coming together. With Lance and Nonna planning the food they'd prepare when Lance's mother and sisters arrived to help, and Star taking charge of decorations and favors—without breathing a hint of what she intended to do—and Michelle and the church ladies lined up to serve, it seemed possible they'd pull it off. Sofie's studio would be open for dancing, both yards for mingling, and plenty of room for people to sit and indulge in Lance and Nonna's cooking.

Unbelievably, she found herself looking forward to it—even to seeing Lance's entire extended family. The neighbors wouldn't complain, because Lance had invited them as well—the nurses across the street, the financier, and whoever else had wandered by at one time or another. The only thing that seemed unresolved was Sofie, and it weighed on Lance with each passing day. It weighed on her too. Had she been wrong to insist he stay?

He came up behind and wrapped her in his arms. "Wow. You're burning enough wood in that skull to heat the West Coast."

Star giggled. "So that's the smoke curling up from your ears."

Rese dropped her head back against him. "Mom's moved to the attic."

"Okay."

"Your parents can have her room."

"Eek." He squeezed and released her. "While we're on that subject, I talked to Rico. He and Chaz want to play live in the garden." He looked over to where he'd hacked out the hedge and built a stone pond and fountain. "Maybe there."

Rese snorted. "Guess I know where you'll be."

"I might sit in for a set or two, but I'm not leaving my bride unattended among the New York contingent." He turned. "You want to sing, Star?"

She fixed her fingertips to her head. "He thinks 'I am easier to be played on than a pipe.'"

"So that means yes?" Lance's grin had a wicked tilt.

Rese cocked her head. "You're in an awfully good mood."

"I heard from Sofie," he told her, his expression softening. "She's coming back with Carly."

Rese released a long breath. "That's great."

"Yeah? Two more mouths."

"And you not moping and praying like a fiend."

"I wasn't moping."

She planted her hands on her hips. "Just try and deny the other part."

"I plead the fifth."

Rese smiled. "Uh-huh. Do you think Sofie'll mind sharing with Carly?"

"Not a bit," he said. "My family commingles with ease."

But she glimpsed a hint of concern still. "What is it?"

He shrugged. "She sounded a little wrung out is all."

"She must be."

"So we'll share the load, hmm?"

She raised her chin. "It's what we do."

His smile took over his face. "Yeah."

Three weeks. Matt leaned back from his desk and frowned. He'd given Sofie space after the first couple calls had left them both confused and frustrated. She'd written a thank-you card for the flowers he sent to the funeral, and while it might satisfy Emily Post, he would have preferred the live connection of a phone call.

He had no reason to expect it. Eric had not taken her physically from the world, but through his daughter, Carly, he'd taken her back under his control. Matt hooked his hands behind his head and wished he could forget as easily. How was it fair that he thought of her every day, missed her every day?

Worse still, the things she'd said seemed to have burrowed into his mind—or soul? She'd challenged his comfortable complacency, opened a faith door that drew him deeper and deeper with each glimpse. He might have worked into a semblance of faith in order to please her, to have her. What impetus could he claim now, except the need to know?

Though he kept his thoughts to himself, Cassinia looked at him as though his defection showed. As his reluctant conviction grew, she voiced her distaste for anything Christian as though she sensed the careful reading he was giving the New Testament he'd found in a used-book store. He had none of the radiant belief Chaz displayed, yet she must perceive something that put her on edge in a way she'd never been with him.

Or maybe she was simply dealing with her mother's death, not having made peace before the end as he'd hoped. She blamed him for blowing the Price case while she was gone, for bringing Annie to Sofie, for—

The phone rang and he picked it up before realizing it was his cell. He got to that just before it went to voicemail. "Matt Hammond."

"Matt, this is Lance Michelli."

His heart thumped. "What's up?"

"Care to join us for dinner tonight?"

He could say he'd left something in the slow cooker, which he had, or had other plans, which he didn't. He could easily beg off, but he imagined the aromas, the ambience, the conversation— even if it would be without Sofie. "That sounds good."

Pathetic to hold on to whatever part of her he could get, especially if what she'd left him was her strange patchwork family. But something inside felt lighter. Might he hear something around their table that would finally dump him into his father's camp whether he wanted it or not? Maybe it had been an overreaction to throw it all out because one representative—or even many— had been such a poor example. Not even Lance claimed to be perfect.

"Good," Lance said. "Come hungry."

He had no idea. Or maybe he did. When Matt pulled up to the villa, the Road King was parked out front, gleaming like a temptress. The last time Matt had seen it, Lance had mentioned ripping his heart out.

From the steps behind the bike, Lance held out his keys. "The marsala's got a while yet."

Matt raised his brows. Baxter whined. Lance rubbed the dog's head, and Matt had the distinct impression he'd just been afforded a rare honor. Twenty minutes later he brought the bike to a growly stop, climbed off, and handed back the keys. "Sweet."

He didn't know why Lance had called, what the magnanimous gesture meant. They hadn't exactly become friends. He'd done his best for Sofie, but it hadn't worked out, and there'd been no reason for contact since, although the things Lance had said were stuck in his mind.

Truthfully it wasn't only the words, but the way they lived, loved, and worshiped. The way they spent themselves in serving God and one another. That was what he couldn't let go, even when his hurt and disappointment should have driven from him all faithful stirrings.

Lance eased the snoozing dog off his thigh and stood up. "I thought you should know Sofie's bringing Carly to live out here for a while."

For a moment he'd thought Lance was saying she was there. "She got custody?"

"The grandma's facing lengthy rehab and permanent disability. She and Sofie are sharing responsibility, but at least for now Sofie has Carly."

Against the odds, she'd gotten what she'd wanted. He wanted to cheer and cry and thank the God she'd trusted. But then he realized there was probably a long road ahead. "How are they?"

"Coping. Sofie's place and the grandma's both have difficult associations. We're hoping a neutral location might help." Lance spread his arms. "And good things have happened here."

"Is she looking for a miracle?"

"Maybe. The miracle of love and family. Whatever we can offer."

We? Matt was unsure he wanted any part of this. It was wrong to blame the child, against everything he stood for. How many times had he counseled against it? Yet Eric had left a burden of guilt, and Carly was using that.

They were two of a kind. Maybe that wasn't her fault. It was all she'd experienced, that manipulation that smothers and binds. But she knew its power over Sofie. Of that, he was sure.

"When are they coming?"

"Day after tomorrow. Come on." Lance drew him inside, where aromas and laughter wafted. The excellence of the meal disarmed him, the warmth and friendship embracing him once more. Had God instructed Lance to set the hook and reel in Matt Hammond once and for all? Star said he fixed people, but what did he think he could do with an unbeliever, a broken child, and a woman who loved a dead man?

Throat tight, he looked across the table, caught Star's turquoise gaze. She reminded him of Carly—brittle, damaged, and excruciatingly insightful—as she proved with the insensitive and accurate quote, "'He that is strucken blind cannot forget the precious treasure of his eyesight lost.'"

He hated that his loss showed. Gloom descended. He wished he'd gone home to his slow cooker. He'd committed his life to helping kids in bad situations, but he potently resented Carly. As long as Sofie's first allegiance was to Eric's child, she could not break free of the past or contemplate a future.

Lance, of all people, should see that. He turned to question him, and realized that was exactly what the man saw. Then the rest of it hit him. Did they think there was something he could do, something he hadn't tried already, words that hadn't been said?

He no longer argued the validity of faith, was opening himself to the power and presence of God, but Sofie had all that without him. She had them, and now she had Carly. What did they think he could offer?

He got up from the table and thanked them for dinner. "When Sofie comes, tell her . . . well, she knows where I am."

If she sought him out, what then? Carly stirred the animosity he'd felt for Jacky, the weight of responsibility. The weight of failure. Those things were as real as his feelings for Sofie, and he wouldn't be any good to them until he'd dealt with it. But how?

Back at his house, he played his phone messages, staring, stunned, when his mother's voice emerged from the machine. Irony of ironies. *I thought you should know Dad's going in for a heart procedure. He'd appreciate your prayers.*

"Huh. Won't they be surprised when they find he doesn't have one." He deleted the message.

His house was empty, silent. He turned on the entertainment system, but the music grated. He grabbed his jacket and walked to Murphy's. Halfway into his second beer, he felt a hand slide up his back, a fall of hair across his neck.

"Mmm. You smell good."

He ducked his chin as Sybil slid onto the stool next to him. From one extreme to the other. If that wasn't a picture of his condition, he didn't know what was. He slid her a glance. "Buy you something?"

"I'll have what you're having."

The bartender caught his hand motion, popped the cap on a beer, and placed it in front of her.

She took a long drink, set the bottle on the bar. "I heard a rumor."

"Really."

"I heard Lance Michelli healed a cleft palate." When he didn't bite she added, "Did he?"

He rubbed his face. "I wasn't there."

"You've been there a lot since."

"How do you know?"

"Becca."

He should not have told Becca anything, but in a pique over Sofie he'd divulged too much. "If you want to know something, ask Lance."

"I don't think that would go over too well."

"With his fiancée?"

"With him."

"I'm sure he'd let bygones be bygones. What's a little murder between ancestors?"

She arched an eyebrow. "You're funnier than I realized."

"Don't let it fool you. Underneath I'm a serious guy."

She laughed. "Why haven't we hooked up?"

"Because we're friends." He felt sorry for her, but anything more was asking for trouble.

"I can fix that." She slid her hand over the back of his shirt.

"Sybil."

She breathed into his ear. "Let's take this to my place."

"Nice try, but unless you serve sodium pentothal, you won't learn anything from me." He did not intend to revisit the miracle issue. Not when his defenses were down. "I don't believe it anyway."

"Why don't you let me decide?"

"What's the deal? You got a thing for Lance?" He narrowed his eyes. "He is your type. Edgy. Dangerous." Not the religious part. Definitely not that. But he saw in her eyes that he'd hit the mark.

She deflected it. "What if I said you're my type?"

"Come on."

She looked him up and down with a smile that made a greater impact than it should have. Part of him wanted to get back at Sofie, to prove he could let go as she had. He'd better be careful or he'd wind up somewhere he did not want to be.

She leaned her elbow on the bar. "Why did you call Lance dangerous? He has supernatural powers?"

"I'm not getting into it, Sybil." After spending the evening with Sofie's family, he felt a sudden acute protectiveness. "No matter how nicely you ask."

She hiked the eyebrow even higher. "Because of Sofie?"

"Because some things are better left alone."

And some wouldn't leave him alone no matter how he tried. The message light was flashing again when he got home.

CHAPTER THIRTY-SEVEN

Sofie let Carly out of the car and gave her an encouraging smile that covered her own trepidation. *Please let this be the right thing.* Because she was running out of ideas and short of energy. "Well? What do you think?"

Carly looked at the house and garden in the same way she'd observed the landscape on the drive from the airport. Silently. Punishing her? For what? She needed a place to heal as well.

"Ready to go in?"

But Carly shrank back, so she offered an alternative. "Would you like to see my studio first?"

Carly whispered, "Okay."

Thinking of Matt's excitement, she took her down through the hatch. "This is our secret way in."

No comment. Carly descended wordlessly, followed her into the newly finished studio and looked up at the ceiling. "Cool."

"Star painted it."

Carly had said all she intended to.

"I'll teach you to dance if you want."

She nodded, but it was hard to tell whether from interest or in order to please.

"Only if you want." She had to know she was free now, to say no or to embrace something new. The expectations they placed on each other had to be reasonable, but so far they merely clung. Without Eric governing everything, they were adrift. "Are you tired?"

Carly nodded.

"Hungry?"

She shook her head.

Food was going to be touch-and-go until she got the child stabilized emotionally. She brought her out of the studios through the new main doors and into the house through the kitchen. Nonna was there with a hug for both of them.

"Who is this beautiful girl? Little Carly?"

Sensing her panic, Sofie wrapped the child's shoulders. "Carly, this is Nonna Antonia. You won't remember her, but she knew you when you were just a baby."

Carly stood there, wordless. Not even a greeting. Sofie's heart sank. She had hoped these introductions would snap Carly out of her self-imposed silence. Since the accident, she had spoken to no one but her. Not even the judge had gotten a word from her.

Whether that was Carly's way of assuring they stayed together or a true inability to respond, she didn't know. Selective mutism was unusual, but given Carly's isolation before the incident, not as huge a leap as it might seem. Their communication had remained open to the point of excess—until this trip. Taking her out of her familiar city might be stressing her, but Sofie had hoped once they arrived it would be different.

"Is Lance home?"

"He and Rese are still at work."

She had hoped he'd be there to joke and jostle a response so all the weight would not be on her. She hated to admit it, but she didn't know Carly anymore. Six years had changed too much. She could hardly be more than a dream in the girl's mind. And reality hardly ever matched up.

"Come on. I'll show you our room." At some point they might rearrange or create a separate place for Carly, but the nightmares were so constant they'd slept in the same bed since the funeral. Gradually, she would create some distance so Carly could start dealing on her own, but so far it hadn't been possible.

Sofie led her up the stairs, hoping in this neutral place, this healing place, things would get better—for both of them. They washed and changed and climbed into the big bed. Unorthodox maybe, but the child's night terrors were violent enough she had to be right there to soothe her back to reality. Then reality had a sorrow of its own that required what comfort they could give each other.

Guilt was breaking them, and she didn't know how to stop it. Carly refused to be treated by any other professional. "Only you can help me, Sofie." The tearful assertion dichotomously broke and mended her heart. Somewhere, somehow, healing had to come.

As Carly rode with Sofie to the private school Grandma was paying for, dread encased her. It had hardly any students compared to some of her other schools. Like ten kids per teacher. Her whole grade had fifty-four. Sofie and Grandma thought that was a good thing. But she could not get lost in the crowd. How could she be invisible with so few?

Ms. Warrick, the guidance counselor they'd met the day before, had tested her to figure out what she knew and what she'd missed in all the changes from Daddy's erratic work and all their moves—and his death. The woman had looked at her curiously but kindly when Sofie explained as much of the situation as they'd agreed to tell, saying for her the words that wouldn't come.

With Sofie beside her she approached the building. She didn't want Ms. Warrick's kindness. Didn't want caring, understanding teachers. Didn't want friends. The thought of friends made her stomach knot like a fist. She could hurt anyone who tried.

She stopped at the doors, making one last plea. "Please, Sofie. I want you to teach me." If ten to one was good, wouldn't one to one be better?

Sofie's voice was gentle. "You'll be fine."

They both knew that wasn't true. "My stomach hurts."

Sofie drew her into a hug. "It's okay to be nervous. Even scared."

"I think I'm sick."

"Sweetie, you're not sick. You're bright and capable." And then the phrase she'd said over and over. "You are loved. You are beautiful. You are a child of God."

"But I'm not. Any of those things."

"You're all of them and more."

Carly shook her head, unable, unwilling to believe it. The person who had loved her completely was gone because of her. Who would want her now? Only Sofie. Because Sofie *knew*. She'd been there. She'd seen . . .

"There's the bell, Carly. You have your room number. Go on in, honey."

She turned with feet that felt like blocks. All her words clogged up in her throat. When she hadn't been allowed to make friends, she'd wanted them more than anything. Now she had to keep them out, keep everyone out. She couldn't let them see what she was.

She thought about going inside, then sneaking out when Sofie left, but if she made trouble they might not let Sofie keep her. And Grandma couldn't, and Daddy—

Tears filled her eyes. She gulped back sobs. *I am loved. I am beautiful. I am a child of God.* Lies. All lies.

Exhausted, physically and emotionally, Sofie sighed as the doors closed behind her child. She had agonized over this decision, resisted Carly's pleas. If anything could get her to speak again, a consistent social situation where participation was rewarded should be it. And yet the last glance Carly had sent her sank inside like a knife piercing. Such desolation.

Maybe she'd been wrong. Should she have let Carly decide? Others homeschooled with positive results. But they hadn't come out of Carly's situation. If she didn't learn the give-and-take of social relationships now, how and when would it happen?

Or was she pushing her too soon? In the two days at the villa, Star and Rese and Lance and Nonna had all reached out and attempted conversation—without success. Carly didn't mean to be rude. She just couldn't communicate with people she didn't know, didn't trust. The only person Carly trusted had just let her down.

Sofie stared at the closed doors and refrained from snatching her back. Why was she forcing this? Because she needed space herself? She hated to think it could be as selfish as that. Had she gone six years pining for the child only to force a separation when Carly was most vulnerable?

Maybe Eric had seen that, realized she didn't have the commitment to Carly he'd expected. The commitment he'd had. She hated to think it, but maybe he was right. Being Carly's only source of strength and comfort was harder than anything she'd ever done—except for losing them.

She swallowed the doubt and frustration. No matter how overwhelmed, how insufficient she felt, she would do whatever it took. She only wished she knew what that was.

She turned from the door and saw Matt leaning on her car, dressed in slacks and a dress shirt, sleeves rolled, arms crossed. Her heart lodged in her throat. She had pushed thoughts of him behind the imminent needs of each day, blocked feelings that felt traitorous. But there he was, and for too long she stood, taking him in.

He straightened when she finally approached. "Hi."

She moistened her lips, but her throat went dry as memories of him on the roof crashed into her mind. Eric's grip, his panic . . . his fall. If Matt had just let Carly go to him. . . .

"How are you?" His voice graveled.

She couldn't begin to ponder that. She was as she had to be. "I'm . . . getting Carly into school."

"I saw."

"She's nervous."

"New place, new people."

"So much change." She noted the way his hair had grown out

of its cut, giving him a looser, more carefree aspect, but his face didn't look carefree. She could only guess what was going through his mind. "How did you . . ."

"On my way to work." He motioned up the street.

"Oh." Another workday, answering cries for help, swooping in like the man of steel to save the world. Only he hadn't. "Lance told me you came for dinner last week."

He nodded. "I like good food."

"And Harleys?"

"Anything you don't know?"

She sighed. "Too much."

"Ribs still hurt?"

His dive had kept her and Carly from falling, but it had been too late. Something in them had broken when Eric died, and Matt was connected to it, whether they wanted that or not. "Lots of things hurt."

"Yeah."

"Matt . . ." She folded her arms. "I don't know how this is going to be."

"How do you want it to be?"

"In a perfect world?"

"In the one we live in."

She looked down at the ground. "There's a lot to deal with."

"For you? Or Carly?"

"For all of us."

"We could work it out together." His tone was cautiously optimistic.

The thought of someone to lean on, even just to walk beside her, nearly brought tears. "I'm not sure that's possible right now."

"Why don't we have dinner and talk about it?"

"She's not—"

"I don't mean Carly. You've got people to watch her."

Her heart sank. He wanted to pick up their relationship where she'd dropped it. She saw it in his face. But how could she give more than she was giving? "I can't leave her. She won't speak to anyone but me. It's a form of mutism."

"Selective."

That was the term, but it made it sound manipulative. "She has no more control over it than a stutterer."

"Why can't Lance . . ."

"Heal her?" An edge came into her voice.

"I'm not being flippant." The sincerity in his eyes showed that much.

"What Carly needs is love."

He looked at the school into which the girl had disappeared. "Carly needs to know you can't hoard love."

That stung. They weren't hoarding love, they were surviving it.

He wanted her to say something, but what could she say? Things were too complicated, too painful. She felt as though she'd been to war and shells were still breaking overhead. The past six years had been an illusion, and she'd been thrust back into the reality of Eric and Carly and her own inadequacy.

There was only one way through. Matt didn't understand she had to do everything she could for the child. Nothing else mattered. Only in loving Carly did she find absolution.

He could have driven past. But he'd stepped into the punch instead of waiting to be hit unexpectedly. Sofie had looked so achingly lovely with her hair silky-soft around her neck, her slacks and fitted top setting off her supple figure, her smooth olive skin and expressive eyes. He'd wanted so badly to take her into his arms, but that wasn't why he'd stopped.

He had gotten out and approached her because he'd wanted to fight for her, wanted her to fight for herself. But her expressions and body language had been as conflicted as his own, and he'd given up. Just as he hadn't stopped Jacky from walking away, he hadn't blocked Sofie's spiraling back into destructive patterns of thought and behavior. Maybe Chaz was right. Flight was his first response.

As he parked outside the office, his phone rang. He read the caller ID and decided it was time to stop running. "Hi, Mom."

"Oh, thank God. I thought you were out of the country or something."

"I've never been out of the country." Since Dad didn't believe in spending American dollars in foreign economies, no vacation they'd taken had crossed a border. He hadn't had time or reason to since.

"But I've tried to reach you."

"How serious are things?"

"They're going to open up his heart. He could die. Why haven't you answered my calls?"

"When's the surgery?"

"Tomorrow morning. You'd have been here already if you'd returned my first call."

Been there? "I don't know that I can get away."

"Your father is having open-heart surgery. You're all he has, and you don't think you can be there?"

He'd sprung for an expensive last-minute ticket to New York to be there for Sofie. He had far less inclination now, but he might never get the chance to make Jacky's case if he didn't go. "I'll see what I can do."

Nine hours later, he landed in Phoenix, then met his mother at the hospital. He'd sent flowers on her birthdays, cards for Mother's Day, but he hadn't seen her in five years. Her face had lost its sharp definition, her waist thickened. Her limbs were still thin, but the skin hung loose. Her hair was blonder than it had ever been in real life, her eyes a nondescript blue, not brightened by any inner illumination.

She was neither vague nor unintelligent, merely trained to appear both. The submissive wife. Once again his antireligious bias rose up, but this time he didn't reach for an equally useless philosophy. He'd seen faith in action, a sweating, serving, loving faith. It sprang from freedom, not domination.

"Oh, Matthew, I'm glad you're here." Her hug was not the bold embrace of Doria Michelli. Mom's was an insecure, artificial contact after the archetypal enfolding of Sofie's mother's love. Maybe it was her diminutive size and softness, or that she was afraid to show she had substance. Hugging her, he felt sorry more than anything else.

And that surprised him. He'd expected to be angry. But that would come. With Dad. If the man was going to die, he'd make sure he didn't go with a clear conscience. Seeing Sofie's decline had sharpened his resolve. One bully would face himself in the mirror, even if it was the last thing he saw.

His mother's arms slipped away. She stepped back and observed him. "You're so like Webb, it takes me back."

His jaw clenched. "Where is he?"

They went into the room where the giant, Webb Hammond, lay diminished. He worked hard for oxygen, a scowl carving a furrow between his brows until he turned. Matt's stomach clenched at the pride and pleasure that came to his father's face.

"Matty." His florid throat sounded congested. "Get over here where I don't have to strain to see you."

Matt moved to the bedside. "Broken pump?"

"Nothing they can't fix. I'll pay enough for it. Send all their kids to Harvard." The bravado didn't work as well with the tube in his nose and the flimsy gown tied around his chest.

"When did this start?"

Webb shrugged. "Few months ago." He turned. "Leave us alone, Liz. You're hovering."

"I'll get Matt some coffee."

He didn't want coffee, but he also didn't want his mother there for what he meant to say. He waited for the door to close, but before he could speak, his dad said, "Listen up. If I don't come through this, you're in charge of your mother."

"I thought you said—"

"They're cutting open my heart," he growled. "Think there are any guarantees here?"

Matt swallowed. "You're in the geriatric capital of the world. I imagine they do plenty of heart procedures."

"Procedures." He spit the word. "They don't have any idea why my heart is only doing half its job."

As far as Matt could tell it had never done even that much.

"Whatever they find, it won't be good. When it comes, you take your mother with you to Sonoma. She didn't want to move out here anyway."

"Then why did you?"

His father scowled. "Too many memories back home."

He'd been searching for a way to introduce the subject, and now Dad had handed it to him. "Of Jacky?"

His father's jaw snapped shut. Years of clamping down on that name had caused an automatic reflex. "It wasn't healthy for your mother."

Right.

"Point is, she can't stay in Phoenix alone. You'll need to get her located near you."

"That's not as easy as it sounds. Sonoma has limited real estate and elevated property values."

"She'll get something from insurance. I kept a paying job and have something to show for it. Unlike you, quitting the sure thing you had for some namby-pamby social work. Should have asked my advice. I'd have saved you the regrets."

"I have no regrets."

"Sure you don't. Lousy pay. No gratitude. No respect."

"You're wrong." He seethed. "What I do is important. It gets kids safe before bad things happen."

"Well, I've got news for you. Bad things happen."

"They shouldn't."

His dad glared. "I thought I raised you tougher than that."

"What did you think about Jacky?"

His fists balled. "Enough with Jacky."

"Enough? You wouldn't talk about him, wouldn't let Mom."

"She went through it, okay? What good would dragging up the accident—"

"Accident? At least call it what it was."

His father's voice chilled. "What are you talking about?"

"The way you drove him, drove both of us. Someone should have held you accountable years ago for the things you did."

"Things I did? I made you the man you are."

That was the sad truth. "And Jacky? What did you make him? Besides dead."

For the first time ever, his dad had no response.

"You're the one with regrets, Dad. Or you should be. He never had a chance."

"You don't know anything."

All he wanted was for the man to acknowledge the wrongs against his son. But he saw that would never happen. "How do you sleep at night?"

Blood rushed to his father's face. A monitor started to wail. He rasped, "You hear that?"

"Yeah." Matt looked him straight in the eye. "Sounds like a train whistle."

CHAPTER THIRTY-EIGHT

Sofie startled awake and caught Carly before she bolted, screaming, out of bed.

Carly thrashed, yanking against her hold. "No. No, please."

"Shh, Carly. Wake up."

Carly clawed herself loose. "Stop. Don't hurt them."

Sofie turned on the light. "Carly. It's all right, honey."

Her eyes were open, but she kept flailing until reality finally penetrated her dream. Then she sank back into her pillow, heart pounding. "I'm sorry."

"It's all right, honey."

"It was Grandma's little dogs, on their back legs begging. And he . . . he . . ." She gulped. "Matt pushed them over the edge."

She couldn't tell if Carly had actually dreamed Matt as the aggressor or if she switched it with her waking mind. Either way it troubled her. While it might make the dreams easier to bear, it would not help for Carly to transfer Eric's cruelty onto someone who had only tried to help.

"Matt would never hurt Grandma Beth's dogs." Or anything, or anyone.

"But he did. He pushed them over. I couldn't catch them." She started to sob.

"Shh." Sofie pressed her cheek to Carly's hair, drew the child tight against her. That might be the form her dream took, but the real event that triggered it was right there too. Now was not the time to defend Matt, only to bring Carly the comfort she so badly needed.

"I tried. I tried but he held me back."

Sofie kissed her head and let her cry.

"Why wouldn't he let go?"

Now she was dealing with reality. "He didn't want you hurt."

"No." She shook her head hard. "He doesn't care about me. He wanted you."

"He wanted me safe, yes. Wanted us all safe."

"Not Daddy."

Sofie swallowed the ache. Matt had probably not been concerned with Eric's safety. He'd seen a bully and transferred his animosity. If not for that, would he have caught Eric too? Could he have?

"I hate him. Those poor little dogs."

"Matt didn't hurt the dogs."

Carly pressed her face into the pillow. "I hate him. I hate him. I'm glad he's gone."

Sofie rubbed her back. So much anger, so much hurt had to come out. But she would not allow Matt to bear the blame—not in Carly's mind, not in her own. Of them all, only Matt had acted solely for the good of others.

"I wish he was dead," Carly hissed.

Sofie rose up to her elbow and turned the child to face her. "Don't ever say that again." Death was too final, too painfully eternal. "Do you hear me, Carly?"

Carly stared, dismayed. She looked so much like Eric, intense, mercurial. But in her eyes, Sofie saw remorse, or at least regret. She hoped and prayed it was not feigned.

"Go to sleep. You have school tomorrow." Sofie lay down and rolled to her side.

So far she had thought only of the child's loss, of her pain and grief and guilt. God knew that was crushing them both. Matt's words pressed in. *"Carly needs to know you can't hoard love."* She had resented it, but now she wondered if he could be right. Was Carly using grief and guilt to separate the person whose love she wanted from everyone else?

Her chest constricted. She didn't want to think it. Didn't want to believe she'd fallen into that again. Was there more of Eric in Carly than she wanted to believe? She pressed her hands to her eyes. How could she begin to handle this?

Something stirred inside, an inner knowing that she wasn't alone. The One who'd been there through everything, who knew her inside and out, had weathered her doubts and justifications. God had not failed her. There must be a way, would be a way through this valley. Please, God, let there be a way.

Carly closed her eyes. No way could she say anything, even if she wanted to. She'd made Sofie mad. There'd been no hard, cold rage, but she could tell. Why, why had she said it? She should only have thought it. With everyone else it was easy. It happened without trying, and she could not change it even if she wanted to. But Sofie had been her one safe place. Now there was not even that. Now there was no one.

Because of Matt.

Hatred rose up so strong it was almost alive inside her. She did wish he was dead, wished he was dead and Daddy was alive. She wished it so hard it hurt. And she wanted to hurt him. Just like Daddy had hurt those others. Her stomach clenched but she didn't want to throw up. This bad feeling could stay right where it was. She wanted it.

Matt stood in the hall with his trembling mother. He'd said his piece, but it didn't feel as good as he'd thought it would. It felt like a sucker punch, and he'd never been a dirty fighter, had only defended himself and others. Or had he?

His jaw clenched. It had been too easy to take the superior position, to let Jacky be the disappointment. Too easy to play the champion instead of teaching Jacky to defend himself. He had thrived on Jacky's weakness, his need, his admiration. Rightly seeing that neither parent was safe, Jacky had looked to him for everything. And he'd liked it that way.

Pain seized him. Dad had driven them both too hard, but it wasn't Dad's repudiation that had broken Jacky. It was his.

His mother wrung her hands. "I don't know what I'd do without you here."

She didn't know what he'd done, that this crisis was his creation. He stood in silence, knowing it would stay that way if he let it. He and Dad would deal with it man to man—if he came through. But as they wheeled him into surgery, hours before the scheduled time, he said, "I upset him."

"Oh no, honey."

"Yes. I confronted him about Jacky."

She looked up at him. "You . . ."

"I told him it was no accident. That he drove Jacky into that train."

She pressed a hand to her mouth. "What?"

"But the truth is, we all did. If any one of us had been what that hurting kid needed, he'd be here today."

"You can't mean . . ."

Matt swallowed. He hadn't meant to upset her further. But maybe lancing was the only way now. "If you hadn't denied Dad's abuse and I hadn't profited by it, if Dad hadn't thrown his weight and power around like a God-given right, Jacky might not have despaired."

"Please. Stop."

He wished he could. "You know it wasn't an accident. We knew that field, that track, even the train schedule." He shook his head. "Any one of us could have stopped it, but we didn't."

Tears filled her eyes. "Why are you doing this?"

"Because you're living a lie. And you deserve the truth."

She covered her face with her hands. "I wasn't home. I didn't see—"

"You saw it all for nine years. It was just easier to look away."

She crumpled. He caught her. He was on a roll now, breaking both parents at a vulnerable time. But it wasn't vindictive. The righteous anger he'd felt, the self-satisfaction had drained away, and all he wanted now was peace. Peace had a price, and the price was truth. But truth had a price too. That price was love. He had gone there to confront. Now he needed to bind up. God help him, he needed to forgive.

He eased his mother into a chair and crouched before her. "Listen to me, Mom."

She shook her head. "No. You've said enough."

"More than you wanted to hear, I know. You'll do with it what you want." She was probably already painting it a different shade. "But there's one more thing I need to tell you."

Sofie had learned not to hold a grudge, that it made the wound grow deep. The grudge he'd borne against both parents had formed a scab over his own betrayal. He'd carried a token guilt that paled against theirs and became, in a way, a badge of honor. Maybe his responsibility was less since he'd been a kid, bullied and abandoned to his own defenses, but it was time to stop blaming and try to bring what healing he could.

He swallowed the tightness in his throat, his very physiology resisting what he had to say. "I forgive you. I forgive Dad, and with God's mercy, I may one day forgive myself."

Her mouth worked. Her eyes streamed. She gathered herself and rasped, "It would be better if you weren't here when your father wakes up."

He hadn't anticipated the blow, and so it caught him full force. He picked up his overnight bag, gave her one last look, and caught a cab back to the airport.

———————

Lance stood in the driveway. Rese thought he wasn't taking seriously the situation with Star and Rico, but she had it wrong. He knew all too well how hot-headed Rico could be. He'd gotten bruises and a knife wound thanks to Rico's propensity to provoke the large and angry. He knew, too, how fragile Star was under her zany façade. But he gave them credit for being able to behave like adults in a potentially volatile situation. At least he hoped so.

He couldn't ignore the apprehension, though, when Chaz pulled the maroon van into the drive. Rico rode shotgun. Their band equipment would be in the back. Chaz emerged and they hooked hands and hugged. The greeting was a little more active and prolonged with Rico. Grinning, he stepped back and eyed them both.

Rico spread his arms. "You doing this thing, 'mano?"

Lance nodded. "I'm doing this thing."

Chaz laughed. "Did you think we would get here and he'd say never mind?"

"Thought Rese might. She's a clever *chica*. How come she hasn't figured you out?"

Lance shrugged. "You can ask her. She's inside with Star."

Rico's focus slid to the house. "I just might."

"Come on in. We'll unload later." Better to get any fireworks over with and have time for repair if necessary. He opened the door.

Star stood in a knotted blue dress, arms folded over her head. Her gaze fixed on Rico. She wrapped one ankle around the other. "'Alack, there lies more peril in thine eye than twenty of their swords.'"

Rico stood a long moment, then answered, "'Excellent wretch! Perdition catch my soul, but I do love thee.'"

She gasped, her hands flying down and clasping beneath her chin. "'Hear my soul speak: the very instant that I saw you, did my heart fly to your service.'"

He laughed softly. "I don't know any more, chica. I only learned one."

Lance ducked aside as she flew to Rico and took his hands. "I have something to show you." As she pulled him up the stairs, Rico tossed him a wry glance. Then they disappeared from sight.

"Think it's safe to leave them?" Lance asked Chaz.

Chaz spread his hands. "What is the alternative, mon?"

"Good point. Come say hi to Rese." He led Chaz to the kitchen.

Watching his good friend embrace the woman he loved, it didn't seem things could be much better. But then he caught sight of Carly, and her face told a different story. She turned and ran out the back door.

With the déjà vu of Maria's ordeal, he rushed out after her. "Hey, Carly, hold on."

She clenched the pencil she'd been using for her homework and glared.

"What's up?" He moved closer, hoping she'd get mad and break her silence, but her face got stony as she backed into the carriage house wall and slid to the ground.

"If you don't tell me what's wrong, I can't help." Not true. If God wanted to reveal it, her silence wouldn't matter. But so far, nothing.

Sofie came up beside him. "Thanks, Lance. I'll take care of her."

"Wouldn't hurt to let me have a shot."

"It's Chaz. He was on the roof when—He was part of it."

"It doesn't all have to fall on you, Sofie."

She went past and sat down next to the girl. She might get nothing out of her, either, but as long as he stood there it was guaranteed. He went back into the house.

Chaz wore a look of concern. "Things have not improved."

"Getting worse," Lance said. "Now she won't even talk to Sofie."

"She is perhaps too close."

He had told her that. But Sofie claimed that unless Carly was able to participate in the process, there wasn't much anyone else could do. "It's taking a toll Sofie doesn't want to admit."

"I hope I will not frighten her every time we meet."

Rese leaned on the counter. "Anything that reminds her sets her off, but it isn't much better the rest of the time."

She didn't say that with annoyance, just the frustration they all felt. Himself included. "Hard to know what she needs."

"Sofie seemed to think you might heal her," Chaz said.

Lance slacked his hip. "She told you about Diego?"

Chaz nodded. "No small thing, mon. Where much is given, much is expected."

"I know." He could hardly believe he was having this conversation with a man who'd walked much more righteously. Shouldn't Chaz be the one doing amazing things? Then he thought of the financial support he sent down to his father's church and guessed some amazing things were happening through that. They all had a part to play.

"That healing seems to have been God's way of getting my attention. There hasn't been anything so dramatic since. Just little stuff."

"Like Randy's headaches?" Rese asked softly. "And Maria's rebound. And all the things you see or know."

He sighed. "Sometimes there's nothing at all, like with Carly. Yeah, I can pray. We all can. But I haven't . . . Nothing obvious happens."

Chaz cocked his head. "Sometimes it is observable?"

"To the rest of us," Rese said. "Lance is swept off somewhere oblivious."

"Like the night we prayed for Star." Chaz's expression deepened as he remembered.

"Only longer," Rese said. "The last time a couple hours."

Lance wanted Chaz to understand, but at the same time for it not to change the dynamic of their friendship. He'd always looked to Chaz for wisdom, not vice versa. "I just start to pray and God takes over the rest."

"You have been gifted, mon. What are you going to do with it?"

"Do? If God's got something else in mind, He hasn't shown me. I have my hands full, taking care of my family and those extras that seem to turn up here."

"Ah." Chaz looked around. "I feel it. A place of blessing."

Lance nodded. "He's given us this place and the house next door." He looked at Rese. "We're open to whatever plan He has."

"It's good you are listening." Chaz smiled. "Instead of running ahead."

"Yeah, well . . ." Lance ran a hand through his hair. "That running ahead doesn't work so well."

Rese crossed the space and took his hand. "The hardest part for Lance is to stand back and let someone else have a shot."

Wasn't that the truth. He turned to Chaz. "This whole thing with Sof, I can't help thinking Matt's part of it."

Chaz nodded slowly. "But does he agree?"

Rico joined them with Star in tow. "Come on. Let's get the stuff." He started for the van. "Star thought we should practice in the studio until the big day."

Lance shared a look with Chaz and Rese. Rico and Star must have either said what needed saying or found words unnecessary.

———

Matt looked at the invitation on his counter. He had not sent the RSVP because each time he started to write that one person would attend, he almost wrote zero, and each time he almost wrote zero, he started to write one. And then he wondered why Rese and Lance wanted him there when Sofie would be there, and why, if Sofie would be there, he'd want to be anywhere else. But the answer to that was the key to it all. If she didn't want him there—He pushed away from the counter.

He needed to see Sofie without Carly, but that was harder to accomplish than it should have been. He didn't want to go to the house and compromise what Carly must consider a safe place. He couldn't go there while the child was in school since he was bogged down at work and skating on thin ice with his supervisor. He couldn't take a lunch break without someone looking over his shoulder, and his dad's words rankled. If he was making the income he'd thrown away he could tell them to take a flying leap.

As it was, he'd been assigned a mountain of paper work that kept him at his desk and out of trouble. Cassinia had been gone twice as long and violated more protocol issues with Maria than he had with Annie, but he hadn't blown a whistle on her. The lawsuit had been dropped, but not before his supervisor and Cassinia had found him a convenient fall guy. For the first time ever, he'd begun to know how Jacky felt. Nothing he could do was right.

Sofie and Carly blamed him. Mom and Dad blamed him, as evidenced by the fact that no one had called to say his father had made it through surgery. He'd contacted the hospital and learned that much, though they would not discuss the prognosis. And now even his work was being scrutinized, his thoughts and beliefs suspected.

It looked a lot like persecution. He'd read Jesus' words about having tribulation in this world, with the assurance He had overcome it. But Christ had been speaking to His followers, His disciples. Did he fall into that camp?

There'd been no huge moment of truth, only small moments along the way. Little nudges back in line. Small confirmations of things he'd once believed enough to get baptized. Or had that only been one more expectation he'd fulfilled? Like law school, proving he could do enough, be good enough for two sons.

He opened the refrigerator and took out the pitcher of green tea he'd brewed that morning, poured a glass and set it on the table. He ladled a bowl of stewed chicken and vegetables and set it beside the glass. He sat down and considered blessing it. Was it by God's grace he had even that?

He didn't know the formal blessing they all said together at Sofie's so he simply said, "Please bless this food that you've provided, Lord God. Amen." It didn't feel as weird as it might have. But then, no one was there to observe and pass judgment one way or the other. Solitude was a good thing after some of his days. But now he just felt alone.

He'd alienated so many people. Or himself from them, as with Sybil. He'd probably find her at Murphy's with some of the others doing happy hour after work. All he could feel was sorry for all of them. What was wrong with him? What he wanted, what he wished he could do was go hang out at the villa. What if he showed up at the door?

He took a bite of the stewed chicken seasoned with fresh rosemary. Not bad. Good actually. Maybe not fancy, but wholesome and tasty. He turned on the iPod in its docking station and set it to play a random selection. When he'd finished eating he went for a walk. The evening resonated with the sounds of spring birds, dogs yipping, voices of other strollers.

He went back and picked up his novel where he'd left off the night before, too tired to hold his eyes open. The writing was tight, fast paced and packed with activity, but it lacked elements he could savor. Like his life.

He sat back and rubbed his jaw. Nothing had changed except him. His job, his home, his choices; they were all there. Just as before. He still wanted to make a difference, still stood against wrongs. But somehow he was out of step with himself.

He set the book on the end table, leaned his head back against the couch, and closed his eyes. *What do you want from me?* But he knew. The ambiguity of no-man's-land no longer accepted vagrants. He had to pitch his tent in one camp or the other.

Both promised imperfect neighbors. Both boasted emphatic leadership, zealous disciples, and hearty opposition. It wasn't a question of faith or no faith. It was a decision to put his faith in God or man.

His former arguments clamored. Why would God let Jacky die? But as he'd made clear in the hospital, it was the rest of them who'd failed Jacky. Why did God give jerks control over others? But it was believing friends and colleagues who'd empowered Webb Hammond to torment his sons and dehumanize his wife.

On judgment day, the people who cried "Lord, Lord" would be the ones who'd done things in God's name but never knew him. Matt didn't have to hold them accountable now with his own rejection of the truth. It wasn't his job to judge.

"Okay. I'll do this your way." He went down on his knees. "For my rebellion, please forgive me. From self-righteous antagonism toward you and your people and all my other failings, set me free." Maybe in heaven angels and saints were rejoicing over a lost lamb found. He only felt a lightening of the heaviness and a joy that crept over him like a warm blanket on a cold winter night.

CHAPTER THIRTY-NINE

Rese stood in her suite, hands pressed to her face. She had expected the chaos, anticipated the crowd, the noise, the effusiveness. She'd even convinced herself she would enjoy it. But the kids running rampant, the mothers scolding, Lance's brothers-in-law, cousins, and uncles posturing, Roman grumbling, and Doria dominating it all, drove her into the relative solitude of her space—relative because Star had surrendered her room and moved into the office portion of the suite, where she'd fit a futon for sleeping and heaps of colorful clothes for ambience.

Star slipped in with her now and giggled. "What are you doing?"

"Trying to think."

"'There is nothing either good or bad, but thinking makes it so.'"

"Well, not thinking is worse."

"Hmm." She flounced down on the bed. "It's served me pretty well."

Rese settled in next to her, leaning against the headboard. "How long before they miss me, do you think?"

"Long enough, I'd say. They're fairly self-centered."

Rese smiled. "Never thought of that as a good thing."

"Oh, it's very good when you're trying not to be noticed."

"So, how long before Rico misses you?"

"Long enough. He and Lance are playing handball against the shed."

"Working off Roman's insults, no doubt."

"What's with that, anyway?" Star ran her fingers through her fine blond curls.

"He's not Tony."

"What was his first clue?" She drew her knees up. "Why can't people accept others for who they are?"

"Not every place is like this house, Star. Most of the world is like Roman, expecting people to be like them."

"Well, I'm never leaving these walls."

"What if Rico wants to marry you?"

Star faced her with sober eyes. "I'll move the frogs."

Rese shook her head. "I don't think I could stand Lance and Rico under the same roof for long. Too much testosterone."

"Then we'll move next door."

Rese puckered her brow. "Did he . . ."

Star giggled. "No."

"But he's not homicidal anymore? You've made up?"

"'The quality of mercy is not strain'd. It droppeth as the gentle rain from heaven upon the place beneath. It is twice blest: it blesseth him that gives and him that takes.'"

"Good," Rese said with a bob of her head. "I'll take bloodshed off my list of concerns."

———————

Matt finished reading the study and closed the psychological journal. Maybe it was none of his business, but what he'd read had some real promise. Before Sofie could begin to teach Carly normal relationship skills, she had to get her past the trauma of her dad's death, her own near miss, and Sofie's. If Eye Movement Desensitization and Reprocessing worked half as well as case studies suggested, it might be the key to unlocking Carly's communication.

It made sense that the trauma of seeing her dad fall to his death—and almost falling with him—had lodged in an emotionally charged survival portion of the brain that conjured the event in vivid detail when anything triggered the memory, or she felt threatened, or even in her sleep, where the incident created night terrors as her mind tried unsuccessfully to process the trauma. Getting it out of there was the key. He sat back. EMDR might not be the whole solution by a long shot, but maybe a starting point?

Discussing elements of the trauma was usually part of the treatment, but practitioners had worked around that in language-delayed and preverbal kids. The side-to-side eye movements or other bilateral stimuli activated the memory network where the trauma was stored in frozen detail, simultaneously with the informational networks that allowed the child to process the event. The end result was to replace fear, panic, grief, and despair with some degree of peace and resolution. What more could they ask?

He picked up the phone and started down the list of people he regularly worked with. If they told him he was crazy, all right. But the first woman he called verified the positive results of documented studies and referred him to a specialist. He hadn't expected it to be that easy, wasn't even sure what had turned him in this direction—a small chain of events for which he couldn't take credit and was inclined to ascribe to God. Now if he could only get a few minutes alone with Sofie.

Sofie could not believe the beauty of Lance and Rese's wedding day, as the mists lifted to a balmy spring morning, fragrant with honeysuckle, grape blossoms on the old vines, and herbs and flowers in every single pot and bed. Star had forbidden Lance and Rese to set foot in the garden. Since dawn, around all the rented tables and chairs, from every vine and branch, she and Elaine had hung hundreds, maybe thousands, of glass prisms that scattered the sunlight into dazzling rainbows.

What better image of hope and promise could there be?

"Look, Carly. How beautiful it is."

Carly nodded.

Sofie encircled her with a hug. "Won't you talk to me, sweetie? This is a day to forget sadness for a while."

Carly returned the hug fervently, and for once Sofie felt the silence was as painful for the child as for her. She straightened the ribbon that had slipped in her hair. "That's all right. You decide when you're ready."

She found their seats near the arched honeysuckle trellis beneath which Lance and Rese would make their covenant. Guests and family filled the chairs, but she kept her focus on the little girl she loved so deeply, watching for signs that the strain was too much. Maybe the rainbows worked a little cheerful magic, though, because Carly gazed from one prism to another, all shapes and sizes; long round teardrops, spheres, and diamonds. Triangular and rectangular prisms, and even, Sofie noticed, some small glass birds. "Look." She pointed. "A hummingbird."

Carly smiled—the most brilliant sight in the garden. Leave it to Star to create this wonderland. In her chair across the stone path, Elaine sat bemused by the light and color. Beside her, Nonna dozed with a smile on her face.

A trio of violin, flute, and cello played near the carriage house as the chairs filled and other guests found places to stand. She and Carly had a bird-finding contest until the music signified the start of the ceremony. Lance had flown in Father Agostino, the jovial silver-haired priest who had taught him to altar serve and would now officiate. He took his place behind the honeysuckle arch.

Rico, with his hair tied into a ponytail, and Chaz, with his shaved coffee-colored scalp, lined up on one side of the bower, debonair in their elegant charcoal morning coats and cravats. Striking in a softer gray morning coat, Lance took his place in front of Rico. If he had one overactive nerve, it didn't show.

His stance had a hint of self-satisfaction, but when she met his gaze, all she saw was joyful anticipation. Her little brother had found his heart's desire, his anchor. No easy thing in his case. Pride blossomed in her chest.

Michelle came down the stone path in a blue sheath, her brown hair curled and pinned to flatter her sweet, plain face. Star's pale blond hair curled naturally into short, soft spirals as she came next in a blue and turquoise gossamer wrap dress with handkerchief layers and tiny bells sewn onto the tips. Sofie couldn't suppress a smile. Neither could Rico.

Uncomfortable in a matching charcoal tux and cravat, Brad started down with Rese. Sofie hardly recognized her in the ivory lace gown that draped her slender figure in idyllic loveliness. Lance could hardly contain himself, and in fact tears glistened in his eyes.

When Father Agostino asked, "Who gives this woman to be married?" Brad answered, "Her mother, Elaine, her father, Vernon, if he could"—he turned to Lance with a touch of a smirk—"and I do." That brought the tears to Rese's eyes. Brad kissed her cheek and took his seat.

Rese's dress was embroidered with seed pearls that caught the rainbows from the prisms. She seemed to shimmer, or maybe she did. A circlet wreathed her head, culminating in the veil below that hung in soft tulle layers to the base of her dress. She carried white calla lilies with Dutch iris, lavender delphiniums, and purple sweet peas Sofie could smell from her seat.

She hadn't imagined Rese in a traditional gown with a veil, looking so delicate and lovely. No wonder Lance beamed. As they spoke their vows and exchanged rings and lit the unity candle, the joy she felt was pure gift, like a spigot suddenly opened. Momma had worried that being the last unmarried sibling would depress her, but how could she think of herself in the midst of this?

Lance kissed his bride and left them all breathless. They stood and applauded when the priest introduced them as Mr. and Mrs. Michelli. Even Carly clapped, a smile again tugging her sweet mouth. Sofie squeezed her shoulders.

As soon as Lance and Rese passed the last row of chairs, guys swooped in to put the chairs around the tables. Typically groomsmen did not provide entertainment, but there was no stopping

Chaz and Rico with an audience already in attendance. It still upset Carly to see them, so Sofie took her into the kitchen to fill trays with rabbit-and-fennel-sausage meatballs, prosciutto rolled with fresh mozzarella, pesto-and-crab ravioli, roasted peppers, and thin, crisp eggplant.

Nonna shooed her out, but surprisingly kept Carly. Even more astonishing, Carly stayed. Sofie went back outside. Matt stood talking to Lance. Her heart quickened. What was he doing there, looking so fine in a tailored suit and silk tie?

He glanced over and his gaze snagged. Her feet started toward him without conscious effort as though they knew any moment this opportunity could be lost. Lance looked from one to the other and walked away.

She moistened her lips. "How are you, Matt?"

"This moment's pretty good." His eyes had that liquid-chocolate warmth that had undone her from the start. "I hope you don't mind that I came."

"I'm glad you came. I didn't know you'd been invited." Or she might have looked for him—and been disappointed if he hadn't.

"I swear I didn't crash the party."

She smiled. "You'd hardly go unnoticed." She touched the sleeve of his coat. "Not looking this fantastic."

"You're the one looking fantastic." His inspection was long and thorough.

She'd chosen the buttercup chiffon that deepened to mustard because she'd needed something cheerful, not because it high-lighted her copper green eyes and olive skin. But she was glad now that it did.

"Matt, last time—"

"I'm not—" They spoke at once.

She slid her fingers from his sleeve to his hand, and they joined effortlessly. "I know you were trying to help, and I appreciate it. You've been right about everything, but it's hard to know what to do."

He nodded. "I found something that might hel—"

A shriek made them both jump. Carly stood four feet away with a look of stricken rage.

"Carly—"

The child lunged at her, fists clenched and pounding. Sofie took the blows until Matt caught and lifted Carly away. Her screams intensified, and people turned and stared.

Carly's ferocity had surprised her, but Sofie raised her hands. "Wait, Matt."

"Leave it, Sofie. I want to talk to her."

"But she can't."

"I said *I* want to talk to *her*. Trust me."

He had dealt with angry, damaged kids. It was what he did. But could she trust him with Carly? She drew a breath and nodded. Clutching her hands beneath her chin, she allowed Matt to carry Carly away, screaming and biting his shoulder. Though it broke her heart to see the child so hysterical, there was something supremely comforting in turning her over—however briefly—to someone so much bigger and stronger.

Was she wrong? She searched her heart. It didn't feel selfish. It felt . . . right.

Though her teeth didn't penetrate his suit coat, the pressure of her jaws clamping down on his shoulder was uncomfortable enough to make him move quickly into the house. He had no intention of intensifying her panic and fury by removing her from the safe zone Sofie had created. But he hauled her up the stairs and into the white room where Sofie had stayed with Diego. By the books on the shelf and a number of stuffed animals, he guessed it was Carly's room now.

In spite of the noise, he left the door open. To avoid any hint of sexual misconduct, and because it was easier to keep her contained, he sat her in a chair instead of the bed. She had not spoken, but the guttural noises were clear in meaning. If she could rip his head off, she would.

He squatted a long time in front of the chair, blocking her escape but making no attempt to stop either the noise or her thrashing. It was unfortunate he'd been required to touch her at all. That would have reinforced memories of his restraint that day on the roof. But he would not allow her to assault Sofie.

Elfin in appearance, Carly managed to contort herself into an impish gremlin before losing steam and collapsing in the chair. She had probably released a pressure valve that must have been near bursting already. When she'd regained a measure of self-control, he said, "I don't expect you to talk. In fact, I'd appreciate it if you didn't. But I have a few things to say, and this will go quicker and nicer if you listen."

She jutted her lip and jaw. Sofie was probably right that her mutism was out of her control, because she certainly looked as though she'd give him a piece of her mind if it were possible.

"I know you're in a bad place. You feel worse than you ever thought you could. It was that way when my little brother got killed by a train. The hurt is there and you can't make it go away no matter how you try."

She shuddered with sobs, but kept glaring.

"I think you would talk if you could, but you're afraid what you say might make things worse. Maybe you think something you said caused this trouble already. You're afraid to lose Sofie, but treating her the way your dad treated you can only cause resentment."

She gasped, fresh tears starting in her eyes.

"You know it. Inside, you know how Sofie will feel if you keep her from anyone else, if you make her love only you and refuse to make other friends yourself."

She looked away, sullen, but he glimpsed a chink in her conviction.

"It won't be easy. You can't blame your dad if someone doesn't like you. You'll have to make and keep your friends by what you say and do. And Sofie loves you, but frankly everyone gets sick of someone sometimes."

She flicked him a glance, then swiped a hand over her face and shoved her fists underneath her thighs.

"Now I'm going outside to tell Sofie about something that

might help you. I expect you to respect our conversation. If you don't, I have a lot more things to say to you, and we'll come right back up here and finish what we started. I have all day."

Her chin trembled, but she merely watched him rise and walk to the door. He glanced over his shoulder, then descended the stairs where Elaine sat at the foot.

"Let me know if Carly leaves, okay?"

Elaine nodded. He got the feeling she'd already been watchful. "Thanks, Elaine. Your daughter is a beautiful bride."

"She wore my dress."

"It was perfect."

"But she didn't put the green with the green. And they'll know." She jerked a glance over her shoulder. "They always know."

"Tell me if Carly comes down."

She nodded solemnly. He went back to the garden, where he'd left Sofie.

Doria Michelli stood with her and saw him coming. "There," she said. "I told you."

Sofie spun. "Where's Carly?"

"Inside. Elaine's guarding the stairs. She'll let me know if Carly leaves."

"What did you . . ."

Chaz and Rico started a new song, and Star took up the mic and sang with them in an ethereal Enya kind of way, though her voice had a surprising fullness.

He drew her from her mother and to a quieter part of the yard. "We had some straight talk about what she's been doing. But I wanted to tell you I found something that might help her process the trauma." He described what he'd learned.

"I've studied it," she told him. "You think this is post-traumatic stress disorder?"

"What did you think?"

"I've focused on grief therapy."

Hands on his hips, he looked toward the house and back. "I'm not sure she's grieving, Sofie."

She stared up at him, troubled but listening.

"That might be in there somewhere, but what she's really about right now is taking control." Sofie's silence told him he'd hit the mark. "Her whole life she's been utterly dominated. Not terrorized or tortured, but Eric used love as a tool, as a weapon."

Her throat worked. "And now you think Carly is?"

"Do you think she's not?"

Sofie drew a truncated breath.

"I don't know how much she actually remembers," he went on, "but she's internalized the way Eric controlled you. If she can get the upper position, she'll have the love and attention she craves without the domination she hates."

Sofie pressed a hand to her cheek. "And you think EMDR . . ."

He shook his head. "I think it will help her process the trauma of what happened on the roof, so the real work can begin."

She pondered that. At last she looked up. "I've missed you."

It caught him in the throat. "Yeah. There's a hole inside I've been trying to ignore, but I keep stepping smack into it."

She slid her hand into his. "I miss wondering whether you'll call."

"I'm an equal opportunity suitor. I accept calls too."

"I miss knocking heads over religion and—"

"Knocking heads might not happen. You and your family have more influence than you know."

"Oh, Matt, I'm glad."

"Next time you try to defect, you'll have to get by me."

She laughed. "I'm a pretty sharp stepper."

"I'm a pretty good roadblock."

"What about Carly?"

"I like kids."

"But she's Eric's."

He rubbed his face. "I don't expect any of this to be easy. But we've all got baggage. Maybe if we throw it into the same cart we can take turns pushing."

She took his hands. "You're a big, strong guy. Maybe Carly and I should ride."

"Right. I'll be fighting to hold my own with the two of you."

A string of children jostled him, playing tag.

She smiled at them, then up at him. "It's supposed to be a celebration day."

"I don't know about you, but my heart's dancing triple time."

She laid her palm against his chest. "Is it?"

His voice graveled. "You know it is."

Behind them Star began an Irish ballad with all the angst and pathos of the isle. The look that came into Sofie's eyes took what self-restraint he had left. He encircled and kissed her, caught her face between his hands and kissed her again. He groaned. "Tell me I'm not dreaming this."

"Don't wake up, if you are."

"I love you, Sofie."

"I can't help loving you." She searched his eyes. "But I have to—"

He pressed his fingers to her mouth. "We'll figure it out. Together."

"See where it goes?"

"See where God takes it." He locked his fingers behind her neck. "It's no accident you came into my life."

She covered his hands with hers, trembling. "I don't deserve this gift."

"It's nonrefundable."

She laughed through the tears sparkling in her incredible eyes. "Exchanges?"

"No way."

"How about store credit?"

"All sales final."

She slid her arms around his waist and rested her cheek against his chest. "Okay, I'll take it."

Carly watched out the window. She had crept from Sofie's room to the pink one and saw Sofie and Matt kissing and hugging. Her stomach ached. She'd ruined everything. Her anger had all blown up and left only the sadness and fear, but it was too late. She gulped back fresh tears. It didn't matter now if she talked or not. No one would care.

She had *hit* Sofie. She had tried to hurt her the way Daddy hurt the others. She pressed her hands to her head. Like Daddy with the poor little pets. Like Ms. Baker's car and Mr. Hill on the icy stairs. Sofie must *hate* her. She wasn't just sick of her; she'd want to be rid of her.

Carly ran to the bathroom and threw up. She splashed water in her mouth, then stared into the mirror. Was Matt right? Was she like Daddy to Sofie? Did Sofie resent her and plan ways to get away from her? She didn't want to believe anything he said. But his eyes weren't cold when he said it. They were like nothing she'd seen, not even Sofie's.

Sofie's eyes always needed something, for her to talk, for her to be all right. But she wasn't all right. Matt knew. He'd said how she felt, how she couldn't make the hurt go away. She wanted to hate him, but he'd said it, like it was all inside him, too, like they shared a secret.

"Maybe you think something you said caused this trouble." Not only what she said, but everything she'd done. Matt had looked like he knew, like he got it, like maybe he'd been responsible too. His brother got killed by a train. That was as bad as falling off a roof. Making someone fall. When it was an accident. When she'd never meant—

She threw herself onto the bed, sobbing. Someone came in behind her. Carly rolled to her side. Rese's mother, Elaine, came and sat on the bed—her bed. Carly swiped her hand under her runny nose and started to get up, but Elaine patted her shoulder.

"I had a little girl."

Carly sniffed and nodded. Duh, it was Rese.

"She turned into a butterfly. Once she flew onto the roof and we played in the clouds."

Carly sat up.

Elaine stared up at the ceiling. "We played and played in the clouds. But they took her away. They always take them away. She's gone. Gone, gone." Elaine lay down, murmuring, "Gone."

Carly wished she could say Rese was right outside, but words still wouldn't come, and anyway, the girl who turned into the butterfly was gone. Sad and lonely, Carly got off the bed. Nothing stayed the same. Once something changed everything else came tumbling down.

"Carly?" Sofie stood in the doorway.

Carly started to shake. How would she say it? Maybe "I don't ever want to see you again." That's what friends had said when they thought she'd done something, even if she didn't. But this time she had.

Sofie spread her arms. "Come here."

Maybe she'd say it nicely. *It's for the best.*

She reached her and looked up. Sofie squatted down and hugged her. "Come on, sweetie. Let's have some cake."

Wait a minute. What about what happened? Carly resisted.

Sofie slid a gentle hand over her hair and raised her chin. "It's going to be okay."

She searched Sofie's face. Wasn't she mad? Hurt?

"We are going to get through this. All of us. Together."

Carly drew a jagged breath, hardly daring, but wanting so much to believe.

CHAPTER FORTY

The drill whirred and stilled, fixing the sign above the front door on the blue house. Lance murmured, "Careful," as Rese climbed down the ladder and cocked him a glance. Sofie suppressed a smile. Rese wasn't even showing, but he couldn't help himself.

The last eight months had held heartache, hard work, long days and longer nights, tears and laughter, and more tears. But through it, or because of it, they had found a purpose. Matt's hand warmed the small of her back as she read the letters Rese had carved.

Jack Hammond Children's Center. And inscribed beneath it: *Where there's life, there's hope.* There'd been no question on the name, honoring the little boy who had been lost by bringing hope and life to others.

Sofie looked down at Carly. "What do you think?"

"It's nice." Carly smiled up at her, then Matt. "Nice for Jacky too."

Matt stroked her head. "Every place needs a guardian."

Sofie imagined Matt's brother looking down from heaven, watching over the ones who came for help and healing. Carly reached around and took his hand. Sofie basked in the kinship her little girl had found with the man she loved so much.

Having studied for and passed the California bar, he would wear both a social work and legal hat in the foundation he'd set up. She had created a dance therapy program and nearly completed a very different dissertation than she had once intended. With Star and Rico's creative energy, Rese's strength and practicality, Lance's musical and spiritual gifts, they would keep making this a place where healing happened.

Rico, Star, and Elaine joined them, along with Nonna, who had loaded the basket Star carried with a loaf of bread, that all who hungered would be filled, a shaker of salt, that life would have flavor, and wine, for joy and prosperity.

"Ready?" Lance opened the door and they filed in.

Rese had overhauled every rickety, chipped, dull, and dingy inch of it and repainted in creamy yellows, purples, and sage greens. Once it was furnished, Sofie could not imagine one element that would make it more welcoming, comforting, or cheerful.

Carly turned in the center of the big, empty front room, arms outstretched. "Hello! Echoes, hello!"

Walls and ceiling resounded. Watching her, Sofie's heart filled to capacity and overflowed. They were all echoes of a great love—some loud, some soft, some reverberating—repeating in some way what had been done for them. Blessings would spill from this place like a fountain of hope. She felt the promise inside her, turned and saw it in Matt's eyes. She slipped her hand into his, closed her eyes, and raised her face to heaven as Lance spoke a blessing over the present and future and even the generations to come.

As always, I would like to thank the usual suspects who have read, prayed, and borne with me through the process of bringing this book to life. You know who you are.

You are all in my heart always.

Glory to God.

Looking for More Good Books to Read?

You can find out what is new and exciting with previews, descriptions, and reviews by signing up for Bethany House newsletters at

www.bethanynewsletters.com

We will send you updates for as many authors or categories as you desire so you get only the information you really want.

Sign up today!